NEON NOIR

The Cyber City Saga: Book 1

Nina Voss

Maroon Ink Press

Acknowledgements

Samuel, alpha
Karen, beta
Allison, beta
Elisa, gamma
Robin, mu
Rick + Jo, kings
Sam + Carl, queens
And Finn, for taking very long naps

For You

Contents

1

Acid Trips

The obsidian skinsuit slipped through the crowd of meandering pedestrians with purpose to avoid arousing any suspicion. Not that there was anything to be suspicious of. She just really wanted to beat the rain.

The glowing signs beckoned for people to "COME ON IN" and eat "Hot *Spicy* Ramen", their thick aromas competing with the musky smog in a sickening battle of the stenches. Evenings were prime dining time for any place, especially for the Third Ward. But Xia needed to make it home before the dreaded storm.

A rumbling groan of thunder billowed in the dark horizon. Xia let out her own matching grumble and glanced upward. Nothing was visible, as per usual. One can't see anything above the smog. Thick and heavy and perpetually weighing down upon the citizens below. She quickened her pace once more, her slender body squeezing between brutish metalheads and modded cyborgs. Her black skinsuit allowed for the tightest of maneuvering.

"Watch it," barked a golem of a man. Although at this point he was more metal than man. Xia wondered if there was an ounce of flesh left on him. She was waiting for that trend to die. The pendulum was close to swinging, so to speak. Discreet and functional modifications were more readily available, to Xia's satisfaction. But the standard still stood: the more mods you had, the more money you had, and the more superior you were perceived.

Xia paid him no mind as she continued on her way. In just a few moments the lonely sprinkles turned into a downpour. The people in the crowd instantaneously adapted to the change in weather, pressing buttons and triggering various water-repellent mechanisms. Xia didn't need to press any buttons. Her suit was already waterproof, and her hair would dry in a matter of moments. To her mild surprise, she spotted a few umbrellas. It was rare to find such an outdated thing these days.

Nobody else in the clog of pedestrians seemed to be aware of the impending storm. Maybe the ones who did had already taken shelter in one of the shops? But Xia didn't want to spend the remainder of her night stuck in some soup parlor waiting out the storm. She wanted to get home. She had a hell of a long day, and she was ready for a drink and a snooze.

This rain wasn't the storm Xia was worried about. Rain came often enough in Cyber City, usually unannounced and unsuspected since the true nature of the heavens lay hidden by layers of fog and pollution and a plasma barrier. She didn't mind the rain. Others did— especially ones with cheap mods. Just a few feet ahead, a flurry of sparks danced above a woman's head as the rain made contact with her cheap modded hair. An umbrella could have come in handy for her.

On any other given day, Xia liked to count how many malfunctioning mods she could find when it rained. Under the breadth of smog, it was harder to tell the low from the mid-range stuff. But the cleansing waters of rain shed light to it all. Tonight, however, with an impending storm, games were the last thing on her mind.

Xia tapped her temple three times, long-short-long, accessing the radar on her eye screen. The radar floated in her vision, electric blue predictions of weather and warning. But just like a half hour ago, the warning still only read *"INCOMING"*. She paid an entire month's rent for this damn upgrade and it couldn't even give a time estimate. Still, it was a newer mod and most people didn't have it, evidenced by the indifferent and carefree strides of the people around her.

And then it happened. An electric razor sliced through the sky, its voltage crackling through the rumbles of the current rainstorm. Cries, yelps, and *"Fuck!"*s rippled through the crowd. In just three seconds, the crowd transformed from a lackadaisical herd of lemmings to a frantic stampede. Shops reacted just as instantly, switching their neon signs from "Open" to "Closed" and hurriedly attempting to shut their doors to the influx of people trying to get in and seek shelter. Nobody wants acid rain in their shop.

Xia let out her own muttered "fuck". She thought she had more time. It was moments like this she was thankful that she splurged the extra money on her titan suit, even if it did cause her to go hungry for several weeks. She tugged on her sleeve, extending the right hand into a glove to match the permanent one on the left, and then did the same to her collar, transforming the top into a hood. Her hair was technically also acid-resistant, but she didn't want to test it if she didn't have to.

Xia raced through the crowd, now with others racing alongside her. A tailless black lizard skidding through the ranks. Every man for himself.

Mayhem was expected on a night of acid rain. Only the best of skin-suits and body armor would fully protect against the stuff. After one particularly awful storm, Xia vowed she'd do anything for a top-tier suit. The scars on her back and left hand acted as a reminder of the importance of that purchase. Being as deadly and unpredictable as it is, everyone in Cyber City had some level of protection. Something is better than nothing. If you have nothing—

A shrill scream split through the commotion of the crowd. Xia instinctively whipped her head in the direction of the sound. Her eyes fell on the pitiful source.

Shit. A Virgin.

The cowering girl hunched into a ball, the acid slowly burning through the back of her jacket.

Xia stopped in her steps, a stationary rock in a free-flowing torrent of a stream.

"Fuck me," she muttered, splitting to the right and towards the girl. Two, three, four people of varying sizes and mod installs banged into her, but Xia managed to remain upright and get to the girl in a few brisk breaths.

"Hey, you need to get to shelter," Xia shouted as she placed her hands on the girl. The girl whipped her head towards Xia, only for a moment, the falling rain landing on her unscarred cheeks. She let out another scream as the pain sunk in. Xia only caught her face for a split second, but she could tell the girl couldn't have been much older than twelve.

"Come on," she said as she pulled the girl up and wrapped her own body around her. There wasn't much she could do. Luckily the girl was much shorter than Xia. Her 4-and-a-half foot frame made her a somewhat easy little spoon. Xia scanned the surrounding area. Nothing stood out as an immediate source of shelter. No metal overhangs, no open buildings.

Plan 2. Her least favorite kind, as it involved talking to strangers. She scanned the area once more, this time collecting information on the owners. Scanning, scanning... 23 results in the immediate area. She sifted through the results, swiping upwards on her temple to scroll through the options of potential good samaritans.

Perfect. Ginhua Xing. Grandmother. Family-owned dumpling eatery. Minimal known mods. 33.25 yards East.

Xia tapped on her temple once more and set the small restaurant as her destination.

"Run with me," she shouted in the girl's ear. The girl's head bobbed rapidly, and with a forceful push from Xia, the two scuttled alongside the edge of the crowd. Closer, closer, closer the Dumpling sign came into view. A chubby pig holding chopsticks smiled at them endearingly, unbothered by the fat globules of acid that fell around it. The overhang from the building was slight, but it held just enough protection for Xia to ease up her hold on the girl. It was dark on the inside, but Xia could see the people enjoying their safety from the acid hell outside.

She banged on the door with both fists.

"Hey! Ginhua! Help this girl! She's a Virgin! A *Virgin!*"

Xia wondered if they could even hear her. The swarm of people outside was enough to drown out her voice, let alone the walls between them. She pointed at the small girl and mouthed once more, *Virgin.* The people inside glanced worriedly at each other, but nobody made a move. Xia grabbed the girl's chin and lifted it, the girl's black hair falling backward.

A stout woman came from behind the counter and approached the locked door.

"Just her," the woman said, pointing at the girl. Xia could barely make out the words, but relief flooded over her as she understood. She nodded, took her hands off the girl, and backed away. Within three seconds, the door was unlocked and the girl was pulled inside to safety. The girl was able to send Xia one glance, and in that glance, Xia saw gratitude in her unmodded eyes.

Xia exhaled, pulled her hood tighter, and sprinted once more.

By the time she made it to her home district on the outskirts of the city, the air was safe and dry. She flipped back her hood with a breath of fresh air. Well, as fresh as the wards could get. There was a perpetual musk and metallic tang that liked to hang heavy. She glanced towards the direction of her home, debating if she wanted to call it quits for the night or if she earned a reward. The image of the teen from a mile earlier flashed in her mind. She earned a reward.

Xia checked her eye screen. No rain, acid or not, was in the forecast for her district. She walked along the empty street. Much darker and lonelier than usual. People likely heard about the acid storm and opted to stay inside for the night. Lonely night. Perfect time to head over to Mickey's.

She entered the grimy establishment, swapping the musky city air for a different flavor of musky tavern air. The dark floors matched the dark tables, matching the dark walls, illuminated by a few dim bulbs that shed light on the fat dust particles floating like buzzing flies. The floor was sticky along with the tables, but Mickey insisted the glasses were clean and that's all that mattered.

She made her way to the near-empty bar. A few other stragglers occupied the other side, which Xia was thankful for. She didn't like full bars, but she didn't like them completely empty either. She wondered who would be bartending tonight. On weekend nights it could be any of them.

"Xia," her favorite greeted as he appeared from behind the bar. The hanging martini glasses shook with each of his thunderous steps. She was used to his size, but his seven-foot frame still slightly jarred her when he first rumbled into view.

"Dames," she greeted with a nod.

"What'll the little lady have tonight? Usual?"

She nodded. Dames was the only one who could call her a "little lady" and not earn a side-eye in response. She watched as he delicately poured the whiskey and orange liqueur into a glass, swirled it with skill, and then plucked a cherry the size of his fingernail. For hands the size of a giant's, he was careful and meticulous and made a damn good cocktail. He garnished the top and placed the glass gingerly before her.

"Should have known you were working tonight. Bar top's not so sticky."

He smirked. "By the looks of tonight, they'll stay that way. Nobody wants to go out 'cause of the acid over in the second and third wards. Might have even reached Midpoint. You hear about that?"

Xia sipped her drink, wanting nothing more than to suck it all down. But she knew better than to waste it all at once. Especially with *real* liquor, not the synthetic spirits that most places sell. "Yeah, got stuck in it on the way home."

"No shit? Are you okay?" His gravelly voice was one of friendliness and concern, not matching his gruff exterior at all. Scarred and hairy and too tall for a man, Dames was a walking contradiction and Xia loved it.

She nodded again. "Suit held up just fine."

"Did it now?" Amusement replaced the concern in his voice. He motioned with his pointer finger for her to turn around. Wordlessly, she obliged and displayed the back of her titan skinsuit. "Still looks brand new. How much I owe you?"

She remembered the bet they wagered when she first bought the suit. He didn't think it would be able to hold up in an acid storm, and they bet accordingly. Xia didn't know another soul that would stay true to their word and bring up the bet if it meant them losing some coin.

She waved her hand dismissively.

"Come on, you should be demanding your share. Wasn't it a hundred zeCoin?"

"Next round can be on you," she said.

He sighed with a lopsided snicker and made the rounds with the other patrons. Xia couldn't help but notice the discreet glances that Dames sent back her way. She couldn't quite place the emotion behind them. Was it nervousness? Apprehension? She was about to replay the moment and scan on her eyescreen when he beat her to it.

"I'll do you one better than zeCoin," he said as he handed her another drink. "Info." His voice dropped near above a whisper.

"What kind?" Her heartbeat thumped in anticipation. Dames loved to tell Xia *everything* he knew. From new inventions to politics, he got his fair share of juicy information being the bartender he was in an establishment like this. His lack of filter was one of her favorite qualities of his. Considering he hadn't already spilled whatever this tidbit was meant it must have been *very* good.

His onyx eyes darted from side to side before leaning on the counter towards her. She noticed a small blemish under his left eye. The closest proximity they ever held.

"Modular? Medical? Either way, it's a game-changer. Brain transplants." He leaned back, a smile lingering on his lips as the words hung in the air.

Xia tapped the mechanics in her inner ear and replayed Dames' words, wanting to make sure she heard correctly. She knew better than to question his source. Of all the information he'd been feeding her over the years, he'd never steered her in an unfruitful direction.

"No shit?" She muttered as the words replayed in her ear. *Brain transplants.*

"Mhmm", he nodded as he leaned back, proud of himself. "Hell of a tidbit, eh?"

The next second he was off tending to one of the few patrons left in the dim bar, leaving Xia alone. After finishing her drink and feeling a slight warm buzz, she got up from her stool before Dames could make her another. She tapped at her cellchip, the essential device on her wrist, in an attempt to pay for the drinks. He waved her off. Then she nodded, gave the glass one last swig (although it was only ice), and left the bar. While she didn't like owing people, she'd never turn down a free drink.

2

Radio Secrets

It wasn't for another three months that something would come of Dames' information. And it wasn't for lack of perception. Each of Xia's senses were attuned to any inkling of a sign that would lead back to the news of brain transplants. How would they be used? Were they in the beginning stages and in need of testers? Or were they past that, and ready to profit? Who were *they?* Xia needed to know so that she could be one step ahead. After all, that's how she made the most of her money.

It all started back in primary school. She was only eleven years old, towering above the other students her age. Her frame would plateau eventually, but at the time, she felt freakishly large. It was recess time, a time where all the kids would run freely outside and play together— and stick to their groups they had formed. Xia wasn't in any group. She didn't have anything fun to show, and she never had the right things to say, so she had nothing to offer the other kids in exchange for acceptance.

She sat on the school steps, observing the nearby hub of students. She called them *The Snobbies.* But only in her head. They were the richest of the students, which meant they were some of the richest in the city. After all, only the rich went to school. Except Xia. None of the students knew how someone like Xia could attend school. She didn't know either. But there she was.

Xia liked observing The Snobbies. They had the most tech, since they were so rich. They had the most insight, since they came from important families. And they were the loudest, making them the easiest to hear.

Even from a comfortable distance and a feigned look of disinterest, Xia could hear every word, even without a hearing mod.

"My daddy says they're gonna 'limit calories', whatever that means. When he saw I was listening, he shut the door and I couldn't hear anymore."

"Dang," blonde Snobby said.

"What's a calorie?" tiny Snobby said.

Something you might need more of, Xia thought to herself, staring at tiny Snobby. That's what her grandfather always worried about. Xia not getting enough calories. That and 'nutrients'. She didn't really know what these 'calories' and 'nutrients' were exactly, but she knew that it was why her grandfather always plated her food twice the size of his, despite him being twice the size of her. So that she could get bigger. When she hit her growth spurt and got tall, she tried to stop eating. Her grandfather whacked her on the head and shoved her a bowl of soup. *"Not taller, wider. Meat on your bones."*

She had the urge to interject and tell them what she knew, but she bit her tongue. Talking with the likes of the Snobbies made for awkward interactions, and she'd do anything to avoid those.

"I don't know, but I'm guessing it's something important if he didn't want me to hear! I guess I need to be better at sneaking."

The group laughed, but the racing thoughts in Xia's brain tuned out their high pitched giggles. Loud Snobby's dad was the headmaster of the school. He was a man of big and frequent changes, most of which affected the students negatively. Banning the funnest games, firing favorite teachers. If Xia had a hit list, Loud Snobby's dad would be at the top. If "limiting calories" was a new idea for the school, what kind of changes would that entail?

She tapped her chin as she leaned forward on her bony knees. She thought of the school's lunch program, with its decadent buffet and plethora of options for sweets and snacks. Could some of that go away? The thought made her frown. Lunchtime was the best part of her day, as the food in the lunch program was miles ahead of anything her grandfather could supply. And she wasn't alone in her sentiments. The students went crazy for the cheese rolls, the honey grahams, and *especially* the mochi balls. What would they do without the mochi balls?

A rebellion, rampaging the halls. It wouldn't be pretty. Xia knew this. The students loved their mochi balls. *Needed* their mochi balls. It was funny, because it was the one thing that she could easily get on her own, since her neighbor, Lotani, had her own mochi ball stand in Midpoint, the slice of city that transitioned between the bustling Third and the impoverished Fourth Ward.

It hit her. She could sell them to the students. Lotani could make her mochi balls. And she could sell them. And for once, she could have decent pocket money. Maybe even buy her grandfather something. Maybe even have *steak* for dinner. The possibilities were endless. A smile spread.

Three days later, the cries and moans in the lunchroom echoed through the school halls, reverberating the students' horror and dismay. The counter that usually hosted the array of delectable mochi balls was replaced with a vegetable tray.

Xia was a good 10 yards away from the lunchroom when the cries met her ears. And with those cries she smiled in satisfaction— those cries meant she was right. Her insight paid off. And soon, it would pay off *literally*.

She went to work that very day after school, haggling with Lotani. It was surprisingly easy to convince the pudgy woman to make so many of her goods without any initial payment. Xia didn't know, but Lotani was itching at the chance to help out Youle's skinny, reclusive granddaughter. Within days, Xia was running her own illicit business, selling mochi balls out of her bag to the rich and privileged kids of Greikko Academy. Her name once obscurely known by the others in her grade quickly became the most sought out. Well, her name was still obscure. Most just called her "The Mochi Ball Girl". But Xia didn't mind. She was making money, all on her own wit and skill.

A month later, she bought a rib-eye steak and brought it home. Her grandfather shed two tears of ecstasy and nostalgia at the taste. It was the only time she had seen him cry.

Xia lay on her bed— a thin mattress that barely raised her six inches off the floor— with the memory of her grandfather and that steak. The pure bliss in his eyes when he cooked the slab of meat. The smell that seemed to linger in their kitchen for days. How her grandfather had uttered a bewildered "how" but raised no other questions, because he had complete trust in his granddaughter. Yet the face that was always so clear had grown hazy. A mere outline in the depths of her mind. Her heart panged. Damn, did she miss him.

She rolled onto her side and stared out the tall window of a wall. The lights from the city below cast an electric glow into her tiny studio, a room almost as tall as it was wide. Xia didn't mind the constant stream of light. It kept her company. Made her feel warm. Alive. She'd rather bask in the neon gleams of the city that never dies than in darkness. Darkness is where the hidden things like to appear. She preferred them hidden.

Her radio crackled as the time evolved from 2:59 to 3 a.m. She leaned a little closer to hear the prizory console better. A radio in Cyber City was a commodity that'd literally cost an arm, leg, and several mods. They didn't make them anymore, and the use of radios, specifically transmitters, were one of the few contraband that was heavily punished. Most didn't know why. Something about how they were used in the rebellion back in her grandfather's time. Which meant that the few brave souls who used such devices and broadcast their own words and wisdom over the air were a rare breed. And the things they had to say were valuable. And for Xia, valuable info was her livelihood.

Xia got to know the various voices that showcased their insights. And every voice that popped up was soon never heard from again. Xia figured the slags, soldiers of the Freesian Military Force, tracked their transmitted signals and dealt with them accordingly. Some lasted longer than others. But there was one who stood the test of time, one who never fell into silence.

A distorted voice crackled from the radio. The Nightcrawler. *"3:00, Night four of the seventh moon. Dusty today. Dusty, dusty, dusty."* Xia smirked. She liked how his whimsical words contrasted the robotically baritone voice. It reminded her of Dames. In a world where everyone modded their outsides to match their insides, she appreciated the enigmas.

"What if there was an escape from the dust? From the pollution, the crime, from the misery of this hellhole of a city." Xia looked down towards the city below with endearing eyes. Hellhole? Maybe to some. Maybe for most. Maybe even for her. But it was also home.

"An escape will be coming. But not for everyone. In fact, for barely anyone. What am I talking about? Well, I'm talking about a new utopia, supposedly. Our lovely FRF government heads have been working on a new place. What 'working on' means, I haven't got one smitten clue. Knowing our lovely republic, it means a mountain's worth of shit has been put into this new shiny place, leaving us to further rot in our dust. Dusty, dusty d ust."

FRF: The Federal Republic of Freesia. It was the official name for the established homeland, but the name was rarely used colloquially. As soon as the plasma dome shut everyone inside eight decades prior, the name *Cyber City* was dubbed.

"So who gets to venture to this new place? This place that, supposedly, will be clean and fresh and prosperous and free from all the grime of Cyber City? Do you have a guess? Come on, guess for me."

Several ideas flit into thought. The government officials? They were already safely residing outside the city walls in protected hubs, sheltered little creatures that'd choke on the city's dust after a mere day. The wealthiest? Xia doubted that as well, as wealth meant nothing outside the walls, and the delicate balance of hierarchy relied and thrived on the rich here inside. Two more seconds and she'd have had the answer on her own, but the distorted voice rang through and beat her nimble mind.

"Nope, whatever guess you had was wrong, and if you're right, I'll never know because I can't hear you. Hahaha! The golden ticket answer is: The Virgins. The Virgins will be the lucky few to travel to this Utopia. This mod-free utopia, free of our robot claws and techno-vision and all our jaded technology. That's the catch. That's what makes this new place so perfect. The government wants to start from scratch. They've grown tired of us. Tired? Angry? Bored? Who the lovely hell knows. Apparently we've come too far with the mods. As for when this new world opens, or the protocol for how our lucky Virgins will get to venture there, I don't have a clue. I'm just the messenger, and not a very good one. I give good word, as my few listeners

know, but the word is minimal. That's all I got. Rest is speculation." Xia could hear his spittle on the last word. *"So while I don't know when it'll happen, it will. Keep an eye out. A modded one. Unless you're one of the lucky few that don't have one of those, HA HA HA!"* Even with the voice distortion, the laugh cackled at a delicate, high pitch. *"Well, that's all I got, my friends. Get some sleep. And, as always, never trust the government! Judgment comes one day, FRF."*

The Virgins were a small community, and a skeptical one at that. Characterized most simply by their lack of mods, they rejected Freesia's current lifestyle and the populace's dependency on technology. While they still used tech to varying degrees, they drew the line at mods: the cybernetic devices installed directly into the body.

Xia couldn't see how the government could convince them to do anything.

Judgment comes one day, FRF. You'd never hear such brazen statements in everyday life. For all its crime and corruption, people steered clear of government criticism. Wasn't worth the trouble. There's enough trouble to deal with as it is. Only the zealous radioheads had the gall for such audacious words.

Xia slapped the top of her radio and shut it off, then curled herself into a ball like a silver sphynx. Her body was exhausted, but her mind would keep her awake for several hours with the news of this "utopia". It wasn't until the sun battled the smog that she finally drifted off.

3

Broken Promises and Broken Noses

Xia left Calypso's with a moon tea in one hand and a honey graham in the other. It was her usual breakfast from the quaint tea café ever since Calypso insisted on a heavy discount after Xia helped get some debtors off her back.

"You will always have a place in here, and I'll always have a graham in there," the cocoa-skinned woman had told Xia with a trace of an accent of another time and place, pointing to the assortment of goodies in the glass display case. Since then, Xia stopped there religiously before venturing on to the rest of her day. Prior to winning that prized discount, she'd never have wasted her coin on such a luxury. Tea drinks and sweets, especially ones with *real* sugar, were an expensive commodity. She'd wondered who Calypso's sugar supplier was but knew better than to ask.

The day was as close to beautiful as the city could get. The smog was thinner than usual, allowing some of the sun's precious rays to break through. Despite the sun's glow, it wasn't too hot, meaning the stink of sweat was kept to a minimum. The S-trees ("s" for *synthetic,* as authentic trees had difficulty growing underneath the plasma dome) that lined the street looked barely artificial today, their leaves bright and emitting no off-putting frequencies. She could actually smell the herbal notes of her tea. Refreshing.

Xia had just finished her daily morning workout (which, depending on the time of her awakening for the day, often took place in the early afternoon) and steroid regimen. Her line of work required peak physical fitness. Exercise was one necessity. The suboptimal food quality made vitaroids, a vitamin-infused steroid injection, another one.

It was tough work as a freelancer, but Xia would have it no other way. The work could be hard to come by, sure. And the pay was sporadic and unpredictable. But the independence and self-reliance was an invaluable perk that she'd never give up. Yesterday was her self-made day off, and she was ready to get back to her routine today.

Her black boots were silent as she rounded the corner of Mint and Seventh, a sprawling alley bazaar in Midpoint selling a hodgepodge of gems and junk. She primed her ears for Lutno. Lutno, The Modless Maniac. The Soapbox Virgin. Lunatic Lutno. But to Xia, he was just Lutno—an outspoken pariah who preached the woes of society and the dangers of mods. Xia made it a habit to cross past his soapbox—a small wooden crate— each day. She'd never admit it, but her steps lingered each time she sauntered past his outcries. His words had grown louder and more manic over the years, but the ring of truth never faded.

But when she rounded the corner, there was no Lutno. His wooden crate sat on the side of the street, alone against the concrete wall. The lack of Lutno was jarring. She had never seen an empty soapbox. Like clockwork, he was there, every morning. But not today. She glanced around, wondering if anyone else had the same reaction. She was the only one to stop in her steps. She furrowed her eyebrows, cocked her head, and continued on her way.

By the time she made it to the Steel House, her tea cup was empty and her honey graham was half digested. She was already craving another one, but her stomach was used to waiting long stretches of time between meals. The Steel House was a monstrous thing, its name both characteristic and not. Made entirely of steel both inside and out, the looming structure looked nothing like a house. A cold metal monster.

Xia entered the building, glanced towards the purple-haired pixie seated at the front desk who paid her no mind, and took the creaking elevator up to the 11th floor. The hall reeked of illicit herbs and must.

A nose mod would come in handy in situations like this, but Xia's nose remained a Virgin's.

"It's about damn time," a cracked voice rang out. A large head peeked out from down the hall, her eyes glowing and hair redder than blood. Xia continued down the hall and brushed past the flame-haired woman into her place.

"So, what's the trouble today?" Xia asked, positioning herself as close to the door as possible.

"Not even a hello?" Flamehair mused. She let out a lurid, discolored smile, her teeth a nasty gray. She tossed Xia an even nastier crumb bar. Xia reluctantly stuffed it into her mouth. The taste was foul, but food was fuel.

"Thanks," Xia said. "So, what's the trouble?"

"Not what, but who. And not who's the trouble, but rather who's *in* trouble. You want to take a seat? I got more crumb bars-"

"I'm good. Who's in trouble?"

"Are you sure? I got some different flavors—"

"Katia," Xia cut her off. "I'm on a schedule."

She wasn't. This was the only job Xia had for the day.

"Right," Katia said, looking slightly dejected. "You're a busy bitch. I know. It's my cousin. Garren. He got robbed last week. They took all his zeCoin, almost 6000, and he's got rent due. Dumb bastard's already been late twice. If he's late again, he's out on the streets. And that boy can't handle the streets. Meaning I gotta take him in. And I ain't takin' him. The bastard stinks. And he talks so damn much. You can't get a word in edgewise. And this is coming from me. Imagine that."

"Details of the robbers?" Xia said, simultaneously tapping her earlobe so she could record what Katia was about to say.

"Not much. They attacked him at night, over by The Duck Palace. He had spent a few hours there, gotten hella wasted, and walked home. Robbed right off the corner of Doti Street. He put up quite the struggle, so he says. Looks like he did too. Got two black eyes and a busted lip, and he's walkin' with a limp."

"No weapons?" Xia asked.

"They didn't use any, but I'd be shocked if they didn't have any. My cousin is small and ain't much of a fighter. Got the spirit of one. But not the skill. I have his address here so you can go talk to him—"

"Don't need it," Xia said, waving off the suggestion like a bug. "What's the payment?"

"Are you sure? I know I'm missing some—"

"Payment."

Katia sighed. "A third of his retrieved zeCoin, should be about 2000. And I'll throw in a dozen crumb bars."

Her stomach churned, the taste of said bars lingering unpleasantly. "2200 and skip the crumb bars."

Katia rolled her eyes. "Deal."

Xia counted her few blessings for another easy one. A robbery by the Duck Palace? With no weapons? When would they ever learn?

It was a three-mile trek from the Steel House to the Duck Palace. Xia opted for the trek over a bus ride. The buses reeked and cost money that could be spent on a drink. In the Before Times, buses and trains were the standard form of travel around the city. But at some point during the war, several underground tunnels fell to their demise—and the train system fell along with it. For years they lay abandoned until they were cleared out completely. Only the buses were left. And with that, the bus prices shot upward.

Xia's scarlet modded eyes glanced up towards the restaurant sign. It was a dingy place that was anything but a palace. Seedy, with seedy characters. She couldn't speak for the quality of the duck.

She skipped the main entrance and headed towards the deserted back alley. In one swift motion, she leapt up and grabbed onto the metal overhang extending from the roof. Her gloved hands just barely made a decent grip. Using every ounce of upper body strength she could muster, she pulled herself up and over the edge. Grunt, pull, hoist. One down, two to go. She jogged forward to the next overhang. Xia versus the three-tiered Duck Palace. This jump was slightly shorter. Smaller grunt, pull, and hoist. Heavy breaths. Last one. The final overhang stood a solid 10 feet above her, taunting her. She made a mental note to intensify her upper arm workouts to make situations like this easier— a mental note that was consistently made and consistently unfulfilled.

She scanned the surrounding area as her nimble frame crouched along the side of the roof. Her eyescreen identified no surrounding lifeforms except for a lone pigeon on the opposite side of the roof. Xia expected this. She delved into her settings and scanned again, this time looking for modified frequencies. The eyescreen filled with numerous numbers and codes. Gibberish to the untrained eye, but she had years of training. Her eyes were quick to scroll and quick to find the type of frequency that didn't match the rest. Bingo.

She highlighted the frequency and pinpointed the source. And scoffed. They couldn't even move from the last time? Xia scuttled further upwards on the sloping roof, higher and higher until she could see her destination. Without any hesitation, she jumped off the edge, her agile body surging forward. A black cat abound. She landed on the neighboring building with ease.

Xia paused for a moment as she considered which route to take. Cautious and careful? Bold and brazen? She usually erred on the side of the former, but the ease of the mission made her consider the latter. She scanned a final time to confirm her plan of action. Then she ran.

Her sleek black body flashed across the roof of the building, agility her learned strong suit. Her steps were silent, the distant bustling of the streets below the only sounds that could be heard. Her silver hair flowed behind her like a horse from the yester years. The sight was almost majestic, yet there was no one there to witness. Closer, closer. Then she reached the edge of the roof. Choosing the element of surprise, she jumped once more, launching herself forward. Her adrenaline fueled her arms for some extra upper body strength, and she hung off the edge of the next building over. Swing, swing, kick. What looked like a solid wooden barricade was nothing more than measly plywood. In one swift motion, she landed inside a small room laden with empty bowls of food and garbage, several mats and pillows strewn about, and a plethora of tech. *Stolen* tech.

All the mats lay empty save for one. The body that occupied it sprang up at the sound of Xia's smash through the flimsy wall. His groggy eyes attempted to comprehend what was going on, but Xia had already placed him in a solid choke hold.

Once in her hold, the memories came back quickly. "Y-you again?"

She squeezed her arm tighter. "Why the hell are you guys still here?"

He sputtered incoherently.

"A week ago. You robbed Garren. 6000 zeCoin."

He sputtered. "What of it?!"

"Give it back." Her voice clipped. A part of her felt disappointed that they hadn't learned from the first time she raided their place. Everything remained identical to the last time. Except there seemed to be a few extra empty bowls. Her nose shriveled at the smell.

"Okay, okay, okay!"

Xia slowly released her hold. The man took a few wobbly steps forward, his hands rubbing at the inevitable bruise forming on his neck. She eyed him carefully. His steps were slow. A little too slow. Then his hand reached not towards the computer holding all the stolen zeCoin, but instead towards his pocket.

Xia's disappointment deepened as he spun around and pulled out a gun. But not just any gun, an *Enforcer*. The disappointment evolved into fear.

"Get out or I'll shoot!"

The slight quiver at the end of his command quelled Xia's worries. There was a reason this gang never used weapons when they robbed unsuspecting drunkards. They were nothing more than a band of skeevy brutes who used theft as a means to make their living. Murder wasn't in their skillset. No doubt the Enforcer was a stolen good that they figured to use as a defense for their hideout. And she doubted they had much practice with it.

She slowly raised her hands. "Okay, okay. I'll go." She backed up towards the broken wall. The thief's shoulders began to relax. But instead of retreating further and leaving the thief in safety, she dropped to the ground and leapt forward, attacking with a low spinning sweep kick. Her dagger of a leg knocked the man off his feet and he crashed onto the ground. Then she climbed on top of him and straddled his stunned body. The man gripped the gun tightly against his chest, the weight of both his and Xia's bodies crushing on top of it.

"What the hell was that?"

The man groaned. She lifted his head only to slam it back onto the floor.

"I asked you a question. What the hell was that?"

"I-I-I'm sorry!"

"Are you?" Her voice dripped incredulity. "So, if I let you up, you're not gonna try to shoot me?"

The man attempted to shake his head. "No. No, I swear."

"And you'll give me the money you stole?"

"Yes!"

"Really? You promise?"

"Yes, yes, I promise! Please. Just let me go."

"Give me the gun."

He made his best attempt at a nod as his nose crushed into the floor. Xia eased her weight in order for him to bring his arm out from beneath and to the side, allowing her to take the gun. But as she moved to grab it, he used all his strength to swing the gun-wielding hand for momentum as he rolled over.

They struggled for a moment before the splitting sound of the Enforcer shot through the air. Xia regained her tight straddle over him, now staring down at his cowering face. In a surge of strength, the man shot again, his second attempt just a hair away from Xia's cheek.

Crack. The man screamed as Xia snapped his wrist. His grasp loosened as his hand lay limp at his side.

"You promised." Her palm strike cut off another plea for mercy, smashing his nose into his brain.

4

Where's Lutno?

"Fuck," Xia muttered. She kicked the thief's lifeless body. Too bad he wasn't able to feel it.

The computer stood before her, demanding a password. Guessing was pointless. Hacking wasn't her favorite sport, but it was a necessary one. It wasn't a matter of if she'd be able to do it, but if she'd have the time.

She pulled out her Medusa, a mid-range hacking device that utilized a combination of dictionary and brute-force attacking to hash trillions of passwords. A race against the clock. She scanned the keyboard to gather data on which keys were used most frequently, and that's when she discovered one odd key on the top left that was used exponentially more than the rest of the odd keys. G1. She tapped it and a preloaded string of characters entered into the password box. Was it that easy? She hit enter and the monitor displayed the home screen. It was. Leave it to this ragtag group of thieves to be too lazy to manually input their own password. Now they'd pay the price for it.

She stuck the Medusa back in her pocket and activated her wrist's cellchip in order to begin the transfer of funds. She scanned the surrounding area to check for frequencies when the distant sound of voices halted her. Her hand moved towards the Enforcer in her pocket. Despite it being foreign, she was ready to make use of it if necessary.

Come on. Come ON. The computer was slow, only transferring 500 zeCoin at a time, and with each transfer was a verification of "Are you sure?" that Xia repeatedly jammed with impatience. After the eighth jam and transfer, the door clicked. By the time it opened, Xia was at the window.

"What the- YOU!"

Damn. She almost had her escape. But they saw her. And that was too much of a risk.

The first one was easy. Two strides forward and a dagger to the jugular. The second one got a fight. Jab, slip, cross, head kick. He was short enough for a solid one. Almost knocked out, but not quite. Knife to the jugular. The third was scrambling, but heading towards her fast. Three knives? Or the gun? She caught the glint of silver in his hand. A third knife to the jugular.

The blood pooled with the leftovers on the floor, a concoction of rotting food with soon-to-be rotting flesh. How long before the stench would reach the floors below and they'd be found? No concern of hers. She checked each of their pulses. Dead, dead, almost dead. She was about to snap the neck, but her hand traced the gun at her side. She withdrew the Enforcer and pulled the trigger, half expecting nothing to happen. But the hairs on the back of her neck tingled as electricity sliced through the air and a gaping hole burned through his head. Fully dead.

Out the window she jumped. Another day's work.

She wiped the blood onto her black skinsuit, the material expelling it instantly. A day of work for Xia was never dull. But some days were a little too thrilling. And today was one of them. She did not like killing. But if the alternative were a risk to her own life, that was not a risk she'd ever take.

Nobody passing on the busy avenue would have presumed that the dull-eyed, silver-haired vixen, face seemingly muted with boredom, would be holding such anxious, conflicting thoughts. Did she do the right thing? True, they had seen her and had recognized her instantly. But as Xia had assessed, they were nothing more than a lowly group of scummy thieves. Not murderers.

The memory of the thief shooting at her sprung. She shook her head. They were clearly capable of it, however sloppy their attempts were. And revenge was a hell of a drug.

Her fingers stroked the new object at her side. The deaths were worth it for an Enforcer. They were only used by the Freesian military and could blast a hole through damn near anything. With the amount of bullet-repelling gear available, standard firearms no longer held the edge they had in ages past. But an Enforcer? There was no protecting against its plasma beams.

"Well cut off my third eye, you did it, you tiny bitch!"

"Like you could ever afford a third eye," Xia mused.

She winced at Katia's guffaw of a laugh. "Is that *humor?* The silver bitch has got some humor! Here I thought you were as boring on the inside as you were on the outside."

The backhanded remark glided right through her. "Payment, please."

"You want a transfer? Otherwise I got enough phys."

Phys. Physical zeCoin. Her grandfather called it 'cash'. Said it was safer. *"You can trust what you can feel."* It was clunky and took up valuable space in her pockets, but she couldn't help but think of her grandfather whenever she had some on her.

"I'll take the hard stuff." Katia dropped 22 glowing obsidian beads into the palm of Xia's hand. A quick glance and she confirmed it was 22. In the pocket they went.

"I wanna hear all the details! Sit down, I'll get you a crumb bar. The new flavors aren't nearly as bad."

By the time Katia turned back around with several crumb bars in hand, Xia was already out the door.

Her day ended on the daylight side rather than the twilight. After picking up some cheap noodles from Fenuk, her usual noodle guy, she made her way to Mickey's. But not before passing by Lutno. Her whole day felt lopsided without the fulfillment of her daily routine of seeing Lutno and absorbing some of his crazy yet veritable semantics. She needed to straighten that out. But as she reached the corner of Mint and 7th, the day further fell out of kilter. Lutno wasn't there. Just his lonely soap box.

Xia stood there, frozen in her tracks, staring at the lone box. Where was Lutno? Every day, without fail, the small framed, wacky old man boasted his knowledge and warned of the dooms of society. Every single day. But not today. A lopsided day.

"Watch it," a nasally woman grunted as she banged right into Xia.

She shook her head. Was probably nothing. Everyone needs a day off, even crazy Lutno. Her grasp tightened with the bag of noodles while her other hand went for her upper pocket. Her empty upper pocket-

"Hey!" She yelled. Rage and panic rose as she realized all her phys was gone. The woman who bumped into her. She cursed herself for being so damn stupid. Her eyes darted along the street, but the thief was nowhere in sight. She sprinted and took a hard left down an alley. Needed higher ground. Spotting a large dumpster, she climbed atop and hoisted herself onto the ledge of the closest building. Her arms would surely be sore tomorrow.

Tap tap, tap tap tap. The scene from a few seconds prior replayed on her eye screen. Why did she have to zone out on that stupid box? She barely got a good look at the gal. But there, in the replay out of the corner of her eye, she noticed a dark-haired woman take a hurried right at the end of the block.

Xia scolded herself once more for not checking her memory screen before she made the sprint. She took a left. How many mistakes could she make? She glanced at her now dripping bag. The noodles had spilled. Today was not her day.

Two hours of searching, sprinting, and cursing later, Xia gave up. She slumped against the wall of a smoked meat shop, the delicious fumes taunting her nose. Her eyes watered in anger. Half her job involved getting back what people rightly deserved, and she couldn't even do that for herself? Bested by a lowly pickpocket. It was her own fault for choosing phys.

She debated for several minutes on whether or not the smell of smoked pork had won her over. It had not. She made her way to Mickey's.

"What the hell is that?" Dames asked as she plopped the soupy bag onto the bar counter.

"Can I get a bowl or something? Some of the noodles are salvageable."

He snickered. "What happened? Can't picture you dropping your food."

"Got robbed. Can I get the usual?"

Dames' eyes widened. "Robbed? Can't picture you getting robbed, either."

"Yeah. So. The bowl and the drink, please."

"How much did they take?"

"Too much. Drink. Bowl."

Dames clicked his tongue and walked towards the back. Xia let out a sigh housed deep in her bones. She was tired. Sore. And so hungry. She should have taken one of the nasty crumb bars. It would have been worth having to listen to Katia's rambles.

Dames returned with a large bowl. But it wasn't empty.

"Here."

Xia shook her head, but she couldn't help herself from salivating. "No, I can't—"

"Come on. It was leftovers. Just take it. Seems you could use some good luck today."

She eyed sideways, as if someone were to snatch the goods away from her. Nope, not even a glance in her direction. She took a bite.

"Thank you."

"Now, one glass of the usual. Coming right up."

The food was good. Damn good. She didn't bother throwing in the rest of her noodles. *Leftovers my ass.* There's no way somebody could start eating this and not finish it. She tried her best to savor it, but minutes later the bowl was empty and she was sucking down the drink before her.

"So," Dames said as his monstrous frame leaned against the bar. "Another big day in the life of Xia. Care to share some of the adventures had today?"

Sip. "Not really." The silence weighed down, thickening like the smog outside. "I didn't see Lutno today."

A flash of something on his face. "Really?"

"Yeah. This morning, and just a few hours ago. No Lutno. There's never no Lutno."

Dames hummed. He never hummed. That flash of something. Xia replayed the moment in her eye screen. Zoom. Analyze expression. 82% worry.

"What's wrong? You're not telling me something."

His eyes narrowed. "I hate those fuckin' memory replay thingies."

"Dames," she almost pleaded. "What is it?"

He leaned closer, his voice now a low rumble. A scratchy puma purr. "I heard something may have happened to him. Apparently his ramblings yesterday were…what was it? 'Increasingly frantic'. Swore somebody was going to get him, so that they could 'get away'."

The gears began to turn. "Who's they?"

"Have no idea. Got my hypotheses. Not sure what the motive would be though. Unless his ramblings got too offensive and the gov' got 'im. Slags never bothered with him before, though."

Xia knew a motive. Dames had never led her astray, and neither had the Nightcrawler on the radio. Brain transplants and a new utopia where only Virgins were allowed had a clear logical conclusion. And Lutno was the proof of it happening.

"You told me a while back," Xia dropped her voice down. The bar was practically empty, but one could never be too careful. "About the brain transplants."

"Right. No news about when they'll gain movement. Right now only certain elites have access, as far as I know."

"You didn't hear about anything else?

"No. Why?"

A stare-off. Xia considered. Then she cut it short. "If you do, let me know."

1 a.m. Xia stared out at the flashing pinks and blues of the city lights below as she injected the vitaroids into her bloodstream.

Dames didn't know about the Utopia. Did he not have a radio? She always wondered where he got his information, but she knew better than to ask. She didn't share the newfound information with him. She never did. She received information, never shared it. Knew better than that. But if she were to share it, Dames was the person she trusted the most. For now, though, she decided to keep it to herself.

She had the dots connected. Now, how to turn those dots into money?

She pulled out the thin needle with ease and grabbed the next one. Mod adapter solution. Finding the same spot, she placed her thumb on the end, ready to push—

Her footing stumbled as the room shook beneath her. Her scarred hand jolted forward and steadied herself on the tall glass. A few passersby knocked into each other on the ground below as the land reverberated with uncontrolled vibrations. A Rumbling.

This one wasn't too bad. It was over almost as soon as it began. The timing was less than ideal. Placement was important with injections. She paused and waited a few moments, ensuring the quake was truly over, before sliding the long needle back into her arm. The needle that allowed her to use mods and prevent her body from rejecting the technology. Something that was as ingrained in her life as going to sleep, and yet there was a whole subset of people that rejected it all. People like her grandfather. People like Lutno.

She didn't know too much about Lutno's life. His home was a mystery; he could have lived on that soapbox for all she knew. But she did know of some of his followers.

Lutno had a decent following. A small one, sure, compiled of other Virgins and regretful people modded beyond humanity. Somehow, Lutno had caught on that someone was after his unmodded body. How did he know? Had other people been taken? Further recon was needed to uncover just how deep this pit went. She couldn't go straight to the source, but she could go to his biggest fans. One of which happened to live right in the building.

5

VIRGIN CONNECTIONS

K nock Knock, knock knock knock.

Her grandfather taught her that knock. That was the knock Virgins used with each other. A little white lie was sometimes necessary.

An eye through the peephole. "Who's there?"

Xia glanced around. Scanned. Nobody in earshot distance except for the eye in the peephole.

"I'm Xia. I live on the 25th floor. I want to talk to you about Lutno."

"I don't know who you are talking about—"

"My grandfather is Youle."

A pause. She should have led with that. The click of the door sounded as it opened ever so slightly, revealing a gangly old woman, hair grayer than the smog. Her cloudy eyes traveled up Xia's lean frame, slow and suspicious, until they rested on Xia's face. Her eyes softened. "You have his mouth." She turned around and walked further into her home. Xia followed.

The place was cozy. Nothing like Xia's place. A kettle brewing tea gave the home a botanical spice. Mismatched but well-kept upholstery and real wood filled the room, allowing for minimal walking space. Plenty of places to sit, though. She chose the end of the brown woven couch.

"Lutno wasn't out yesterday."

The woman took a seat in a crimson red armchair, arm's length from the kettle. "Mhmm."

"Do you know why?"

The woman glanced from side to side with anxiety. Palms clammy. Her breath hitched. "Why are you asking me this?"

Xia wiped her own moistening palms on her black suit. Then she leaned forward, her eyes following the swirls of the carpet, her mind drifting from her grandfather to Lutno. "I like Lutno. I think there's a lot of value in what he has to say." The woman nodded subconsciously. "I walk past him every day when I'm working. He's always been there. But not yesterday. And two days ago, I heard he was worried that somebody might be after him."

Palms clammier. "Not just him. All of us."

"You mean, Virgins."

Her eyes widened. "We prefer the term Humans."

She stopped herself from rolling her eyes. "Right. Somebody is after humans. Can you tell me what you know? What else has Lutno told you in your private meetings? That he can't say in public because it's too dangerous?" She paused, perhaps coming off too strong. "My grandfather, Youle. You knew him. You didn't know me, but he raised me. You can trust me." She hoped those words would be enough to diminish the woman's hesitance.

A long pause before the words poured from her mouth. "He said they were going to slice open our brains and steal our bodies!" Her face paled in terror at what she had just said. Her bony hand grabbed the kettle and poured into the small yunomi before her. Tea to calm the nerves. One of the first lessons Xia remembered from her grandfather.

"And do you know why?"

The woman shook her head. If the tea was burning her, she didn't show it.

"Who else knows about this?"

"Word is spreading fast. We're all terrified. If Lutno is really gone...who knows who will be next?"

Xia leaned over and rested her hand over the trembling woman. The touch sent a slithering snake up her arm and down her spine. When was the last time she touched someone like this?

"Thank you for telling me this. If you need anything—" she pulled out a small card from her pocket. "—you can call this contact. If you hear anything, call this contact. And if you want me to check in on somebody, I can do that too."

The woman's tremble lessened slightly. "Thank you. You really are Youle's granddaughter."

Two days later, a call.

"Name." She answered.

"Who? I don't...I think I have the wrong contact."

Xia recognized the rattling tone. "Ah." She turned off the voice adapter, which warped her usual tone two octaves lower. "This is Xia."

"Oh. Hi. Yes. Youle's granddaughter. This is Impani." Xia realized she hadn't caught the woman's name prior. Impani. She liked it. "You said to call you if I heard anything."

"Yes. What have you heard?"

"It's my friend. Botan. He is Lutno's nephew. It's just horrible. He doesn't know if it's Lutno or not. But you cyborgs have ways."

Xia glossed over the crypticness.

"Where shall I meet him?"

Impani gave the address to Lutno's home. It was on the opposite side of town, which was to be expected. Virgins like Impani and Xia's grandfather were a rarity. They tended to live in clusters on the outskirts of the city, mainly towards the Southeast side of town. Due to the fact that Xia practically never dealt business with Virgins, she seldom set foot in that part of the city. She made her way from the West side of the Fourth Ward, through sprawling Midpoint, past the bustling skyscrapers and clogs of people in the Third Ward, and towards the Southeastern First W ard.

Excitement prickled at the prospect of seeing where and how Lutno lived. Was his home as intense and haphazard as his spiels?

The answer was no. Lutno kept a clean and tidy home, reminiscent of the Before Times. Before the Ultima War. Before the end of globalized, interconnected, free civilization. Photographs of a young boy with glasses playing ball. A teenager grimacing beside a bright-eyed middle-aged man and woman. A young Lutno? His parents? And the books. Xia had never seen so many books. So proudly on display. Had Lutno no discretion? A single slag's eye on this would mean a one-way ticket to the Void.

Nobody knew what the Void was like. Nobody had ever gone there and come back to tell it. A few had made wild claims, but they were nothing short of drunken tall tales meant to impress. Some questioned its existence. Xia was one to question every declaration from the FRF. But she knew of the government's potential for the terrible, so the existence of the Void was not one she would question. And with the amount of lawbreakers and so-called "criminals" that got rounded up and sent off to never be heard from again, there was no reason to discredit its existence.

"So, you are friends with Impani," Botan said. Xia could barely see his face behind the wrinkles, glasses, and thick black beard.

'Friends' was a stretch. "Yes." She picked up one of the books on the shelf. Woodworking: The Complete Step-by-Step Manual. Another. The Mysteries of World War II: Secrets in the Trenches. Another. 50 Ways to Cook a Zucchini.

A cough. "Can I show you?"

"Right." She quickly stuffed the book back and followed Botan into the bedroom of the small house. Bed made, clothes folded.

"Over here." Botan grunted as he bent down and pointed to the corner of the Perisian rug. It was a beautiful piece from another land and time. A crimson tapestry with intricate blue and beige shapes dancing around each other in perfect symmetrical harmony. Her eyes followed his finger. At the edge, the beige prematurely blended into the crimson.

"Blood. And you think it's Lutno's?"

Botan nodded. "We figured you had one of those mods that could confirm for us."

"You figured right." It was a stretch for them to assume any modded person would have a DNA matcher. Most people had no use for it. But in Xia's line of work it was a necessity. She touched his pillow with her forefinger and scanned, and then repeated with one of his shirts. DNA match. Onto the blood. Within seconds, she corroborated the sad truth. "Yes. This is Lutno's blood."

A small sigh. "I figured as much. Um, here." He dug around in his pockets and pulled out a few phys, his hand trembling as he offered it to her. "For your trouble."

Xia waved him off. "No need. This was easy enough. Besides, I got to see the home of the infamous Lutno."

Botan's eyes widened. A cyborg, refusing payment? Being charitable? It was nearly impossible to believe in his biased eyes. "Are you sure?"

"Yes." The information she was giving to Botan was just as useful for herself. And her current goal was to build rapport with the Virgin community. She pulled out her contact card. "Here. Call me if you hear anything else about Lutno, or you need help. I know what Lutno was telling you all, and I think there's truth to it. You'll need to protect yourselves. I can help."

More evidence for her horrible hypothesis. The brain transplants were happening, and Virgins were targeted. Was Lutno one of the first?

The prospect of brain transplants had been tossed around since Xia was a child. Her grandfather's Virgin friends warned of the decline of society, the irreversibility of mods. How they'd only get worse and worse, that people would only grow more reliant on them. An addiction that would overtake humanity until there was none left. Keep modding yourself until what's left to mod? But even that has limitations. The human body can only undergo so much. Xia had minimal modding compared to so much of the population, but even she couldn't skip an injection. That mistake only needed to be made once.

Two years ago. She had stumbled into her apartment at two in the morning. Lips buzzing, room spinning. Dames sure makes a good drink. The mattress on the floor called to her like a siren in the sea. How could she refuse? She collapsed on top and fell into deep slumber, and it wasn't until the following afternoon that she was released from it.

Did I take my injection? The question came like a bullet. She couldn't remember. She checked her supply. She had not. Panic rose. She quickly rolled up her sleeve and jammed the needle up her arm, praying that it wouldn't be too late. It took 6 hours for the injection to fully take effect. So if she had none of the fabled side effects for just a few more hours, she'd be in the clear.

It was on hour three. It started with the shakes. Came on slowly. Just the twitch of a finger. But it kept on twitching. Then it was her hand. Then up her arm. Minutes later her arms trembled violently as she held onto herself for stability.

By hour four, she was a rattling mess. She lay on her mattress, willing the injection to hurry the fuck up. Her head throbbed. Her teeth ached. And then came the splintering pain of little fireworks in her eyes. Most of Xia's mods related to her eye screen, so as her cells rejected the foreign technology, her eyes took the brunt of the pain. She moaned in agony.

On the fifth hour, the fireworks subsided. The shakes became a vibration. Deep, heavy breaths replaced her moans. She passed out for another 12 hours. And she never missed another injection.

Without injections, Cyber City would crumble in a day. While the mod-adapting injection was by far the most populous and important, injections had managed to capitalize on every market to fix every problem. It had started as a public health endeavor. Coralex Pharmaceutical had swooped in to save the day when a bacterial virus causing hemorrhaging plagued the city. The city was saved. But that wasn't the only problem. Malnutrition from a lack of decent food and real sunlight became an increasing issue. White knight Coralex saves the day with vitamin injections to supply you with everything your body is missing. A "small" (but actually quite hefty) price increase and you could have your vitamins infused with steroids, allowing the meager human frame to better survive in the harsh demands of Cyber City. They attempted a high-calorie protein synthesized injection to replace food altogether, but that didn't quite catch on. People love the taste of a good carb.

And the taste of a good drink. No chance in Hell she'd ever take an alcohol injection, she thought as she took a sip of the murky cocktail before her. Dames wasn't working today, evidenced by the sub-par quality of the spritz. No cherry.

"Back out on the soapbox?"

Her ears perked. Then she tapped twice up the ear to amplify the sound as she honed in on the conversation of two men at the end of the bar.

"No, just walkin' around. I swear it was him. Looked way more...normal though."

"Lutno? Normal?" The taller man laughed, almost sounding mechanical.

"Yeah. Clean shaven, clothes more modern. No crazy antics. Was weirder to see him like that than his usual self though."

"Lutno doesn't do normal. You're mistaken, Al."

"I'm not," the shorter man said, his demeanor growing defensive. "I got two damn good eyes, and ten even better mods, and you know damn well—"

"Oh, here we go again—"

The two bickered and Xia tapped out of the conversation, the useful bits coming to an end. She had no doubt that the man really had seen Lutno.

Or rather, Lutno's body. That was no longer Lutno.

6

Vroom Vroom

It was only a matter of time before the promise of this Utopia would become common knowledge. But which would come first? That or the access to routine brain transplants?

Xia didn't know, and it didn't quite matter. The fact that it was already happening meant that she was running behind. For now, she was working on building a network so that when the time came, and Virgins were the ticket out of this hellhole, she would be the first one called for aid— for a nice little price.

Her name had spread in the Virgin community, mostly thanks to Botan. Refusing payment was the right choice. She told Botan that she was a freelancer, taking on any and all odd jobs that needed doing. *"Have you ever killed someone?"* He had asked. *"Yes."* She had answered. She couldn't quite read his expression, and even her facial mood recognition software had put an even split between worry, curiosity, and "unknown". She told him she'd offer bodyguard services, check in on homes for safety, and, most importantly, sell fake mods.

Fake mods were not a commodity. Knock off mods, sure. But it was still a mod. What's the use of a device that looks like it could enhance functions, but couldn't do anything at all? Well, now there was a huge one.

He had asked how these fake mods would work. Xia explained that there would be no installation process, no actual alterations of the human body, and no need for injections. Just wearable pieces of technology that radiate frequencies mimicking those of mods. Visually, the wearer would appear the same. But a quick scan would show them to be (poorly) modded.

He had seemed hesitant. But he agreed to spread the word, and spread the word he did. That night, Xia stayed up all night tinkering and soldering, testing and scanning. Who knew a fake mod would be so much work? But by the following morning she had it. A perfect modular chip, to be clipped over the ear. She held it between her slender fingers, eyeing it with satisfaction and exhaustion. Hopefully the next one would be quicker to make. If Lutno was already replaced, she'd need more fake mods.

It had been three weeks since Lutno's disappearance. Besides the man at the bar supposedly catching a glance of him, nobody else had heard from the Soapbox Speaker. In that time, Xia had become a household name in the Virgin community. Her hours were filled with meeting new people, gaining their trust, and fake modding. She was getting better at it, each finished product taking less time to complete than the day before. So far, her business only consisted of the faux mods and the occasional household security enhancement. Until she got a call.

"Name."

"The smog is quite dusty today," a frazzled voice on the other end whimpered. A code greeting was needed for her circle of clientele.

"This is Xia. What do you need?"

"Yes, I— uh…I need your help." The stranger's voice broke as if about to cry. "My husband. He's missing. I don't— I don't know what to do. I think he, he kept saying…I think he—"

"Where can we meet?"

The woman gave her address, and Xia arrived two hours later.

The apartment was possibly the shabbiest Xia had ever set foot in. With each step forward, the prospect of any decent payment dwindled. She reached the designated room number and knocked, the door rattling from the contact.

A young woman answered the door, eyes bloodshot and puffy, face still wet from tears. But the swollen face did little to mask the woman's natural beauty. She beckoned Xia to come in, which she did. Xia was about to break the ice when the woman began to cry once more.

"It's – my – husband," she uttered between gasps.

Xia waited, painfully, for the woman to continue.

"He never – came home last night. He's never *not* come – home. He must have been — *taken*!"

Xia waited again, but the woman only continued to cry. "I need you to try to calm down. I can't help you if you can't tell me the details."

"There ARE no details! He's simply — *gone!*"

Of all the skills Xia had cultivated over the years, social was not one of them. "Do you want my help or not? Then I need you to tone it down and tell me what you want me to do." The sobs continued, but with some slight restraint. "What's your name?"

"L-L-Leiko."

"And your husband's?"

"Ettaro." Her voice gained some hidden strength at the mention of her husband's name.

"And you last saw him yesterday?"

"Yes," she nodded.

"Where did he go?"

"He went to work. He is a waiter at the Friar's Den. I called and they said he left w-work as usual. B-but he never came home!" The tears threatened to erupt again.

"Can I take a look around?"

"Y-yes. Go ahead." Leikko followed at Xia's heels like a lost puppy, sniffling and hiccupping behind her.

There wasn't much to look at. The living room and kitchen spanned a measly 15 feet, and what would have fit better as a closet was the couple's bedroom.

"Any weapons?"

"Just a knife. Under his pillow."

Xia flipped the pillow over, revealing the small dagger. "So he is unarmed when he leaves for work each day?"

"Y-yes."

Xia couldn't fathom venturing around the city unarmed. But she kept that to herself.

"Was there any—" she stopped as the sound of the apartment door opened. Leikko whipped her head around, eyes wide with hope.

"Ettaro!" She shrieked as she sprinted from the closet bedroom into the arms of the man at the door.

The man enveloped her in his arms, but Xia caught the momentary surprise in his eyes. She replayed the moment. Yep. *Confusion,* followed by realization.

That man was no longer Ettaro.

Xia stared between the reunited couple. The feeling was bizarre. She had the sudden urge to run before him and slice his throat. End the life of the sicko who stole the poor husband's body. But she wasn't about to further scar the emotional woman. She suppressed the dangerous urge and waited for Leikko's ecstatic frenzy to calm before announcing her departure. "If you need anything, Leikko, feel free to call me."

"Yes, yes, right. Thank you." She paid Xia barely any attention. "Ettaro, let me make you something. You must be starving. Where were you?! I've been crying non-stop! Do you want some fried rice? I can thaw some of the beef tip rolls. I think we have a few left."

Leikko continued to babble as Xia stepped towards the door to leave, passing Ettaro on the way out. "Good to see you again," she said, her voice just soft enough that Leikko couldn't hear.

Ettaro nodded back. "Good to see you too."

Xia's mind raced the entire three-mile walk home, replaying the encounter in her mind. How nonchalantly he greeted her back, despite them never meeting before. How his hand adjusted to the cap on his head, likely hiding the scar of a brain procedure. How long before Leikko would notice that that was not her beloved? How many others had lost their friends and family without even realizing it? How many others had lost their bodies? Most likely they were killed. She hoped they were. She didn't want to imagine the potential experiments conducted on Virgin brains. Yes, death was the kinder option.

These people, whoever they were, were moving fast. Who were they? They were operating secretly, as evidenced by Ettaro returning back home to roleplay as Leikko's loving husband. They had insider knowl-edge, considering they knew about the Utopia *and* had access to brain transplants. And since they had access to undergo such a procedure, they clearly had money. But the richest in Cyber City lived cushy lives as top dogs. Xia found it unlikely that they'd want to leave. Unless this Utopia was really just that: a perfect new world.

With the FRF behind it, chances were slim.

"Carry me, Grandpa!"

"Oh, alright, but it's the last time. You're getting too big for these old bones." That was the third time he'd said that this week. The girl called his bluff. But it wasn't a bluff. With each lift, Youle believed it was his last.

He walked out of the apartment into the stuffy air, the skinny girl wrapped atop his shoulders. He remembered how the air once was: crisp, with different flavors depending on the seasons. There were animals, there were smiles. He tried to give the girl as many of those as he could. Even when it was the last thing in this god-forsaken world he'd wanted to do.

In just a few more days, Xia's network boomed. She continued to make more fake mods, which she now dubbed *fods*, but her mind lin-gered on Leikko. With every call she received, she hoped to hear that trembling voice on the other line. But no, it was always a different voice with varying trembles. They all trembled to some degree. There was a lingering apprehension between Xia and each new Virgin. By the end of her work with a client, the apprehension had somewhat dissipated and they'd spread the word to other Virgins they knew. And the cycle continued.

Xia wasn't used to so much business. They weren't the wealthiest of clients, but the sheer volume made up for it. And as her tinkering skills improved, she began to build up a supply.

"Here, I can transfer. 1200 zeCoin."

Xia tapped away at her cellchip and accepted the transfer. When it was complete, her eyes trailed to the total funds. Her eyes widened.

"Is everything alright?" The skinny Virgin asked.

"Yes. Everything is fine. Call me if you need anything else." She prac-tically ran out of the man's apartment, her heart giddy. She hadn't ex-pected to reach her goal so soon. The day was finally here. She skipped the bar and went straight to a place that filled her with envy every time she walked past.

Unassuming on the outside, the aqua neon lights allowed for the naked eye to make out subtle shadows within the small shop. Inside was glorious. For Xia, she was a kid in a candy shop.

It was a small shop for its kind. There were others selling larger varieties, but Xia only wanted the best and this shop in Midpoint had it. Three models stood brilliantly on display. She inspected the first. Too hefty, too masculine, and likely too expensive. The second was flashy. It caught her eye, and the metal seemed to sparkle under the shop's low light. But the third. Oh, the third. She could have drooled. Slapping the tank, she called out to the motorsmith in the back. "I'll take him."

The sleek, matte finish rejected the blaring, luminescent glow of the city around them. She revved the engine, propelling herself even faster, feeling the beautiful beast roar beneath her with each throttle. She smiled. Leaning forward even further, body becoming one with the machine at a perfect 90-degree angle, she sailed off into the night.

Xia tended to stick to the heart of the city. It's where her work was done, it's where the drinks were poured. It was louder, and more crowded, but there was no reason to head out to the backroads. Not until now. Here she let out a gleeful howl, muffled by the matte black helmet that fully enveloped her head in a sleek, sharp bubble. Ant head with a snake body. Riding a dragon. Alone on the backroads, Xia was on top of the world.

Owning a motorcycle was uncommon in Cyber City for several reasons. First was the cost. It was a massive chunk of change, which people tended to use on other purchases. Gaming experiences, next-generation mods (most were still stuck on V2.5), pleasure dens. Or just a decent meal. Not only was the initial cost high, but maintenance was a pricey endeavor. They frequently needed tinkering, and a decent motorsmith charged an arm and two legs. Second was the convenience. Most people lived in cramped apartments. Where to store the bike? But the final reason, and perhaps the strongest, was that it made people a target.

If you rode a motorcycle, it meant that you had money. *You* became a target. But Xia didn't care. She'd deal with that. And anyone would be quick to find that she was not the loaded victim that they believed, but a penny-pinching freelancer who slept on the floor.

And being a freelancer, she made connections. One connection being quite useful. And she was driving to them right now. The barren road kicked up dust as she whizzed along, barely visible in the darkness of night. In the distance grew two bright bulbs of light, growing larger, larger, then flashing past her. Another motorist. A bubble of camaraderie. Xia smiled.

After what felt like two minutes, Xia stood at the door to what appeared to be a rusted, abandoned ranch house, save for the smoke escaping the chimney. She knocked.

"Russel? It's me."

A few seconds later the door swung open, revealing a lanky man with strong hands and eyes ridden with mods.

"Xia," he said, a cigarette hanging out of his mouth, ash mixed in his stubble. "Got your message." His eyes darted to the helmet at her hip. "Lemme see her."

"*He's* right over there," Xia corrected, pointing towards her new baby.

"Wheeewie!" he whistled as he jogged towards the bike. His hand glossed over the finish, fingers delicate and respectful of the beast's novelty. "Absolutely beautiful. Not too big, but not a tiny thing either." He examined more closely, fiddling with his eye mods. "Proton solid-state battery, pulse width modulation controller, fire throttle, all the good stuff. Solidly constructed. This Neyo's work?"

Xia nodded.

"And I get to store her?"

"Yes, if you could store *him*. And you'll bring him to me once a week when I'm too busy to come get him."

"Once a week? C'mon, these legs ain't gonna want to run back all them miles-"

"You owe me."

He took a heavy puff from his cig and thought back to the time he first met the silver-haired rascal. She seemed too skinny and too bored to get the job done. How many anti-theft mechanisms did he have on his damn ride? But after two too many drinks at Mickey's, his beloved

Luella was gone. He had tracked it down, but there was no way he'd get it himself. Didn't have a fighting bone in his body. And he'd never trust the government to get it back. So he called up this freelancer that his friend swore by. And in less than a day, his beloved Luella was back at home, sweet and sound.

"That I do, that I do. Alright Xi, you got it."

7

The Revitalization Project

As Xia ran home, she felt a longing the farther she went. A magnetic pull, calling her back to her cycle. Is this what mothers felt towards their infants? The thought was silly, but she wondered if this was a microscopic version of that. Xia didn't have a lot of grandiose hopes and dreams. But she did dream of owning a motorcycle. And now that dream was fulfilled.

Technically, they weren't even considered motorcycles anymore. The old ones, in the Before Times, used actual gas and had a manual transmission. Her grandfather had told her about the old fabled machines. How you could taste the freedom as the air whipped around you. Then, when Xia was six years old, she was walking along Grand Avenue with her grandfather when she saw it in person. It lasted only a few seconds, but Xia would forever remember those flashing moments. The scurrying of people getting out of the road, the swears of a few burly modded men, and the gleam of blinding headlights as it came closer, and then passed her, neon lines racing away.

"*Wow,*" she had uttered. Never had she seen something move so fast. And then the stories of grandfather's fabled motorcycle took physical form. And in that moment, she knew that someday, she'd have to have one.

The run home was a measly two miles if you cut through some back buildings in the mangier part of the city. Xia didn't mind. The sleezier the area, the more she was grateful for her own tiny place in the Fourth Ward. Russel could handle it. And he could use the exercise.

She ran past a string of crumbling, dilapidated buildings and a few sad drugged souls lingering about when she heard a man's voice echo.

"Hey, you!"

She kept running, but scanned the surrounding area. Dria Flock, age 22, moderate modage, currently under the influence of nexanine. Peia Korin, severe modage- dysfunctional, age unknown, currently under the influence of nexanine. Troy Deleur, age 51, mods unknown, age unknown, currently under the influence of nexanine...The list continued. Whole lot of nexanine. Nobody posing a serious threat or a sincere purpose. She kept running.

"You bitch!"

She instinctively scanned again and found a life form following behind her. Their scan blockers were effective. Most outlaws and misdoers had them, Xia included. Her hands glossed over the Enforcer in her side pocket. She hadn't yet had the pleasure of using it since she acquired it, but it was always at the ready. She picked up the pace.

"I know what you did to Draxel!"

Xia didn't know who that was and didn't care. She kept sprinting until the unknown person had quit tailing her, then dropped her pace back to her comfortable jog. She never even glanced back.

As Xia lay on her bed that night, she dreamed of the bike that she'd been forced to stash with Russel. In the Before Times, most people had their own garage, or they could simply park it on the street without much worry. But private transportation had become pretty much obsolete unless you were the elite. Everyone rode the buses or they simply walked. And there were a plethora of mods to assist with that. One particularly popular one, albeit expensive, was the Auto-Walk mod. A very simple and self-explanatory name. Placed in both kneecaps, it triggered the nerves and aided the muscles in the leg to walk with electrical impulses, allowing one to walk with half the physical effort. Xia'd never get one of those. She liked walking—*and* the effort that came with it.

Blip. Blip. Blip. An incoming call. She expected another worried Virgin, and was surprised to see the familiar call card.

"Name," she answered.

"You always gotta answer with that?"

"You can never be too careful."

Dames' low voice let out a rumble that sounded like exasperation, but Xia could see the smirk on his rectangle of a jaw. "So, somebody got themselves a fancy bike? Is that why I didn't see you at the bar today?"

"Word travels fast."

"You know damn well Russel called me immediately. Shame you gotta leave it all the way over there."

"It's not too far."

"Well, I may have a solution for you. But if it's not too far, I guess you don't need it."

Xia sat up from her mattress and turned to look at the city lights below. She could just make out the glinting outline of the bar's open sign. "Spit it out."

"Come on, say please."

Xia smirked. "Please."

Dames' guffaw rang out, a cacophony of low singing birds getting trampled through the gravel. Frankly, it was a bit scary-sounding. She pictured a girl cowering under the resonance. She loved his laugh. "I know a guy who makes personalized electro-magnetic defense forcefields. I like to call them electro-bubbles. He won't call 'em that though. Scolds me whenever I do. Got an ego."

"Electro-bubbles?"

"That's right! But like I said, don't call them that in front of him. He only recently perfected it, only selling them off-market. Also *very* dangerous. But you'd be able to handle it just fine."

"How exactly does it work?"

"Well, I can't really explain that part. But think of it like a magic bubble that can surround an object and only a person with the right signal can disable it."

Xia's eyes glossed over the lambent metropolis below. She imagined herself zipping through the crowded streets, flashing past the glimmering lights, and being able to drop off her bike in any of the twisted alleys that tangled through the area. "Where can I meet him?"

The next morning, Xia stood inside a small office across from the Electro-bubble creator, Flux. Clearly not his given name, but perfectly fitting for his persona. His large desk lay covered with gadgets and equipment: old electronics, control panels, pump sources, laser diodes, soldering tools. It slightly resembled the small station she had set up at her place to create fods, but scaled tenfold. And this was only a fraction of it. The door behind them led to his workshop, which was where the "real work" happens, he told her.

"Very cool," she said as her eyes scanned over all the equipment.

"Yes, it's *quite* cool," he corrected, his voice nasally and somewhat high-pitched. "You seem decent. I'll show you."

Xia followed behind him, her 5'9 frame towering over his measly 4'10. The hunch in his back knocked him down a few inches further. He shuffled forward and opened the door, the smell of burnt plastic and metal smacking Xia in her nose. She fleetingly wished for a smell-inhibiting mod. She followed Flux through the large room, past half-finished projects and colossal pieces of machinery that did God knows what, to the back. There the projects took a shift towards the smaller scale. But something told Xia these minuscule pieces of tech were just as, if not more, deadly than the massive machinery behind her. Her eyes swept over multiple small tables, one labeled *nanotech*. But Flux walked right past that one to a small table in the corner. A little lone chip lay atop. Before Xia could get any closer, Flux put a quick hand to her chest.

"Er- sorry," he said, hand lowering and cheeks reddening. The first time his pompous exterior crumbled. "But you need to stand back while I reprogram it." Xia nodded and watched as he tapped the small chip. A translucent screen appeared above, and his nimble, feminine fingers danced in the air as he went through each menu option, listing off each step to Xia. "And finally, the most important piece. You'll scan your fingerprint, iris, and saliva to imprint on the device. Only you will be able to access the Defochip."

He stared at her, his expression blank. "I don't have all day."

Her eyes widened. "You want me to do it right now? I haven't even paid you."

He scoffed. "What are you gonna do, snatch it and run off?"

"I could."

"Nah, you wouldn't. No way Dames would send you over here if you would."

Xia leaned in closer, examining the small chip more closely. Then her gaze shifted down towards Flux. "You trust him that much?"

He turned to face her, eyes unwavering. "If there's one person I trust in this god-forsaken city, it's Dames. Now," he tapped the floating screen once more. "Your eye and your spit, if you would."

Xia leaned forward and pressed her thumb to the screen, and then her eye, and then her tongue. A few seconds later, a checkmark floated down from the screen, signaling that the process was complete. Then the screen disappeared.

"Now, tap the chip," Flux said, his voice noticeably farther behind Xia. She turned to see him standing several feet away. Obeying, she turned back around and tapped the Defochip. Immediately, a brilliant electric blue bubble appeared around her, the rest of the room wobbling through its translucence. The hairs on the back of her neck stood up. She tingled.

"So, what happens if someone touches it?"

Flux grinned. "Let me show ya."

Before Xia could raise a brow, Flux stepped towards the bubble and reached out to touch it. As soon as his pointer finger made contact, his body flew backward like a rock in a slingshot, narrowly missing one of his massive machine inventions.

Xia jogged out of the translucent bubble and over to Flux. "You alright?" she asked. The smile on his face answered her question.

"Phew! Works pretty damn well, doesn't it. But see, I'm wearing this." He extended his wrist and showed her a thick black band. "Shock absorber. If someone ain't wearing one of these bad boys, they'd get a nasty shock."

"How nasty?"

His grin widened like a devious child. "*Nasty.*"

Xia nodded and glanced back towards the glowing blue sphere. "So, this'll happen to anyone who gets too close? No warning or anything?" She imagined a small child wandering too close, innocent with curiosity.

"Yes."

Children need to learn the harsh cruelties of their world at some point. "What's the payment?"

That night, Xia sat at her small desk, soldering away. She was getting the hang of these fods. But every time she got caught up, three more Virgins wanted to buy some more.

She hadn't yet heard of any other people being taken. Then again, it's likely many Virgins wouldn't disclose that to her. At this point, they mainly trusted her for buying protection, but not much else. Her mind flashed back to Leikko and the man that was no longer her husband. Leikko hadn't made contact with her since, but it was only a matter of time before she realized that that man was no longer her beloved spouse.

A loud beeping interrupted her wiring. She glanced at her cellchip. An SOS from Dames.

CHECK NEWS NOW.

She dropped the two wires and hastened to the black screen in the corner of her room, turned it on, and changed to the news station. Sinnie Soto, the primary newscaster who had more beauty mods than Xia had mods altogether, graced the screen. Her hair was a deep mauve tonight, and her eyelashes nearly crept through the display. Her literally sparkling eyes looked heavy under the sheer mass of lashes, fluttering with each new sentence.

"—all thanks to Coralex Industries. It is through their innovation that we have the bustling and advanced metropolis that we do. And it is through their technological advancements that we are able to enjoy so many pleasures and revelries, bringing out the best of the human form."

In other words, mods, Xia thought. She rolled her eyes.

"However, the spectacular technological advances have left little room for other endeavors. Agriculture and livestock is limited, and technology is our leading innovation. Due to Prime Minister Zoke's visionary endeavors, the Freesian Republic's Modernization Sector has been pursuing a rather promising endeavor known as *The Revitalization Project.*

This project houses a society reminiscent of the Pre-Recovery Era, with the eventual goal of Freesia profiting from the physical fruits of this place, and possible reintegration."

The image of a portly gentleman in a navy suit gazing proudly into the distance displayed behind Sinnie Soto. They always used the same image of the Prime Minister. His actual live appearances were a rarity, and with each appearance the likeness between this old stock photo and his true visage grew starker and starker. Xia couldn't remember the last time she saw actual footage of Zoke. To her knowledge, he hadn't stepped into the city proper in years. He, along with the rest of the government committees and military officials, were housed in the enviable Outer City Hubs.

"Removed from our current society, this Project focuses on horticulture, agriculture, aquatics, and forestry. This space has been revitalized and is now safe for habitation. Due to the nature of this place, only people without modular devices or enhancements are permitted to partake in this project and leave Freesia. If you are interested, you are encouraged to reach out to your nearest FRF Affairs Office.

"What an exciting prospect for our city! Prime Minister Zoke continues to work diligently in bettering our everyday lives, with—"

Xia muted the screen. It was finally official. The magical place away from this hell hole was open for business, but only for Virgins. Her heart pounded in her chest. Business was about to get very busy.

8

FILTERED CHEMISTRY

Xia woke up to numerous messages and missed calls from old Virgins, new Virgins, and Dames. She opened that one first.

Swing by the bar tonight?

She responded a simple *yes* and then scrolled through the rest, thankful that she silenced her cellchip. There were worried messages asking for more help, and one even asking for advice on what to do about the news segment and the prospect of leaving Cyber City behind.

She didn't respond. She would, but not yet. The day was too busy. She had spent the entirety of the previous one working on fods, so today was delivery day. And she was going to make those deliveries on her brand-new bike.

After picking up her favorite tea and honey graham from Calypso, she made her way to Russel's secluded home off the backroads. She took the longer, safer route. She wanted to get a solid walk in, especially since she was about to start walking a lot less. The farther she went away from the heart of the city, the less the air smelled. Felt lighter. She never noticed just how heavy the air was until moments like this. Is this what the air was like in the Before Times? Before the Great Global Warming Collapse? Before the Ultima War?

Youle had done his best to tell Xia as much as he could of the world before this current one. He was no historian, but anything was better than what the FRF told the people. There were some nuggets of truth, but they lay hidden under piles of steaming bullshit.

Once upon a time, the world was completely interconnected. There were no walls keeping people inside. People were free to go where they wanted. Sure, there were monetary and societal limitations, but the option was there. People could hop on a train or plane and go somewhere completely new. And they could run in fields, hike mountains, order a coffee on any corner. They could even see the sun in the sky. And the sky was blue! Xia stared at the orange sky above. This orange was the nicest they could get. Usually it was a muddy gray. She tried to imagine a blue sky, with a yellow sun. Were eyes meant to see such brightness?

This was the world her grandfather knew when he was young. But the world was deteriorating. The world had known about the climate issues for decades, but change wasn't made fast enough. And in some parts of the world, no change was made at all. As technology accelerated more rapidly, the world governments utilized artificial intelligence—AI—in their decision-making on how to reverse the impending climate-driven doom: geoengineering, carbon capture and storage, banning of fossil fuels, and a complete ban on all importing and exporting with countries that did not agree to such climate endeavors. But the ecological disasters increased by tenfold in a mere decade, with entire countries demolished by earthquakes, hurricanes, and viruses. Mass migration occurred, and with it, disease.

It reached a catalyst 80 years prior. Nobody quite knows the truth of it. The two leading world superpowers, the United Provinces and the Eastern Coalition, held a standoff. A cold war that quickly turned hot. Both countries decimated each other, and many others, through just a few well-timed nukes. And it was during this time that the FRF was established from the ruins of the Eastern Coalition, and the safe haven of Freesia closed its walls to the rest of the world, not letting anyone in— or out. There was a brief rebellion to the restrictions the government put in place. It was swiftly, and brutally, squashed.

According to the FRF, the rest of the world is practically a barren wasteland with uninhabitable levels of radiation. There are other societies established, but they are few and far between, and as the FRF continuously pounds into its civilians' heads- *They are not to be trusted.* Add to that mix the prospect of viruses that the current public is not immune to, the radiation, and the constant threat of being sent to The Void, not everyone is eager to venture outside the walls. Practically nobody is.

If it weren't for Youle's grandiose tales of the times before, Xia wondered if she'd even care about a life outside the walls. Amazing how accustomed people become to the familiar. The unknown spurs fear, especially when the government does nothing but tout its dangers. But she wasn't dense. There was no reason to blindly trust in the FRF.

Then again, Xia actually liked Cyber City, in a twisted kind of way. A dog-eat-dog world, she became a basenji. She managed to adapt to the hectic and difficult way of life, and she couldn't help but feel some satisfaction in that. But with the purchase of that damn bike, Xia felt a spur of something new deep in her gut. Or was it her soul? She never felt such a level of longing, of fulfillment, of *freedom*. A slice of heaven in a hellscape. She gazed back up towards the burnt orange sky and imagined it blue. Blinding.

She approached Russel's place. He stood there, already waiting for her, his gangly frame leaning against the front door, a cigarette hanging from his mouth.

"So, ya dumping me already?" He called out to her.

"Thought you didn't want to make the walk."

He smiled, his cigarette drooping, and walked towards her. "I'll admit, I wasn't too keen on making that trek back home, but I could have brought it up to you today. Didn't even get a chance to ride it."

Xia raised an eyebrow. "Never even took him for a joyride?"

Russel frowned, insulted. "I'd never. I respect a man's cycle. Would only ride it if you needed me to." He tossed her helmet to her. "Unless you'd let me take her for a spin right now."

Xia popped the helmet on and swung her leg over the side of the bike. She gave him a two-fingered wave, and with a small nod, she sped away. Russel took another puff and grinned.

How the hell did she manage to work before? Getting around town took a quarter of the time, and was actually *fun*. She wasn't used to having so much fun. Would the novelty wear off? She couldn't see how. She zipped and weaved through the city, flying past dirty looks unbothered.

When she delivered the first fod, the man stood there in shock as she pulled up. The second delivery was more chatty. He wanted to know every detail about the bike, of which Xia did not share. The third delivery wasn't fazed, but they wanted to confer about the news from the night prior. Her helmet still on, she offered no insight. Just got the money and went on her way. She didn't want to talk about it. Not until she met with Dames. And not until she had some more fun with the bike.

"You know, you're not supposed to drink and drive." Dames slid the drink across the bar.

"What?"

He shrugged. "Just some old saying. From before."

She hummed and took a swig. Even the drink tasted more succulent than usual. She was on a high, the electric adrenaline still buzzing through her veins. "What's the talk been like in here? Since the news last night?"

"It's been something. People seem to have lost their filters. Not that they had much of 'em before. Some are lamenting over how they want in on this project, mainly because of the possibility of fresh water and meat. People love their meat."

No surprise there. Water straight from the tap was practically undrinkable. Tasted metallic. Like blood. Most people drank tea, boiling the water sometimes three times for good measure. And meat cost as much as a decent mod. Those cows had seen brighter days. Quite literally, since they were kept inside locked-down facilities. No way they could be kept in the open—not enough space, and too many people trying to steal them. Or even just parts of them. The prospect of fresh meat and fresh water was enough to make even the most well-off cyborg want to get away.

Xia pictured jumping into a pool of fresh water, body fully immersed in cool cleanliness. Emerging to clean air, blinding and brilliant blue cast above her. It was an enticing prospect.

"Some trashed the Virgins, either upset that they were the lucky ones to get to go or happy that they'd leave altogether. The ones without any filter trashed the FRF." He glanced both ways. "Some said the whole project was a front for something else entirely."

"Do you think it is?"

The question was brazen, but Xia was curious if there was something Dames wasn't telling her. He shrugged and started cleaning a glass. She could tell he wasn't hiding anything. That was the scope of what he knew. "Do *you*?" He countered.

Xia leaned forward and took another sip, her silver hair hanging over her face. While she didn't trust the FRF, others clearly had reason to. Reason enough to implant their own brains into new bodies just so they could get there. That seemed like a good reason to believe that there must be some truth to this 'Revitalization Project.'

She shrugged back. She hadn't yet disclosed to him the business she'd created. With the way word traveled in her circle, she expected him to bring it up to her, and then she'd spill it all at once. But he hadn't. The Virgin circle was a tightly woven knit. She hesitated, then scanned the room. Nobody appeared to be listening. The people that frequented Mickey's weren't the listening type, either. That's how Dames got so much information in the first place.

"You remember that info you gave me a while back?" She tapped her head.

"Mmhmm," he said, leaning closer, still cleaning the already spotless glass.

"It's happening already. To Virgins."

Xia sipped again, letting the gears shift in Dames' own brain, waiting 'til they clicked into place. His eyes widened.

"Since when? Since—Lutno?"

Xia nodded. "I've been helping them out."

"Helping who? Virgins? With what?"

The question was quiet, but it hung in the air like a viper, waiting to strike. Xia felt exposed. This was not the conversation for the bar. Of all the secret and covert tidbits of information exchanged between the two of them, this was the most severe.

"Not here." She paused. A heavy pause. Nervousness fluttered inside her, unable to escape under the weight of the massive, uncomfortable pause. "Come to my place after your shift?"

A flicker of something passed over Dames' face, but Xia didn't dare replay the moment. "Sure. Must be quite the ops."

"You remember where I live?"

He nodded. "I'll call when I'm there."

She flicked some phys at him and downed the rest of her drink. Then she left the bar, hopped on her bike, and rode home.

Dames had offered to walk Xia home once, just once, after a particularly rowdy night at the bar. She had drunk too much, and some not-too-kind patrons seemed to be eyeing her a little too closely. But even then, he had only dropped her off at the main building doors.

It's not that Xia and Dames weren't close. In fact, that was the issue. Dames was the closest person Xia had, other than her late grandfather. But Dames was her friend and her bartender. Nothing more. And she knew of how things could end up...of where expectations often led.

That was something her grandfather didn't teach her; it was explicitly all around her. It was the reason why beauty mods were the most popular variety of mods, and why the Red Light District was frequented more than any other area of the city. Of the minimal pleasures in Cyber City, sex thrusted at the top.

Xia had never done it. Had no desire to. The act alone seemed disgusting to her, and she never felt that fluttery desire that removes the disgust and replaces it with passion. The closest she had felt was an admiration for the human form. A lean body sprinting past, jawline sharp and eyes like a cat. She couldn't tell if it was a man, woman, or something in between. The physique struck her, and she stood in the bustling street and just stared at their retreating figure.

Other than that one fleeting androgynous encounter, Xia had never felt lust for another person. And the prospect of it made her shudder. She hoped Dames wouldn't get the wrong idea.

Here. The message came like an electric shock, causing Xia to jump up from her chair and nearly drop her recently constructed fod.

She met him in the apartment lobby, a dingy room with a few busted chairs and a couple of doors to some offices. The ceiling was high, but it did little to shrink Dames' figure. She beckoned him to come in the elevator without a word, instantly regretting not saying hello. The silence deepened the awkwardness. Even Dames looked a little off. Almost, bashful? She hated it. She needed him to be his usual confident, suave self. She could feed off that. But instead, he seemed to feel the same tension.

She glanced up towards his tower of a figure. "You look even taller in here."

"I'll probably look even taller in your place."

The words reddened her cheeks. Why? She hated situations like this. A fight to the death with an outlaw seemed more comfortable. The lift to the 25th floor couldn't move any slower.

Dames was right; despite Xia's apartment reaching a solid 10 feet tall, Dames was massive inside. But that was because he wasn't just tall, he was wide as well.

"Wow, that's quite a view," he said, taking in the window of a wall.

"Pretty standard," she said. Which was true; most people lived in high-rise apartments. There wasn't room for much else.

"I live on the second floor. Don't get to see much." His pupils contracted as he gazed at the luminescent horizon. "How do you sleep?"

"It's basically a nightlight."

He let out one of his gravel laughs. It felt out of place to hear in Xia's home.

"Come here," she motioned towards the table in the corner, her equipment splayed about. She picked up the completed chip. "This is what I wanted to tell you about." She placed it in his bulky hand, the tiny thing lost in his palm. "Don't break it."

He held it up to the city light between his index finger and thumb, examining it through his eye screens.

"A mod?"

"A fod," she corrected. He looked at her quizzically. "A fake mod." It felt uneasy showing the little pieces of work to Dames. She knew they worked, and she had done a solid job selling them. She didn't realize it until that moment, but she wanted Dames' approval.

"Who'd want a fake mod? Oh," the answer came to him as quickly as the question. "Virgins."

"Yes. Virgins," Xia said, gaining some traction. "After Lutno wasn't out on his soapbox, I was suspicious. The Virgins keep close, so I asked around. He was missing. And apparently, he thought someone was after him. I pieced together that brain transplants might be used to be able to access this 'Utopia', and so when Lutno—"

"Wait, you knew about the Revitalization Project?" He looked down at her, a shrivel of hurt in his onyx eyes.

"Y-yeah." A pause. To tell or not to tell about the radio? She chose not to. "Anyways, I confirmed that Lutno was gone, so I offered services to different Virgins. Built a network. I'd check their homes for potential ways to break in, offer to help look for missing family, but most importantly, sell them these." She pointed to the fod.

Dames nodded, soaking in the words. "You help find any missing people?"

Xia turned towards the window. "No. Not really. I only got called to help with that once. And when I met with the girl, the missing husband came home. Except it wasn't actually him."

"You mean, someone else in his body?"

She nodded. "The girl didn't notice. She was too ecstatic he was home. I thought she'd have figured it out by now. I keep expecting a call from her. Never got one."

"If the husband was taken and had his mind replaced, the girl would be the next easy target."

A hole opened deep in Xia's stomach and dread pooled in. How had she not thought of that? Of course, whatever abhorrent soul kidnapped that man and stole his body wasn't going to play House with the wife. He would have someone else snatch her too. And Xia had just left. She felt sick.

Dames noticed the color fade from Xia's already pale face. "Hey, you okay? Don't feel guilty."

"Easy to say, not easy to do."

Xia continued to stare out the window, but she wasn't looking at the city. Her mind roared with images of Leikko. Strapped to a chair as they injected her, as they sawed open the top of her beautiful head. She knew Leikko for a whole ten minutes, but in those ten minutes, she knew Leikko held nothing but pure, unadulterated love for her husband. And as they tossed her brain, or whatever they did with the sole remnants of those poor Virgins, gone was that love.

The images broke and Xia was snapped back to reality by the feeling of physical touch on her shoulder. Dames' monstrous hand lay gingerly. It was the first time he had actually touched her. A bubble of something. Excitement? Heat? Repulsion? Xia couldn't sort through them all. She turned back towards him and, in doing so, shook off his clasp.

"So, since they're targeting Virgins, the best defense would be to not appear as one. And these devices can do that."

"I see. Well, you've made quite the setup here. It's pretty genius, honestly."

She couldn't help the smile that gushed from her gut. "Thanks."

"I just can't believe it's come to this. That people would be doing something like this. Kidnapping people and putting their own brains inside them." A gravelly exhale. "That's not true. I can believe it. I just don't want to."

Xia nodded. The capacity for vile behavior knew no bounds. She saw it firsthand. The lengths one would go to for money, for beauty, hell, for a decent meal. Screwing anyone and everyone over in the process. What made her so different? Was she different? She thought so. She didn't like pain. She didn't like to feel it, and she didn't like to see other people feel it either. But even she could acknowledge that those feelings had subsided over the years. The first dead body she saw haunted her for weeks. She couldn't sleep. She'd close her eyes and instead of darkness, she saw the bloody mangled face. Now she'd walk past the same scene, make a solemn nod, and forget about it after two drinks.

"You called it a 'Utopia'. Before, when mentioning the Revitalization Project. You really think it's all that great? Sinnie Soto seemed to downplay it."

It was true. The newscast made sure not to diminish the "greatness" of Cyber City, and they did little to sell the Project.

"It's because they're targeting Virgins. Things like 'agriculture' mean little to us, but that is the exact society that Virgins want to go back to. And since they're only targeting Virgins, they have to keep up with their 'Freesia is the best' propaganda for the rest of us."

Dames nodded slowly. She gazed up towards his towering frame, a stoic pillar of hard reason. In that moment, Xia thanked the universe for allowing her to find another soul that felt the same way she did. That she could actually share her thoughts with someone. That wasn't something she could do very often. Especially after Youle's passing.

"You're doing good work." The words were simple, succinct. But they hung in the air like a flowering explosion that only Xia could see.

"Thanks."

Dames looked down at Xia, his eyes uncharacteristically soft. "So, you got anything to drink?"

How the tides turned. But Xia knew what that question entailed. And she couldn't predict the ending.

"I better get some sleep." And with that, she let Dames out the door, the jittery bug of unease still flapping its excited wings in the pit of her stomach.

She slept little.

9

Rose Gold

Xia walked down the bustling avenue, scarlet flashing lights blinding and penetrating her vision. They took their name too literally. Why so much blazing red? Was this supposed to instill passion? It only gave her a headache.

Xia hated the Red Light District. The blatant public displays of sexual advances and groping, the heavy smell of perfume and smoke, the distant groans and moans floating from the bellies of the seedy establishments. She narrowly avoided bumping into two figures, a large woman with hands the size of dinner plates massaging the groin of a man half her size. Her nose shriveled.

Despite being the most populated district on any given day, Xia avoided it when she could. But she had a delivery. She approached a smaller shop, its wooden, candlelit entrance standing out among the sea of electricity. A painted sign hung above the curtain doors: The Virgins' Lair.

She pulled the curtain aside, revealing two intimidating blocks of men. Security. They patted her down, efficiently but forcefully, then scanned her.

"No Scan Blockers," the shorter of the two said. His solid metal teeth glinted under the candlelight's warm glow.

Xia looked past them and made eye contact with the woman at the end of the room. She made a silent "oh" and rushed over, her ruby silk robe floating behind her. It took everything in Xia to maintain eye contact and not glance down toward the woman's bare chest, but even in her lower visual field she could make out the massive mounds. Two nipple eyes with areola eyeshadow beckoning Look at me! Look at me! She did not.

"It's alright boys, she's meeting with me," she said. Her voice was light, feathery, yet there was a finality to it that demanded respect.

The men stepped aside and Xia followed the flittering red robe in front of her, past the sea of satin pillows and flickering flames. Half, three-quarters, and fully nude women lay about, their poses seductive but their eyes curious towards the silver-haired puma slinking past. Xia returned their glances, but only for a second. So much skin.

Down the hallway they went, past the fabricated moans of performative pleasure, until they reached the last room. Inside was a man seated behind a large mahogany desk.

He stood immediately. "Fine to meet you in the flesh, Xia," he said with sincerity, but Xia didn't like his tone. He seemed to fit right into this establishment. Black hair, blacker beard, eyes glowing with hunger. He clearly enjoyed his line of work as the owner of the most successful brothel in the city. She did a quick scan. Levi Lionhart. Definitely not his birth name. Age 55. Owner of The Virgins' Lair. One known mod. She scanned his pelvis. Erectile Enhancement V2 .8. Fitting.

He walked in front of Xia and gave a low bow, then gave the red-robed woman a kiss and a squeeze. She fluttered her spidery eyelashes and giggled a breezy melody that could make any man weak in the knees. Then she turned on her heel and left the room.

"Please, have a seat."

Xia obliged and sat in the massive violet armchair before the desk. Her body relaxed and melted into the cushion. Is this what it felt like to sit on a cloud? What she would do to have this in her apartment after a long day of work.

"How are you doing this lovely evening, my friend?"

Not her friend. "I'm fine. I have the fods." She pulled out a small black case, but he waved his hand dismissively.

"Yes, we'll get to that. I wanted to speak with you a little more first. Get to know you better."

"There's no reason for that," she said. The comfort of the chair did little to ease her discomfort at his tone.

"I beg to differ. You've become quite the household name in our community."

"Your community?"

"Yes, the human community. Silly name. The Virgins. " She couldn't help but smirk, but she kept her mouth shut. What would his community think if they knew of the blood flow maximizing mod in his penis? A mod's a mod. She wondered how many other Virgins had secret mods. What an oxymoron that was. "My girls were the ones who told me about you. How you've been helping with protection after some…threats have been introduced."

Xia's eyes narrowed. Was that all he knew? Or was it possible he had more information on who exactly was targeting them? She played dumb. "Threats?"

He let out a laugh, equally suave as his speaking voice. "Ah, so we are doing this dance. Who knows more? I will confess, my friend, that I truly know nothing except for what my girls tell me. Aside from them, I don't involve myself much with my community."

She didn't catch it before, but there was a trace of contempt at the word community. She eyed him with suspicion, then replayed the moment and scanned his face. It seemed he was telling the truth. He didn't know much else.

He leaned across his desk. "You see, Xia, my girls are my livelihood. They are water and I am but a tree. If anything were to happen to them, that would affect me quite terribly. I need them to be safe. Here. And while I do my best, this is not the safest of professions. They are in close contact with all types of folks. Ones who, I have learned, may now have ulterior motives."

Yes. If any of "his girls" were taken, that would mean one less body to sell. One less stream of income.

"Levi, if you—"

He clasped his hands together. "Ah, what sweet melody to hear you say my name like that. I'd pay you good to do a little more."

She stared at him. The silence said enough.

"Just a joke, just a joke, my friend!" There was some charm to him, but it was dripping with slime.

"If you use these," she gestured to the fods, "won't that mess with your entire business plan? If people come here and see that these women aren't actually Virgins, but have mods, doesn't that defeat the whole purpose?" This had struck her the moment she got the call from him two days prior, but she wasn't going to question a decent buck. Not until she was in the buck owner's office.

"Yes, I was waiting for you to ask me this. Such an observant entrepreneur. You've got many good qualities, it's quite apparent. They won't be able to wear them here, no, it is mainly for their walks home. The girls have become increasingly paranoid. Some threatened to quit. Said I need to do something. And they were right, of course. I have an obligation as their mentor to ensure their safety. So these are for them to use whenever they are not here. And, one for myself, of course. The girls are only as safe as I am."

Except he didn't need it. She glanced at his groin. "Sure."

"I appreciate your understanding. Now, I have to ask. Can you tell me anything about who exactly is targeting people like me and my girls? I can pay you double."

She shook her head. "Apparently, some people just really want to get out of here. And are willing to do anything. Including becoming you."

For the first time since meeting him, Levi appeared visibly uncomfortable. "I see. Yes. Not everyone has found their place in this world. The FRF Project does sound enticing. Especially to my people. But as you can see, I have found my place here. And I will do anything to keep it that way. Now," he beckoned her to pass him the case.

She tapped at her wrist and rested it above the desk. "First."

"Smart girl, smart girl. I'd expect nothing less." He pulled back his sleeve and tapped the band on his wrist, then hovered it above her own. Xia watched as 5000 zeCoin filled her bank account, and then another 500.

"A little extra, for your time. Use it to get yourself something nice, would you? You'd look lovely with a lavender lip."

She'd have paid a thousand zeCoin for him to have never said that. "I want to speak with the girls."

She expected a little pushback, and at the very least, an inquisition from him. But he nodded. "You'd do best to speak with Mai. She's the most sensible of the girls. She'll have the most to say. You can find her two doors down, the door behind the rose gold curtain."

Xia nodded. As soon as she rose from the chair, her tense muscles begged to return to the cloud. Levi bowed again, this time even deeper, and Xia returned a stiff nod before exiting his extravagant office.

Two doors down. Each door lay hidden behind a satin curtain. Past the aqua blue, across from the emerald green, hung a soft pink curtain. She pulled it back, about to open the door when the rhythmic sound of dainty "ah"s stopped her. The ball of uncomfortable ooze returned in the pit of her stomach. She dropped the curtain and spun to the side, resting against the wall. This was not how she wanted to meet this "Mai".

She heard another door click open. Levi emerged from his office, his expression quickly growing comical. "Ah yes, she may be busy. If you would, please wait until her business is finished." He walked past, his snicker growing into a full-bodied laugh. Embarrassment filled her bones. She waited, and waited, until the grotesque moan of a dying man signaled that business was complete. A few minutes later, the very much alive but satisfied man left the room and down the hall, ignoring Xia, much to her relief.

The uncomfortable ooze remained, although smaller. Xia squashed it down and knocked.

"Yes?" A voice called out.

Xia opened the door and entered. The room was surprisingly large, with a queen-sized four-poster bed and a lilac canopy draping over the sides. A woman sat at her vanity in a matching lilac silk robe and turned to face Xia, her jet-black hair flowing behind her.

"Something tells me you're not my next client," she said.

"No," Xia said, her voice stiff. "I just spoke with Levi. Delivered him some fods, which are meant for you guys."

The small smirk on her puckered lips widened into a smile. "You are Xia! I figured you were, but didn't want to assume. I'm the one who told Levi about you in the first place."

"I see." Xia stood there, feeling awkward. She'd never been in someone else's bedroom. Although, technically, this wasn't exactly someone's bedroom. But it was a room with a bed. And the bed wasn't hers. And the things that happened on that bed were not things that ever happened in her bed.

"Hey, you alright?" Her gaze snapped back to Mai. "You kinda zoned out for a second there."

"Yeah, I'm fine." Xia took a few steps towards her. "I wanted to talk to you. All the girls, really. It seems my name's been getting around."

"That it has. I expected you to be a bit...I'm not sure. Older, maybe? You seem pretty young. Although you've got some wrinkles around the corners of your mouth. I'm guessing frowns come with your line of work. Beauty mods ain't your thing, huh?" So candid, so upfront. Xia just stared. "Although that's definitely not your hair! You've got one of those hair color-changing mods. Can it change texture, too? Can you show me?"

Xia guessed that this Mai didn't interact much with non-Virgins, except for the ones that came looking to get off. And they probably didn't care much to share about the intricacies of their own mods.

"No," Xia said.

"No, it doesn't change texture?"

"No, I can't show you—"

"You can't? Or you won't?"

Xia exhaled out her nose. "Doesn't matter. Look, there's some serious shit going on with your people. People being taken." She paused, not indulging anything more. "I'm helping you guys out, but I don't know much about who is doing the taking. Do you have any idea? Have you heard anything?"

Mai turned back towards her mirror, brushing her long locks, but Xia could see the girl's darkened reflection. "It's all just speculation. Nobody knows who exactly. But with the news that came out the other day, it's pretty obvious why it's happening. There's a new shiny place to go, and we're the ticket out." The bubbliness that Mai exuded from the get-go dissipated just as quickly. She turned back towards Xia. "And with the news public now, you can expect to be a lot busier."

10

A New Resolve

Xia left the brothel and walked back down the crimson avenue, the path twice as packed as when she arrived. The later it got, the hornier people became. Sidestepping and skirting nearly a dozen public displays of lust, she made it to the secluded alley where she parked her bike. The sight of the glowing electric blue bubble brought her immediate relief. She trusted Flux's work, but it still wrecked her nerves to leave something so precious completely exposed. She scanned the bubble, a feature Flux had shown her, to reveal how many times someone came into contact with it. Zero. Good.

Levi was right about Mai being the most insightful. While she didn't have much new information for Xia, she had a solid head on her shoulders. The other girls either seemed too scared or too angry to really talk with her. The distrust towards non-Virgins was real. Before Xia would have deemed it misplaced, but considering there were boogeymen out there kidnapping and taking over Virgins' bodies, she couldn't blame them.

As she rode along the city streets, she could feel her cell chip buzzing against her wrist. Forgot to mute it. It was her own fault; she never did respond to the numerous past and new potential clients. She'd been sidetracked. Working on fods. Enjoying her new bike—

The blaring screech of an electric siren crashed her eardrums and she quickly skidded to a stop. That sound only signaled one thing.

"STEP DOWN FROM THE CYCLE."

A warped, robotic voice commanded her. Xia reluctantly obeyed. *"REMOVE THE HELMET."*

She raised her arms slowly and then removed her helmet, set it down, and returned her hands to the air.

Two figures in obsidian armored bodysuits, limbs glowing with various neon tech, approached her. Faces fully covered with opaque visors and plating, they looked anything but human. FRF Protection Force: the government's precious military. Or as Xia and others like her called them, *slags.* She remained stationary, but her heartbeat threatened to pulse out of her chest.

"SCANNING," one of them said while the other closed the distance and stood right before Xia. She gazed upwards, staring right where their eyes should be, into their soulless black visor. They leaned down and frisked her. Movements methodical, never lingering for a second too long. The hand neared the Enforcer in her back pocket. *Shit, no no no.* The fear was two-fold. She really didn't want to lose the thing. She'd never gotten the chance to use it, but she'd grown accustomed to the feeling of its slick curvature against her thigh. But even greater was the fact that an Enforcer was contraband with extremely severe consequences.

An Enforcer was a particularly dangerous type of contraband due to the fact that only FRF personnel, mainly the military, may use them. Their effects were beyond dangerous. Even with the most protective of mods, a shot from a laser gun would ensure a pure gaping hole through the body. But with little to no protective mods, you'd be disintegrated. There lay a chunk of the reason people will not mess with Force members. That and the Void.

She needed to do something. Anything. Her arms still hovering in the air, she moved her hand closer to her temple until she could swipe with her thumb, gentle but quick flicks in an attempt to move through the options menu on her eye screen. If she could activate her bike's forcefield, maybe that could allow for an escape? That'd ensure a pursuit. Call someone? That'd do nothing. She flicked too long and accidentally began recording. *Fuck.* There was nothing she could do. The hand moved closer, closer until—

BANG. The two onyx heads simultaneously snapped to the left, and in perfect unison, ran off towards the noise. Sweet relief cascaded over Xia, but she didn't linger one second to enjoy it. She mounted the bike and raced away.

Why had they stopped her? She'd never know. She'd only been stopped twice before, but it was still just as nerve-wracking. If they wanted to, they'd find something to stick you with. Just depended on the mood and agenda of the slag that got you. Which was impossible to figure out, since there was nothing to read. Not an ounce of visible humanity. Every time she stared into that soulless void, she tried to imagine herself in their place. She couldn't, and yet it easily could have been her trajectory.

Going to school and completing an education unlocked career opportunities that were not accessible to the rest of the population. Military was a difficult yet coveted position to an uneducated person, but was practically expected if you received an education. There were other options, most involving working for the government in some capacity. But the military was the shiniest option. They lived cushy lives in the neighboring sector right outside the walls along with the other government officials, but were able to exert power and control over the citizens of Cyber City. Power-hungry, government-loving robots with all the tech you could dream of.

She had considered joining them herself, until she discovered the ghost of truth.

Growing up, Xia had never given her lack of parents much thought. It was common to have only one parent in Cyber City, and having both parents gone wasn't far behind. Group homes were one of the few social services that the FRF established after extreme necessity. Hard to sell Freesia as a superior metropolis when there are dead kids on every corner. She had asked about them when she was younger, but Youle's simple and vague answer of "They died when you were seven months old," was satisfactory enough for her. She never pried much more. She was content with Youle. He provided just enough to quell any inquisitions. Until she came home from school one day.

"So, what did you learn today?"

"We drew what we want to be when we grow up," she had said with exuberance, something the girl rarely did.

"Can I see?" Youle had asked, his eyes sparkling behind his rectangular spectacles.

Xia rifled through her scraggly bag and pulled out her drawing. Youle took the paper, and as soon as his eyes laid on the black-suited figures, his heart sank.

"What do you think? I even drew the little lights on their arms." She pointed, then jabbed the paper a few more times for good measure, since Youle had gone quiet.

"Xia," he said as he dropped the paper onto the table, "you don't want to join the Military."

"Yes I do! They make lots of money, and they always have lots of food to eat, and they get to wear super cool clothes—"

"Yes, darling, I know. Those seem like very nice things. But the thing is, the Military does very bad things. And they do them to nice people. People like us."

Xia frowned. "But some of the siblings of my classmates are military. I don't think they'd do bad things to us." But then Xia thought of how her classmates don't play with her at recess, or how they made fun of her long skinny legs. Doubt bubbled.

"They do. And they have. You know your parents died when you were young, and that is why you are with me."

She glanced down at her big feet. "I like being with you."

"And I love having you. And raising you. You are my perfect star. But you would have also had your mother, and your father. But the military killed them."

Her eyes shot upward, green orbs exuding scared incredulity. "Why?"

Youle pulled the gangly girl into his warm arms. "Because your parents wanted freedom."

That night, as she lay on her bed, the creeping dread of what was happening crawled up from the floor and tangled her limbs, immobilizing her. She'd been floating on the winds of entrepreneurship and making good money. She'd eaten more this week than she had in the entirety of the previous month. And that was on top of the purchase of her bike. But the encounter with the slag rattled her. Checked her. Reminded her of her place in this abysmal city. Of how in a matter of seconds, everything you've worked for, your entire life as you know it, could be taken away.

And the poor Virgins felt that tenfold. The image of Mai's darkened eyes, of Leikko. A spur of energy caused Xia to make the call.

Unable to complete call. Invalid contact digit.

Xia's hand collapsed back onto the bed. Dames' words from the night prior came ringing back. *"If the husband was taken and had his mind replaced, the girl would be the next easy target."* Guilt and regret replaced the dread. Why didn't she do anything more? How could she have been so stupid?

Perhaps the money was no longer her main priority.

Her cellchip buzzed and a glimpse of hope simmered. She answered quickly. "Name."

"Hi, is this Xia? This is Mai. From the pleasure den."

The hope left as quickly as it came. "Yes, this is she."

"Weird voice thingy! It's cool, though. Makes sense. You've really got all the bells and whistles." A pause as she exhaled. "Right. So, I want to hire you. Weird request, but I'm hoping you can come and meet with my father. He's, well, he doesn't want to use your fods. And he's telling others not to. Goes against 'our beliefs', he says. A bunch of BS. But he never listens to me anyways. I'm hoping if he hears it straight from you, he might get a different idea."

Xia doubted it. She wasn't exactly convincing. But she couldn't help but feel some slight indignation at the prospect of someone convincing Virgins against protection simply because it resembled a mod. "I get paid either way?"

"Of course.

"Alright. I can come tomorrow. Where am I meeting him?"

There was a brief pause before Mai answered, "The Korin Pagoda."

Xia blinked, as if that would clarify if she heard correctly. "Is someone gonna let me in?"

"I'll be there. I can let you in."

"You can do that?" How could a prostitute like Mai have access to the Pagoda?

"Yes. Third hour, come by?"

"Ok." The simple response masked her excitement.

The next day, she delivered that day's worth of fods and took some extra time to talk with each Virgin. None had any useful information for her, and instead were filled with the usual worries and concerns and some hopes that Xia might have the ability to quell some of it. Besides the fods, she really didn't. She gave her usual spiel: making sure the device stays hidden on the ear, never leave the home unarmed, to call her if there are ever any attempts on their safety or if they hear anything out of the ordinary. Then she'd make a quick scan of their home, checking for foreign DNA or markers of any kind. And then she'd leave. Her spiels were absent-minded, and her answers to the Virgins' nagging questions thoughtless. Her mind was preoccupied with the meeting at the Pagoda.

Xia had never stepped foot in the place, along with the vast majority of Cyber City's populace. It was one of the few places, if not the only place, that a modded person truly did not have access to. A pride of the Virgin people. It remained a sanctuary only for their kind.

After her final delivery, she made the ride across town to the Ko-rin Pagoda, a treasure that she usually only saw decorating the distant horizon. Its seven majestic tiers reached towards the invisible heavens above the smog, its entrance hidden behind the massive stucco wall that encompassed the structure. And Xia would get to enter it herself. She wondered who Mai's father might be, that both of them would have access to be there. Entrance to the Pagoda was a privilege reserved for the most devout of their community. But perhaps that had changed with the recent disappearings. Would she enter to find masses of unmodded people seeking shelter? She was about to find out.

She parked her bike and activated the electro-bubble, then walked towards the small gate on the southern part of the wall. The gate looked completely out of place, its heavy-duty metal doors clashing against the classical charm of the solid stucco. It served its purpose for protection and nothing more. Standing on either side of the doors were two slags. Nobody quite knew how or why they would guard the place, but it was suspected that the Virgins paid a hefty sum to buy that level of protection. It certainly worked. A wall and some heavy doors would be nothing to an outlaw with the intention to loot, but FRF military was a nasty enough presence to deter even the most determined of criminals.

She sent a quick message to Mai and waited, hoping she didn't have to talk with the slags. Her Enforcer was safe at home, but she still wanted to avoid an encounter with them if she could. Luckily, Mai's reply was instantaneous, and just a minute later the gate doors opened.

Mai stood beyond the two slags on the path and raised her hand and waved. Xia nodded and the two slags wordlessly stepped aside, allowing her to enter the forbidden place.

She wasn't sure what she was expecting, but it wasn't this. Her eyes adjusted to the color scheme before her. She'd only seen such vibrancy from the artificial neon projections from electricity, but this was pure. Pure green grass, pure purple flowers, pure red strawberries. Was this the color fruit was supposed to be? She thought of the dull fruits and vegetables sold at the markets. Of the brownish burgundy cherries Dames used in his drinks. How much better they'd be with one of those sanguine berries. Did they taste as vibrant as their color?

She glanced up and looked towards Mai. Standing on the stone path that split the green garden in two, her black locks flowing behind her, she looked so much more youthful here than in the sex den. The question sat on Xia's tongue, begging to be asked. Her eyes returned to the fruit. She didn't see Mai snicker.

"You can have one! Part of your payment," Mai called out, reading her mind. Although it wasn't hard to do. She was practically drooling.

She leaned down and grabbed one. Her tongue screamed in anticipation, but she made it wait as she held the fruit up to her eye. She scanned it, but minimal information appeared. She turned off the eye screen and simply stared at it. Tiny little seeds, a sprite of leafy green growth, a perfect ruby curve. Then she popped the berry into her mouth. The sweetness was so different from anything she had tasted before. So fresh, pure, bright. She could have eaten a bucketful.

Her eyes snapped back to Mai, who patiently stared on in amusement. Then she wiped her hand on her leg and approached Mai.

"Good?" Mai asked, eyes twinkling.

She nodded. "Your father?"

"Right. This way." Xia followed Mai through the Pagoda's entrance, but as Mai continued towards the stairs, Xia's legs stopped as she took in the room before her. Unlike the scarlet blares of the Red Light District, this crimson inspired awe. The intricate gold danced along the pillars and walls like flowering dragons. Incense coated the silky air. Several people in long, flowing robes sat at the center of the room, their heads bowed and legs crossed. Were they meditating? Praying? A lost art in Cyber City. At the back of the room, Xia could just make out some figures sparring outside. Could the Daimyo be back there? Her blood ran hot at the mere thought.

The pagoda was one thing. But the Daimyo was another. The leader of the Samurai, he was also the last of them. It was a dying art. Or rather, a barely revived one. The practice had died long ago, but the Virgins had resurrected it and bled its practices into a form of Zen Buddhism. Her grandfather had filled her head with tales of samurai past, and the line between fiction and not lay as elusive as its true legacy. But there was, reportedly, a Daimyo that resided at the Pagoda. If there was any type of "leader" of the Virgin community, one would consider it to be the Daimyo. From him imparted the virtues of bushido and Zen Buddhism, and from there came the core values that tied the Virgins together.

"Xia?" Mai called. Xia hastened to follow, her eyes leaving the distant sparring. She followed Mai up the stairs, passing floor after floor, until they reached the seventh and final. At the sound of Xia's step onto the hardwood floor, a figure rose from the end of the small room, his deep blue kimono flowing over his muscular, aging frame. The Daimyo.

"Father, I want you to meet Xia."

11

THE DAIMYO

He stood not much taller than Xia, but his presence loomed over her like a lone citadel in a cloudy expanse. Such an aura demanded reverence. A human embodiment of the Pagoda itself. Xia bowed. She was gifted a small head nod in return.

"You are the silver fox."

Xia blinked. "Silver fox?"

"It is what many have been calling you. Smart, cunning, nocturnal. Silver." He glanced towards her silver strands.

Silence dominated as the man stared at Xia, his deep brown eyes penetrating Xia's red. He seemed unbothered by it. Xia was quite bothered. She felt herself shrivel underneath it.

"I had no desire to meet with you. This is my daughter's doing."

She looked over towards Mai, catching the tail end of an eye roll. This quick-lipped prostitute was the daughter of the last samurai, the most revered man in the city. The only Virgin that warranted admiration from the rest of the populace, a man whose presence was a fable. Yet the resemblance was as clear as the sky from the Before Times. The same pursed lips, the same widened nose, the same espresso orbs. She was her father's daughter.

"She told me you don't approve of what I'm doing."

"I could not care less what you are doing. I simply don't approve of my people acting on it." He turned from Xia and gazed out the window towards the sparring men below. "To appear as those who have altered themselves from our true nature is as atrocious as to actually do it."

Xia considered his words and the solemnity behind them. "But if it meant protecting yourselves from death, isn't it worth it?"

"Not if it means compromising our true values." He looked back towards Xia, eyes filled with a loathing disappointment at the mere presence of her various mods. As if to say, *look at what you've done to yourself.* She didn't need her memory screen replay to tell her of the disapproval in his stare.

"What do you think they should do, then?"

His answer came slowly. "Every soul is in charge of their own journey, their own destiny. I trust each soul to protect themselves, but I cannot tell anyone what to do."

Getting kidnapped and having their bodies stolen didn't seem like being in charge of one's own destiny to Xia. "So, everyone fend for themselves, basically? Why not let people do that by wearing an imitation mod?"

"Perhaps you are mistaken of my role. I do not 'let' anyone do anything. I only share the true path, and others may choose to follow it."

"That's not true!" Mai exclaimed. Xia had nearly forgotten she was there. "You wouldn't even let Fuello inside here the other day when you heard he had been using a fod."

Fuello. The name didn't ring a bell. Her fods were really making the rounds, her clientele expanding past the people she'd met with.

"This is my dojo. And only those who adhere to our principles may practice inside."

Mai gulped, the words stinging. Xia didn't see how she could possibly persuade the man. His entire being oozed authority and resolve. This citadel would bow to no wind. Especially not a gust like Xia. She felt more like a wisp.

"At least Xia is doing something! Meanwhile you stay up here, in your ivory tower. You tell people not to use these fods yet you have two Freesian military standing at the fucking doors!"

"Language."

Xia stepped back, feeling awkward in the family exchange.

"People are dying! Or worse! We don't even know what's really happening to them. And she's out here actually making a difference. You're the best damn fighter in this place and yet you do nothing—"

He stepped forward, his authority manifesting tenfold, his words heavier than obsidian. "I am here. Every day. Training our people. From dawn to dusk. I will not compromise our truths for any threat, no matter how dangerous." He pointed a long finger at the people sparring below. "You could have been one of them. But you have abandoned those values."

Prostitution didn't align with bushido, supposedly. Mai seethed, and her warm brown eyes blazed hot.

"Values mean nothing if we are dead!"

"Values do not care if you are dead. And their meaning remains obstinate no matter our state of being. They simply are." His gaze returned to Xia. "What do you believe will happen when they catch on?"

She blinked.

"The people who have been targeting us. They are not of simple mind. They have been targeting us since before the knowledge of the Revitalization Project was made public. They have access to technology not yet revealed to the public. How long will these measly little devices outsmart them? How long until they catch on?"

She stood there, feeling like a child scolded by their teacher for their poor performance.

"Your devices are a quick bandage that's doomed to peel off. I will not abandon a life's worth of principles for such a thing." His eyes hardened at Mai before returning to Xia. "I have entertained this conversation for too long. I must return to my vassals." Her bow was quicker this time, as was the Daimyo's head nod. He brushed past her, sending an electric jolt through Xia at the touch. Despite the talking down to, she felt nothing but awe for him.

Mai looked as if she wanted to throw something, but the only throwable objects in the room were what looked to be very sacred texts, and even Mai's rage wouldn't risk breaking one of those. She crouched down on the ground and let out a loud exhale, her hands curled into fists on her cheeks. Then she sprung back up and whirled towards Xia.

"You weren't very convincing! The hell am I paying you for, anyways?"

Xia raised a brow at the misdirected anger. "I never said I was. This isn't my forte. You owe me nonetheless."

Mai turned towards the window and looked down below at her father, his kimono swaying with each powerful step. Without even a glance at Xia, she tossed the freelancer some phys. Xia caught it and stood for a moment, waiting for Mai to say something. When the words never came, Xia descended the stairs.

When she reached the bottom floor, it struck her that this was likely the last time she'd ever set foot in this stunning structure. She had to make the most of it. She walked the length of the crimson room, past the meditating men and figurines of famous souls from the Before Times, and stood at the back entryway. At the bottom of the steps were a dozen men in black keikogi, hair in tight buns, and faces firm with resolve, training with bokken.

She gazed on, almost in a trance as the men sparred, their movements like a perfect dance. Feet stepping with purpose and ease, arms fluid with grace. A silk ribbon of a flowing current filled with ferocity. Motions slow and controlled, then quicker than a biting viper.

Mai's father called something indiscernible and then entered the fray of sparring. One after the other, a samurai entered combat with the Daimyo, the Daimyo shouting a quick critique when the other inevitably fell to the ground. It was clear why he was the leader. Despite his age, his skills stood miles ahead of the training men.

An image of a young Xia. Training with this legend. No silver hair, no red eyes, but body moving as agile and swift as a snake in the sea. Inspiration spurred in her chest, and her mind traveled to Mai. How could the girl throw all this away? And to work in as slimy a place as the Virgins' Lair? Xia had felt out of place before, in the awkward encounter between Mai and her father, but here, she felt even further displaced. Her tight suit, her silver hair, her red modded eyes. These warriors, clothes flowing free in the cool air, their hair organic black, their eyes clear with nothing but human resolve. It was mesmerizing, and Xia was entranced.

The Daimyo caught Xia's stare. She broke from the trance, quickly turned on her heel, and left the training grounds. As she walked back through the Pagoda, she tried to take it all in. Every intricate swirl of gold, each statue's pensive face. And as she ventured through the front garden, she snatched one more berry for the road. Then she walked past the two slags, not paying them a glance, accepting the fact that she'd never set foot in that palace ever again.

Over the next few days, business had slowed for Xia. She wasn't sure if it was due to the Daimyo's influence or because she was reaching the end of her prospective pool of clients. Or perhaps the Daimyo was right, and his prediction already occurred.

She couldn't deny his words. These people who were targeting the Virgins clearly had connections as well as a level head on their shoulders. The word of her fods had spread so quickly in the Virgin circle. Like wildfire. And wildfire isn't contained. It could have easily spread outside that circle. And if it hadn't yet, it would eventually.

Despite the presence of The Revitalization Project now being made public, Xia still didn't know much about it. She decided to check out what she could for herself. She parked her bike in a nearby alley, only just starting to get accustomed to leaving it in strange places, and made her way to the Southeast Block's FRF Office. Normally these offices didn't get much traffic. Mod certification and social service registration were the two main orders of business, and a good chunk of people with mods didn't certify them anyway. (Xia only certified a few—enough to not be bothered by slags, but not enough that they had access to everything about her.) Since the news of the Revitalization Project, the place gained a bit more traffic. But even then, Xia didn't have to wait long in the small line outside the squat building, and after five short minutes she approached the front desk where a thin man sat behind protective glass.

"Can I help you?" He asked, eyes glued to his monitor.

"I'm here for information on the Revitalization Project."

He unpeeled his gaze and looked her up and down. "You're not of the desired clientele for the project."

"I know. I just want some information is all."

The man stared, feeling bothered, and wanting nothing more than to be unbothered. "First door on your right."

These clerks were the lowest on the FRF totem pole, and due to that, were a bit more apathetic towards their roles. And Xia thanked them for that apathy. She followed the man's instruction and knocked on the door, and a moment later entered as a soft voice beckoned.

Jina Grovo, according to the placard on her desk, sat behind a massive monitor and an even more massive amount of paperwork. The dozen eye mods couldn't hide her tiredness. Her thick brown hair was pulled back into a tight bun, stretching the rest of her wide face with it. It looked painful. Or maybe it was the job that was painful.

"How can I help you?" her voice drawled as Xia took a seat.

"I want to know about the Revitalization Project."

The woman barely looked up from the papers before her when answering. "You're ineligible."

"It's not for me. My friend and her family want to go," she lied.

"Then they can come here and ask about it themselves."

"They are too scared. There's six of them."

Jina finally looked up and gave Xia her undivided attention. Families were painfully small in Freesia. Having a child was becoming more and more uncommon, and having multiple children even more so. But four children? That was the jackpot. Of the millions living in Cyber City, a minuscule fraction were Virgins, and a smaller fraction of those would actually leave to join this project.

"How many children?"

"Four," Xia responded. The woman's eyes didn't look so tired anymore. "They want to know the criteria to leave and the logistics."

The woman cleared her throat and began her spiel. "The Project features a community located safely outside the walls that has been revived from its prior desolate state due to the Great Ultima War. Its water sources have been decontaminated, multiple farms for livestock and crops have been prepared, and purification plants run to continuously sterilize and monitor air quality, all residing under a transparent plasma photon dome for protection."

Xia paused, considering how to best continue the conversation. What route would be most fruitful? What route would end the meeting prematurely? She studied Jina's face. *Hopeful.* Xia guessed that of the people coming in, few were actually eligible, and fewer signed up.

"My friend is a bartender. How will his skills transfer to the project? He knows nothing about farming or livestock and the rest."

Jina's voice perked up. "Machines currently do the brunt of the work. Minimal physical labor is needed. People are just needed to enjoy the fruits of their labor and test the success of the project as a whole."

"Why are Virgins needed? Why would having a mod mess with that?"

A shift in Jina's seat. "The project is meant to test the efficacy and potential of the lifestyle from prior to the Great Liberation, and the use of any modular devices hinders the accuracy of testing that."

"If machines are doing most of the work, why do you need anyone?"

"The machines function to bear the majority of the workload, but people are still needed to test and verify the capability to live in such a manner."

"Like, 'do the berries taste okay' kind of deal?"

Jina breathed out in visible relief. "Yes, exactly."

"How do the the purification plants work?"

"The purification plant works to suck in and filter the air, with activated charcoal at its core for adsorption to remove the radiation. After filtration, the air is disinfected via ultraviolet light and released back into the open."

"How many plants are there?"

Jina's mouth opened and hung there. Then the answer came quickly. "Four."

Xia tilted her head. "And how many lakes?"

"Two."

"Can people see the space before committing to the move?"

"I'm afraid not," Jina's tone was sickeningly reassuring. "Once an unmodded individual makes the commitment to enter the project, they must participate in its entirety."

"You can see why people would be skeptical. To uproot their lives and head somewhere they've never been."

"Yes, I can see how that would be inhibiting. But you may be rest assured that the FRF holds true to its promises, and that the Project lives up to its name."

"Have you seen the space?"

Jina's eyes flickered. "Excuse me?"

"Wherever the Project takes place. Have you been there?"

"Yes, of course I have. Now, I'm afraid that's all the time I have. Please, relay this to the family of six." Her eyes hungered at the number. Then she returned to the papers before her, and Xia left the office. As she passed the people in the short line, her eyes lingered on one person in particular. A girl, no older than 12. Soft brown eyes and chestnut hair. The same girl that Xia saved in the acid storm so many days ago. Their eyes locked. And as the girl recognized the silver sphynx, Xia gave a meaningful shake of the head.

No.

12

Two Lakes or One?

Xia sat in her apartment, the sun attempting to break through the smog and grace the city with its glittering rays. Some of the beams broke through, its gray gleams casting a haze through the window.

The conversation she had recorded between her and Jina Grovo replayed on her screen. Every slight facial impression, every shift of the body, every pause in her words, Xia was able to study it all. And it became abundantly clear what was said with clear confidence, and what seemed like a lie.

Xia doubted the woman had ever seen the Project. And when asked of the explicit details of the place itself, there was no weight behind her words. But what was the meaning behind those potential lies? Was she just trying to sell the place, and knew that if she didn't have answers, that that would turn away prospective volunteers? Or was the reason more sinister? Was the Project a front for something else entirely? If it were a front, it was fooling whoever was targeting Virgins. Xia decided that she didn't need to know the answer, she just knew that this Project was not to be trusted.

Xia had been avoiding the bar. There was a lingering tension from the night Dames had come over. Was she imagining it? Probably. But she still felt it. And it was strong enough to drive a wedge between her and one of her few joys on the planet: alcohol. But the wedge was growing thinner, and the longing became stronger than the tension, so she ended up back at Mickey's that night. She prayed that Dames wouldn't be the one bartending, but as soon as she stepped past the entrance, she noted the thinner layer of dust and grime. The colossal figure at the back of the bar confirmed her disappointment; Dames was working.

She took a seat at the bar, thankful that it was a bit busier than usual. She sat next to a strikingly attractive couple that was a little too handsy. The man slipped his fingers around and squeezed the blonde woman's thigh, and her thick pink lips drunkenly squealed at the touch. Xia regretted her seat choice immediately.

"Well hello there little lady," Dames smiled as he sauntered over. "Been a few days."

"I've been busy."

"Usual business? Or old stuff?"

"The usual." How she wanted to spill some more, to tell him how she got to enter the infamous Korin Pagoda. How she met the even more infamous Daimyo. How money was no longer her main prerogative. Her tight lips remained sealed.

"Speaking of usual," his massive finger pointed towards the drink in front of the couple as he raised his eyebrows.

"Yeah, the usual."

A few moments later, Dames brought her the signature cocktail, a small cherry sunken at the bottom. Xia reached into her pocket and took out the strawberry from the Pagoda garden. Even in the dingy lighting, she could see the difference in shade and quality between Dames' cherry and the berry between her fingers.

"Woah, where'd you get that?"

Xia quickly plopped it into the drink. "Part of a payment. For a job."

His lips curled into a mischievous smirk. "You know, I heard about one of your jobs. Well, I'm assuming it was a job. Unless you've got a kink I don't know about." He glanced towards the handsy couple beside her, who now had begun to neck each other. Bile rose in her throat.

"What?" She sputtered.

"Paco saw you. Remember him? Helped him with taking on that gang in the Fifth Ward. Nice guy, but hornier than a devil. Spends a whole lot of time in the Red Light District. And he spotted you immediately. Said he's always wanted to show you a good time. Seeing you there was the cherry on top." Her cheeks reddened, resembling the berry in her drink. "Which begs the question. What were you doing there? Letting off some steam after a hard day?"

His banter was playful. A little too playful. He really did want to know. She was quick to clear the air. "I had business at the Virgins' Lair. You can imagine why." She gulped her drink, pleading for the alcohol to hurry up and take the edge off this conversation.

"Of course. That checks out. What was it like inside?"

"What?"

"I've never been. I'm curious."

Another gulp. "Ask them." She bobbed her head towards the couple next to her. She didn't look at them, but she could hear the smacking of their lips as they made out.

Dames let out his gravel laugh and snapped his clubs of fingers together. "Save that for the Red Light District. Keep it in your pants."

The man looked up, face redder than Xia's. The blonde woman's face contorted. "Get your fingers out of my face," she snapped back. Xia was impressed at the woman's gall. Dames didn't look like someone to bite back at. The scarlet-cheeked man looked towards his girl with horror, but Dames kept his cool. A rottweiler amused by a chihuahua.

A yell from down the bar interrupted the exchange.

"Crank the volume!"

Dames turned towards the telescreen hanging above. A breaking news segment. He tapped the band on his wrist a few times. The sound from the screen loudened and cut through the bar, causing everyone to immediately quiet.

A different voice. "Go back, go back!"

A few more taps and the screen replayed. Sinnie Soto graced the screen, her hair a soft blue tonight. While her lips and eyes and hair were different, the same fluttery eyelashes pulsed with each word.

"The Freesian Republic's Modernization Sector continues to report the stellar success of the Revitalization Project. With its rapid success, more volunteers are still needed to sustain and profit from the project. The Sector recognizes that while it is a fantastic and unparalleled opportunity, it is a commitment that can be difficult to choose to make. Which is why the Modernization Sector has sent us, just today, this exclusive footage of the project."

Exclusive doesn't mean much when it's sent to the only mainstream news source in the city, but Xia kept that thought to herself.

The camera panned to an aerial view of a small compound, grass as green as the Pagoda's garden. The colors were so clear. The water as blue as the sky. There was no smog to block the sun's rays. The shot zoomed in on a large brown cow with a man standing beside it. The bar murmured at the sight of him.

"Lunatic Lutno!" someone exclaimed.

"So that's where the crazy son of a bitch went. I wondered—"

"Shhh!" The handsy blonde shushed, a jeweled finger raised to her pink lips, her eyes glued to the screen.

Sinnie Soto rambled on about the pure water, the warm temperatures, the fresh taste of eggs as the sun kissed your skin in the morning. Camera cut to Lutno eating eggs. An infomercial for a move into the country. Camera cut back to the landscape. She continued to ramble. But Xia wasn't paying attention to the words, she was busy analyzing the landscape.

One lake. Not two. Five purification plants, not four.

"— space is limited in this Project, but there is still plenty of need currently. All unmodded individuals are encouraged to visit their local FRF Affairs Office. We thank you for listening, and will now return to your designated channel shows." She gave a final glittering smile before the screen clipped back to a cybernetic wrestling match, and Dames quickly turned the volume down to avoid the loud grunting and shouting that came with those.

The blonde whined beside her. "Ohhh, how I want to go there! I'd give up all these stupid mods if it meant I could go skinny dipping in that lake."

"I just want the food," a burly man a few seats down piped up. "You see that cow? Twice as big as the ones they got in the meat plants."

"And speaking of plants!" A woman covered in tattoos said. "That greenery! Just gorgeous. Nothing like that here."

"Bunch of bullshit that they're only letting those Virgins up in there. I'll be a damn better farmer than those snivelly bitches."

The bar's chatter livened, and soon everyone was talking about the Project and whether or not they'd want to go. And from what Xia could hear, most people did. She wasn't too surprised. Even she was mesmerized by the clarity of the water.

It was at that moment a sad realization dawned on her. As the bar patrons longed for an escape to this land, and voiced their ill wishes towards the Virgins, the threat that had been facing the Virgins became more apparent. This project wasn't to be trusted. Meaning the body-snatchers were likely ill-informed. But the body snatchers came from a greater pool of people. As Xia listened to the blonde whore beside her lament over her exclusion from this society, she realized that this woman could be willing to do the same—to take over a Virgin's body to get there. The threat wasn't an ominous group; it was the people all around her.

"Want another?" Like clockwork. She looked up at Dames, and his lips thinned in a knowing stare.

"I better get going." She paid and left, the chatter muffling behind her as the door swung shut.

There was no denying that the footage of the Project had an enticing effect. A stroll past the FRF office displayed a line snaking out the door. But not filled with Virgins. Everyone wanted to shoot their shot. As Xia continued with her deliveries with the fods, she was relieved to learn that they were not as easily swayed. The presence of Lutno in the footage seemed to have a deterrent effect.

"If it's too good to be true, it probably is. And there's no way Lutno would run off there. Absolutely no way in Hell," an older Virgin resembling a mushroom told Xia as he paid for the fod. He examined the piece in his stubby hand. "Is this small thing really enough to no longer appear a Virgin?"

The question was asked often. That along with concerns over what happened if it fell off, if someone noticed the small piece set behind the ear lobe, whether or not it was actually a mod and Xia was scamming them. All valid concerns.

"This device emits the same frequencies that all V1 and V2 mods emit and will show up via any basic modular scan. You will still appear to be a Virgin to the naked eye, so there will be no noticeable change to your appearance. You won't need any injections or mod adapters. As soon as it is no longer making contact with your skin, you won't be emitting the frequencies anymore. Any buzzing or static noises are abnormal, so call me and I can fix it." She finished her spiel with a perfunctory "Any questions?"

"No, no, that sounds alright," the mushroom man replied. "And even if it doesn't do the trick, if it'll make my wife feel safer, that's the most important thing to me."

Xia left the mushroom man's home with a pit of dread in her stomach. It had been there for weeks now, growing with each encounter with a Virgin. This endeavor for some easy cash had evolved into so much more. Simple families being ripped apart. And for what?

She disabled the electro bubble just as her cell chip rang. She tapped her wrist.

"Name."

"Xia, it's Mai. I need to see you." Her voice broke on the last word.

"Can it wait?" She still had two more deliveries.

"No, no. Please. You need to come now. I'll pay—"
"Where should we meet?"

So it wasn't the last time Xia would set foot in the majesty that was the Korin Pagoda. Despite the heartbreak in Mai's tone, Xia couldn't help but feel a prickle of excitement at the prospect of going back. Her mouth salivated at the thought of those precious berries. She drove a little faster.

The two slags stepped to the side as soon as Xia approached, and the doors opened just as quickly. Everything looked the same: same lush grass, same bright berries, and yet something felt *off*. The air almost heavier. A coldness that didn't belong. Something, but she couldn't quite place it. She scanned the surrounding area. Nothing out of the ordinary, no modded people. She walked up the stone path and entered the pagoda.

It felt different inside, too. No praying monks, no distant chants. She peered out the back entryway and saw it was empty. No sparring. Her hand instinctively went to her pocket as she took a defensive stance. Was this some sort of trap?

"Xia," Mai called as she raced down the stairs. Her pale skin was sickeningly white, a stark contrast to her onyx locks, which tangled around her in a frizzy mess. Her eyes were bloodshot and puffy. A sobbing ghost. "It's my father. Masato. The Daimyo. He's gone."

13

THE CALL TO ACTION

"Gone?"

Mai nodded frantically, her unkempt hair bobbing with each vibration of the head. She rubbed her eyes with her palms. "Yes. He never arrived here today. He messaged me last night and told me not to come home. I tried calling, but he didn't answer. And it's my fault."

"Your fault?"

She groaned. "So, my dad *had* been helping a bit. He would walk people home if they felt unsafe. He'd been walking some of the monks here, and I begged him to walk one of the girls from the VL home. She kept saying that she felt like someone was watching her."

"VL?"

"Virgins' Lair. She's one of the sex workers. Prisha. And my dad agreed. He walked her home last night, and sure enough, she got jumped. But he fought them off. She ran off and called me. She wasn't sure if he made it out alive. I assumed he had, because he messaged me and told me not to come home. So I stayed at the VL. But when I came here this morning, I find out he never showed up here. I think, I think—" her voice broke. "I think he was snatched too."

The mere possibility of the infamous Daimyo getting captured hit Xia like a falling dumbbell. There was no way. "Are you sure?"

"I could barely believe it myself. But there's no other explanation. My father would never miss coming here. And if he was attacked…"

"It's hard to picture your father getting taken. Not being able to defend himself."

Mai's eyes hardened. "He may be the Daimyo, but he is still human. And without any technology, if there were enough of them…" Her eyes wandered off, as if imagining the scene taking place. Her father fighting mercilessly against hooded figure after hooded figure, but the sheer number being too many. One sneaking up behind at just the right time and injecting him. His body falling to the ground, only to be scooped up by the hooded figures. Carried away. Never to be seen by her again. Her eyes watered once more.

Even though Xia had only met the Daimyo a few days prior, the thought of something happening to him shook her foundation. This threat seemed so much larger, so much more daunting. If they could take the Daimyo, how much protection could she really offer? He was right; Xia's actions were a small bandage on a massive hemorrhage.

Mai cleared her throat. "It's not going to be good. The monks and samurai are already talking. Saying they can't stay here. That if we stay, we'll all be hunted. That we must go."

"You mean, enter the Project?"

Mai shook her head vigorously. Xia imagined the girl would get a headache soon enough. "No. We don't trust what the FRF says. Especially after seeing Lutno on the news yesterday. Lutno didn't stand so straight. And he never smiled like that."

"You knew Lutno?"

"We all do. Or, did. He butted heads with my father a lot. They had the same ideas, but Lutno was much more…zealous, I guess. But still, he was one of us and he helped keep our community strong. Now he's gone. And so is my father. Who is left to hold us true to our ideals? Nobody." She exhaled once more. "Come upstairs, they are talking now."

Xia nodded and followed Mai up to the third floor. A circle of a dozen people sat on the floor, all male save for one old woman with cat like eyes and a lopsided mouth. Once again, Xia felt incredibly out of place.

A samurai with beady eyes talked rapidly, but Mai cut him off. "Everyone, this is Xia. Or as you call her, The Silver Fox."

Xia cringed.

"What is she doing here?" Another samurai spat.

"Quiet, Buko. Sit, Xia," commanded an old man sitting beside the lone woman. His thin gray beard wisped down to his torso like a cloudy vine, and the wrinkles on his face made his eyes barely visible. There was a warmth to him reminiscent of her grandfather. She obeyed and sat down across from him, as did Mai. "Perhaps Mai has made you aware of our situation."

"Yes," Xia replied, her voice tentative.

"I am curious. What is your judgment of the government's Revitalization Project?"

"Um, well," She glanced around the circle, a dozen piercing sets of eyes burrowing into her vision like daggers. She focused her gaze towards the man with the question. "Yes—well, I don't think it's an offer that anyone should take up."

"How have you come to this judgment?" His tone was inquisitive and light. Comforting.

"Well, you should always be wary of what the FRF says. But this Project in particular, there seems to be some red flags. The fact that nobody can see the place ahead of time, the fact that they only want Virgins." She didn't disclose the inconsistencies from the footage to what Jina at the FRF Office had described. She felt she had already said too much. "Too many doubts for something you'd have to uproot your life to pursue. Even if it did mean decent food."

A smile from a samurai to her left. A nod of approval from a monk on the right. Xia eased slightly.

"A wise assessment," the old man replied, "that we share whole-heartedly. It is suspected that the recent news broadcast is an attempt to further entice our community, since the acceptance of the project has been minimal. But still, it does nothing to aid our current predicament. Consequently, it further endangers us. And with Lord Daimyo gone, the danger deepens. I am afraid our meager home in this land is further shaken. It is time to travel the road that we have been anticipating."

A silence loomed over the circle. Faces flashed with various emotions. Resolve, uncertainty, despair.

"We can't! It's been a fairytale for so long. We have nothing to stand upon," Buko finally exclaimed.

"Time waits for no one. Whether or not the soil is ready, the rain always comes."

Xia's eyes darted around the circle, attempting to read clues. She had no idea what they were talking about. The old man read her puzzled eyes.

"Since the dawn of the Freesian Republic, and the movement to hold steady to our roots began, we knew our time here was limited. The foundation for our home was never strong enough to hold us. And it is crumbling as we speak. We've always known that we must leave, someday. And that fateful day has arrived. We must leave the Freesian Republic. We must leave the city. And it is you who can help us." Grunts and grumbles rippled through the circle, the loudest landing with Buko.

Xia stared back incredulously. "Me?"

"As proven with the falling of Lord Daimyo, and the confirmed capture of the Zealous Lutno, we are quick to be targeted and even quicker to fall. We cannot stand on our own, and yet our values bind us to our weak humanity. You have proven yourself strong and competent, but above all, you have proven yourself an ally. I am afraid we don't have many of those outside our community." A crooked smile perched on his thin lips.

The words were daunting. And yet Xia couldn't imagine saying anything but 'yes, of course' to his kind face. A face that ever so likened her grandfather. And the more he spoke, the more she could hear her grandfather's voice.

"But what can I do? I'm just a freelancer. I've made the fods, sure. But that's the extent to what I've done, really."

"Blessings, my child, you ooze humility. Your physical capabilities are strong. I have heard of your countless endeavors. Gang fights, recovered goods, and connections with parts of society that lay hidden to the most modded of eyes."

It was true. Being a freelancer, especially an experienced one as Xia, meant she had rapport with all types of characters. Characters that were more than useful in illicit activities. But still, what the old man was asking was nothing like anything she had done before.

"So, when you say help, you mean what? Help you to escape the walls?"

"That is exactly my intent."

Buko's outburst overshadowed Xia's lack of response. "Lord Daimyo would never allow this! She is not one of us. She is not one to be trusted. Her body is painted with the very thing that seeks to destroy us."

"And yet, Lord Daimyo did allow for two Freesian Force members to guard our gates each day," a slim samurai with heavy bags under his eyes piped up.

Buko glared. "Do not speak with such negativity about Lord Daimyo!"

"There was no ill will in my words, Buko."

"Lord Daimyo hated walking past those two Force members each day, I assure you," another voice said.

"And yet, he did allow it. Circumstances have only grown more severe, so this may be allowed too, no?" The slim samurai spoke again.

"This is different," another voice spoke. "To have someone by the likes of her actively work with us, learning of our protected secrets. The thought is detestable."

The voices clashed back and forth, rebuttal after rebuttal. It was only broken when the lone monk woman raised her dainty, frail hand and uttered a meager cough. Everyone immediately silenced. Despite the delicacy of her frame and features, her voice carried a vigor and hardness that forced its way through the circle like a boulder downstream.

"Your bickering irks the spirit. Calm yourselves." The circle collectively breathed in and out, then silence returned. "The silver girl holds a twisted spirit. In her eyes are foreign blood and violations of the body's purity. And yet, the intentions are pure. The actions are pure. Trust has been laid. We may accept it. We may dance with the silver fox."

Xia blinked. Never had she felt self-conscious of her eyes before. Or was the woman speaking metaphorically? Or both? Everyone seemed to know except her. They hung their heads in acceptance of the old woman's words. The old man with a likeness of Youle smiled.

"Do you accept this dance?" He asked, his tone playful.

The image of Leikko's enamored face. Of Lutno standing in that open field, eyes hollow. Of the Daimyo. But one thing returned. Her grandfather's eyes of ardor. Xia nodded. "I'll do what I can."

Buko tensed, but everyone else nodded. The old man stood, followed by the old woman, followed by the rest of the group. As each person stood, the old man's figure seemed to shrink and shrink, until Xia stood and saw just how meager the man's frame was.

"Speak with me," he motioned. Xia gulped and followed him up the stairs, leaving the silent group behind, until they reached the room where Xia had met the Daimyo just a few days prior.

The view that looked full and majestic before seemed empty now. As if, without the Daimyo's presence, it lost its grandeur.

"My child. I thank you. You may call me Kibou. The others call me Roshi, but many moons have passed since another called me by my birth name. I would feel happiness if you did so."

Xia nodded. "Sure, Kibou." She'd have preferred to also call him Roshi.

"I am sure you find us odd," he said as he straightened the sleeves of his maroon kimono. "How we hold so strongly to convictions that seem to fail us. But believe me, my child, they give us strength. It is needed in a world such as our own."

The air stilled at his words.

"I do not like the word 'Virgin'. Before the fall of our society, this term was used to describe one who hadn't experienced the joys of sexual pleasure with another soul. Perhaps that is why we were dubbed with the name. We shun the technological pleasures that could enhance our untouched bodies. We object. And for what? Why do we do it?"

He turned to face Xia, a twinkle in his eye. A secret that only he knew the answer to.

"Many in our community share the sentiment, and call ourselves human. I do not like this, either. For I see the humanity in you, as I know you do in me. Your flesh feels, your blood runs, your heart beats. But the little sparks in your eyes—". He lifted two long fingers. "The mods. The little CPUs that you, both physically and mentally, have grown so reliant on. They are a barrier. A wall separating you from your true humanity."

The twinkle in his eye sparkled. "But I am not here to lecture you. Nor to chastise you. You are your own person, who has chosen to help us."

The responsibility outweighed her confidence. "Do you really think I can actually help you?"

"I don't think this, I know this."

14

Adopted Puppy

The little girl stood in the empty park, staring at the bars looming above her. They seemed so high, yet her short grandfather could easily touch them.

"I don't think I can do it," she trembled.

"I know you can. I believe in you. Let's give it a try."

The girl stared up into her grandfather's twinkling eyes. Besides the neon lights of the city, his eyes were the brightest things she had ever seen. She climbed the stout ladder and, with every ounce of deep-rooted courage, launched herself onto the bar. But as she hung there, the courage dissipated into doubt.

"Look at you! Alright, now swing your arm and grab the next one."

She stared towards the paint-chipped metal bar. It seemed so far away. Then she glanced down at the ground. Her grandfather seemed far away, too. She obeyed him and swung her arm forward, but she hadn't anticipated the loss of strength.

"Ah!" She landed with a perfunctory thud. It was only a few feet, but to the small girl it felt like a mile. "You said I could do it..." She gazed at the ground forlornly.

The grandfather crouched down and lifted the girl's chin with careful affection. "You can do it. Just not yet."

Kibou eyed Xia with a similar twinkle. "Fleeing the city must sound preposterous to you, correct?"

"A little." A lot.

"Of course. The plasma field that enshrines our city, holding us inside, it is all-encompassing. Only the military holds the freedom to pass through. How fortunate for them, how unfortunate for us." A coy smile on his lips. "Now tell me, do you know of a soul by the name of Opell Doksen?"

Xia shook her head.

"He will aid us in our quest. You will take me to him. Tomorrow. Come here to fetch me, and we will go together."

"Where is this guy? What does he do?"

"In due time, the unknown will be made known. Tomorrow." He bowed, signaling the end of the conversation. "Farewell, Xia."

She bowed in return, head swimming with unanswered questions. Then she descended the stairs, completely different from when she ascended them.

"Xia, wait!" She turned, halfway down the courtyard, and saw a breathless Mai chasing after her, almost tripping on the stony path. "I'm coming with," she breathed as she caught up to Xia.

"What?"

"I can't go back home. I just can't. Not without Father."

"Don't you want to be there in case he returns?"

Mai shook her head for the umpteenth time. "No. He won't return. And if he does, it won't be him. And if that's the case, I don't know what will happen to me."

Xia realized that Mai was right. If the Daimyo was snatched and returned with a different brain, they would likely snatch Mai too. Like Leikko inevitably was. Which is why it was the one thing the Daimyo had communicated to Mai. 'Don't come home.' She looked into Mai's pleading eyes, wanting nothing less than for her to follow. But a pang of intuition trembled in the depths of her gut. Perhaps this was a chance to make things right, to make up for her lack of action with Leikko. If it were, she'd let fate decide.

"Try to keep up." Xia turned on her heel and began making her exit.

"Wait, really?"

"Come on," Xia said, not looking back. Mai followed behind at her heels, counting her lucky stars that Xia didn't need much persuasion.

As they exited the gate, Xia noticed the gaze of one of the slags linger on them as they walked by. What was going through their metal head?

They approached Xia's bike, the fluorescent blue bubble glowing. "Woah," Mai muttered. Xia disabled the forcefield and checked for any attempts to bypass the barrier. Zero, as usual. She swung her leg over the side and slid on her helmet.

"Get on," she motioned.

"W-what?" For the first time, Mai looked scared.

"Unless you want to walk."

Mai stood there and weighed her options. She glanced around her, hoping that an alternative would spring out of the air. When nothing did, she approached the back of the bike with hesitance.

"But I don't have a helmet," she whined.

"Keep your head pressed into my back, it'll block the wind."

"But what if we crash?"

"We won't."

Mai gave one glance back towards the Pagoda, took a steady breath, and clambered onto the back of the bike. There was barely enough room for the two of them, but Mai was small enough that she could just fit. She wrapped her arms tightly around Xia's waist and pressed her face in between Xia's shoulder blades.

The added weight made Xia feel clunky and lopsided. She didn't like it. Hopefully this wouldn't be a regular occurrence. "Ready?" She registered the nuzzling of Mai's face further into her back as a yes. And with that, she sped off.

As Xia flew through the city, she made sure to drive with increased caution due to the additional cargo. Slower speeds, more controlled turns. Because of this, the signs and lights that were normally blurs in her accelerated rushes were visible; her surroundings were clear. At first, it was jarring. She could see the stares as she drove past. It wasn't too common to see a cycle in the first place, but a cycle with two passengers was even less so. But the stares weren't unfriendly. There was curiosity, inquisitiveness, amusement. She caught the eye of a little boy— his fluffy brown hair dancing with each enthusiastic jump as he pointed excitedly to the passing cycle. Time slowed as Xia stared back at the boy. His hair floating as the brightest of smiles graced his naive face. Although he couldn't see, Xia smiled back. A second later, the moment was gone, but Xia could have sworn she heard Mai laughing, the sound swept away in the racing winds.

They zipped through the Third Ward, through Midpoint, and into Xia's home Fourth Ward. When walking this route, the change from bustling metropolis to the dilapidated ward was gradual. But on a bike, it was almost jarring how much the city changed. She parked her bike in one of the neighboring alleyways and activated the electro bubble.

"That...was...amazing!" Mai breathed excitedly in between her words. Her hands vibrated with adrenaline.

Xia smirked. "This way." They exited the alley towards the main street, walking past a stench-inducing gear factory. The closer they got to Xia's place, the more the street filled with warehouses, factories, and apartment buildings. Not a place for visiting. The closest bar was Mickey's, but that was enough for Xia. They reached the tallest of the neighboring buildings and entered the lobby. There were only three busted chairs instead of the usual four. Maybe one of them got *too* busted? Mai took it all in, although there wasn't much.

"Come on," Xia said, right before the elevator doors began to close. Mai scurried inside.

"Don't tell me you've never been in a high rise," Xia said as she pressed the 25 button.

"Not in a long, long time. You know they've been using elevators for hundreds of years? This one seems like it's from the Before Times. Pretty old and slow," Mai mused.

Xia hummed in response. The lift slowly raised them to the 25th floor, and Mai followed Xia as she entered her apartment. Unlike the lobby, there was a lot to take in in here.

"Wow," Mai gasped. The sky was darkening, preparing for the signature neon haze cast from the city beyond.

A few times, Xia had sat on her mattress and watched outside as the sky slowly grew darker and darker, and the city grew brighter and brighter, a gradual shift from day to night. There was only one point in which she actually noticed the shift. A sudden twist of lighting from a warm haze to a cool one. She wondered if that was the moment the sun fully escaped for the evening. "This is amazing."

Xia didn't respond, but instead went straight to her small fridge. From there she took a small vial and poured a slight amount into a syringe. Never hurt to take an injection early, but always hurt to take it late. She peeled back the length of her tight black sleeve and injected the serum into her forearm. Her maroon eyes squinted as black appeared in her peripheral, along with warmth— Mai stood right over her shoulder.

"What," Xia barked.

"Can I see?" Her eyes gleamed with genuine curiosity. This was likely her first time seeing an injection. So commonplace for all of society, but not for Virgins. Xia turned so the girl could get a better view.

"There's not much to see." Slowly the needle fed the fluid into Xia's bloodstream. When the syringe was empty, she rubbed the spot a few times and then pulled her sleeve back down. "There."

"Wow," Mai muttered.

Xia walked over to the fod setup. A second later, the warmth and black in her peripheral returned. "Can you quit that?"

"What's all this?" Mai's curiosity burned brighter.

"This is where I make the fods."

"Really? At this small little table?"

First the comments about the dingy elevator, and now the 'small little'. She didn't expect it, but they rubbed her the wrong way. Xia was protective over her domain. It wasn't perfect by any means, but it did well enough. "What did you expect?"

"I don't know. A big machine or something. Or a lab."

"A lab? To make a small tech device?"

Mai shrugged. "I don't know how any of it works." She bounced over to the fridge. "You don't have much in here. Where's all your food? You don't even have crumb bars. Everyone has crumb bars."

Xia rolled her eyes. Wasn't this girl supposed to be grieving her father? Maybe this is how she coped. An on and off switch from negative to positive. Either way, she needed a break from the girl.

"I'll be back later," Xia said as she walked towards the door.

"Wait, what? You're not leaving me here alone, are you?"

Xia stared at her, letting the silly question answer itself.

"What am I supposed to do?"

Xia turned to fully face the black-haired girl, arms crossed at her chest. "You do realize you were the one who decided to follow me around like a lost puppy?"

Mai's lip puckered, but she recovered quickly. "Well, you're not going to leave a lost puppy all alone? Puppies chew things up. Break things."

An eyebrow raised. "You're not going to break anything."

The lip puckered again. "Well I don't want to sit here all alone! I'm coming with. Where are we going?"

Xia blew out her cheeks. No energy to argue. "A bar."

Mai's eyes lit up like the skyline below. "Perfect!"

15

Bar Talk

Xia had wanted to walk. She needed the solitude. Wanted to clear her head a bit. But with Mai at her side, the decision was quickly regretted.

"What's that building over there?"

"Where do you get your groceries?"

"Don't you grow anything?" And a long tangent about how difficult it is to grow anything in general.

"Do you worry about your motorcycle getting stolen?" Long tangent about the rarity of cycles, and how she'd never believed she'd ride one.

"What's the bar we're going to?" Tangent about the dangers of drinking.

"Do you drink a lot?" The tangent continued.

One block from Mickey's and Xia wanted to grab her Enforcer and blow Mai's brains out. Or her own brains out. Or maybe both. Either way, it had to stop.

"Can you just, stop talking?"

Mai looked up at Xia, her innocent brown eyes growing dejected. "Y-yeah, sorry. This is all just really exciting to me."

"Yeah, well, this is just another day for me. And I didn't ask for you to be here. I don't even know why I let you come."

"I don't know either. I was surprised when you said yes."

"Yeah, well..." Xia pointed to the fat brown block before them. "We're here." She swung the door open and Mai followed behind.

Xia was used to the thick musty air, but it hit Mai like a ton of bricks. Her nose shriveled, wanting to recoil inside her face. "What is that smell?"

Years of grime, rust, smoke, occasional vomit, and a lack of adequate cleaning supplies resulted in a unique concoction of a smell that Xia learned to enjoy. "Anything and everything." She noted the lack of dust on the tables. "Dames is working tonight."

"Who's Dames?"

As if on cue, the large man entered from the swinging doors behind the bar, a dozen glasses balanced in his meaty hands. She nodded her head towards him.

"He's huge! I'd expect him to...well, *not* be a bartender. He'd make a great fighter. Like those cyber wrestlers."

Xia had often thought the same thing. "He's good at what he does."

The bar wasn't very busy, so the duo had their pick of spots at the bar. "Let's sit here!" Mai said, patting down a spot at the very center, directly under one of the few buzzing lights. The exact spot that Xia made an effort to avoid.

Xia ignored her and instead took a spot towards the end at one of the darkest corners of the bar. A few moments later, the dejected puppy followed and took a spot next to her, feet sticky. Mai's hand hesitantly touched the counter and was visibly relieved when it wasn't nearly as sticky as the floor.

"No way, absolutely no way. The little lady's got herself a friend tonight?" Dames sauntered over to them, his eyes shining with pure amusement.

"Not exactly—"

Mai straightened with a newfound energy. "That's right! So you're Dames?"

Dames leaned on the counter, his amusement multiplying. "That I am. What has she told you about me?"

Her smile grew. "Oh, that you're the most handsome bartender here, and that your big strong hands make the best drinks—OW!" Mai rubbed the side of her face, which Xia's hand had just flung across in a light but forceful backhand. "Gosh, you are no fun."

Dames let out his gravel laugh, causing Mai's eyes to momentarily widen, the guffaw catching her off guard. But then her eyes squinted as she laughed along, finding the entire situation just the funniest thing. Xia found it repulsive.

"If you can get this little lady to let loose and have a little fun, both your drinks are on me tonight." He looked towards Xia, catching her annoyed eye. He raised his eyebrow with an amused smirk before turning back to her new 'friend.' "In the meantime, what can I get you ladies? The usual?" Another glance toward Xia. She nodded, not meeting his eyes.

"Um..." Mai leaned over the counter to get a better view behind the bar, lifting herself off the seat. Where did this spunk and audacity spur from? The girl hadn't even had a drink yet. She had presumably just lost her father. Xia didn't understand, and the whole thing was annoying her very core. "Got anything sweet?"

Dames turned around and scanned the bar, as if viewing it for the very first time. "Sweet, hmmm...He pulled out two bottles Xia had never seen before and noticed the dusty film covering one. Mai pretended not to notice. He poured equal parts into a dainty glass that should have broken between his massive fingers and swirled it in a hypnotic circular motion, the two liquids dancing together and becoming one. He then dropped in a single small cherry and placed the glass in front of Mai. "There you are, my dear."

She picked up the glass and sniffed it, her wide nose wrinkling slightly. "What is it?"

"Taste and tell me."

She took a sip. Her face contorted for a second, but then relaxed just as quickly. "It bites at first, but is smooth on the way down." She giggled. "My stomach feels all warm! Could be sweeter, though."

"Yeah, not too many folks like the sweet stuff. The more you drink, the less you'll like it too. Back in the day we had a nice mead. You'd have loved that. But bees are hard to come by. Have to charge a mod and a leg. Not worth it. Speaking of. I can't help but notice you lack those."

"Legs?" She quipped.

"You're cute. We don't get a lot of Virgins in here. Honestly, I can't remember the last time we did."

Mai looked around the place. The dust particles floating around the few hazy lights, the tech-covered patrons sulking over grungy tables. "Yeah, this isn't really the type of place we frequent. We tend to stick together."

"So what got you with Xia over here?"

"Can you get me my drink already?" Xia asked.

"Right, I'll be right back." Dames meandered off to the other side of the bar, while Mai turned towards the glowering Xia with exasperation.

"Would you lighten up already?"

Xia stared at her, expression blank.

Mai's eyes intensified. "Look at what just happened to my dad, and yet I'm still able to joke around. Would it kill you to crack a smile?"

Xia turned away from her and watched Dames. Even from afar, she noticed the care in which he poured each part of liquor. How vigorously he shook the mixer, the ice rattling inside the metal tin. He continued to shake as he talked with a jovial looking patron with a hunk of metal for an arm. He smiled, the patron smiled, and a small bud of content fluttered in Xia's gut at Dames' happy exchange. He gingerly poured the liquid into a freshly washed scotch glass and then held the glass up to the light, observing for any imperfections. Did he handle each drink with such attention?

He sauntered over and placed the glass before her.

"Yes," she finally answered. Then she took a sip. "Where's the cherry?"

"Sorry, used the last one on your friend." He cocked his head towards Mai. The straight face lasted for about a second and a half, and then the smile broke out once more. "I'm just kidding you!" He grabbed underneath the bar and plopped in the small fruit. Mai's spunk seemed to be rubbing off on Dames. It made Xia incredibly uncomfortable.

"Are you done?"

"Yes, yes I'm done. Holler if you need something. And remember," he looked back at Mai. "The mission for free drinks still stands." And back to work he went.

"What a fun guy. I like him."

Another sip. "Everyone does."

"Especially you."

Xia didn't take the bait. Her eyes remained on the drink. Mai took another gulp of hers. No wince this time.

"So, Xia, we're going to be spending some time together. I'm curious about you. I want to know more about you. What do you like to do in your free time? Do you drink often?"

"My whole life is free time. I'm a freelancer."

Mai let out an exasperated sigh. "Yes I know that, but when you're not running around beating people up and making fods, what are you doing?"

"Is that what you think I do? Run around and beat people up?"

"I know you can, and I know you have. Answer the question."

She thought for a moment, the question foreign to her. "I come here."

"So you do drink often."

"Wow, you really cracked the code on that one. Who would have guessed?" Another gulp.

Mai's mouth transformed from a shocked 'o' into a maniacal smile. "A joke! Sarcasm! I'm absolutely amazed. Wow. This is incredible."

Annoyance flooded over Xia once more. Did this girl ever let up? All she had wanted was some alone time and to get a nice buzz going. She made eye contact with Dames from across the bar and tapped her drink, signaling that she was going to need another one lined up. There was one positive to the Virgin body snatching. She made so much money that she could get as many drinks as she wanted.

Mai caught the exchange. "I'll have one too!" She shouted. Then she swung her head back and gulped the rest of the drink. The jovial metal-armed man let out a howl.

"Relax, would you?" Xia muttered.

"I'm just having some fun. I've never been to a bar like this. A bar at all, really. If we want to drink, we tend to make wines at home with fermented fruits. Most Virgins do, if they are going to drink. But many prefer eating the fruit itself to fermenting it. The rest of the city drinks a lot of moonshine, right?"

"Moonshine, gin, or sake. So if your goal is to get drunk, you're gonna get one of those three. Moonshine will do it quickest," Xia answered, the most she had really said all night.

"What's in yours?"

Xia shook the glass, the ice cubes rattling. "Whiskey, something orange, and something else I don't know."

"You've never asked?"

Xia's shoulders raised in the slightest shrug. "Makes it mysterious."

"So you like mystery, then?"

She downed the rest of her drink. "No."

It wasn't long before Dames had dropped off two full new glasses, but it was barely quick enough for Xia. Mai was happy with her progress. It was the most she had gotten Xia to say all night. And all day. Actually, it was the most she had said since the girl had met the silver-haired rebel. And the key to getting more was the very thing that Xia could talk about. A couple more drinks.

"Come on, you must be at least a little curious about me."

It was true. Xia was *very* curious. How did the daughter of the Daimyo fall into prostitution? Where did she get such vivacious gumption? But she didn't want to humor her. "Not interested."

Mai rolled her eyes. "Let's see." Her fingers drummed along the bartop. "If you were any mythological creature, which one would you be?"

"What?"

"You heard me. Like a mermaid or a banshee. I think you'd be..." She tapped her chin with her forefinger, milking the moment. "Not a dragon, that's a bit too *grand* for you. I say a valkyrie. Yes, you'd be a valkyrie. What do you think?"

"I think I'd be a mole."

"Those aren't mythological! Those are real."

Xia shrugged again. "I've never seen one."

The corner of Mai's lips twitched as she held back her smile. "Alright, a mole. Now do me. What would I be?"

"A gremlin."

"What? Oh come on."

"You asked me. I answered."

Mai eyed her playfully, the smile breaking through her tight lips. "I'm much too pretty to be a gremlin."

Xia finally quit staring at the glass before her and turned slightly towards Mai, glancing her up and down. She was right. The girl was much too pretty to be considered a gremlin. The joke was practically absurd. The way her black locks flowed gracefully over the slender curvature of her back, the way her rosy lips parted whenever she wasn't talking. The big eyes, the dainty hands, the even daintier feet. She likely received a lot of business at the Virgins' Lair.

"A sprite," Xia answered finally. Then she turned back to her drink to take a swig.

"A sprite? Like a little fairy?"

"Mmhm."

"Okay, okay. I can see that. I can work with that. Because I'm so small and cute?"

"Sure."

"So, why are you a mole then? I personally think you are much too pretty to be a mole."

Xia thought for a moment, letting the silence linger. "They just burrow into the ground to be alone. Sounds cozy."

"So you'd want to hide away underground and be alone?"

Another sip. Honestly, no. She was no good at talking to people, but she still liked to be around them. She enjoyed the bustling of the city and the liveliness that came with Ferinday nights. People-watching was a solid pastime. There's something she liked to do in her free time. Another sip. What was the question again?

"Xia?" Mai repeated. Xia glanced over. Had Dames made it extra strong? She was only halfway done and her head already had little bees buzzing inside.

"Yeah, um, the mole? No I guess not. I don't know. It's a stupid question."

Mai humphed. "I disagree! It's a fun question and speaks a bit to your character. Well, if not a mole, maybe a fox? What do you think of being called the silver fox?"

She shrugged. "Don't care."

"Better than the silver mole?"

The faintest ghost of a smirk. "Sure."

Mai was about to revel in that ghost but was interrupted by the glowing metal arm that rubbed up against her. The patron that had been sitting across the bar now stood directly beside Mai.

"How are you two gorgeous women doing tonight?" He addressed it to both of them, but he only had eyes for Mai.

She turned towards the man with a sweet but coy smile. "Oh we're doing just fine, how are you, handsome?"

Xia puzzled at the reciprocity. The man grinned revealing a set of dilapidated teeth. "I'm Peles. What's your name?"

"This is Mola," Mai nodded towards Xia, a hint towards Xia's 'mole' joke. "And I'm Eri. I like this," she said as she stroked his metal contraption of an arm, taking the attention off herself. Streams of light pulsed from his forearm to his bicep: yellow, green, blue, violet.

The man raised his arm and showed it off with pride. "Just got it. Cyntro Model 3."

"What does it do?" Mai asked, her tone light and flirty, but her curiosity was genuine.

"Various cybernetic enhancements. Makes me extra strong. Got lots of cool gadgets in there, some are secret though. But maybe, if you play your cards right, I could show you." His arm moved to touch the small of her back. Whether he dumbed down his explanation because she was a Virgin or because he thought her to be some ditzy girl, Xia wasn't sure. But either way, he was sure laying it on thick.

Mai leaned into his touch with a pout. "Oh, I would love that. But—" she snatched Xia's hand. "My girl here wouldn't like that."

The man lifted his hand and stared at Xia, looking at her for the first time. "You two are together?"

"Yeah," Mai said, deepening her pout. "While I do swing that way, she doesn't, and she's *very* possessive." Mai let go of Xia's hand and brushed her cheek with a delicate graze of the fingers. It took everything in Xia to not recoil at the touch.

"Well if she changes her mind," he slid forward a contact card. "You call me anytime."

Mai picked up the card and gave it a little kiss before sliding it into her back pocket. "You bet I will."

Peles' eyes hungered with pure lust. Reluctantly, he removed his ravenous eyes from her and waved towards Dames. "I'll see you next time, my man."

Xia waited for him to leave the bar before turning to Mai. "What the hell was that?"

"Whatever do you mean?" Mai blinked her eyes with faux surprise, tone mocking.

Xia could have slapped her again. This time for real. "All that touchy shit. And why did you tell him we were together?"

Mai clicked her tongue, shaking her head with exasperation. "Xia, you've got a lot to learn about men. Not just men. People in general. They want to feel special. Wanted. You can't just reject them. You've got to play along. Because when people are told no, that's when they get dangerous. Anyways, I've got to use the restroom. Please tell me they have one of those?"

Xia pointed towards the opposite side of the bar. Mai hopped off the barstool and made her way towards the bathroom, leaving Xia to mull over the conversation that just transpired.

Of course Mai could navigate situations like that; her job made it a necessity. All she did was deal with horny men. On top of that, she was a natural beauty, *and* a Virgin. She was likely approached very frequently. Xia never would have dreamed of handling the situation like that. She didn't think it was possible. There wasn't a flirtatious bone in her body.

Without asking for it, another drink appeared before her. She looked up into Dames' onyx eyes. Eyes that would be menacing if it weren't for the crinkles that lined them from years of smiling.

"You alright? Sorry about Peles. Obnoxious, but a decent guy."

Xia looked off towards the bathroom, then back down at the drink Dames just made. This was her opportunity for an escape. Mai had proven herself more than capable, and Dames would make sure she got back okay. Xia could leave, right now. Free herself from the black-haired sprite.

"Xia?"

She grabbed the drink and took a sip, letting the opportunity slip away.

16

Recovery

By the time Mai came back and began her babbling again, Xia was leaving tipsy land and entering drunk territory. They were no longer on the solid ground of the bar but on a ship sailing into rocky waters. She hadn't eaten enough. Normally she'd try to wolf down something prior to a night at Mickey's, but Mai had caused her to skip that. She now understood the adage Dames had told her from the Before Times: 'Don't drink and drive'. She couldn't imagine operating her bike when the floor was moving beneath her.

"So what do you think of that?"

Xia's heavy head turned towards Mai. "What?"

"Were you even listening to me?"

"No."

Mai groaned. And repeated her babbling story. Which once again, Xia did not listen to. How could she listen when the bees were now buzzing in her ears and not just her brain? And some of the bees had arms, pulling her eyes down. It was a workout to keep them open. Another sip. Head getting heavier.

"Dames!" Mai called out. "I think it's time for us to get going. Um, how much do we owe you?"

Dames waved a hand. "I heard you yell something about sarcasm. Seems she really lightened up." He looked at Xia, whose face drooped closer and closer to the bartop. "Don't worry about it."

Mai didn't press. "You are just lovely, you know that?" Despite her drooping head, Xia reached out for one more sip but Mai pushed the glass away.

"Come on girl. Let's go get you home."

She couldn't even protest. By the time her mind registered the words, Mai was half lifting, half pulling her out the door. And by the time she registered the hands on her, they were outside. Dames looked on as the two left, feeling incredibly guilty about his heavy-handed pouring.

"Alright, now which way was it again?" Mai looked to her right towards the increasing neon, the number of signs and people snowballing the further the street went. Midpoint. Then she looked to her left, the street a barren gray block by comparison. She took the left.

The walk seemed ten times longer to Mai than on the way there. Xia was slim, but there was a lot of weight to her. How much muscle was she hiding under that black suit? Mai wondered if it was uncomfortable, or if she got hot. She was drunk enough that she might even tell her. But Mai kept the questions to herself.

They walked past the occasional person, but nobody paid them much attention. Drunk walks home from Mickey's were a commonality. That was until they were just a few blocks from Xia's apartment, when two lanky young men spotted them from across the street.

"Hey, what's the matter? Your friend need some help?"

"No, we're fine!" Mai shouted, desperately hoping that would end it. But as the one man smirked towards the other and began closing the distance between them, she knew their intentions were anything but to help.

"She doesn't look fine," the taller of the two said. Everything about him screamed cocky. The way the corner of his mouth upturned into a permanent smirk, the way his blue eyes stared down with condescension, the way his body leaned back in arrogance. All he needed was some chewing gum to complete the picture.

Mai continued walking, with Xia leaning against her for support. Was she listening to any of this? Mai looked towards the tall girl, but her silver hair clouded her face. The two men followed behind, then began walking on either side of them.

"You know, I've seen her around here," the tall boy said, pointing at Xia. "But you. I've never seen you before." He reached out and touched Mai's arm.

"We're just trying to get home. Maybe we can get to know each other some other time?"

"Nah, I think tonight's gonna work the best for us." His grip tightened on Mai. She jammed a defensive elbow to his stomach, which caught the sandy boy off guard, but only for a moment. The cocky smirk left his face, replaced by a disgusted rage. He pulled Mai into him and wrapped his arm around her neck, the veins in his arm popping as he placed her in a tight choke hold. "You fucking—"

But he was cut off just as quickly. It was a flurry of motion that sandy boy had barely caught from the corner of his eye— the drunken Xia using her weight to slam into the shorter man, catching him off guard, before stabbing his side. He only had a moment to look at the blood pooling underneath his friend's falling body. His attention shifted to the silver-haired rogue who was now pointing a gun at him. But not just any gun. His eyes widened in terror as Mai spluttered under his hold. It was an Enforcer.

"Let go of her," Xia said.

He didn't need telling twice. He gave a sorrowful glance towards the body on the ground and ran off, leaving his friend behind, as well as his own cockiness.

Xia slammed the gun back into her pocket and glanced down toward the body. The man groaned and Xia vomited a steady stream of brownish, wretched juice. Then she wiped her mouth, turned around, and began walking home, every other step wobbling under the moving street.

Mai stood stationary. Her heart pounded in her chest. She stared at the body, the blood now mixing with Xia's alcoholic bile. A lump grew in her throat. She wanted to vomit. She wanted to cry. After a thick moment, she chased after Xia, her steps wobbling as well. "Xia...Xia!" She caught up, but Xia kept walking.

"You ok?" Xia mumbled.

Mai nodded. A lie. "Are you?"

Xia kept shuffling. "I want to go to bed."

***

Five hours later, an army of slags marched into Xia's apartment, their heavy feet made of steel. A drummer drummed along with each step. The apartment shook with every pound. But when Xia opened her eyes, she realized that they weren't in her apartment. They were in her head. Shaking her brain and pushing against her eyes as her ears rang from their mods' high-pitched frequencies.

God, she was hungover. And still a little drunk, judging by the spinning window. The lights blinded her. She shut her eyes once more and let out a garbled groan.

"You're awake!" The voice was needles in her ears.

Xia slowly lifted herself up. She looked around, noticing a smell. Mai appeared at her side holding a bowl of noodles.

"I got you some—"

In one swift motion, Xia grabbed the bowl and stuffed a fistful of noodles into her mouth.

"For hell's sake, use chopsticks!" Mai scolded, but a smile traced her rosy lips. Xia grabbed the metal chopsticks from her with equal ferocity.

"There's really not many food places around here. Had to go back past Mickey's. I stopped in and told Dames I got you back just fine, and he told me the best place to get you some food. That was a whopping..." She checked her cell chip. "Four hours ago. I would have offered to heat it up, but..."

The half-empty bowl proved that wasn't necessary. Xia continued to chomp it down, as ravenous as a starved wolf.

"Dames said he *may* have made your drinks a little extra strong."

So that's why she had gotten so inebriated. Fucking Dames. She set the bowl down and rubbed her eyes. "Wanted me to 'lighten up'?" She grumbled.

Mai let out a nervous laugh. "Yeah, I guess."

Xia stood—the motion was a little too quick and the room rocked sideways—and walked over to her small bathroom. Once the door shut behind her, she unzipped herself from her black skinsuit and hung it up on the back of the door, activating its self-cleaning process. She skipped the squatting pan; she'd piss in the shower. It was almost the end of the month, and she had been saving up her water supply. But as she noticed the wet tile, her eyes widened in horror.

"No," she muttered. She turned the shower handle and the horror spiked when no water came out. "MAI!" She shrieked, her voice cracking in pure despair.

"Xia?" Mai's voice grew equally panicked. "Are you alright?!"

Xia nearly swung open the door to kill Mai but the sight of her nude self in the reflection stopped her. She grabbed the towel, which was damp, and wrapped it around herself before exiting the room to complete her assassination.

"You showered? You took a shower?!"

Mai backed up, her hands raised defensively. Never had she seen such rage in Xia. This was the most emotion the freelancer had shown since Mai had met her. It was terrifying.

"I-I'm sorry, I didn't know. Is there no hot water left or something?"

"No hot water, no hot water?" Xia laughed, devoid of all humor and filled with incredulous indignation. "Try no water at all! How long did you fucking shower?"

"It was only—"

"I had been saving it all month. All month! Wiping myself down at Mickey's! Getting in and out faster than it took to get undressed! And now there's none left at all, because of *you*! Who I didn't even ask to be here! Who won't give me a damn second to myself. And now you took this away too!"

She raised her hands and brought them to her head, asking the heavens why they cursed her with this devil sprite. The sudden motion loosened the hold on her towel, and the poor fabric fell to the floor in a thunderous thump.

Mai let out a tiny "oh," before covering both her eyes with her dainty hands.

Xia let out her own reaction, the sound a cross between a groan, a cry, and a yell, before darting back into the bathroom. She slammed the door behind her and leaned against it, wishing this hell of a night to be over.

After several long moments to calm herself down and question her life's purpose, she grabbed a baggy t-shirt and some shorts from the small closet and put them on, her movements sad and perfunctory. She glanced at her reflection in the mirror. Her sclera was nearly as red as her irises. She looked absolutely miserable. Taking a few more deep breaths, she wiped her eyes and exited the bathroom. Mai startled at her entrance and stood from the corner chair.

"Xia, I'm so sorry—"

"You didn't think I might need a shower? After stabbing someone and vomiting?" Her words were much quieter and more controlled, but the same fury lay underneath them.

Mai gulped. "I didn't know that it cut off— that you had a limited water supply. I really didn't think I showered for that long."

"Yeah, well, you did. Everyone has controlled water usage. Especially in apartment buildings like this. I don't know how you and your fancy father got around that, but yes. We peasants don't get to shower all day. And we don't have fridges full of food. And we drink away our pain, no matter how unhealthy it is. And we use mods because that's our society and it's how you live in it!" Xia winced at the last word as she bit her tongue so hard it nearly bled. She babbled too much. She barely knew what she was saying until after she already said it. The alcohol unlocked the gate between her brain and her tongue. Or maybe Mai had just worn her down too hard. She groaned and shuffled over to the small sink by the fridge and grabbed a glass. Filling it with lukewarm water and ignoring its beige tint from contaminants, she gulped it down. She was too exhausted to boil it right now.

"If you're out of water, how can you use the sink?" Even under the circumstances, Mai couldn't help her questions.

"Bath and kitchen supply lines are different."

"Okay, okay." She said to herself. Then she came over by Xia and began opening and rifling through cupboards.

"What are you doing?"

"Let's see, where was it? I know I saw it earlier...aha!" She grabbed a small container that Xia hadn't touched in ages.

"That stuff tastes awful."

Mai chuckled. "You're not supposed to drink it, silly." Then she squatted down and pulled out the few pots and bowls Xia owned. "Go lay down. I'll make this right. Or at least, better than it is now."

Xia had no energy to protest. Shuffling back over to her bed by the window, she fell atop it, and fell asleep less than a minute later.

Water usage limitations were one of many on the long list of government restrictions. Mandatory resource allocation, traffic restrictions, surveillance measures, stop and frisks. The list had actually shortened in the last decade. Technically there were energy limits, but the limit kept increasing over the years due to the energy-reliant nature of living in Cyber City. And surveillance via cameras and facial recognition became pointless when people kept using mods to alter their faces.

Xia had assumed those restrictions were the same for most people, save for those that had enough money to buy inspectors and military off. Apparently, it was different for the Daimyo as well. Or maybe that's how it was for people who didn't live in apartments, which was a small minority of the population. She didn't know how it all worked. Most people didn't. They knew the rules, and knew to follow them. Well, most of them. Some crimes reaped amazing benefits. And others just weren't worth breaking.

The battalion of slags had left and were replaced by—a sauna? No, the room wasn't nearly hot enough. But she felt warm and wet. Her eyes flitted open.

"Perfect timing! Now I can get your back."

Xia's eyes widened as she saw Mai dip a towel in a wok and bring it close to her face.

"What are you doing?" She sat up abruptly, almost spilling the large pan in the process.

"Careful!" Mai stabilized the wok and dipped the towel once more. "Those tea leaves you had sitting in your cupboard. They're aromatherapeutic. Fantastic for your skin. It's *not* for drinking." She lifted the towel once more and hovered it near Xia's cheek. When Xia didn't retaliate, she gingerly wiped and patted the hungover girl's face. "See, doesn't that feel nice?"

It did, much to Xia's chagrin.

"You don't use this thing very much," Mai gestured towards the wok. "Had to give it a real nice cleaning before I could use it. The thing was covered in dust."

"Yeah, I don't cook much."

"I can tell!" She dipped the towel back into the bowl and pulled back her playful tone. "Why is that? Is that how most people around here live?"

Xia eased as the warm water seeped into her pores, the aroma calming her heightened nerves. The soothing was so therapeutic that the question didn't even bother her.

"It's near impossible to grow anything yourself in apartments like this. Closest you can get is a hydroponics system. But that's a lot of time and effort that most don't have. The only market in the Fourth Ward is absolute trash. The closest decent one is in Midpoint. Otherwise you'd have to go to the Third Ward. And in the end, it makes more fiscal sense to just use nutrient injections and buy ready made food. Markets are expensive." Her eyes were closed as she spoke. Better to take in the scent.

Mai hummed, finding the information kind of sad, but also pleased that Xia shared so much. "Well, that's something I can do. Cook. I can make myself useful."

"You talk like you're sticking around for a while." When Mai didn't respond, Xia opened her eyes. "How long were you going to stick around?"

Mai straightened up, gathering courage for her response. "Until my community is safe."

In that moment, Xia saw her life flash before her eyes. The solemn and comfortable nights alone, the electric rides through the city, the casual drinks at the bar. It all disappeared as Mai's face popped up, her looming presence and constant streams of questions invading the solitary lifestyle Xia had grown to appreciate. "You're messing with me."

She wrung out the towel once more, her words strong with conviction. "No. I have nowhere to go. Nowhere to be. And I can help you. I need to help you. You'll see." She wiped Xia's face once more. Maybe it was the warmth of the water, maybe it was the aromatherapy, or maybe it was something else that Xia hadn't yet recognized, but she didn't have the spirit in her to object.

17

The Letter

Xia woke late the next morning on her small cot. The day was gray, with only the ghost of the sun attempting to haunt them. She stretched out, the tips of her toes just hanging off the edge. She felt incredibly well rested. Which was unheard of after a night of drinking. In fact, she actually felt relaxed. Her muscles held no tension. Her skin felt soft and smooth.

Some of the tension returned when she remembered her new roommate. She sat up and looked around for the source of her new obnoxious problem. The culprit lay curled up in the lone lounge chair Xia owned, head and knees scrunched into her chest. The towel used for Xia's sponge bath hung over the chair, partially covering Mai's eyes so as to block the light from the window wall. It seemed Xia was the only one able to sleep without a shade.

Xia was going to revel in her companion's slumber and enjoy the moments alone. She tiptoed just three steps when Mai began to stir. Cursing to herself, she tiptoed two more steps, but Mai fully awoke, the towel falling to the floor. She let out her own big stretch like a waking cat, accompanied with a loud yawn, before her groggy eyes met Xia's.

"Good morning," she said with a smile.

"Morning."

"Grumpy in the mornings too? Sheesh." She stood. "But come on, don't you feel great? That yochi tea works wonders."

"What are you wearing?" Xia looked down at Mai's baggy ensemble.

"Found it in your closet."

Xia's eyes burned with indignation. Of all the clothes in her closet, Mai had to pick the one set of pajamas she still owned from her late grandfather. "Change."

Thankfully, Mai didn't put up a fight. "Fine. Not like I was going to wear it all day. But first, I'll make breakfast—"

"Look, Mai. We need to talk about last night."

Mai froze.

"You said you were going to stick around here until the Virgins are safe. Well, that may never happen. And I'm not—"

Mai eased and cut Xia off. "Oh don't worry, I know. You didn't sign up for a roommate. I get it. Believe me. I'm aware of the burden I'm imposing. But here's the thing. Aside from my own selfish reasons for wanting to accompany you with this, I can help you. Not only am I a phenomenal cook," she smiled proudly before dropping her tone, becoming serious. "But I am a Virgin. And you know how tight knit our community is. As much as Roshi—or, *Kibou* as he's allowed you to call him, and the other elders may believe you can accomplish this, it will be so difficult on your own because we have a hard time with trust. I'm sure you've noticed that when selling your fods."

It was true. It was a trait that Xia recognized, and was inherently grateful for since it made interactions short. Many bought the fods with reluctance or on behalf of worried family, but the distrust was always there.

"You may not realize it, but our community is much larger than you think. We aren't around much on this side of town. We're very good at keeping to ourselves. If it weren't for that distrust, you wouldn't be able to keep up with selling those fods. You'd have triple the clients."

Virgins were known to be a small minority of the population. But just how small, Xia never knew exactly. Perhaps it wasn't as small as she thought.

"So today, I'm going with you and Roshi to meet Opell Doksen. And if you aren't convinced now, you will be after I make breakfast."

She winked, but Xia's mind was elsewhere. She had nearly forgotten about the plan to meet this Opell character with the old monk. Yesterday felt like ages ago. The images from the night prior flashed before her. The drinks, the bloody body, the towel dropping. A cringe ran through her body like a centipede. Mai didn't notice. She began working with the few ingredients in Xia's kitchen along with the leftovers. Xia took a seat at the small two-person table and waited, her mind mulling over the events of the last few days. She already felt in over her head.

"Mai. Your father. You said he walked a girl from the VL home. And she was jumped, but he fought them off. Right?"

Mai faced the small stove, her back to Xia. "Right."

"And then the next day, he never made it to the Pagoda."

"Right."

"Did he tell you anything about the attackers?"

She shook her head as she stirred the pot. "All he told me was not to come home."

Xia hummed. The Daimyo was cryptic, but if he could he would have told Mai more. But he didn't even want her to come home. If he was able to fend off the attackers, he assumed that they would target him next. "We need to go to your house."

Mai hesitated, weighing her options. "Do we have to today? I just feel—"

"Yes. It has to be today. Before we get Kibou. Besides, you need a change of clothes."

The corner of Mai's mouth twitched into the daintiest of smiles. She nodded, plating Xia a serving of breakfast: a concoction of flour, spices, old dried vegetables, and leftovers from the night prior.

Xia would have demanded they leave right then and there, but the smell of the food forced her to linger. And as she took a bite, the taste confirmed it. Maybe she could put up with the sprite for just a little longer.

Mai lived on the opposite side of the city. But with Xia's cycle, the trek barely took half an hour. Throughout that time, the grip Mai had around Xia's waist lessened from a choking death grip to a moderate clutch, and by the end Xia worried the girl was going to fall off since she was barely holding on at all.

The houses that lined the street were unassuming and small, many barely visible behind the stone walls that shielded them. But at the end of the street, one home towered above the stone palisade. Simple yet enticing, the sloping copper tiled roof stood faultlessly over the second story, shoji screens lining the walls and allowing the minimal sunlight that Cyber City received to enter into the home.

"Damn," Xia muttered into her helmet. *That* was a house.

Xia parked right out front. She doubted she even needed the electro bubble, but she set it up for good measure anyway. Mai gazed towards her home, her eyes saying more than words ever could.

"Ready?" Xia asked. It took a moment for Mai to acknowledge her. When she did, she gave a hasty nod and a sad smile before unlocking the gate. There was another garden, this one much smaller but just as vibrant as the one at the Pagoda.

"What do you do when there's acid rain?" Xia asked as they walked past the budding plants.

Mai shrugged. "Try to cover it up the best we can. We have metal tarps that we can use. Luckily the closer you get to the city's walls, the chance of acid rain becomes less likely. I can't remember the last time we got hit with it."

Mai unlocked the front door but froze as soon as they entered.

"What is it?" From Xia's point of view, everything looked normal. The home was very traditional, with tatami-style rooms and intricate tapestries featuring birds from the Before Times.

"Something's...not right."

Xia scanned the surrounding area. No people, no abnormal frequencies, no life forms except for a pigeon out in the garden. Mai took a few hesitant steps forward, as if a monster were to pop up from around the corner.

"There's nothing immediately out of the ordinary here that I scanned."

Mai waved her hand dismissively. "Not like that. It's too...something's missing. My home always had this smell. Not very strong or anything. But it smelled like home. The smell isn't here."

Xia thought for a moment, looking around the pristine house. "You never returned here after you left yesterday?"

"No."

"I'm guessing that whoever took your father came here, too. Maybe to look for you. But maybe to look for something else. They likely fumigated the house to remove their trace. That way nothing would come up on scanners. They'd get rid of any fingerprints they leave behind, DNA, as well as smells. Hence why the house doesn't have the signature home smell."

"So we can't find any trace of who was here?"

"Didn't say that. Where's your father's room?"

Mai took Xia upstairs and led her to the bedroom. For all of the Daimyo's reverence and glory, he slept simply. Like Xia, the Daimyo also slept on a bed directly on the floor, although this one looked much more comfortable. The room was illuminated by four hanging lanterns, casting a warm glow on the near-empty room. Xia opened the unassuming closet and scanned, finding nothing out of the ordinary. Then she moved the lone partition in the corner of the room, revealing his desk, along with several large books.

"Did your father write much?" She asked, noting the calligraphy set.

"Almost every night," Mai answered.

"Last night, too?"

"Maybe."

Xia scanned the desk and opened the drawers. It was completely empty. Uncharacteristically so, for the desk of a man who wrote every night. Mai noticed this as well.

"It's been cleared out," she said.

The last thing the Daimyo was, was a fool. "If your father were to write something, something that he wanted you to see but only you could find, where would he put it?" She expected Mai to think for a while, or to say that she didn't know. But immediately Mai's eyes widened and she beckoned Xia to follow her. The two left the bedroom and went down the hall, a furor in Mai's steps.

This bedroom was the opposite of the Daimyo's, and very clearly Mai's. The room was essentially one blooming blossom of a flower. Rosy embroidered quilts adorned the massive bed, sakura paintings and tapestries and dried blossoms decorating the walls. Prior to the intruders' fumigation, Xia expected the room to smell like the flower itself.

Mai opened her bottom drawer dresser and pulled out a small wooden box. She opened it, revealing its contents to be empty.

"They really cleared the place out," Mai mused. "I kept my mother's old jewelry in here. What a shame." She breathed out, letting the disappointment slide off her. "Luckily, your fancy scanners didn't pick up on this." She slid her finger along the bottom and pushed, allowing her finger to hook inside. Then she pulled out a small wooden key that fit flawlessly inside the box.

"Smart."

Mai smiled and walked over to her vanity. Simple makeup and various perfumes aligned the desk. She picked up one of the bottles and dipped the key inside, letting it soak. "Needs oil. If you try to unlock it without, it won't fit right." As she let it soak further, she pulled open her top right drawer. "At least they didn't take my hairbrush," she joked, her small brush being the lone content inside. After another moment, Mai pulled out the slicked key and pulled her vanity away from the wall. Barely visible to the naked eye was a small hole at the very base of the structure. She slid the key inside and turned, and Xia watched as the back of the drawer holding the hairbrush pulled down, revealing a secret compartment.

"That's quite a setup."

Mai returned to her feet and checked the back of the drawer, pulling out a folded piece of paper. "But it worked, see?"

Mai's eyes grew hungrily at the note. They morphed from the eager hunger into sadness, into hurt, and finally into an angered resolve. Xia was dying to know what it said, but she waited behind Mai with her arms crossed until the girl handed the precious memo to her.

My Dear Mai,

You are a clever girl, and so I have faith that this letter will reach you. By the time you read this, I will be gone. These words are too precious to be spoken aloud, and so I have condemned them to this mere piece of parchment.

As you have likely heard from your friend, I was ambushed as I escorted her. And as I fought them, I sealed my own fate. I am ashamed to write that they took me by surprise. Their vile modage hid their steps, hid their sounds, even hid their faces. They were not of the military. I believe them to be hired brutes, nothing but muscle and mods. I killed them. They did not expect a fight.

I examined their bodies, and there laid my fault. If I had left immediately, perhaps I wouldn't be writing this letter. I found nothing worth noting as I inspected them. But time was not an ally. Two more brutes came, and they were not alone. They came with a man. A man whom I recognized immediately, and who recognized me. Dr. Iro Nagawa.

You were not meant for this world, my dear Mai. Even as a fetus, you rejected it. I faced the hardest decision of my life with your birth. To embrace the technology of our corrupted world if it meant saving your life, as well as your mother's? Or to stay true to our values if it meant your demise?

I admit, I was a coward, because I did not make the decision. I left it for your mother. Your poor, vibrant mother, who was too precious for this world. As you grew inside her, and her health declined, and your fates grew dimmer, I became a coward. I let your mother decide your fate. And she, like the brave and vigorous soul she was, rejected a blood transfusion that would save her life, all because the blood came from modded souls. But you, she chose to save you by any means.

It was a miracle your mother graced this world as long as she did, and this was all due to the efforts of Dr. Nagawa. One of the most skilled surgeons of our time, and one who's specialty lay with our Human community. It was through his skill that you were saved.

When I saw him, I must admit, I rejected the truth that lay so blatantly exposed. He recognized me instantly. My garments allowed for it easily. I left that instant. But with that recognition, I sealed my fate. There lay my second mistake and possibly the greatest of my life: that I did not kill him right there and then.

I confess. It has been difficult to choose my path. I know they will kill me, now that I know Dr. Nagawa to be the one conducting the procedures that terrorize our people. He will be suspecting I will target him. He will come to the house with countless more brutes. I will fight, and I will lose. But I will not allow them to take me. You know what that entails.

I would write more, but time is of the essence. They will be here soon. What I will say is this.

I have nothing but love for you. Farewell, sweet Mai.

As Xia read the final line, tears welled in Mai's eyes. Xia pretended not to notice.

"What does he mean here, you know what that entails?"

A few tears spilled out. "It means he will commit suicide rather than be taken."

Xia nodded, scanning over the letter once more. "And this Dr. Nagawa? Have you met him?"

Mai shook her head. "Not that I remember. I think I saw him a few times when I was young, but ties were cut. I never knew why. But I can guess as much now."

So the surgeon behind these brain transplants came to the scene of the kidnappings himself. The Daimyo seemed to have pieced everything together; he knew that the doctor needed his living body for a brain transplant, and if he couldn't defeat the intruders, he'd defeat himself.

"If your father had an intruder, where might he fight him?"

"Not inside the house. Probably in the front garden."

Xia stuffed the letter into one of her many hidden pockets and left the room, going exactly there. Mai followed behind. As they stood in the garden, Xia scanned back and forth. No signs of the doctor, or of anyone for that matter.

"I thought the intruders used your fancy tech to wipe the place clean."

"They did." Xia swiped up and down, tapping her temples, all invisible to Mai.

"It looks like you've got an itch."

Xia glanced over at Mai. "What?"

A mischievous grin grew despite the circumstances. Mai mimicked Xia, scratching her temple and tapping the air in a silly mock.

Xia ignored her. "They wiped the DNA and all unsuited materials. Blood, sweat, prints. But I'm hoping they didn't think to..." A small smile crept up at the accuracy of her hunch. "Over here." They walked off the side of the stone path into the grassy expanse of plants and fruits. "You can see leaves have been torn off, as well as patches of dirt where grass should be. Signs of a struggle covered up. She continued to examine the array of greenery, noting each individual missing leaf and misplaced patch of dirt. Once she knew what to look out for, it all appeared so obvious.

"The struggle ended here." She gestured towards the fragile, untouched berry plants. The same ones that grew so lushly at the Pagoda. How she wanted to snatch every single fruit. They hung there so limply, practically begging to be plucked. She averted her eyes and walked away from the greenery and back onto the stone path, leaving the berries alone, and leaving Mai to have a moment to herself in the place where her father snuffed his own life. And as she waited in the empty home, she could hear the distant wail of a heartbroken daughter carried away in the wind.

18

Opell Doksen

Initially, Xia did her due diligence and continued to scan and scrutinize the house for any other pertinent information. After finding nothing, she ended up in the kitchen, scanning the contents of their fridge and pantries. There was tea of every variety, fresh fruits and vegetables, rice and bread. It was near the upper end of affluence by Cyber City's standards, and for what Xia was used to, it was beyond impressive. Was this due to the Daimyo's standard? Or was it a result of Mai's success at the brothel?

She examined a leafy green plant with odd white speckles when Mai appeared at her side.

"I suppose we should pack this all up."

Xia glanced up.

"Since I'm staying with you. And I'm going to be cooking." She attempted a wink, but with her bloodshot puffy eyes, it looked pathetic rather than playful.

"You should also pack up some clothes. And anything else you might want to bring. Keep it light. I don't want the bike to tip over."

Mai nodded. Xia waited outside, letting Mai have some more solitude as she packed her things, but also to keep herself away. Happy-go-lucky Mai was obnoxious, but sad-depressed Mai made her uncomfortable.

Xia wandered through the pristine garden and admired its ability to grow. All her life, she had assumed such an endeavor pointless in the polluted city. Yet here were the literal fruits of such cultivation. Her eyes lingered on the strawberry plant. Then her fingers floated towards them. Before she knew it, she had stuffed three in her mouth.

"Ready," a voice rang behind her.

Xia whipped around startled, red juice dribbling down her chin.

Mai genuinely smiled for the first time that day.

The ride to the Pagoda was short, thankfully, as Mai had not heeded Xia's advice to 'pack light'. Or maybe she did, and this truly was packing light for Mai. Either way, the bike almost tipped over.

The two approached the gate of the Pagoda and entered to find Kibou examining the same strawberry plant that Xia now loved so much.

"Shall we?" He turned with a strawberry in hand.

Mai ran up the stone path with her bag to drop it off for safekeeping until they returned. "Be right back!"

Kibou offered the berry to Xia. She took it with care and resisted immediately shoving it into her mouth. "She is a vibrant soul, is she not?"

That was one way to put it. "Yes."

"Vibrancy requires energy. It can be quite draining. Can it not?"

"Yes." Xia threw the berry into her mouth.

A moment later, Mai came crashing down the path. "Where are we headed?"

Kibou strode past the two of them. "Follow and you shall see."

The trio walked in silence through the streets, leaving the tranquil area surrounding the Pagoda and into the heart of the city. Mai continuously attempted to catch Xia's eye, and Xia continuously acted as if she didn't notice.

The further they went, the busier the streets grew, and with that, the more out of place they looked. Seeing Virgins out and about in the city was uncommon itself. But a monk? His flowing maroon robes stuck out like a peacock in a chicken coup. With that came many stares, and many comments— most of them derogatory.

Mai hated the attention, and with each odd or outright nasty comment she shot back her own nasty glare. But none of it phased Kibou. If it weren't for a small smile at a foolish joke about what he was hiding under those robes, it would appear that he genuinely didn't hear any of it at all.

They continued through the city, past the food stands, past the holographic advertisements of gaming systems and new modular devices, past cybernetic enhancement clinics. If they were to travel into the Second Ward, why not take a bus? Did Virgins avoid those too? She didn't ask. She followed wordlessly behind Kibou. And eventually, she began to question his route. It was after they left the Second Ward and entered the Outer Slums that Xia became concerned over where the hell Kibou was taking them. Mai's glances grew more frantic. She'd never been in the Slums before. It made Xia's home ward look like a paradise.

"Kibou, is this—"

"We have almost arrived, my child." And just a block later, standing before a crumbling building with cobwebs littering the entrance, he confirmed their arrival and opened the door.

The entryway held a large staircase traveling upwards and a skinny staircase around the corner leading downwards. Kibou bypassed the larger one and began to descend the stairs to the basement level below. Xia finally caught Mai's apprehensive eye. Then they followed behind. The building was silent save for the electric buzzing of the flickering overhead light, barely illuminating their descent. Out of the corner of her vision, Xia noticed a skinny shadow scuttle up the wall.

She covered her mouth to muffle her yelp as her legs froze. Her eyes followed the shadow, which continued to scuttle until it reached the ceiling, daring to crawl right above her head. Fear and disgust tensed in her chest and bubbled in her throat.

Mai whipped around. She'd never seen Xia like this. "What's wrong?" Her eyes followed Xia's gaze and when she saw the culprit for Xia's terror, a laugh burst.

"A centipede? You're scared of a centipede?"

The sound of Mai's voice seemed to aggravate the small creature, and its dozens of legs scurried forward until it slithered into a crack in the ceiling. Xia clenched her hands into fists and willed her body to calm down. Each second brought a small bit of relief as her heart rate slowly returned to baseline.

"Oh come on, it's just a bug! They are icky, sure, but they won't hurt you." Mai wanted to joke further, but she noted Xia's lack of annoyed response. The silver girl seemed genuinely perturbed.

Kibou gazed on from the bottom of the stairs, a wistful look on his sage face. "The greatest of enemies are often the smallest of foes. Come. We have almost arrived at our journey's end."

As the fear left, embarrassment replaced it. Xia brushed past Mai and followed Kibou down the hall, avoiding even the slightest glance in Mai's direction. She couldn't stand to see the girl's reaction. At the end of the hall, Kibou knocked on a small door, his feeble hand barely making a sound on the steel. Nonetheless, it swung open a few moments later.

Xia wasn't sure what to expect, but she wasn't expecting this. One eye, one arm, one ear, and a quick scan showed his legs were bionic. She'd never seen someone with so many missing parts.

"Opell," Kibou greeted with a low bow.

Opell simply nodded. "You the girl?" He asked, staring down at Xia. His dark cocoa skin held patches of milky white, matching his white teeth. For teeth so white, he didn't seem the type to smile.

"Yes, this is our silver friend," Kibou said warmly. He walked inside, pushing himself past Opell. Opell gave her a once over, his jaundiced eye glancing up and down like a yoyo. Then he burst out in a high-pitched laugh. Mai startled.

"Is something funny?" Xia asked with a drawl.

He cut his laugh as abruptly as he started it. "Nope. Inside, inside."

"He's weird," Mai muttered as they followed him inside into the flat. Even though she barely whispered it, Opell whirled his head around and flashed a devilish grin.

"Oh, am I?" He laughed once more.

Xia'd never met the man. Of that, she was certain. And yet that high-pitched laugh sounded oddly familiar. Where had she heard it?

Kibou had already made himself at home, standing at the stove and boiling some tea. "T'was a long walk," he mused. Xia was getting used to seeing the wise old man in places he didn't belong, and Opell's kitchen was one of those places.

Xia wondered how Kibou had gotten himself acquainted with some-one like Opell. The man wasn't a Virgin, yet he opted to keep himself one-armed. And one-eyed. Perhaps due to low funds? As evidenced by his flat, Opell was not a wealthy man by any means.

"Xia, you hold many questions as to why we are here. Opell, shall we quell them? May we head into the room?"

Kibou glanced down the dark hallway leading off the living room. She imagined centipedes hiding in the shadows and shuddered.

"Yes, lets. Lets lets lets."

Kibou ambled over with a tea in hand. "I'd offer you a cup but I'm afraid our friend isn't keen on having liquids in the room." He took a long sip, clearly the exception to the rule, then followed behind Opell. The girls followed suit. The hallway grew darker and darker until they reached the end. Opell turned around and cast his wicked smile once more, his teeth practically glowing in the dark. "You ready?" Then he swung the door open with dramatic flair.

Xia registered the sounds before the sights. Electronic buzzing, sta-tic, and various user interface blips of varying frequencies and pitches danced around the darkness. Gradually, her eyes adjusted to the low-lit room. She'd never seen something like it. The room was riddled with tech; every surface and corner held some type of machine or monitor, and yet most of it she couldn't place what it was. Except she recognized the device on the main desk instantly. A radio transmitter.

The high-pitched cackle registered. "You're the Nightcrawler! On the radio!"

Opell's head turned ever so slowly, as if he were a haunted doll. "Why yes, yes I am. How ever did you figure that out, little girl?"

"Your laugh." She expected him to laugh in response, but he didn't. Instead he turned his attention towards Kibou.

"She's got some smarts."

Kibou nodded. "That she does, that she does."

Opell's manic smile grew larger as he bent down closer, closer, too close to Xia's face. She stood motionless. Then she felt the tiniest ping at the back of her scalp as he plucked one of her long hairs. "Silver smarts on a silver head."

Xia hurriedly sidestepped him and glanced around the room. Beige boxes with black screens, wheels with shiny black tape, tubes with wires sticking out, and dozens of old monitors lining the walls, some on, some off. "What is all this stuff?"

"Golden tech from golden times." Opell puffed his chest out with pride as he sauntered around the room, pointing out each device. "We got here your movie reels, your record player, cathode ray tubes-those go in the computers. Speaking of, we got your Akari 900, your Pineapple 3, your Commander 64. Your gaming systems: Akari, Z-Box, Gamestation, Nuntindo. VHS tapes, cassette tapes, landline phones, floppy discs. And, as you already know, your radio. But we had to change it up a bit. This ain't no ordinary radio."

He gleamed with the glittery joy of a crazed lunatic, mouth nearly frothing at the words. "Can't have them catch me. No, no, no. And they always catch 'em. I'm sure you've noticed. You're smart. Real smart. You must hear 'em. They get on here. And soon they don't. Because they're caught. Because them slags. They catch 'em. They track the signal. But me? My signal doesn't lead here. No, no, no. It leads to a place way out West. Far, far, away. Outside the city."

"How?"

"Quantum mechanics." He smacked his lips before widening his grin once more. "This radio is fitted with a quantum entanglement interface, which encodes anything I transmit to the entangled particles way out West. Outside this dusty city."

Xia had wondered how he was able to continue broadcasting. "That's amazing," she said honestly.

"Yes, yes yes yes, precisely. Yes yes yes. Isn't it all just beautiful?" His eyes sparkled with absolute love for his vintage collection.

It was nothing short of impressive. Most of this stuff, Xia had never even heard of. How had he got his hands on it all? One glance at this room by a slag and he'd be carted off to the Void. All tech and literature from the Before Times was strictly forbidden in an attempt to wipe away the memory of the past. But for people like Opell, it did the opposite. It birthed a passion and furthered an obsession. And now he was the

Nightcrawler, spreading illicit news over radio waves to the few people who had and used radio transmitters.

Mai stood at the table in the corner, inspecting one of the gadgets. "I had one of these when I was young. A CD player." A sad smile graced her lips. "Sure does bring back memories."

Opell's smile threatened to rip his face open. He hadn't shared his collection in a long time, and seeing someone else appreciate it brought him pure, unadulterated joy.

"Let us continue the purpose of this visit," Kibou said as he took a long sip of tea. "Opell is an old friend. But a hidden one. He has been a useful tool and ally. It is he who uncovered the truth of the world outside."

The blazing grin returned. "Let me show you." He motioned over to one of his many monitors and began typing away. "This computer is connected to a digital satellite receiver. It connects to a satellite waaay up there." His long index finger pointed upwards. "Up above this little city. Above the smog, above the clouds. Way up in space. It circles around and around and around. And it takes very pretty pictures. Pictures that I get to see."

He tapped away on his keyboard, screens opening and closing, then entered coordinates into the search box. A moment later, an image of lush green grass and a peaceful mountainside filled the screen.

"Where is this?" Mai asked.

He clicked further, the screen traveling through the mountainside as if they were eagles soaring right above. A pristine river fed into a lake, its massive waters a glittering blue that no neon light could quite emulate. Some type of large animal stood at its banks. Xia wanted to pause the screen and look at the animal, but Opell continued to move through the land. On and on they traveled, until a massive gray wall could be seen in the distance, with a gray cloud doming above it.

Xia's eyes widened, and Mai let out a gasp. "Is that—"

"Our beloved Cyber City, yes."

19

PROOF IN THE PUDDING

Kibou had implied that the world outside was inhabitable. Their entire goal depended on it. And yet that did nothing to diminish the shock Xia felt seeing it on the screen.

"The world out there ain't no 'barren wasteland'. They shove that down our throats since we're babies. But they're shoving lies. Stinky, dusty, lies. The world out there is shiny, see?"

"Can you still be sure it's inhabitable? Is it possible the radiation levels are still dangerous?"

Opell shook his head, his thick dreads swaying with each shake. "The proof is in the pudding." He tapped on the screen a few more times, returning to the animal at the lake. "See this? This here is a sika deer. And if you see here…" His fingers tapped some more and he opened a file on his computer. "This is also a sika deer. Notice any differences?"

Xia examined the two identical animals and shook her head.

"Exactly. This file here is from the good old days. That's what they looked like back then. And yet here they are, decades later, with no changes. If the radiation was really that bad, there wouldn't be deer runnin' around. And not the same deer from before then. It would be significantly genetically mutated."

Opell read the skepticism in Xia's eyes. "Not convinced? I have more. Let's see here…" He entered new coordinates and traveled around the screen once more. "Where are you…where are you…here! This forest. See these big guys?"

Xia examined the black and white creatures on the screen.

"Pandas!" Mai exclaimed.

"Yes, pandas! And here's the thing- pandas don't come around here. The bamboo forest is a bit a ways away. Never have pandas been around this area. And pandas don't like to move around. For them to come all the way over here means this was a better place for them to be. Meaning not only is it safe here, but safer than other places. And yet they stick us here. In this dusty, dusty, bubble."

"Can you get closer to the city?" Xia asked. She wanted to quell the last ounce of skepticism that sat in the back of her head like a lone itch begging to be scratched.

"Unfortunately," Opell said as he input new coordinates, "this is the closest we can get. If I try to move any closer—" he inched the screen further along, but it was no longer a seamless zoom. The images cut in and out like jagged shards of glass until it froze completely. "That happens." He moved the screen farther away until the image grew clear again. Even from that distance, the image was daunting. "And you see this?" He zoomed in on an emblem on the far side of the massive wall: thin red lines depicting a hawk ascending above a pyramid.

"The FRF Insignia," Mai muttered.

"Is that enough proof for you, silver girl?"

The weed was barely a seedling. She gave a solemn nod. "So, this satellite. Can you see images of anywhere? Anywhere around the world?"

Opell laughed again. There was no rhyme or reason to when he released the guffaw, but Xia was already getting used to it. "That would be something, wouldn't it? And the tragic thing is, you used to be able to. But alas, I can only see for a limited distance around here. A radius of about 200 miles, give or take. A lot of it is water. Plenty of ruins. Lots of animals. And our dusty city."

"And when were these images taken?"

"Every 36 hours, I get new images."

"What about the Revitalization Project?" Mai piped in, her question echoing Xia's thoughts.

A dangerous fire lit behind his crazed eyes, and his smile twisted into something crazed. "Nope. No sign of this perfect little paradise. This perfect little place that you—" he jabbed a long finger into Mai's chest, pushing her small frame back, "—are supposed to be sprinting towards. Why aren't you sprinting, little girl?"

Mai gave a nervous chuckle.

"Manners, Opell," Kibou scolded, his tone as light as a feather.

"Even if the outside world is inhabitable, is that enough?" Xia turned towards Kibou. "Say we somehow get you outside the walls, away from FRF control. What will you do? Where will you go? Seek shelter in the trees and eat wild berries? That can only get you so far. Not to mention the fact that the FRF would come after you eventually."

"I was awaiting this question. Opell, you've forgotten to show them the most important piece."

"Oops! Why, yes I did. Forgetful, forgotten, forget, forgoth," he mumbled to himself as he typed away, fingers furious with fervor. "Hold onto your hat, silver girl. It's about to blow away." He gave the keyboard a loud tap as he hit enter and a new image filled the screen.

At first, nothing seemed out of the ordinary. A swath of trees made up a forest. Lush and green, but nothing different from the rest of the images. Until she noticed a deeper batch of brown. And when she noticed the brown, she noticed the cloudy mist that hung above it.

"Is that smoke?"

"Ding ding ding! Yes 'tis! And if we zoom in here, you can see where it's coming from." The screen zoomed further onto the batch of brown, revealing the nature of the out-of-place patches. Roofs. They were houses, and judging by the smoke, they were inhabited. Not only was life inhabitable right outside the walls, it was already inhabited.

Xia continued to stare at the screen, the reality sinking deeper and deeper. So deep that it settled in the very pit of her stomach like a boulder in a pond, its ripples stirring worries and notions that had been laid to rest in the comfortable pool of her body. There was an entire fresh world outside, yet they were trapped in the cybernetic cage of Freesia. And with this new truth, the objective to help the Virgins escape became more than a mere pipe dream, it became solid. An attainable goal that Xia was meant to achieve.

"How far away is this... settlement?" Xia asked, her eyes still glued to the screen.

"About 70 kilometers. It's a trek, but doable. Ready to sprint, little girl?" He flashed yet another grin towards Mai, and this time she returned it in earnest.

Xia cocked her head to the side, her body filled with reticence. "How do we know we can even trust these...inhabitants?"

"Opell, zoom in closer on the side of the house," Kibou commanded. Opell obliged, and the fuzzy image of a tri-pointed symbol inside a circle filled the screen. It scratched at a faint coil deep in Xia's memory banks.

Mai's jaw hung open. "Is-is that—"

"Yes, yes it is, my child," Kibou replied with deep satisfaction.

Xia waited for an explanation. Kibou took a small sigh before beginning his tale. "Our Lord Daimyo, while formidable and well-deserving of his role, was not the original soul for the task. No, that soul was someone else entirely. A prodigy of their time, he excelled in every domain. Linguistics, the arts, philosophy, and of course, his physical capabilities. The best swordsman I'd ever laid my eyes on. Even superior to the current Lord Daimyo.

"A week before his proclamation ceremony, where he was to accept his responsibility as Daimyo and lead the current samurai, he disappeared without a trace. I cannot iterate the absolute shock and confusion this caused for our community. Unlike the current Daimyo's disappearance, where the primary reaction has been *fear*, this Daimyo-to-Be's vanishing caused utter bewilderment. He was searched for, and nothing was uncovered. But we had our inklings. For this legendary samurai had high hopes to escape the walls. And for the months leading up to his proclamation ceremony, he became further and further withdrawn. He'd disappear for hours at a time. Until one day, he disappeared forever. Perhaps he was taken by the government for his illicit ambitions? Or perhaps he was all too successful?

"This symbol, an ancient one used by our lineage of Daimyos, offers evidence to the latter. You bring us to the world outside, and we may find the Lost Samurai. I trust that he holds the key."

He let the story sink in. The prospect of a Virgin escaping and making a life for themselves outside the walls was beyond absurd. Yet she lived in a world where the absurd found new ways to manifest every day.

"The night shall greet us soon. Xia, do any more questions swim in your mind?"

Her mind was an ocean of questions, and if she allowed herself a minute to wallow in them she'd drown. Was it really just a few months ago that she was drinking milk teas on her way to bust up gangs and retrieve cash, ending her nights with a single cocktail that she could barely afford? The world had seemed so large then, and she was reminded of it every time she stared at the glimmering city from her apartment window. The massive skyscrapers that towered above the crowds of people below, the neon lights that reflected and bounced off each other's gleams in a hazy glow of luminescence. Yet that life felt so far away. So insignificant. So inconsequential compared to the life that swept her up and she was swimming in now. How long until she drowned?

"So life is possible outside the walls. But that still doesn't explain how we get out there."

Kibou's old eyes glinted. "That is up to you, my dear. I feel the answer is on the tip of your very nose."

Xia escorted the old monk back to the Pagoda, facing just as many odd stares and remarks as the way there. This time she didn't notice them. Her mind was preoccupied. The identity of the Nightcrawler, the gadgets, the revelation of life outside the walls.

The city looked foreign to her, the people like ants milling around a hill. How pointless it all seemed. The blazing sun that Xia pictured when she'd let her mind wander was real and bright and shining on a beautiful world outside while they were all trapped inside this cyber-clogged bubble. People looked longingly at the Revitalization Project, and yet that was the whole world outside. It was obvious why the FRF government would do anything to keep that knowledge hidden. People were already killing Virgins to get to this Project; imagine what they'd do if they found out that was the whole outside world?

As they entered the gates of the Pagoda, and Mai retrieved her things to take to Xia's, Kibou gave Xia a low farewell bow, but she wasn't quite done with their visit.

"Kibou, do you know of a Dr. Iro Nagawa?"

His gentle fingers twirled the wisps of his beard. "Ah, Dr. Nagawa. There is a name I have not heard in quite some time and a face I haven't seen even longer."

Xia looked towards Mai for approval. She hesitated, eyes furrowing, before giving a clipped nod. Xia pulled out the letter. "Read this."

Kibou gingerly took the letter and read it thoroughly, not exhibiting the slightest change in expression. Finally, he lifted his gaze and gave a small, sad smile to Mai. "I think," he turned towards Xia, "that we should keep this letter private." He offered the letter back to Xia, but Mai snatched it back, more hastily than she meant to.

"Where can I find this Nagawa?" Xia asked.

Kibou shook his head. "Leave the hidden predator to its hiding, lest we become prey ourselves. There are more pressing matters for you to attend to. Like finding us a way out."

Xia was about to rebut, but Kibou's deep bow cut her off. He was finished with this conversation. He spun on his heel towards the Pagoda, his robe billowing behind him.

Mai exhaled a breath from deep in her bones that she had been holding the entire day. Despite Kibou's small stature and perpetually calm demeanor, he added a level of anxiety that Mai did not enjoy.

"Let's go," Xia said, walking back towards the gate.

"Wait, can we talk—"

"Not here." Nobody was around, but she still felt exposed.

Mai didn't protest, and the two exited the gate. Xia eyed the two slags as they walked passed. While she couldn't see anything behind their voids of visors, she couldn't help but feel the eyes of the slag on her right burrow into her. She didn't know the intention behind the eyes. But whatever it was, it was strong as it followed behind her.

It was hard enough not to tip the bike on the way to the Pagoda, but it was a miracle they hadn't on the way back. It was a Ferinday night, meaning the streets were even busier—and drunker— than usual. Drunk and busy made for slow and audacious movements. Not friendly for two people on a cycle with a massive bag of stuff.

After Xia had barely dodged a hefty man that jumped into the middle of the road, calling out for Xia to "give him a ride, if you know what I mean", she was a second away from pulling over and kicking Mai off. But then her stomach growled, and she thought of the various foods in Mai's bag, and she continued the strenuous ride.

The walk from the cycle to the apartment was silent, which Xia was thankful for. Even Mai knew to hold her tongue about such secretive matters when there were other people around. But as soon as the apartment door swung shut, Xia braced herself for the barrage of questions and statements from her black-haired sprite.

"Oh my gosh, what a day. For the first time in my life, I can actually say: 'I need a drink!'" She flung open the contents of her bag, covering up the small table in Xia's kitchenette corner. "That Opell dude was kind of a creep."

The ghost of a smile. "I kind of liked him."

"Really? He's just so, *odd*. I suppose you are too." She laughed as she began picking through ingredients, prepping for dinner. Xia looked on with mild interest, wondering what succulent creation she'd get to taste. "It's been a big day, so I think we deserve a big meal." She glanced up. "Why don't you change? Is that skinsuit even comfortable?"

Xia crossed her arms. "Very."

Mai shook her head, her black hair falling from behind her shoulders. "Always putting up a fight."

Xia paused, sifting through the retorts in her mind. She cast them all aside. "It's not that. I'm not used to having someone else around. Or having someone tell me what to do."

Mai's face brightened at the lack of retort and glimpse of introspection. "I get that. Having someone always tell you what you should be doing... it often has the opposite effect. I know that firsthand."

Mai chopped away, her hand a blur as she sliced through a carrot with rapid precision. The girl was skilled. Xia felt a few pounds of weight leave her shoulders at the sight of Mai being useful instead of her usual nuisance. There were some perks involved in having the sprite around.

Xia changed into a loose tee and shorts (much to Mai's smug satisfaction), took her nightly injection, and grabbed one of the few canned moonshine mixtures she had. They were nothing compared to Dames' concoctions— part of the reason why she frequented the bar so often. But they were better than nothing. She stared a few moments before grabbing another for Mai. Then she sat at the table as Mai finished preparing their supper.

"What's this?" She said, picking up the can. "Moon Juice?"

"Try it," Xia replied as she took a sip.

Mai recoiled as soon as the liquid attacked her taste buds. "This is disgusting."

"It's not that bad."

"Yes, yes it is. I'll drink it, though. Maybe it'll taste better with food."

It didn't. Xia's mouth screamed in ecstasy at the first mouthful. She didn't know how food could taste so good. This was better than the steak she had bought so many years ago, and the ghost of that steak still haunted her salivary glands to this day.

"So, Xia. I feel like a lot has happened today... and it's all just happened. We haven't exactly been able to debrief."

Xia nodded with a mouth full of mushroom.

"So life outside the walls isn't just possible, it's already happening. And Kibou has left it to you to figure out how to get us outside. So, big question. Are you?"

"Am I what?"

"Going to help us?"

Xia leaned back in the small chair. "I already gave my word."

"I know, and for the life of me I can't figure out why. This is an incredible task for anyone, especially someone who's not even a Virgin. You kind of got sucked into this. But not really, because there's nothing holding you to it. This mission could very well end in your death. Why agree to help us in the first place?"

"I've got my reasons." Another swig of the canned cocktail and the face of her grandfather flit to the forefront of her mind. "I chose to seek you guys out and sell the fods. It spiraled a bit, but that's just life, right? I could never have planned for this. But I'm in it. So I'll adapt."

Mai stared at Xia, her large eyes squinting as if discovering a part of the silver girl she'd never seen before. Uncovering a hidden gem in a sea of coarse sand. Mai wanted to find more gems, and she was certain there were many. She smiled. "Well, thank you. Truly."

Xia nodded and took another massive bite. Manners evaporating.

"Well then, the big question. Do you have any idea how you are going to do it?"

"I got a lead."

"And Dr. Nagawa. Roshi—I mean, Kibou, he told you not to inspect that further."

That didn't make sense. This Doctor was the reason the Virgins were disappearing in the first place. Take him out, the threat is gone. Why would Kibou tell her not to go after him? There must be something that he wasn't telling her. Still, she had her own reasons to go see him. And for Mai, it was personal.

"Like I said, I don't like others telling me what to do."

Excitement and hope flickered in Mai's eyes. "You mean, you want to go see him?"

"Yes, he's certainly on the to-do list."

The flicker grew into a flame. "We should go tomorrow!"

Xia rolled her eyes. "This constant spontaneity. You need to reign it in. No, we can't just up and go tomorrow."

"But—"

"This is the man that caused the death of your father. He is beyond dangerous. We need caution. A careful, meticulous plan. Besides, do you even know where he would be?"

Mai sunk into the chair, her shoulders sagging. "No…"

"Exactly. Besides, our to-do list is long. First, I need to follow up on a lead."

Mai cringed as she took another gulp of the canned moonshine. "I'll be honest Xia. I really don't see how we can do this. The only ones with access are government officials and the Force Military. How are we going to get outside?"

"Well, luckily, that lead stands right outside the Pagoda walls."

Mai's face puzzled. "You mean, the Force Military members?"

Xia smirked. "Those aren't real Military."

20

Acid Memories

Their mere presence had ticked off faint alarm bells in the depths of Xia's mind. She'd hear them faintly, and with each time she passed the two guarded figures the ringing grew louder. There was something off. She couldn't place what. Initially, she chalked it up to the fact that she'd never been in such close proximity to them in a non-hostile encounter. But no, it was something else. The way the one figure's gaze always seemed to follow her.

Her intuition proved fruitful through a clumsy mistake of which Xia didn't even realize until halfway through the walk to Opell's. They had passed a group of pure cyborgs, laughing and drinking in rambunctious but almost threatening glee. Their eyes followed the trio, then their words. Nasty words. Mai shouted back, Kibou kept gliding, and Xia instinctively traced her fingers over the Enforcer in her pocket. Her heart had dropped. The gun was in her pocket. She had forgotten to take it out before walking past the slags at the Pagoda's entrance.

Xia's scan blocker couldn't inhibit the detection of an Enforcer. Was it possible the two Force members hadn't scanned her upon her entrance to the Pagoda?

Normally, Xia'd never take such a blatant risk. But she was riding on the high of her discovery of the lush outside world, and so she decided to take the risk once more. When they returned with Kibou, she let herself walk past the slags with the Enforcer in her pocket. And again, they did not stop her, but the one did stare. What was it about their stare? Then a memory hit her like a lightning strike, the electricity sizzling her skin as she realized how she could confirm her suspicions.

She waited for Mai to get her things from the Pagoda that she had left behind, and in that time, replayed an old recorded memory. One she had made by accident. The night she had first met Mai, when the two slags pulled her over, and in her attempts to do something had accidentally begun recording. She studied that recording, specifically their uniforms as they scanned. Once Mai returned, and they walked past the slags once more, Xia noted these uniforms. And the *difference* between them.

"What do you mean, they aren't military?" Mai asked.

Xia tapped on her wrist, a small display screen hovering above. She swiped through and accessed her saved memories from her eye screen, and selected the night she was stopped by the slags.

"Watch this."

The recording played on the floating screen above Xia's wrist. "You were stopped by the FRF Force?!"

"Sh! Watch."

The recording ended, and Mai's eyes furrowed in puzzlement. "So, what does this mean exactly?"

Xia zoomed in as she replayed. "Do you see here? On the visor of the slag? There's a blinking red light. It happens when they are scanning. You can see there's no light on the other slag, and when they both run off, the light is no longer blinking. Now tell me, have you ever seen a blinking red light on the two slags outside the Pagoda when people are coming in and out?"

"I mean, I don't think so? I don't really pay much attention."

"Well, I have not. Which means they aren't scanning. Especially since," she got up, retrieved the Enforcer from her suit, and set it on the table with a thud. "They let me walk past with this into the Pagoda."

Mai paled at the sight of the weapon, a lump in her throat inhibiting decent airflow.

"Tell me, how did you get those slags to stand guard every day?"

Slags for hire *was* an uncommon endeavor, due to both the cost and the general fear around them. Most people avoided them like the plague.

But, in theory, that would make them the perfect defense for a place as sacred as the Pagoda.

She paused. "I'm not actually sure. They've always been there."

"You don't know who hired them?"

"I know my father was the one who OK'd it. When I was young. But that's all I know."

Xia stretched her arms out, satisfied. "Well, it might be worth it to find out who exactly hired them. Otherwise I think I'll just ask them directly."

"Them, you mean, the slags?"

Xia smirked. "I think that's the first time I've heard you call them that. 'FRF Force Members.'"

Mai smirked back. "I think this is the first time you've mocked me."

Xia could feel one of the multiple barriers between the two of them crumbling away. It made her nervous. She took another sip.

Mai's eyes lingered on the gun resting atop the small table, pointing past her half-eaten food, directly at her chest. "You got anything else besides this?" She shook the can of acid moonshine in her hand.

Xia glanced up at the cupboard above her small fridge. Then back at Mai. Then at the cans between them. After a final swig, she stood and grabbed a large bottle from the cupboard, along with two scotch glasses, and sat back down.

"What's this?" Mai asked with intrigue as Xia poured the mysterious caramel-colored liquid into the two small glasses.

"It's good. Good enough that the bottle is half full despite owning it for several years."

"Wouldn't that mean it isn't very good?"

"Meaning I only drink it on special occasions."

"This is a special occasion?"

Xia shrugged. "It's been a day."

Mai's tentative fingers clasped the glass and she raised it to her preemptively puckered lips. She expected it to be bad. Her Virgin tastebuds were used to the sweetest of wines, and the can of moonshine tasted like broken glass. So when the substance hit her tongue, she was surprised that the hit was more like a pet. Maybe even a massage. A harsh massage, but one that she could get used to with enough hits. It slid down her throat with a deep, warm burn.

"That's not bad."

Xia sipped along with her. "No, no it's not."

A silence descended upon them, embracing the warmth of the golden whiskey. Comfortable for Xia, but uncomfortable for Mai as her eyes returned to the gun. "Can you put that thing away?"

Xia cocked her head, eyes questioning, but obliged. She took it over to the safe in the corner of her room and set it alongside the other few valuables she owned: a photo of her grandfather, a tanto and dagger, a stash of phys. When she returned to the table, Mai's face further paled, her glassy eyes drilling into the spot where the gun had laid.

"You okay?"

Mai didn't look up. Had she even heard Xia? Her switch in demeanor was more severe than the many revelations that had unfolded with her father. But as Xia followed Mai's lifeless gaze, she realized she recognized that stare. And when she thought back to the last time Mai had seen that gun, her suspicions were confirmed.

"Was that your first dead body?"

Mai finally lifted her face. "So he did die?"

Xia shrugged. "Probably." Mai drooped at the callous answer. For the first time in a long time, Xia regretted her choice of words. She couldn't stand to look at the wilting flower, especially knowing she caused the drought. Grabbing her small glass, she walked over to the massive window and watched the world below. It was as dark as the city could get. While the city's perpetual fluorescence made for a constant nightlight, the smog somehow allowed for the night sky to retain its darkness. The near-black sky seemed to endlessly stretch above, blanketing the silver stars that supposedly rest outside their bubble. Xia sighed.

"It fades." She continued to look outward. "The memory— it fades. It'll always be there. The first one does. The first dead body, I mean." Like displaced rocks on a bumpy road, it was hard to keep from stumbling over her clumsy words. She took a deep sip to regain her footing. "Because you'll see more of them. It's just a part of life. Especially if you stick around with me, for what we have to do. I'm sorry your first one had to be so bloody. Mine was too. But the first few days are the hardest. It'll pass. I promise."

The reflection in the window showed an empty chair, and when she turned around, a desperate Mai clung to her in a critical embrace. The girl's skinny arms wrapped around her torso like tendrils. Xia's breath hitched as her hands hung stiffly at her sides, almost dropping the precious amber liquor. *Do something with your hands*, she commanded herself. It took some effort, but her hand gradually obeyed, gifting Mai the most awkward of pats on the back.

In what felt like hours but was only a matter of seconds, Mai released Xia from her hazardous hug.

"Thanks for that," she said. Then she snatched the glass from Xia's hand and downed the liquid. The warm fire blazed hot.

"That's meant for sipping," Xia said as Mai sputtered. She'd have been angry at Mai wasting such precious liquor, but her yacking seemed retribution enough. "Get me another."

The yacking subsided, and Mai smiled at the silver girl, and with that, another barrier began to dissolve. Mai had been determined to crack at those walls. To puzzle together some of Xia's elusive pieces. So far she had only managed to piece together a few, but she was getting somewhere.

The two sat cross-legged on the thin cot on the floor, glasses full of liquor, staring into the skyline. Xia'd never admit it, but it was nice to have someone else there to bask in the view. To enjoy a drink with. To just coexist in this god-forsaken city rather than spend another night alone. Or maybe that was just the booze making her sentimental. Her mind wandered to her grandfather like a lackadaisical honeybee, sucking in the nectar of his essence. The crinkling of his eyes that accompanied his free-flowing smiles. The smell of leather and musk with a dollop of tobacco despite him not smoking in years. The bend in his back that grew deeper and deeper through the years. What would he think of her now? She took another sip, warming the tender thoughts even more.

"Xia, can I ask you something?"

She continued staring out the window and nodded.

"Last night, when you were going to shower, but you couldn't...and you came out to give me a piece of your mind. And your towel dropped..."

Xia's face reddened. "What about it?"

"I noticed the scars on your back."

A deep sip. "Acid rain," she said simply. But the mere observation caused the avalanche of a memory to cascade over her, crushing her chest as she remembered the worst day of her life.

Youle was getting old. No matter how many times he tried to hide it from Xia, hide the wheezing breaths as he walked up the stairs, hide the winces as she hugged his arthritic bones too tightly, Xia noticed. And wordlessly, she adapted. The hugs became gentler, the trips outside less frequent, and a good chunk of time was spent brewing and bringing him herbal tea.

Despite the setbacks, Youle insisted on his morning walks, of which Xia was not the greatest fan. She'd choose morning sleep over a morning walk any day. Initially, she did accompany him. But then it became every other day, and eventually once in a blue moon. And so it began as any other ordinary Moonday, with Xia sleeping in until noon. She awoke, and it wasn't until halfway through brewing her grandfather's tea that she noticed he wasn't yet back home.

Panic was instant. Her grandfather was not one for surprises, not one for the unordinary. He had a schedule and he stuck to it. She dashed out of the house without a second thought.

Being of the particular and the unordinary, Youle had a general route that he liked to traverse, away from the crowds and bustle of the city. Xia followed the route away from Midpoint, past a park with rusty play equipment, across a stony bridge crumbling from neglect, until she reached the resting place that Youle always traveled to. The hearth of old trees and abandoned garden had seen better days, but it was a peaceful spot that attracted an array of birds that sang a multitude of melodies and chippering chirps. The tweets grew louder as her footsteps hastily approached. Then she saw him. Her heart momentarily leaped at the sight of him, but then plummeted as she registered his huddled position beside the tree.

"Grandpa!" She shrieked as her bony legs broke into a sprint. Several birds flew away as the young teen ran to her grandfather's side, her knees falling to the dirt with a hard thud. Her hands frantically clutched his sides as she brought her ear to his chest, desperately searching for a heartbeat. Faint and slow.

His eyes gradually opened into a half-lidded gaze. A frail hand reached up to his granddaughter's face, caressing her cheek, soaking in the eyes that so strongly resembled his own son's. He gripped onto life's thin grasp for this moment, and he was so thankful he had. A smile.

The words came hoarse and slow, taking every last bit of life to utter. "Sweet Xia, continue to grow. Continue to grace this world with things that are right. Because so many things are wrong. I love you." A final smile, then he left the physical world.

Xia clung to each word, and then she clung to him, her wails piercing the still air. The birds sailed away, all except one: a lone blackbird perched directly above Youle's lifeless body.

She didn't know how long she lay there, clutching onto her grandfather as if that could bring him back. Her eyes stung from the waterfall of tears. It wasn't until an electric schism pierced the air that Xia lifted herself off of his chest.

"No, no, no, no!" She whipped her head from left to right, frantically searching for a place for cover that she could drag him to. But there were only the trees. She could maybe make it underneath the stone bridge if she ran, but not if she brought Youle. And as she looked down at his face, face so peaceful he could be sleeping, she knew she couldn't leave him. So she covered herself over him, face over his, and braced herself for the first storm she ever had to endure firsthand.

There are two types of acid rain storms. Informally, they are characterized as "drizzles" and "drops". Drizzles are a lighter form of the storm, with the acid droplets being smaller and more frequent, more akin to a typical rainfall. The drops are a different beast. While the acid droplets are less in number, they fall in fat globules that threaten to pierce through everything in its path. Today was a dropstorm. And she found that out when the first globule split into her upper back, burning through her thin gray shirt.

She winced as the burning sensation radiated through her back. And she willed herself not to scream, not to cry. More was coming. She braced herself.

By acid storm standards, it was short. Perhaps the universe had decided that was enough agony for one small adolescent to handle. But it wasn't until seven droplets cleaved her skin, five on the back and two on her hands, that the universe made this decision. She had done her best to protect her head, but at the price of mutilating her left hand.

Once she was sure the storm had stopped, she raised her head and looked down upon her grandfather, his face just as tranquil as before the storm. The pain subsided for a moment as her gaze lingered on him. It was a price worth paying.

Xia glanced down at her scarred hand, now holding the amber liquid that was left by her grandfather, one of the few things he left specifically for her after his impending death. She raised her glass to her lips, not elaborating any further.

"Xia," Mai broke the reverie. "If the world outside is inhabitable, and the air isn't toxic, what causes the acid rain?"

The question hit her like a drop of acid itself. Eyes darkening, she gazed upwards towards the plasma barrier beyond the smog. "I don't know."

21

THE SLAGS' SECRET

Based on her new revelations—with one that needed confirmation—Xia formulated a plan. A *tentative* plan, but a plan nonetheless, to escape Cyber City's walls.

She woke early the next morning to get that confirmation—earlier than usual, especially for the day following an evening of alcohol. She wanted to get a move on this quest by herself. Riding the bike around town with an extra human latched behind sucked out a lot of the joy. She imagined Mai wouldn't be up for it first thing in the morning. Her snoring figure huddled in the chair was confirmation. Xia smirked at the girl's impending pounding headache; Mai had a glass too many.

After eating some of the divine leftovers and changing into her skin-suit, Mai's deep snores rumbling in the background, she checked her cell chip for any messages from the night before. The orders for fods had slowed considerably, so much so that she hadn't had to make any the past few days. She figured that the disappearance of the Daimyo would increase the demand for the product, but it seemed to be having an inverse effect. With no new business, she gave Mai one final glance before leaving the apartment and heading to the Pagoda.

As she rode through the city, the reality of her impending encounter hit her like a block of cement. Her bike jolted as she pulled back the throttle in a physical response. *Get a grip*, she muttered. The spidery nerves jittered in her chest, dancing in a web of uncertainty. What if she was wrong? What if they were authentic FRF military? Force members that grew lazy and a little too trusting, and that was their explanation for not scanning upon entrance? But when Xia considered this possibility, it didn't sit right. Besides, there was no room for doubts now. There was no turning back.

She parked her bike in what was now her usual spot, hitched the helmet, and made her way to the Pagoda's gate, heart electric in her chest.

The two figures stood guard, one on either side, just like any other day. As Xia approached, the figure on the left gave a quick glance in her direction before returning his subhuman gaze forward. This slight out-of-place movement gave Xia a momentary ease, furthering her hypothesis that they weren't the cold and callous military men they were posing as.

Adrenaline ablaze, she started strong. "I need to speak with you both."

She imagined the pure confusion under their masks, never having been approached in such a brazen manner. Likely, they were rarely approached at all.

"What?" The robotic voice spoke. But even with their voice morpher, Xia caught a slight stammer at the beginning of their response. Confidence further replaced her anxiety.

She chose to go bolder. "Yes. I know your secret." She crossed her arms and eyed between them, letting the weight of her words do the job for her. Oh, how she wished she could see their faces behind the visors. Their helmets bobbed between boring into Xia and boring into each other, wordlessly trying to communicate. She bathed in the uneasiness. FRF military wouldn't stand for such brazenness, such disregard for their authority.

"What do you want?" The glancer blurted, the voice morpher unable to hide the urgency in their voice.

"Like I said. I need to speak with both of you."

The non-glancer gave a nod before opening the gate and entering.

Xia knew they'd be unwanted inside the pagoda, but this was not a conversation she'd risk having outside. Still, she didn't expect the fit that would ensue as soon as the Force members stepped inside the walls, just a few yards from the gate's entrance.

Buko emerged from the Pagoda, sprinting down the stone steps, unsheathing his sword. "How *DARE* you bring these foul figures inside our sacred space!"

"Silence, Buko!" A voice called from behind. Kibou. As soon as his soft voice hit the air, the devout samurai froze. Then he sheathed his sword and retreated back inside the Pagoda, throwing murderous glares behind him. Xia was thankful for Kibou's credence. She turned toward the alleged Force members as the gate shut closed.

"Scan me," she said.

The two glanced at each other once more. It was almost comical; such figures had done nothing but instill fear and loathing at their mere presence, and yet here they were, thrown off by Xia's few commands.

She traced the outline of the Enforcer in her pocket, waiting. She heard the small electrical whirring that comes with a deep-scan, and then her heart jolted as she noticed the blinking red light on the visor of the slag to her right.

"You have scan blockers," glancer replied. The figure with the blinking red light whipped their head toward them, as if glaring.

"Any FRF Force member can get past V4 Scan Blockers." Xia said tentatively, looking between them with utter confusion. "Follow me."

They didn't require further stringing, they obeyed. Xia ignored the outbursts from samurai and monks alike when they stepped inside, and Kibou quickly hushed them.

"Is there a space where we can meet privately?" Xia asked.

"Fourth floor," Kibou responded. A few more outbursts, a few more hushes, and Xia and the two supposed slags ascended to the fourth floor.

"How long have you known?" The non-glancer was the first to speak.

Xia wasn't sure what she knew. The glancer was definitely not a slag. But she'd been thrown off by non-glancer's blinking light. Were they a former slag? Better copycat uniform? "Turn off your voice morpher. Feels like I'm talking to a robot."

Surprisingly, they obeyed. They had not put up much of a fight.

"So, like I said, how long have you known?" The one on the right spoke, a deep and feminine voice coming from behind the helmet.

Xia danced around the subject. "Not long. Why don't you tell me exactly how this all came to be? Otherwise, you know what I could do with your little secret."

"Fuck," glancer muttered, his voice deep and husky with a hint of gravel. Not quite Dames' level of concrete. "I knew you were trouble. As soon as I saw you walk through those doors those weeks ago, I knew. I knew, didn't I, Fay?"

Fay, the non-glancer, crossed her arms and popped out her hip. All military motions evaporated. "More like trouble for your dick. We all know why you kept blabbering about her."

Glancer coughed. Xia ignored it. "Who is we all?"

"There's five of us. Well, four doing the rotation. And no, we are not FRF Force members." Her tone hushed at the last part, hesitant to say such incriminating words aloud. Xia relaxed, her initial hypothesis standing tall in its accuracy. "We're freelancers, like yourself. Until we got this gig, that is."

"How long have you been doing this?"

"Gosh, must be what, twelve years now? It was Leonardo who found out about the gig. That the Virgins were wanting some type of protection for their Pagoda, and were willing to pay weekly. It's basically like a tax. They all pay into it. Even those who don't go to the Pagoda. Weird things they'll do for their beliefs."

Glancer ripped his helmet off, exposing his pained dark-skinned face, his small squinted eyes in denial that Fay was revealing their well-kept secret.

"Oh settle down, Grimer." Glancer to Grimer. "This is your fault anyways. Couldn't have made it any more obvious when confronted."

"I got nervous, okay? I forgot what we practiced," his brutish face turned dopey as he shuffled his large feet back and forth in embarrassment.

Fay groaned and removed her own helmet. Her thick cobalt hair was pulled back into a messy ponytail, accentuating the fullness of her features. Sharp yet full navy eyes, strong defined nose, shapely lips covering straight white teeth. Fine lines of age scattered her attractive face. It was a shame a helmet covered it half the day.

"So anyways, the people here were looking to hire straight from the source. Get some slags stationed outside. They're a headstrong bunch, but damn are they naive. You know how much it would cost to get some actual slags out there? But luckily for us, Burgs—that's our boss, so to speak— had a connection. He was former military. Or, about-to-but-dropped-out military? But he still had his old uniform. And he was able to make identicals. Identical in every aspect. Well, except for one piece."

"The scanner."

"Yes, that technology he was unable to copy. He *did* copy the blinking light, but since it didn't actually do anything, we haven't made the habit of using it. So when you told us to scan you, I remembered, but this idiot here—"

Grimer looked as if he was about to cry. "He's going to *kill* me!"

"Yes, he'll probably kill both of us. And it's your damn fault." Fay's ocean eyes pierced through him like a tsunami. It was a pitiful sight.

"Does anyone here know that you two aren't real slags?"

Fay's eyes returned to Xia, softening. She liked the silver girl. Fay knew this shtick couldn't last forever, and she didn't want it to. She was waiting for the day the hourglass ran low. This clever and independent silver gal seemed fitting for the role. "Not anymore. The only one who did know was the Daimyo."

"The Daimyo?" Xia's mouth hung open in surprise.

Fay nodded, cobalt pony bouncing. "He knew it was naive to want real slags out there, and he'd never approve it. This was the perfect compromise. And we still got a beautiful paycheck."

"Well you can kiss those beautiful paychecks goodbye now," Grimer moaned.

"I'm not going to tell anyone," Xia stated. "Unless you don't help me, that is."

"And what exactly is it that we're signing up for?"

Xia's eyes shifted around the room as she took a quick scan, ensuring no ears were listening. Then her gaze returned to the imitation slags, bracing herself for Grimer's whines. "You're going to help me get outside the city walls."

Grimer did whine. And voiced many complaints, as if Xia had never considered them. Like how the task in and of itself was impossible, and how even if it were possible, the endeavor would take you to a barren wasteland. And how if this "Burgs" didn't kill them, the task surely would.

Xia tuned out most of it, and told them she would answer anything and everything *after* they took her to see this Burgs character. She didn't want to explain everything twice.

"He might not go as hard on you if the girl comes with," Fay mused. Grimer reluctantly agreed, and so the duo planned with Xia to meet up at their 'headquarters' after their guard shift. Her cell chip continuously buzzed against her wrist during the interaction, and a quick glimpse confirmed that Mai was the source of the incessant calling.

Running off the high of yet another hunch confirmed correct, and not wanting to face the yippy sprite just yet, Xia took her dear sweet time getting home. A tea from Calypso's, some egg rolls from a street vendor, and a roam through the city streets. These small things would have brought her nuggets of irreplaceable joy a month ago. But as she gazed upward towards the invisible barrier that trapped them all inside, she couldn't help but feel like a fish in a tank. She watched the minnows of cyborgs and modded souls around her, unknowing of the ocean around them, content with their scraps of bait. For so long, she had been one of t hem.

Calypso's tea had lost its sweetness.

"What the hell is that?"

Mai arose from the plush pink cushion, a coy smile lighting her face. "Well, *somebody* decided to leave me alone all day— without any word, mind you— so I had to entertain myself. And I was getting quite sick of sleeping curled up in that little chair. I'm only 22. I shouldn't be having back problems already!"

Xia realized she never knew how old Mai was. She figured the girl was young, but not that young.

"Took forever for the delivery drone to get here. Something tells me they don't prioritize deliveries to the Fourth Ward."

"I'm not paying for that."

Mai rolled her eyes. "Don't worry. I wasn't expecting you to. But look!" She gestured towards the new rosy sofa couch that sat facing the window. "Now you can enjoy that beautiful view while kickin' your feet up. Doesn't that sound nice?"

It did sound nice. Xia shrugged.

"Now come on. Dinner's almost ready, and you're going to tell me where the hell you were today."

So they ate, and she did. A piece of rice spat out of Mai's mouth when she learned her father knew of the imitation slags' secret. By the end of the retelling, and the end of the meal, Mai insisted she was coming along to meet these characters. Xia couldn't quite tell what her sentiments were. Intrigue? Betrayal? There was a twinkle in her eye of *something*. Xia didn't use her facial expression scanner. She'd let the mystery unfold itself.

22

The Synthetic Slag Ops

At midnight, Xia followed the coordinates given to her by Fay, with Mai pressed against her back. Slowly but surely, she was getting used to the added weight on her slim cycle. Xia expected the dwelling place for these rogues to be hidden, perhaps sitting on the outskirts of the city. Instead the coordinates took her to the heart of the Third Ward. A sleek skyscraper offering high-end, luxury housing towered above them, standing tall between a posh bar and a cluster of entertainment hubs hosting VR experiences and mod displays. Most people with extra money to spare came to the likes of these places. Xia found it to be a waste. VR games would only further the stark reality of their trapped bubble here. And why spend your zeCoin on a drink here when you can get ten for the same cost at Mickey's?

She stared at the advertisements for the latest V4 mods and tech: a taste enhancer that promised to make the most unpalatable of gruel taste delicious, a robotic arm that could lift up to 8x a person's weight (and looked identical to the prosthetic worn by the man hitting on Mai at Mickey's), a hoverboard with anti-theft mechanisms *promising* that people wouldn't be able to simply push you over and swipe your board. (That was the largest problem with hoverboards and why they were not a main source of transportation. Incredibly easy to steal.)

"Silver girl," a voice called from behind. Xia turned around from the vivid display to face an amused Fay and nervous-looking Grimer.

"Call me Xia," she answered, growing increasingly sick of all the 'silver' alliterations. "And you know Mai, the Daimyo's daughter."

"Yes, hi. Can't say it's good to be speaking with you without the mask, but here we are. Fay. Grimer."

Mai's eyes bored into Fay, taking in every detail. Eventually, she unpeeled her eyes and turned towards Grimer, who alternated between fidgeting with his thick dark hands and running them through his buzzed hair.

"Shall we?" Fay broke the silence. Xia mused the nonchalance with which Fay had been handling this entire situation. 14 years was a long time to be running such a ruse. And it was more than just a ruse. If the FRF found out, they'd face the most extreme of consequences. A sure ticket to the Void.

The four entered the swanky establishment. Tech littered the walls, from advertisements to colorful displays to help-desk monitors asking if you'd like an espresso, with a machine built into the wall making that wish an instant reality. Xia had never set foot in such a place. Her freelancing work didn't reach this type of clientele.

Xia's apartment elevator took a solid minute to carry her up to the 25th floor. But here they reached the 40th in a spiffy seven seconds. She expected a hallway when the doors opened, but instead it opened right into a large living room, everything ivory and pristine, with a massive window of a wall similar to Xia's facing the city skyline.

"Take a seat. I'll grab the others." Fay left the living room and went down a hallway, but Grimer stayed behind, holding on to every last second he had before having to face Burgs. Mai took a seat on the massive white couch, not a speck or stain in sight, but Xia remained standing, casting the occasional pitiful glance towards Grimer. He could not stop fidgeting.

After a few silent moments, two more men entered the room. One was undeniably handsome, and not in a synthetic mod or plastic surgery kind of way. Just pure genetics blessing him with warm, yet striking hazel eyes and a jawline that could cut a shot glass. Hair too dark to be blonde but too light to be brunet. Lips just plump enough without leaning feminine. And a jagged scar snaking down his left cheek, down the neck, and ending somewhere under his tight white tank. Xia liked scars. Just not her own.

"So, the gig is up, I hear?" The handsome one said with a bittersweet smile. Nothing to smile about, but he seemed to want any excuse to show off his dazzling white teeth. "I'm Leonardo," he said as he approached Xia, offering up a hand. "But I know who you are." He smirked at Grimer. More fidgeting. Then he turned towards the man at his side. "This here's Renjiro. Call him Ren."

Xia couldn't get a good look at Ren because he kept rubbing his eyes, and when he wasn't rubbing his eyes, he was yawning. She gave them each a small nod, while Leonardo's gaze flitted towards Mai.

"I thought I felt some eyes burning into me. You're the Daimyo's daughter."

Mai continued to glare.

"You two aren't the most talkative, I see."

That's not usually the case, Xia thought as she looked towards the glowering Mai. Then Grimer's breath made an audible hitch, signaling the approach of their leader, Burgs.

Burgs was gruff. Every single thing about him, every minute detail, was gruff. Scruffy, unkempt hair, black and gray speckled stubble, burly arms and even burlier legs. His naturally dark-skinned face rested in a scowl, and Xia wasn't sure if that was due to the situation at hand or if that's simply how his face liked to be. He seemed quite comfortable with it.

"So you're Xia," he said, voice just as gruff as his exterior. Their eyes met, heights matching perfectly.

"Yes," Xia bowed slightly. "And you're the head of this...operation?"

"If you can call it that," he said. He shifted his gaze towards Mai. "You the Daimyo's kid?"

The glower Mai had been harboring seethed further as she rose from the couch and marched over. There was a loud *SMACK* as her petite hand flew across the air and slapped him. Grimer gasped, the poor man on the verge of fainting. It was a solid smack, but Burgs didn't flinch. Instead, he narrowed his eyes and smirked, impressed at the girl's gall.

"How dare you. How dare you all! To be masquerading as militant protectors of our Pagoda, taking our people's money all for a charade!"

He crossed his burly arms across his big chest. "Your father was the one who allowed for this charade, honey."

"And if he were here, I'd slap him too!"

Silence hung in the air before the eruption of a howl broke it as Burgs' grin burst into a laugh. "Looks like we got two spicy little ladies here! You'll give Fay a run for her money."

Little lady. She allowed it coming from Dames, but hearing it from Burgs made her want to give him a slap as well.

"Don't call us that. And don't call me Honey!" Mai blurted. Xia cringed.

"Burgs," Xia said, cutting through the layer of banter. "I'm here because I have a task I need to do, and I think you can help me. And I think you're in a position to help me considering I know about your charade."

"Mm-hm," he grunted, nodding his head. "But what if we eliminated that leverage right here and now?"

It happened in a second, but Xia was prepared for it. Burgs lunged forward, his movements swift for such a stocky frame. But Xia was quicker. A quick kick to his gut held him at bay while she pulled out her Enforcer and pointed it directly at him, taking several steps back to give her distance. The smirk returned to Burgs' scruffy mouth.

Her eyes glanced around the room, meeting each one of Burgs' posse. Leonardo held Mai in a standing headlock, his other arm skillfully restraining Mai's own arms, rendering her unable to move. Mai seethed, but Leonardo seemed to be enjoying holding the girl so close to himself. Ren finally quit yawning and Xia was able to see his electric green eyes. Fay looked disappointed— not with Xia, but with the unprovoked attack. Grimer was a few seconds away from a full-blown panic attack. Her mind flashed back to this exact scenario from a week earlier, with Mai in a choke hold while Xia held assailants at bay with her Enforcer. Then she remembered Mai's lifeless stare as she contemplated the dead body. Xia was determined not to recreate that aspect.

"I've already told multiple people where I am. If I don't come back, they'll come here. You don't want that."

"She's bluffing," Renjiro finally spoke. His electric eyes seemed to sizzle as they bore into Xia.

Burgs wasn't looking at Xia. He was looking at the smooth black weapon in her hands. "Is that an Enforcer?"

Xia nodded. "One shot of this and you can kiss your flesh goodbye. Now let her go before she faints." Mai's face paled blue.

Burgs' eyes grew with insatiability as he lifted a hand and motioned Leonardo to drop her. The handsome boy obeyed and gingerly let go of Mai, who fell to her knees in a thunderous *thump* uncharacteristic of her delicate frame, massaging her neck as she coughed.

"What...the hell..." she sputtered, rage building.

"Gimme that gun," Burgs commanded.

Xia lifted the gun towards her shoulder defensively. "Excuse me?"

"You give me that gun and we'll help you. You'll get it back, don't worry."

"You just attacked me. Why the hell would I give you my gun?" She stared at him incredulously. He smirked.

Fay made eye contact with Xia. "Give us a moment," she said as she gave Burgs a tug and pulled him down the hallway.

Xia slowly brought the gun back to a defensive stance and stood, unmoving, as she studied the faces of the men before her. Grimer seemed to be calming down, but only slightly. No matter how many times Leonardo unpeeled his eyes from Mai, who now stood staunchly beside Xia, they wandered back a moment later. But she was most intrigued by Ren. She scanned them all, and while they all had scan blockers, Ren's was the most effective as she couldn't even register him as a life form. How many mods were injected into those glowing eyes? Their fluorescence rivaled the city's own neon.

She had no idea what was said in the other room, or what kind of hold the blue-haired woman had over the gruff leader, but a short minute later Fay and Burgs returned before them.

"Alright. Tell us what you want, Xia."

***

Xia stood before them as Burgs lounged in a thick armchair and the rest sat on the milky couch. While initially there was a comfortable distance between Leonardo and Mai, the stretch between them grew thinner and thinner until Mai was clutching to the end of the couch, Leonardo now only a few inches away.

"And this *Opell Doksen*, you believe the images you saw were true? Isn't it possible he conjured these images himself? I mean, from your description, he sounds like quite the *colorful* character," Leonardo said, stretching his arm out behind Mai. Mai slapped him. Leonardo chuckled.

Xia nodded. "Scanners showed no sign of ill intent or deceit. And the tech that I recognized was authentic." She thought of his late-night broadcasts as The Nightcrawler. "He's credible."

"So you're wondering where we got these fancy suits, then?"

"Precisely."

"But how are the suits enough?" Fay asked. "So you get to the gate disguised. How will you know where to go? The protocol?"

Xia straightened. "A scouting mission. I'll map out their layout and see how they get through their gates. Which will be a lot easier with one of your 'fancy suits'."

Fay nodded, her brow furrowed. "And say you figure out how to get outside. Say you really do complete this mission and get out into the free world. What's the plan then?"

"I'll find the Lost Samurai."

Leonardo clicked his tongue. "Sounds awful risky."

"Of course it's risky. Risks are necessary."

"Why even bother?" Leonardo yawned. "This seems like a whole lot of work for someone who's not the one wanting to escape. Why are you even helping them?"

Xia thought of Lutno, of Leikko, of the Daimyo. But above all, she thought of her grandfather. Throughout her freelancing, there was a constant tickle in the back of her mind. *Would Youle approve?* His final dying wish forever lingered: '*Grace this world with things that are right. Because there are so many things that are wrong.*' With every seemingly righteous theft, every mercy killing, she wondered, would her grandfather be proud of the woman she had become? Proud like the day she brought home that steak? Or was she bringing more wrong into the world? It was a perpetual unanswered question, until now. She knew Youle would swell with pride, and she could see that smile more clearly than she could see the group sitting before her.

"Why wouldn't I?"

Leonardo huffed. "I can think of a thousand reasons."

Mai's eyes burned.

"Your plan is full of holes," Ren spoke, his voice quiet.

"It's nothing but holes," Xia jabbed. "I've—"

Leonardo burst out laughing. "Buttholes!"

Xia rubbed her face with her hands in exasperation. "My point is, I don't have a great plan. Much of a plan at all, really. I've been given this task that's near impossible. But it's necessary. So I'm just figuring it out along the way. Like I always do."

What else could she say? She was aware of the mountain of issues. All she could do was tackle them one at a time. Right now, it was this one.

"So this scouting mission. Which one of us do you want with ya? You can only pick two. The other two'll be at the Pagoda," Burgs said, breaking the silence.

"You're not going back there!" Mai exclaimed.

Burgs snapped back. "Of course we are. With all that's been happening to your folk lately, how do you think they'd feel without us? You might not like us, but the truth of the matter is, we *do* provide protection. We had you all fooled. And that money pays for this place." He gestured towards the lofty place around him. "Now quit that scowling. Not a good look for you. Give you wrinkles. What are you, 21? Do you want wrinkles at 21?"

Her scowl deepened.

Xia barely paid attention to the exchange. Surprise had overcome her. Why did Burgs want to help? A moment ago he was willing to kill her. Now he wanted to help. Either Fay was just that persuasive, or he was hiding something. She chose not to question it for now. Her eyes traveled from one person to the next. The anxious Grimer, who apparently had the hots for her, the laid-back Leonardo who clearly had the hots for Mai. She settled on the mysterious Ren and competent Fay.

"Renjiro and Fay."

Fay nodded. Ren yawned.

"How long until you can get me a suit?"

"Couple days. First I'll need to have you fitted—"

"And for me too," Mai cut in.

Xia rolled her eyes. "You're not goi—"

"We either fight here now, or fight about it later, but either way, I'm not sitting behind."

Xia groaned, envisioning Mai's impending whine fest. "Fine." She turned towards Burgs. "Two suits."

"I can help Mai get fitted," Leonardo smiled with a flutter of his long eyelashes.

"Cut that shit out, Leo," Burgs barked. "Actin' like a creep."

Leonardo sunk into the couch in embarrassment. "Sorry, sir."

"You two. Follow me."

Mai stood, relieved to be away from Leonardo, and followed behind Burgs with Xia down the hall and into a spare room. Now *this* was a tech room that Xia understood.

Burgs took a seat behind a computer with several curved monitors, an advanced holographic display in the middle. "I'll need to scan you both for fits. Xia, you're fine to step right in with that suit you've got. It's tight enough. Mai, your clothes are too baggy so you'll have to strip down."

He said it so matter of factly, and Mai complied so matter of factly, removing the sweatshirt and pants as if she was simply taking off a pair of shoes. Xia averted her eyes.

A large tube stood in the corner. "I guess Mai's first. Take a step in the body scanner."

"That's not really some death tube that'll gas us as soon as we step inside?" Xia asked, eyes lingering on the large cylinder.

Burgs chuckled. "If I wanted to get rid of you two, I already would have. Besides, Fay'd kill me."

Xia wondered the extent of their relationship. It seemed Fay had quite a hold on Burgs. He may be running this op, but Fay was certainly pulling some strings.

Mai opened the curved door into the tall cylinder. Her skin took on a greenish hue, and her white underwear emitted an evanescent glow. Xia shifted her gaze to Burgs' monitors.

"Alright, arms out at a 45-degree angle. This'll take a few seconds." He input a few keys and a moment later a little holograph of Mai hovered in the display before them. "Houston, we may have a problem."

"Houston?" Xia's eyes furrowed.

"Old saying. Point is, FRF military must be a minimum of 5'3. She's only 5'1."

"Does it really matter?" Mai voiced from the tube.

"Yes," Xia and Burgs responded simultaneously.

"If it were an inch or less, I may be able to add it to the footwear. But at two inches, that's cutting it." He looked up from the display towards Mai. "Sorry girl, you're too short to get on this ride."

"No way! There's gotta be some way to make me taller."

Burgs shook his head. "Getting on your tip toes won't be enough. Unless you're willing to kiss your Virginity goodbye and use some good ole' mods, you're stuck at 5'1."

There was a pause as her dismayed face turned into resolve. "What kind of mods are we talking?"

23

GROWING PAINS

"You're not serious," Xia said, finally looking at Mai.

"Like hell I am. I'm in this for the long haul. So, like I said, what kind of mods are we talking?"

Xia grimaced and turned towards Burgs. "I guess the easiest would be, what? Nanobots?"

Burgs nodded. "Surgical implants would be pretty invasive for a measly two inches. Got more risks involved too. Nanobots could get it done. Not sure how fast exactly."

"What are nanobots?"

Burgs motioned Mai to come out. "Get dressed. The scan is done and I don't want to be talkin' to a half-naked girl."

Mai's lip curled as she exited the scanner and threw her clothes back on.

"Nanobots are tiny little robotic devices that operate on the cellular level. They can be injected into your joints, signaling the bones to grow."

Mai gulped. "How long would it take?"

"Can't say. You'll have to check out a Height Tech Specialist. Don't go to any cosmetic mod place, go to one that specializes specifically in height enhancement. You'd likely need to get a meaty injection to grow two entire inches in a short amount of time, though. Now get on in there, Xia."

Xia stepped into the scanner. Just like how Mai appeared green inside, the room outside appeared green as well.

"Oh cool," Mai muttered, staring at the little holograph of Xia. She waved her hand through it, momentarily cutting Xia's figure in half.

"Cut that out," Burgs snapped. "Are you forgetting Leo had you in a chokehold just twenty minutes ago?"

"Oh, I remember. I'll do as I please."

Burgs grabbed her wrist and glared at her, his resting scowl replaced with pure menace. "*No*, you won't. You two are damn lucky I'm helping you out. You're under *my* roof. Your father hired me. You got some mixed feelings about it all, and you'll sort them out yourself. You disrespect me, I'll do a lot worse." He spat on her shoe and released her wrist, a mark already forming.

Mai's consistently carefree demeanor finally shook, and she rubbed her wrist looking like a scolded puppy. Part of Xia was happy to see Mai finally put in her place, but the other part of her felt oddly protective. That was *her* puppy to train, not Burgs.

"Alright, scan's done. You can get on out."

Xia stepped out of the tube and into the tension. "We appreciate what you're doing. It's a lot, I know. I don't like working with others, especially her, so this is an adjustment for me."

"Just remember your place, and remember who's helping who. I'll work on yours first," he glanced towards Xia. "And you two let me know what I should do about the short one's suit. Once it's ready, I'll trade you for that." He motioned towards the Enforcer in her side pocket.

She never got the chance to properly use it, yet the prospect of it leaving her side felt like losing a limb. Still, the suit was needed, and he was proving himself trustworthy. "Will do. Let's go," Xia motioned. Mai gave a curt nod and followed Xia out of the room. Leonardo met them in the hallway.

"So, not picking me for the mission?" He asked with a faux pout, his lip jutting out in a way that some might consider attractive.

"Get serious and next time I'll consider it," Xia said as she brushed past him, not paying him another glance. Mai did, and Leonardo winked back.

Mai lay face down on the operating table, the harsh white lighting casting a sickly glow on her pale back. A thin white sheet covered her from the waist down. It did nothing to help the goosebumps that speckled her skin.

"Cold?" Xia asked from her side.

"Y-yeah," Mai said.

A lie. She was terrified. Xia could tell. She racked her brain for words of comfort. "Don't worry. They do this stuff all the time." Although, she couldn't help but think that if she were the one getting this procedure, she wouldn't have picked this place. But when finding a height prosthetic specialist, they couldn't go just anywhere. It would be easy enough to find a decent place to get the job done. But the job itself raised some red flags. Why would someone want to grow only two inches in such a short amount of time? Pair the question of *why* with the desired height being the minimum height required for a Military Force member and, well, it raised questions. And Xia didn't want any questions raised.

"We'll start with the numbing injection," Tezza, the lead technician said. Not once did she make eye contact. From the screening forms Mai filled out, to the monitors displaying the intricate data for the procedure, to the various equipment, the tech's eyes stayed glued to the task at hand. Even commands to her assistant were made with the quickest nod in his general direction, never meeting the young man's dull eyes. Maybe it was better that way.

Her gloved, spider-like fingers skillfully inserted the injection into the small of Mai's back. Mai tensed, but remained silent.

Tezza pricked various spots on her back. "Feel that?"

"No," Mai muttered.

"Alright then. Jole, position the fluoroscope." The young man obeyed, placing glasses over his wide eyes and positioning the robotic arm over the lumbar section of Mai's back, setting the fluoroscope device atop. As he prepared the machine, Xia saw a grayscale image of close-up vertebrae on the monitors beside Tezza.

Tezza monitored the screen. "Targeting growth-plate region 334. Currently at 332." Jole barely touched the robotic arm with his nimble fingers before Tezza stopped him. "Good. Lock it." She swiveled around to face Mai again and put on some glasses. Then she motioned towards Xia.

"Either stand back there or put on glasses."

"Don't go," Mai muttered through the hole in the face rest. Xia held out her hand and Jole placed a pair of protective glasses in them.

"Alright," Tezza said as she grabbed a long needle from the surgical tray. Xia'd never seen such an odd-looking needle, and that was because it contained the nanobot receptors. Tiny receptors invisible to the naked eye, yet powerful enough to alter the human body.

With meticulous and steady care that came from conducting such a procedure a thousand times, Tezza inserted the nano-needle into the small of Mai's back. "Jole," she commanded. The assistant took over and Tezza swiveled back around to the monitors, observing the placement in the spine.

"Two increments right. One increment right. One increment north. Hold. Hold. Okay, release."

Xia watched on the screen as tiny specks released from the needle tip, then disappeared once more as they latched onto Mai's growth plate.

"Retract," Tezza commanded, and Jole withdrew the nano-needle. "How are you feeling? Still okay to start on the knees?"

Mai's voice wavered. "Yeah, let's do it."

Normally, one would opt for the spine *or* the legs when optimizing their height. Or would opt to have the surgeries on different days, giving the person a chance to recover. But for an entire two inches in one week, this was the quickest way to do it, and Mai wanted to go all in.

They flipped Mai over and repeated the process on her legs, and this time Xia caught the wince as the nano-receptors anchored into her bones. Once the procedure was over, Jole helped to adjust and dress Mai, as her legs were two numb blocks.

"I can send recovery instructions electronically to—"

"Can you give a physical copy? She doesn't have holotech."

For the first time, Tezza stared directly at Xia. "Right, sure."

A moment later, Tezza handed Mai several pages of instructions and signs to watch out for, of which she did not review with the duo. Tezza had one job and one job only: to complete the procedure at hand. There was no small talk, no reviewing of concerns. The procedure was done, so she was ready for the two to leave.

"You have arrangements to take her home?"

"Yes," Xia replied.

"Pay out front." And with that, Tezza motioned for the two to leave.

Xia glanced towards Mai. "Got a wheelchair?"

"You said you have arrangements," Tezza responded coldly.

"Yeah, to get her home. Not out of the room." Xia stared in annoyed disbelief. This place specialized in height enhancements. None of the clients would be able to walk afterwards. Yet the question itself seemed to burden the tech.

Tezza waved her hand dismissively. "Jole," she motioned at her assistant. He nodded and stood, presumably to grab Mai some mode of transportation, but instead walked over to Mai and bent over.

"Excuse me?" Mai exclaimed, just as his hands scooped under her legs.

"Last patient stole our wheelchair. Hefty dude with an even heftier friend," Jole spoke for the first time. His drawl matched his sunken eyes.

"You only have the one?" Xia asked incredulously.

Tezza cocked her head. "Care for our assistance or not?"

Mai glanced between Jole and Xia, his hands hovering, waiting for his next command.

"Xia will carry me. Come on," Mai muttered.

Arguing was fruitless, so Xia wordlessly hoisted the girl up and headed out of the room.

"Payment's at the desk out front," Tezza called out just as they left.

After paying the 2,000 zeCoin to the receptionist, and several complaints about her positioning in Xia's arms, the two stood at the corner of Onaku and 7th, waiting for the med transportation pod.

"You ever used one before?" Mai asked, her first statement since they left that wasn't a complaint.

"No."

Mai hummed. "Me neither. Not that I remember. Hope it gets here soon. I think the anesthesia is wearing off."

"Does that mean I can set you down?" Xia groaned. Mai wasn't heavy, but she wasn't exactly a feather, either.

"No."

Xia huffed as her eyes drifted across the skyline. Orange today. She liked the orange. Mellow, warm, yet there was something otherworldly about it. Daunting.

"Damn it," Mai groaned. The anesthetic was fading fast.

"Don't worry, here it comes." She could just make out the notable electric whirring sound over the multi-layered backdrop of noise that came with every part of the city. The small white pod came floating down the street. Unlike hoverboards, which were a constant source for thievery, hoverpods were a pretty trusted form of transportation, and a necessity for the disabled, which Mai currently was.

Xia scanned her cellchip and input the access code, allowing the top half of the pod to open like a perfectly cracked egg. She laid Mai down in the plush seat.

"Good to go?"

"Yeah," Mai said, her pained expression growing as the anesthetic further faded from her joints.

Xia gave a two-fingered wave as the pod shut closed and hovered the crippled Mai back to the apartment.

Xia had to admire the girl's dedication. She was an interesting character, that was for sure. Initially, the girl was synonymous with annoyance, but the more Xia was forced to endure her presence and learn more about her, the annoyance was slowly replaced with curiosity. And a touch of endearment. And with this latest stunt, there was even some respect.

For Xia, mods were the norm, and procedures and enhancements like this one were a right of passage. Injections were as routine as brushing your teeth, and an operation to change a core part of your being was nothing more than an average Moonday. But not for the Virgins. Their rejection of this world was staunch. Much more than a simple callous rejection, like Xia had always thought. Like the rest of the city thought. Their beliefs ran deep, connecting them with cultures of past, and bearing them fruits that the rest of the city couldn't yield. Like those damn berries.

Mai tried to keep it cool. She truly did. The girl had felt pain before. With her father as Daimyo, she had sparred and learned to take a hit. Pain also came with her line of work. She'd been beaten, she'd been bitten, she'd been fucked so raw she was unable to sit for days. Yet nothing could have prepared her for the agony that the nanobots inflicted inside her bones.

The procedure was a painful one in and of itself. But most people weren't trying to grow two inches in a week. The nanoreceptors usually had much more time to do their job, and the body was able to work symbiotically with the little bots. But for Mai, the bots screamed at the bones to grow faster, faster, and they were screaming at her legs and her spine.

Mai screamed back.

24

The Suit

"Xia, when does the pain stop?"

Mai's voice came out hoarse, croaked. It was the first time she had spoken real words in hours. Nothing but moans and groans and the occasional scream as the nanobots ordered her limbs to stretch. Xia hadn't slept a wink. The ex-Virgin's cries had begun to subside as the hefty amount of painkillers finally gave her some reprieve.

"I wouldn't know. Never had any type of nanotech."

"Not that. From losing someone." Her voice drifted like a lone dandelion carried off in the wind. The drugs seemed to be making her sentimental. Or perhaps they were simply opening the gates, allowing for the locked-up thoughts to come tumbling through.

Xia swirled the amber liquor in her glass, eyeing its clarity. Most spirits, even the best ones from Dames, housed specks of imperfections. Dirt, dust, bits of who-knows-what. But this was nothing but pure, smooth liquor. She took a sip of her third glass of the night. Couldn't sleep, so she drank.

"It never really stops. But it changes. It's the worst now. But it'll fade. Then morph. Then one day, it'll almost be a comfort. A reminder of something *powerful*. Of something worthwhile when nothing else seems to be worth anything at all."

Mai let out a pathetic whimper. "What would he think of me now..."

The perpetual question that rotted in Xia's own head. "He wouldn't like what you are doing. But he'd admire how you're handling it." She didn't know the Daimyo all that long, but she truly believed that the warrior would appreciate Mai's gall and willingness to endure such pain.

"I hope you're right..." Then she was back to groaning before finally succumbing to sleep.

Xia felt for Mai. She did. But at the same time, Xia appreciated the fact that Mai was bedridden, so she could get a move on some things solo. Mai hadn't been hindering her, but she couldn't help but feel physically lighter without the girl's constant presence. No never-ending questions, no eyes burrowing into the side of her skull. She took a deep breath and embraced the thick air, the smog unusually peppery on her tongue today, then swung her long leg over the side of her bike and took off. She had an agenda for the day.

First, to Burgs. Her suit was ready. She was looking forward to meeting him without Mai, especially after the discourse between them two days prior. Trust was everything in a working relationship like this. She needed to build some rapport with the gruff guy. Mai was a hindrance there.

The building looked different in the light of day. Less daunting, more shiny. A silver monolith just begging to sparkle if it were blessed with some of the sun's priceless rays. No sparkles in the burnt orange smog. She messaged Fay and waited in the lobby.

"Where's the Daimyo's girl?" Fay asked as she exited the high-speed elevator. Her hair hung in loose blue waves like the sea itself.

"Writhing on a couch."

Fay raised a brow.

"Nanobot height enhancement."

Fay pursed her lips and nodded, impressed. "You want an espresso?" She gestured towards the flashing machine on the wall.

Xia was about to object, as she always did with offers of crumb bars or vita-juices. But this stuff probably had some actual quality to it. "Sure." She watched as Fay scanned her cell chip to the small display and tapped on the screen, asking for two espressos. A small tray popped out with two small cups, and a second later, the machine filled them with the hot liquid. The entire interaction took no more than ten seconds.

"Careful, it's very hot," Fay warned as she handed the small cup to Xia. She wouldn't have been able to take this on the elevator at her home's apartment. It'd spill by the fourth floor with how rickety it was. But this elevator shot them up more smoothly than the espresso itself.

"Leonardo here?" Xia asked as they entered the apartment. The question answered itself as his dark golden head popped up from behind the couch.

"Hoping I was at the Pagoda, were you? No, it's Grimer and Ren's turn today. You're stuck with me, I'm afraid." He grinned. Was it confidence? Cockiness? Or did he just think he was funny? Maybe he was just overcompensating. Anyway you had it, Xia found it obnoxious. Shame that scar didn't ground him a bit.

"Burgs got your suit in the back," Fay motioned. Xia followed her, leaving Leonardo behind, and entered the same tech-filled room with Burgs sitting behind the same curved monitors.

"You're late," he muttered. He had never given her a time, but Xia simply nodded. "Suit and boots are in the scanner. See 'em in there? They're yours once you complete your part of the trade." He stuck his hand out, motioning for the Enforcer.

"Suit first."

He eyed her, up and down, eye to eye, no scanning involved. Only the mind's gears at play. Then he turned back to the monitors and began typing.

A silence hung and for a moment Xia thought he may have changed his mind about the whole thing. But then he spoke.

"Step on in and try 'em on and I'll scan you once more. Fit needs to be precise."

Xia's eyes darted between the scanner pod and Burgs. His eyes seemed glued to the monitor, but a quick glance up and he'd see Xia completely exposed. Her cheeks reddened. "You want me to change in there?"

His eyes furrowed. "I don't have all day. Get on in there."

"That's a lie. You do have all day," Fay said from behind Xia. Xia glanced back towards her. Did she have to be in the room too? Xia tried to take a step towards the scanner, but her feet were now weighted to the floor.

"There some problem?" Burgs asked.

"N-no." She pulled her feet with everything she had, steps clunky and hesitant as she entered the pod. Her shaky hands picked up the black fabric. If her mind wasn't preoccupied with pure anxiety, she'd have appreciated the simultaneous strength and silkiness of the material, the durability of the armor plates. She'd inspect the glowing tech that illuminated the arms and legs. Instead, she stood there frozen.

"What's wrong with it? What am I even asking, it's perfect. Put it on."

Fay's mouth opened and closed in a sudden realization. Without a word, she stepped in front of Burgs and faced him, disrupting the line of view.

Thank you, Xia could have cried. Her hands continued to tremble as she hastily unzipped the skinsuit from her toned frame and stepped into the military suit. She thought her skinsuit fit well, but it fit like an itchy sack in comparison to the suit that Burgs had crafted. Despite its thickness and durability, it melted over Xia's skin, fitting every curvature of her body with perfect precision. Practically a second skin itself. She was just about to zip up the back when the door clicked open.

"Hey when's the—oh, my bad!" Leonardo exclaimed, leaving the room as hastily as he had entered. Xia cringed as a deep shudder reverberated through her bones. Of all the people to see the scars on her back, Leonardo lay at the bottom of that list. Her trembling hand zipped the suit up.

"Get out the way, Fay," Burgs muttered, oblivious to the woman's intention. "How's it fit?"

Xia raised her arms above her head. "Perfectly."

He tapped a few keys and performed a scan. "Yep, looks like it does. Throw on the boots and visor."

She put on the boots and, just like the suit, they conformed to her body perfectly. Solid yet very comfortable. She could run for miles in them. Then she picked up the visor, the piece of equipment she had secretly been looking forward to the most. Even as it lay there, sitting so unassumingly, it tugged a thread of angst deep within. She picked it up and held it in between her hands. Lightweight and smooth, yet there was some meat to it. Some hidden weight. She pulled up her silver hair and fit the helm over her head. A slight film covered her vision, as if everything she saw was first encoded and decoded before hitting her own pupils. If it weren't for the way her hair pressed in between the helmet and her skull, she'd have doubted she was wearing anything at all.

He scanned once more. "Looks like it all fits just right. Step on out. Need to go over some things with you. And grab the gun. Fay, go outside and keep Leonardo in line, would ya?"

Fay nodded and cast Xia a quick nod before leaving the two of them alone. Xia removed the Enforcer from her skinsuit. Now she looked like a true slag. She stepped out of the tube and approached Burgs at his desk, setting the gun before him.

The dim lighting did little to hide the bags under Burgs' eyes, the monitors illuminating every tired wrinkle. She hadn't caught his tired eyes before. Or perhaps this was thanks to the visor's clarity?

A smile tugged at the corner of Burgs' lips as he felt the gun between his hands. He didn't revel in the moment for long. A second later, he stashed it into his top desk drawer.

"Alright girl," he said, giving her his full attention. "This suit here is worth more than anything you own, and anything you ever will own. Even more than that fancy bike of yours. So I'll expect you to treat it as such. Understand me?"

"Yes, sir." Her voice came out in a low, robotic warble.

"This suit is equipped with Radon V6 Tech. Full vista-armor, V6 shock absorbers, laser-embedded scan chips. Under a Force scan, they'll see your ID number. 747282. That's also written on the inside of your visor. Read it, memorize it, know it better than your own name. This suit here is identical to any slag's, except for one missing piece."

"Their scanner."

"Yes," Burgs nodded, the ghost of disappointment on his face. "It's the one piece I've never been able to get my hands on to successfully recreate. It would be damn nice to have. But more importantly, it'll appear as if you've got one. Inside the V5 scanner are several laser-embedded scan chips which emit frequencies identical to the V6 scanners used by slags.

You just have to remember to activate the red light. That mistake is what led you onto us. You can play around with the different options in your visor. There's a lot of stuff there. You'll just need to sync it with your retina mods. You talk with that Mai girl about that?"

"What do you mean?"

"Well, she's a Virgin. That means she doesn't have any ret-mods. She'll look like a slag, but she won't be able to use any of the suit's features. And she'll be a real burden at that point."

Xia hadn't thought of that. Ret-mods were the most basic of modular devices, acting as a template for any other type of activation mods. They'd be necessary to use the helm's tech. "Considering she went through with the nano-bot injections, I'm assuming that will be no problem for her."

Burgs huffed. "You know, this whole thing would be a lot easier without her."

Xia took off the visor. "I know. But she's stuck with me now. And that's that."

"If I cared, I'd ask how you got tangled up with her." He returned to his keyboard and tapped away some more.

"It wasn't by choice," Xia said as she glanced around the room. Various sources hummed: the scanner pod, the multiple monitors, the small fridge in the corner. Nothing noteworthy, until her eyes landed on the radio in the corner. "Listen to the Nightcrawler?" The question was just as bold as his expression. She had told the crew about Opell Doksen and the images he found, but hadn't linked him to the Nightcrawler.

"The hell?"

Xia walked over to the radio.

"Don't touch that!"

She raised her arms, exhibiting her placidity, hoping to draw a stark difference between her and Mai. "It's in better condition than mine. Yours even has a cassette player."

His expression eased. "Gotta listen to the tunes. Sound quality's shit. But that's what you pay for nostalgia."

She eyed Burgs. He was older than her, but not by *that* much. Somewhere in his 50s. Cassette players were *old* old. Just what was this gruff guy's background?

"What do you listen to?"

"Doubt you've heard of any of it. Mokito, Grayson Lumes, got a couple of Pariva Puarez' beginner stuff."

"Pariva Puarez?" Xia's face lit up. "My grandfather raved about her. He saw her perform when he was very young. In the Before Times."

Burgs leaned back in his chair with the most genuine-looking attempt at a smile Xia had seen on him. "No kidding?"

She nodded. "I never got to hear any of her stuff, though. He didn't have any records of her music. But he told me all about her. Was his first crush, he said."

A small pause sat between them before Burgs opened the bottom drawer of his desk and pulled out a small tape.

"Here," he said, handing it off to her. She took the tape from him, her fingers momentarily brushing against his own. Rougher than sandpaper.

"You trust me to play it?"

"I'm sure you'll figure it out alright. They say you're smart."

Xia smiled to herself for the first time that day. First time in a few. It took a few moments, but she figured out the player, and gingerly placed the tape inside and hit play. The husky, soulful voice of a young woman played through the speakers. The quality was odd. She was used to everything being crisp, clear, perfectly tuned to the ear. But there was this haziness. A steady hiss of fog, veiling the ghost of the dead woman's voice. A piece of the past that Xia wasn't meant to listen to. Yet here she was

.

Burgs hummed along, the gruffness in his voice hindering him from hitting the higher notes.

"It sounds familiar. I think my grandfather used to sing this."

Take me for all I am, this love'll set you free, a heartbeat that beats only for you, and a tongue that's only for me.

He never sang it to her, but to himself in the kitchen, quietly, after one too many drinks of bourbon. Xia remembered thinking that was such an odd thing to say. Why would their tongue only be for her? Her young mind couldn't fathom the intricacies of love and sex. Hell, she still couldn't. But now she could at least understand the intent behind those words.

"Your old man had good taste."

"He did. In a lot of things. Especially a good drink."

Burgs raised a brow. "Yeah? What's your poison?"

"A smooth bourbon. Don't need much else with it. Although the Virgins grow berries better than anything I've tasted in the markets. So put one of those in there and, well, then it's anything but poison."

Burgs stared at her before bursting out into his guffaw. "You, you're funny."

She wasn't sure what the funny part was. But the man was smiling, so that meant the ice laid by Mai was thawing.

"Yours?"

He smacked his lips. "I'm not picky. I'll drink the synth spirits. Just none of this moonshine shit everyone's drinkin'. I understand pickin's are slim if you want the real stuff. But that shit is worse than shit. But a good whiskey? Yeah, that hits the spot. There's a lounge next door that serves the real stuff. No synths. But the prices." He whistled. "Not for me."

Rich coming from someone who lived in the swankiest place Xia had ever set foot in.

The ice was melting, melting, but she didn't want to slip. The question sat on the edge of her tongue waiting to dive in. "Burgs, how are you able to make these suits? How do you know so much about the slags?"

He stretched his back with a loud crack. "I know more about those slags than you think, girl." She waited for him to continue, not letting the silence hinder her. "You want to know my secrets? Come back tonight with a bottle of that good whiskey you're blabbin' about. Then I'll talk."

25

Rejection

The lean man laid back into his emerald green armchair, velvet immaculate, a glass of chartreuse held lazily between his perfectly manicured fingers. He wouldn't be surprised if he were the only one in the city with the stuff. He'd never settle for synth spirits. But even with the good stuff, he had a particular thirst that only chartreuse seemed to quench. He had gone through many bottles throughout the years. Too many to count. Every successful surgery resulted in a victory serving of chartreuse. And recently, those victory servings came much more often. His supply was depleting. He'd have to get some more, because he still had many surgeries to go.

"Sir, your next appointment is here."

He took a long sip, purposely letting the moment linger. "Send them in."

The blonde entered the room. Her eyes widened with hunger at the luxurious upholstery, the smuggled books, the glittering carafes of what could only be expensive liqueur. She shook her head. This is what she was leaving behind.

"What can I do for you," the man in the armchair drawled. Voice and affect lazy, uncaring. It didn't unnerve the blonde. She hadn't been unnerved by a man her entire life.

"I want a Virgin body."

The man trailed his eyes up and down her slender physique. Thin in all the right places, plump in all the better ones. Too plump for this man.

Her breasts seemed to scream at him, and he could see the outline of her derriere from the front. Too disproportional. But a simple injection could fix that. Besides the curvature of her frame, her face was perfection. Thick eyelashes covering big sparkling eyes, nose prim and small, lips luscious. Synthetic perfection- you'd spot this same face ten times over walking down 7th Avenue. Even more in the Red Light District.

"Why's that? Too pretty for your own good?" Of course, he already knew why.

"I want to go to the Revitalization Project."

A bemused smile grew on his thin, aging lips. He lit a cigarette to his mouth. "Yeah? Why's that?"

The woman placed her hands on her hips, demeanor haughty. "I'm sick and tired of this place. The men. Yes, the men." She waved a pointed finger. "And hell, most of the women too. The only decent ones around this shithole are the kids. And nobody has those anymore. Try to find you a decent man who wants a family. You get sleazeballs who want their dick sucked. I'm sick of injections. I'm sick of boiling my water when I'm thirsty. I'm sick of never being able to take a bath because I'll use up my water supply. If this Project is a tenth as glamorous as the News said it is, then it's better than here. So, I want in."

He smirked at the irony of her dilemma. How many mods and surgeries had she undergone to alter everything about her, curating herself into the perfect human sex doll? And then growing resentful when that resulted in nothing but meaningless sex? The people here were so foolish. And yet, there was something about her he admired.

"Are you sure about that? Even if it means giving up your perfect self?"

Her turn to smirk. "This body may be perfect, but it's no longer myself. Better to start from scratch."

"My answer is..." He swirled the liquid in his glass, letting the moment swirl with it. "No."

She fumed, eyes blazing with rage. "No? Why? Don't like what I said about men?"

"Quite the contrary. I agree. But no, you are not the right candidate. Now please." He flicked his fingers towards the front door. "Get out."

Her eyes blazed for a moment. She debated grabbing the crystal carafe and shattering it, but the brute that let her inside likely wouldn't stand for that. So she settled for a pointed "fuck you" before huffing past the brute and slamming the door shut behind her.

He took a sip. Little did the woman know, her naivety had saved her. What better reward for hating your body and the world around you than to be stuck in it? Yes, this was a poetic outcome. Besides, there was no shortage of prospective clients.

"Name."

"G-Gregot Foley. I-I was hoping to buy some t-tea?" His voice rattled as he uttered the code phrase.

Xia turned off her voice modifier. It had been a while since she heard the code phrase. The lack of calls and messages for fods had been odd, but she was busy enough that she had purposely not given it much thought.

"What can I do for you, Gregot?"

"Y-yes. I know I'm not s-supposed to be calling you for anything, but I was hoping you had some fods left."

Xia frowned. "What do you mean you aren't supposed to be calling me for anything?"

"Oh. That's what Roshi told us. W-well, I didn't hear it from him, my d-daughter did. That's who I'm worried about... I fear she's being followed. C-could you still help? I've got money—"

Xia cut him off and asked him for the address and key logistics before ending the call. There was the answer to her lack of inquiries. Apparently, Kibou did not want Xia distracted. At the same time, she needed to make rent. She did not appreciate his meddling. And while she had been planning on meeting with the old man soon enough, it was now an immediate course of action.

Off to the Pagoda.

This was the first time returning to the Pagoda since learning of the slags' secret. As she approached the two figures in mock uniform, she tried to decipher who was underneath. The one on the left was obviously Grimer. He seemed to radiate a nervous energy. The perfect demeanor on the one on the right led her to believe he was Ren. For a brief moment, she had the childish urge to smack them upside the head, simply because she could. She squashed the urge and streamed past them.

"Where's Kibou?" She asked a young Virgin man tending to the garden.

He gazed at the silver girl with a mixture of amazement and disgust. "Top floor."

She ventured up the stairs, ignoring the stares and glances of the various people she passed, and entered the top room which had previously been the Lord Daimyo's.

"Ah, Xia," he turned to greet her before she could get a word in. "I was hoping you would come here. Cell chips are not a favored form of communication for this old man. I trust you've been making progress."

"I have," she replied tentatively. "But what's this about you telling people not to contact me for business?"

"Yes. What about it?"

She blinked. "Why would you do that? My helping you is a priority but I still need to make money."

"I find it hard to believe someone like yourself doesn't have savings."

For the first time, his words really ticked her off. "This will take time. I haven't taken on any of my usual gigs in order to help you all. A venture that could very well cost my life, mind you. People don't work for free."

"Ah yes, unfortunately not. Money. Together the root and answer to all life's problems."

"I don't have time for your philosophical ramblings, Kibou. Either I'm back in business for your folks or you start paying up."

She hoped for him to portray the slightest of annoyance. The flare of a nostril, even just the cock of an eyebrow. But no, like a feather in a breeze, nothing passed his stoicism except the lightest of smiles. "Surely you have other reasons for wanting to meet with me, no?" His eyes rested on hers, two soft doves gracing rough terrain.

Was the old man always right? She breathed out, letting some of her fire release with it. "You knew about the slags. Out front. That they aren't...you know."

The eye crinkles deepened. "Yes."

"And you were waiting to see if I figured it out, because you knew they would be the key to getting out."

"Yes."

"And if I did figure it out, then you knew you could trust me with this entire thing."

"Precisely."

She released a breath that had been caught deep in her chest. She wasn't annoyed that Kibou told people not to reach out to her for fods; it made sense. What was daunting was that if she wasn't working on fods, then she was all in for this mission. A mission that grew more dangerous the more she plotted it. A mission that'd change her life forever.

It already had.

"How can you be so sure we can trust the Lost Samurai outside? How can you be sure he knows a way back in?"

"Haven't I proven the depths of my knowledge already? I fully trust that if you make it out, you can make it to our destination. And there I trust you will learn what we need."

"But if he knows a way in and out, why hasn't he come back?"

"Why would he?" A wry smile graced his lips and his beard twitched. "Time is not our ally. I fear the sands are escaping us." His eyes intensified with a calm ferocity as he held out a small pouch. "May you have no other distractions, my friend."

It was the earliest Xia had ever been to Mickey's. Dames wouldn't be working, but she messaged him and asked him to bring a bottle of authentic, pre-war smoked whiskey. She didn't know who his supplier was for such rare bottles. Luckily, Dames was as trusty a middleman you could get. The cost was normally absurd, but with Kibou's gifted pouch, it was a drop in the ocean. And Burgs was more than just a useful ally. He had the potential to hold crucial knowledge. How else did he know how to make those suits? She wanted him in his corner. And if a bottle of the good stuff would put him there, then she'd pay anything to get it.

On my way, he messaged as Xia sat at the bar. It was nearly empty. Normal for mid-afternoon on a Wheresday. All of a sudden, the door swung open with furious force. She turned in her seat half expecting Dames, but instead saw a vaguely familiar blonde woman.

Was she familiar because Xia had met her before? Or was she familiar because she had the same type of face as every woman following the modular beauty trends? Xia would have assumed it was because of the typical face, but there was something about the glittering rings on her fingers and her scowl. Especially the scowl. That was the scowl of someone faced with perpetual disappointment.

The blonde sat next to a greasy-haired man with aging lines and skinny arms. A man who did not keep up with beauty trends. "What's the matter, Clova? Bad date?"

No joke back. She motioned towards the bartender and ordered a gin and tea.

"You meet with that surgeon guy?"

Her eyes blazed. "Shut up will you?" She seethed quietly, but it was just loud enough for Xia to hear. Something about the anger in her eyes. Then she remembered. This was the same woman with an affinity for PDA at the bar, who had no problem yelling right at Dames. The one who said she'd love to go to the Revitalization Project. Xia turned up her sound frequency mod and isolated the location, allowing herself to hear from them and only them.

"Oh, relax, practically nobody's even here." The man said, although he did hush his tone. Xia swirled her drink and pretended to take great interest in the quality of the glass.

The woman eased once her drink came. "Yes, I met with him. And he said I 'wasn't the right candidate'. What the fuck is that supposed to mean?"

"Maybe he meant because your body is so perfect, you shouldn't want to switch it?"

She rolled her eyes. "No, Toti, that is not what he meant."

"Well, what do you think he meant—"

"I don't fucking know!" Her tone raised slightly.

"Did you give him the spiel on men?" He asked with the faintest of sneers.

"Yes, yes I did. So he probably heard that and wrote me off. I was willing to pay whatever he wanted. Guess I'm stuck here. Stuck with you."

Toti did little to hide his elation. "Yep. Looks like you're stuck with me."

Xia continued to swirl her drink, mulling over the conversation. Besides Toti's obvious infatuation with Clova, something else was also obvious. Clova had met with the surgeon performing the brain surgeries. She was trying to get to the Revitalization Project. And Xia was willing to bet everything that that surgeon was none other than Dr. Iro Nagawa, the man responsible for the Daimyo's death.

A tap on her shoulder jolted her out of her mind's brainstorm, and she turned around to see Dames. She hastily turned off the sound frequencer.

"You alright? You were practically ignoring me."

"Yeah," Xia said, mind still lingering on the blonde. "Just thinking, sorry. You got the bottle?"

"Yeah. Is this why you haven't been to the bar recently? Drinking your own private stash?"

"I was here barely a week ago. And this is actually for someone else."

"I see," Dames stared down at her, eyes inquisitive, but he didn't press any further. "I guess it just seems like longer. Last time you were here was with that friend of yours. What was her name again?"

"Mai," Xia said, glancing back at the blonde.

"Right, Mai. She was a fun one. You still hanging around with her?"

"What? Yeah, she's around."

"Your mind really is elsewhere, yeesh."

"Sorry. How much I owe you?" She took the glass jug from him, the contents a beautiful brown.

"I'll add it to your tab. Just pay the next time you're here."

Xia shook her head. "Come on, Dames. This is way too much. Seriously, how much?"

"It's really no problem—"

"Dames, cut that out. I don't even know the next time I'll be here. How much do I owe you?"

A flash of hurt quickly crossed his face, but Xia still caught it . "3000 zeCoin."

She tapped her wristband a few times and sent the money his way. "I really appreciate you getting this for me."

"Yeah, no problem." His voice lingered. "Xia, I'm sorry about the last time you were here."

She finally dropped her attention from the blonde. "What?"

"With Mai. You were really drunk. I should have cut you off."

"You should have poured with softer hands," Xia rebuked.

He gave a nervous chuckle, something that Xia had never heard him do. "Yeah, well, hard to do with these." He raised his giant hands.

Xia turned back toward the blonde, her attention desperate to leave the memories of that night. The drinking, the attack, the vomit—the dropping of her towel in front of Mai.

He coughed. "Well, I hope to see you around here. Keep yourself safe out there."

Xia felt the disappointment behind his words, and a sickening mixture of pity and regret balled in her stomach. "Yeah, yeah I'll try to come by soon." Empty words. He gave a nod and an equally empty smile before leaving the bar.

Xia ignored the churning ball in her gut and got up from her seat, taking her drink with her, and walked over to Clova.

"Hey," Xia said, taking a seat next to the duo. The bartender had headed into the back, leaving the three of them empty in the seedy joint.

"The hell do you want?" Clova snapped.

"Don't be so rude," Toti chided.

"I heard your conversation earlier," Xia said.

"For fuck's sake, Toti. I told you you were talking too loud!"

"I didn't mean to! Besides, you were talking just as loud as I was—"

Xia cut through the bickering. "It's alright. I already know about the guy. I'm just trying to get to know more. I can pay you for whatever you know." Xia slid some phys towards her.

Clova glanced down toward the money. Then she flicked it back at Xia. "I don't want your money."

Xia was not expecting that. She began to consider a new proposition when Clova continued.

"Why do you want to know about this man?"

Xia thought to herself, considering her choice of words. She remembered the vitriol in which Clova spoke about him, and her route was decided. Easily enough, it also happened to be the truth.

"I want to get rid of him."

Clova's hair swung behind her as she flung her head back in a humorless laugh. "Good luck with that. He's got an army of brutes working for him. I passed three just on my way to my appointment. But I don't see how taking him out would be difficult. He can't weigh much more than you."

"What's the man's name?"

"Nagawa. Don't remember his first name."

"Iro?"

Clova clicked her tongue. "Yeah, that's it. Gave me the creeps. Even more so than most men do."

Toti smirked beside her.

"What was he like?"

"Probably mid-60s or so. You could tell he took care of himself. Pretty thin, but not in a malnourished kind of way. Just kind of lean. Too smug for his own good."

"How did you learn about him? About what he does?"

Clova leaned forward, another sip of gin to her lips. "If I told you that, I'd be a dead woman. You sleep around, you learn all kinds of secrets."

"Can you tell me where he lives?"

Clova nodded while taking another slug, eyes hazy behind her heavy eyelashes. She snatched Xia's wrist, her jeweled fingers grazing Xia's cellchip. Then her eyes glanced toward Xia's other hand, the one perpetually gloved.

"What's up with the one-gloved look? Trying to start a trend? Or are you hiding something under there?"

A wave of discomfort jolted through her. She shrugged.

"Hmm. I take it back. I do want payment. I'll send you the address if you show me what's underneath that glove."

Xia didn't like the power flip of being on the receiving end of a demand. And even more so, she didn't like the prospect of exposing her scars. She brought her gloved hand to her chest protectively.

Clova's brows raised in amusement. "No glove, no address."

Xia's eyes burned down toward her covered hand. She could count on that hand the number of people who'd seen the disfigurement. And here she'd be adding two grunts to that list.

Without making eye contact, she removed the glove.

The back of her hand was warped, resembling the hand of a raw, shriveled corpse. Acid burns from an acid storm were severe, but if treated, the damaging effects could be lessened. Xia didn't treat those burns. She didn't have the knowledge or the energy to do much about them at the time. She had been consumed by the enveloping waves of grief, drowning her, leaving her with little power to do much else.

"No wonder you leave that covered," Clova mused with captivation. She stared for several more moments before returning to Xia's other wrist. She hovered the cellchip on her own wrist over Xia's and tapped a few times. "There's the address."

Xia nodded, feeling exposed but satisfied with the gained knowledge.

Clova glanced back toward Xia's now gloved hand. "You know, I bet that hand could do a lot of fun things. If you're ever up for some fun things."

Xia raised a bemused brow.

"Fun," Clova smiled with a pucker of her thick pink lips, cocking her head slightly. She brought a jeweled finger to Xia's chest and pressed ever so slightly.

Xia recoiled at the touch. The visible recoil was by normal standards extreme, but it was slight compared to the revulsion that imploded in her chest.

Clova laughed. "Not your type, eh? Ah well, had to give it a try." Toti shook his head with exasperation beside her, and Xia made her escape, the bottle of whiskey in a bag slung over her shoulder.

26

GRUFF OLD TALES

The painkillers pulled Mai in and out of painful consciousness. During her wake windows, she moaned and called for Xia, nothing but silence greeting her back. It wasn't until well into the afternoon that one of her groans was met with a response.

"How are you feeling?"

Mai gazed up at her new-found friend. Silver hair almost glittering against the hazy horizon behind the window, skin-tight suit molding her sculpted form. It was a shame, Mai thought. If the woman just learned an ounce of social charm, she'd unlock a whole new arsenal of weaponry.

"Like someone is splitting my back apart."

"And the knees?"

"Knees too."

"Here." Xia tossed her a small pill bottle. Her hands fumbled and barely caught them.

"More? Isn't there like, a cap on how many I can take?"

"You're fine. Just don't take them all at once. Your pain should be subsiding by now anyway. Is it?"

It was still hell, but what had been a fiery inferno was subsiding into a modest blaze. "Barely."

"Barely means we're on the right track. And here, got you this." Xia placed a small bag beside her. "I know it's the last thing on your mind, but you got to eat."

Mai shifted her position on the couch and ignored the food. "Where have you been all day? I want updates."

"Later."

"It's the least you can do for me. I'm stuck on this couch all day."

"I got you food. That was the least I could do. I also got you painkillers. I've gone above and beyond."

"Ha, ha." Mai groaned again. This was the most talkative she had been since the nanobots were first injected. Another good sign. The last thing Xia needed was any adverse reactions from the Virgin girl. Although, she technically wasn't one of those anymore.

"Later. I've got to eat. And work on the fods a bit."

Mai's sweaty face scrunched into confusion. "The fods? Aren't you done with that?"

Xia eyed her with suspicion. "Why would I be done?"

"Well, business has slowed, right?"

"Yeah, and why would that be?"

Mai lost the scrunch. "No reason."

"Kibou told you, didn't he?"

The scrunch returned, but it looked scripted. "Told me what?"

"I don't need a scanner to tell me you're full of it. It's fine, I already know. I went and spoke with him today. There's one of the things I did today."

Mai exhaled in relief. "It wasn't my idea or anything. He just told me to keep you on track. And to spread the word to other Virgins that you were closed for business."

"And did you?"

"No." Mai swallowed one of the pills. "So, where else were you?"

Over the next hour, Xia ate and recounted the various events of the day. Mai's reactions grew lesser and lesser. Xia then mentioned that her bike had a whopping four attempted electro-bubble touches but was met with silence. The silence broke with the faintest of snores, which signaled that Mai's ears were no longer listening, having left for slumberland. So with that, Xia gathered the bottle of liquor and left to meet with Burgs.

This time it was Grimer's turn to escort Xia from the lobby to the group's apartment. Xia didn't mind the silence, but it suffocated Grimer.

"Thought you were at the Pagoda for the day? Or did you guys switch shifts?"

It took a moment for his mouth to form saliva again. His words came slowly after that. "Burgs messaged me. Wanted me to swap with Leonardo."

She gave a silent thank you to the gruff man. The last thing she wanted was to be drinking with Leonardo in the next room over. Loosened inhibitions made violence easier. That is, if Burgs was willing to share the precious liquid.

She expected to meet with Burgs in his tech room, same as prior in the day. Instead, he sat in his armchair, his hefty Black frame clashing with the white chair's sleekness.

"So, Xia, you got the good stuff already?" He called out with amusement. Xia approached him and pulled the bottle out of the pack. As his eyes laid on the bronze liquor, his amusement vanished and a primal hunger replaced it. He snatched the bottle and examined the label. "You can't even get this at the liquory! This is aged from the Before Times. What a bottle, what a bottle. Shall we?"

Xia gave a satisfied nod.

"Grimer. Grab us two glasses."

"Just two?"

"Yes, two. Then get back to work."

"Yes, sir," Grimer replied gloomily, quick to retrieve the glasses and get out of their hair. The butterflies he got from Xia and the fear toward Burgs made for a very sickening combo. It was likely best he didn't partake in the booze.

"Have a seat," Burgs said. The bottle had already seemed to bring something out of the man, and he hadn't even had a taste yet. Xia obliged, taking a seat on the couch. Xia's spine sat straight as an arrow, but Burgs leaned back comfortably. And when Grimer gave him his glass and he took a sip, tongue swirling around his mouth, he sunk back even further.

"Oh, that is good," his voice melted as he melted into the chair. "Like velvet on the tongue. And there's almost a spice to it at the end. A warm spice. Damn. That's better than any of the stuff they serve at The Oasis."

"The Oasis?"

"The lounge next door. One of the swankiest bars here in the city. They got good stuff, no synths. But it ain't from the Before Times. Not like this." He took another sip, not able to keep himself from the spirit.

"So, Burgs," Xia said, taking a deep sip of her own glass, trying to find the right words. "How did you get going with these other four? They don't exactly seem like your type."

"I could say the same for you and the Daimyo's kid."

"She kind of latched on to me. Plus she's not all cons. She's got her advantages." Xia thought of Mai's cooking. How she hadn't had any for just one day because of the surgery, and how her tongue already yearned for it.

"Well, similar things could be said about my crew. Grimer's my son. So he's with me for all his pros and cons."

Xia blinked. "Your son?"

"Yes. It's why I'm particularly tough on the little bastard. Apparently, that hasn't worked in my favor."

"And the others?"

He swished the drink in his glass. "I need a cig." Xia waited as he pulled out a cigarette and a lighter. "Want one?"

"Don't smoke."

"Why not?"

"No reason to."

"No reason not to."

Xia shrugged. Burgs held the cigarette in front of her, a silent command of which Xia was not about to refuse. She took the small roll from him and held it to her mouth while he lit the other end. Then, an inhale. A small cough.

"Well, how's the taste?"

Xia had never smoked before. People smoked all kinds of things in the city. Some altered your way of thinking, but cigarettes were the tamest and just made you feel, well, Xia wasn't sure what it was supposed to make her feel. It just made her cough.

"Tastes like ash."

Burgs chuckled. "Yeah. But then the ash starts tasting good. Then you're addicted to it. It pairs nicely with a drink."

As she took another sip, she had to agree. The next drag didn't make her cough.

"The others?" She asked again.

Burgs topped off his glass and took a long, long drag from his own cigarette as he gazed out the window. "It's quite a story."

She let the silence hang and do the work for her. Eventually, he spoke again.

"I had been freelancing for 10 years. Mainly workin' with gangs, gettin' 'em tech and helpin' 'em avoid slags. The city was overrun with gangs back then. I'm guessing you were a real youngin' at the time. Military wasn't quite as effective in keeping them in check. Nowadays all a slag's gotta do is walk down the street and everyone's cowering in fear. But back then, there was a bit more back and forth. Largely due to me. I was a busy fellow.

"But the thing about being a freelancer is that as soon as you have an off day, as soon as something goes wrong, you're on your own. And if your own ain't enough, then you're in a real shitty position."

He took another drag. Then a gulp. Then he refilled his glass.

"I didn't want kids. Who would want to bring kids into this hell hole? But Fran did. Fran desperately wanted a baby. I suppose at one point the biological urge became so damn strong that it even beat me. I said ok. Bam, after one month of raw doggin' it, the bitch was pregnant."

The crassness of the words did nothing to cover up the pure longing in his eyes. "She begged me to quit freelancin'. Get some real work. I was an engineer. Had more experience and know-it-all than 99% of these buffoons. I could do it. I could support her and the new baby in an 'honest' way. But I couldn't. I couldn't answer to someone. I couldn't work within the confines of the FRF. Couldn't play by their rules. Not after what I discovered."

Xia waited for him to elaborate on this discovery, but he moved on. She put a mental check on that, remembering to reroute the conversation after two more glasses.

"So I continued to work with the gangs. Trading my services for money. But the thing is, when you're helping one gang beat another, the other one doesn't care for you too much. I got cornered. I got beat up. I got told to quit my services to the opposing gang and to help them. And my fuckin' pride. I was about to say no. But I knew they'd kill me. And all I could see was Fran's face, and then her holding our little baby boy. And I knew I had to swallow that pride. So I agreed."

Xia nodded along, leaning forward on the couch, waiting for him to continue. The air prickled with the sharpness of his words. And yet she was dying to hear more.

"What's your deal?"

The words sliced through the air. "What?"

"How'd you get into freelancing?"

She shifted in her seat. Now the air's prickling pinched at her skin, itching, jabbing. She hadn't drunk enough for the questioning to shift. The seconds ticked by more sluggish than a snail. Another gulp. "I was used to being alone. Freelancing made sense," she finally spoke.

"Now *that* is the lamest thing I've ever heard. I give you a golden sneak peek into my past. And you give me a cat turd. Get out of here with that shit. Give me something substantial."

She gazed out the window, the sky a deep maroon as the sun set behind the smog. It took a moment, but eventually she picked out a small, lone building for her eyes to rest upon as she divulged pieces of her that lay locked within her deepest cell.

"I grew up with my grandfather. Both my parents were dead. Never met them. According to my grandfather, my mother was very stoic. No-nonsense. But she was empathetic. Always caring about others. And my father was energetic, very physical, and apparently a good fighter. I think I get my athleticism from him."

"How'd they die?"

She blinked for a moment, losing focus of the small building. "I don't actually know how. Just that it had to do with the military. My parents didn't like how the city was run, I guess. Grandfather told me they 'wanted freedom', but nothing more than that. But you don't need to know much more to figure it out. Slags will do a whole lot worse for a whole lot less."

Burgs hummed to himself. "How old are you, kid?"

"28."

"And your folks died how long ago?"

"When I was less than a year old."

He nodded, his lip jutting out as he worked through the numbers. "What is it?"

He waved his hand and took another sip, downing his second glass. The man sure could put them away. "Nothing. Continue."

"Right. Well, they died. And when I was 13, my grandfather died. So I had to make ends meet. It was hard at first, especially because of school—"

"You went to school?" His eyes widened. "And still became a free-lancer?"

She shrugged. "Yeah, I know. My grandfather didn't want me to join the military. 'Cause of what happened to my parents. And after he died, I wouldn't have been able to live with myself if I joined in spite of that. And I know there were other options, but I don't know. You get by on your own for long enough, that at a certain point, there really seems like no other option. Other roads look blocked, even if they aren't. Plus, I was good at it." She couldn't hold back the little smile that tugged at the corner of her mouth.

"I see, I see." He shook his head, chuckling to himself.

"What's so funny?"

"It's nothin', kid. You're just full of surprises is all. We got into free-lancing for different reasons, but seems like we stayed for the same ones. But like I said before. You work alone, you fall alone, and nobody's there to pick you up. Fay was the one to pick me up. "

Xia eased into her seat, the weight of the spotlight leaving her and shifting back to Burgs. They drank in silence for several minutes, the sky gradually darkening, glasses growing emptier and emptier. If it weren't for the warm buzz softening Xia's senses, the silence would have hung too heavy. Was he waiting for her to ask him to continue? Or was he lost in his own thoughts? Finally, after Xia poured again, he stirred the stillness.

"I told the gang I'd help them out. The Kurogane, they called themselves. A foul bunch. Every one of them. The leader was the tamest. Even though I agreed to help them, I didn't. I couldn't. If I did, I'd be killed by their rivals. No, I made the stupidest decision of my life. I sold them faulty tech in an attempt to take them out. It didn't work. And in retaliation, they killed Fran."

Xia had been expecting this turn, wondering how and when the mother of nervous Grimer passed. And yet, she still felt a pang of sorrow at the words. Perhaps it was the faintest echo of regretful despair in his eyes, or the whiskey, but she truly felt bad for Burgs.

"I was destroyed. I let myself be destroyed. You can't do that when you got a kid. But I did. We were living in an apartment down in Midpoint. It was a rough night. Grimer just kept cryin', throwin' one of his toddler tantrums. Screamin' for mommy. And I snapped. Snapped at him, had a full-on breakdown. And our teen next-door neighbor forced her way in. She took one look at the place and just went to work. Swept Grimer up in her arms, calmed him right down. Then started cleanin'. Place was a pigsty. And she turned it into a home. Came over every day, helpin' with the little rascal. As you can guess, that teen was Fay."

A young Fay, helping an even younger Grimer, taking care of a heartbroken Burgs. She now understood the hold that Fay had on the brusque man. Her tongue heavied, the alcohol tightening its grip.

"And the others?"

He leaned back and lit another cigarette, letting another wave of silence descend upon them. "I'm tired of this room. Let's go." He stood abruptly.

"What?"

"C'mon kid. We're goin' to the Oasis. Don't worry, I'll pay."

"The lounge next door? Why?"

He let out an exasperated grumble. "Because I want to. Quit the questions. You want to know my secrets or not?"

He had been sharing more than Xia expected him to as it was. A drain finally unplugged, now it all poured out. She didn't want to stop the flow.

"Fine," she ceded.

"But you can't go in there wearin' that. They got a dress code. Come on, let's get you gussied up."

Her eyes widened. "Excuse me?"

"You heard me. Quit questioning and just do. I'll grab you something from Fay's closet. She's a bit curvier than you, but we'll find something."

Xia's tongue thickened into a concrete slab, dry and unmoving. Never in her life had she gotten "gussied up". She'd never gone anywhere that required it. And she had never wanted to. But there was a first for everything. Her feet followed Burgs before her mind was able to register her decision. At this point, she was along for the ride.

"Wait here," Burgs commanded. He entered Fay's room, leaving the door open a crack. Through that crack all Xia could see was blue. She thought of Fay's deep blue hair. There seemed to be a theme. A moment later Burgs returned with, lo and behold, a blue dress. But it was the worst blue dress she could hope for.

"I'm not wearing that."

"Come on," he dismissed her and shoved the dress towards her.

Xia held it up against her. "It barely covers my crotch."

"But aren't the sparkles pretty?"

"They hurt my eyes." She flipped the dress over and examined the back. Or rather, the lack of back. She'd expose her legs and chest if she had to, but she wasn't about to showcase her scars. No amount of alcohol could force her to put it on. She looked past Burgs into the room behind her. "There's gotta be something else. Literally anything. Something that covers the back. And won't flash everyone if I take a big enough step."

Burgs snatched the dress with annoyance and turned back around. Her eyes wandered past the crack once more, the various textures and shades of blue swirling around in a calming wave. Once more, her feet were about to move before her mind could register their steps, but Burgs returned, a different dress in tow.

"No, come on—"

Burgs clicked his tongue. "Nope. It's either this one or the one with the sparkles."

Xia stared at the dress, willing it to grow longer, looser, anything. But it stared back, tight and taunting. She took the dress with a severe lack of enthusiasm. "Where do I change?"

27

MELODIES AND MILITARY SECRETS

S he stood in the shiny bathroom, the surfaces sleek and spotless. For having four men in the place, they sure kept a tidy bathroom. There wasn't a hair or speck out of place, and the bright lighting made everything visible. But Xia paid no attention to the glistening bathroom. Her eyes were painfully glued to the reflection of the girl in the mirror.

Xia was used to wearing tight clothing. After all, it was a skinsuit that she donned each day. And yet she couldn't get over the tightness of this damn dress. Her hips were not that wide. So why did the dress seem to give her an hourglass shape? How did it give her cleavage? The blackness of her skinsuit allowed for elusiveness. Yet the black of the dress seemed to command a sexy *"look at me"*.

She hated it. But she couldn't deny that she did look pretty damn good.

Burgs, who had already changed into a dress shirt and slacks, clearly agreed. He let out a low whistle as she stepped out of the bathroom.

"You clean up well. Think these shoes'll fit?" He held up a pair of heels. Heels that, with one glance, Xia could tell would not fit her substantially sized feet.

He followed her gaze and glanced down. "Maybe not. Damn, I thought Fay had big feet."

"You already know how big my feet are. You made the slag boots for me." Her eyes narrowed. "Are you fucking with me?"

He grinned. "Here. These oughtta do." He tossed her a different pair of heels, more modest, and larger. It still looked like a tight squeeze. She bent over and slid (more like forced) them onto her feet. She could hear Burgs chuckling above her.

"Come on already," Xia stood and pushed past Burgs, avoiding his gaze, but it was hard to miss the smile painted on his face.

With the rapid elevator ride, they stood in the low-lit lounge less than a minute later. A tall, handsome man with hair blacker than Xia's dress greeted them at the door with a respectful bow.

"Sir, Madame."

She almost laughed. Madame? These were the types of colloquialisms that came with the wealthy world. Xia belonged to the seedy world. And while she looked the part, she could practically see a blazing sign above her yelling *"Imposter! I don't belong!"*

They passed the greeter and entered the main bar. An ornate chandelier adorned with glittering gems set the mood for the elegant establishment, and the guests responded accordingly. Men in tailored suits sat with women in posh dresses that ranged from chic and sophisticated to downright gaudy. Xia was thankful to be on the reserved side, even if her dress left little to the imagination. She pulled her skirt down.

They took a seat at the curved bar. Mahogany wood without the faintest of scratches curved into a perfect semi-circle, similar in structure to the bar in Mickey's. But there was no spillage, no hazy dust particles, no drunken buffoons hashing it out square and center. Just pure sophistication. A small stage sat in the corner with a lone, empty microphone.

"They got music here?" Xia asked, gesturing towards the stage. Xia hadn't been to a place with live music since she was a child. And even then, it was a rarity. Music was a heavily restricted field. One needed to get a license, and each piece of music needed approval by the FRF Media Committee in order to hit the market. There was a Black Market for music, but Xia didn't frequent it. The risk didn't seem worth the reward. Live music was just as heavily restricted, but the wealthy had easier access to it. Exhibit A: The Oasis.

"Yep. That's the main reason I come here."

The proposition to spend money on lesser drink made more sense. The bartender appeared a moment later, setting a drink menu before them.

Pink Appletini, Marble New Fashioned, Orangedrop... She wanted to mock them, but they all sounded very appetizing. "I'll take a...'Scarlet Bourbon Smash'?" She finished the request like a question.

Burgs ignored the menu. "Sazerac."

A few moments later, the thin bartender returned with two drinks, an ombre red for Xia and a simple caramel with orange twist for Burgs. Then Burgs took a small black cube out of his pocket and pressed down the side.

"What's this?"

"Soundbox. Similar to the voice distortioners that slags use. Warps anything we say into preset dialogue that I have programmed. Anyone outside the parameters of this box will think we are talking about mechanical engineering financials."

"Mechanical engineering financials?" Xia cocked a brow.

"Ensures nobody will pay us any attention." He took a sip of his cocktail. "Perfectly balanced, dances on the tongue, yet I'd still rather have the bottle you brought."

Xia didn't quite agree. Her own drink was by far the best damn drink she'd ever had. She'd never tell Dames.

A moment later, the conversation in the room dimmed as a slender woman in a glittering ruby dress stepped onto the stage. Xia was positive she had never seen the woman before, yet there was an odd familiarity to her. Her dark hair was pinned in a swooping updo, accentuating her sharp eyes and lips that matched the sparkling dress. Xia didn't mind these sparkles. The way they glittered with each small breath and movement of the songstress was absolutely mesmerizing.

A man sat behind her with a tall string instrument.

"What's that?" Xia asked, eyeing the man as he brought out a long stick-like object.

"A cello," Burgs replied.

"What is—"

Burgs shushed her. As if on cue, the man pulled the bow across the strings of the cello, releasing the purest sound of deepest longing. And then the woman joined in.

In Xia's 28 years of life, she had seen many things. Heard many things. The sound of bone crunching metal. The sound of songbirds professing their love. Of wind rushing past ears. Of children laughing in glee. Of children crying in fear. None of it came close to evoking such power as the sound that emanated from the duo on stage.

As the woman sang, Xia felt the sound stir something deep inside her, deep within her aching belly. It chilled her. Little bumps raised on her arms as the sound continued to churn her insides. A witch reciting a spell. A sorceress placing her in a trance. The room tilted to the sound of the songstress' hauntingly beautiful melody. All Xia could do was stare.

One song bled into the next. After what felt like a stop in time but had been over twenty minutes, the woman sang her final note and was met with scattered applause. Burgs gave two thunderous claps and glanced toward Xia. Her body had turned to stone, but her eyes were glossy with emotion.

"Good sound, eh?"

The spell broke. "Y-yeah. That was... really beautiful." She wiped her eyes, turned back to her drink, and downed the last bit. It was beautiful. But she wanted to rid her body of the rousing it had caused. Never had she felt so unsettled.

Burgs signaled at the bartender for two more drinks. The man barely set the glass down before it was in Xia's hand, pouring past her lips.

"Hold your horses, kiddo."

"What horses?"

"Old saying. Slow it down."

She knew he was right. She set the glass down. "So. You were military?"

He leaned forward onto the mahogany bar top. "Yes and no." He flipped over the small black soundbox, ensuring it was on and working. "Before freelancing, I had graduated from Hotoko Academy. Top school. Even beat out Greikko. If you weren't gonna be military, you were lookin' at a cushy government job. But most were military. I had the grades and wherewithal to become an engineering executive with the government. But I opted for the military, as people often do. Those that are naive enough'll join the slags in the hopes of changing it from the inside out. Be the change you would want to see, so to speak. And the rest, which is really the most, join for that very power that everyone on the outside hates."

"Which were you?"

Burgs seemed to consider it for a moment. "Honestly, neither. Didn't care about the whole power and grandeur aspect. But I also didn't care about reinventin' the wheel. I was just fascinated by the technology. The scanners, the weaponry, their uniforms, hell- even the dome that's above us. All of it was, *is* , technology's prime. I wanted to be on the inside of all that. But just how deep that technology went...I never could have imagined." He sipped again. "So the military was my path.

"Once you join, you're in. Death's your way out. So gettin' out was...tricky. To say the least. But once I caught wind of what they were doin', death was the better option."

He kept feeding her scraps and she was dying for the main course. Burgs knew it. He enjoyed the slow burn. She instinctively glanced around the room. Nobody seemed to be paying them any attention. It felt insane to be speaking about such matters like this in the open. The small soundbox made it all possible.

"When you first join the military academy, they divide you up based on your school grades, recommendations by teachers, and your athletic capabilities. S Rank, A Rank, B rank, and C Rank. I had just made the cut for S Rank. You're then put through a 12-month training program before you're officially a slag. That all takes place in the Northern Inner Hub."

"Not outside the walls?" Xia had assumed they were housed along with the rest of the government elite in their safe hubs outside the outer wall. Although, with Xia's recent discovery, those safe sectors didn't actually need any protection.

"Trainees never venture outside the walls. Only government officials and actual Military are gifted the privilege." He scoffed on the last word. "No, we were stuck in our tiny quarters, packed like sardines and slowly startin' to hate each other. The longer the months crept by, the more everyone was desperate to become an official slag. No matter how grueling the work, or how little sleep we got, everyone seemed to have the same goal. But me, I was playin' with the tech'.

"Being in S rank, we weren't quite as packed as the others. Got some privileges, so to speak. The others hated us for it. There was a lot of tension between the S rank and the rest. I didn't pay it any mind. I was off on my own for the most part. While everyone else was buildin' alliances, working out to get ahead, or gettin' into stupid fights, I was tinkerin'. The tech at our disposal was just amazing. Yet nobody else seemed to care all that much. Just me.

"Bein' the odd one out, it meant I was a bit more observant. I had the time for it. I wasn't distracted like the others. Or maybe I'm the observant type. I don't know. I couldn't help but notice that the official slags, the Force members that were training us and leading exercises, there was just something *different* about them. At first, it made sense. They were the trained elite teaching the lowly trainees. But no, it seemed more than that. And as I'd watch groups of 'em enter in and out of the city walls, it stuck with me. There's just somethin' off.

"On month nine, we were gifted with our own slag suits. And that's when I really had fun. I continued tinkerin', especially with the scanners and radio equipment. As everyone knows, radio transmitters are heavily restricted for the lowly populace. So I was having a grand old time playing around with 'em. And that was my gateway to findin' out their secret."

Burgs tapped his glass again, and Xia waited with painful patience as the bartender made him a new drink. He took a very slow slip.

"There was a medical facility very close to the S Rank's quarters. And there was a Doc there that always rubbed me the wrong way. First time I met him, I thought, 'There's somethin' off about this guy.' Somethin' wrong in the eyes. And the skin. It had this almost greenish tint. But the others swore by him. They'd get injured in training exercises and with one trip to this Doc they said they felt better than ever. But my gut was telling me something, and I decided to listen to it.

"It started when I was training in the engineering department, as that was my focus through training. The instructor was not military, but a contractor. Pretty rare even back then, but it meant I was learning things face to face— not face to slag mask. She liked me. A lot. Might have had some romantic interest there, which certainly helped. She let me stay late after class to use the equipment. And one area of equipment was especially of interest to me. *Nanotech.*

"I had always hated the constant watching. The constant *listening.* But being able to listen back. That was enticing. And I was in the perfect place for it. Nanobot tech is pretty advanced now, but back when I was in the military program, it wasn't quite where it is today. Still in the more early stages. So I spent a good amount of time working with the nanotech. I was careful not to only work with my little nanobot. From the outside, I was tinkering around with everything. But my focus was on the nanobots. After a solid month of late nights, I had it. The perfect little bug."

He lifted his pinky finger. "The thing was half the size of my fingernail. Outside used a camo sensor to blend in with the surroundings, avoiding visual detection. Barely used any power, avoiding any heat signatures or abnormal energy patterns. And then used frequency hopping to mask the wireless signal. After a final layer of encryption and an anti-radiation shell, I tuned it with a receiver so that I was the only one who could access and decode the audio signal. I was proud of my device then, and still proud now. Although those types of little bugs are used all the time by the FRF now. But to my knowledge, I did it first."

And Xia had been proud of her fods. Those were a child's toy compared to this.

"I purposely got myself banged up so that I'd end up with the creepy Doc. It was a quick visit, and he did fix me up nicely. I noticed that he preferred to sit. He kept rollin' around the room in his dumb chair. Even stitched me up while sittin'. So I stuck the bug on the underside of his chair. And from that day on, I listened. I never heard anything quite good until a fateful day where my roommate got spliced up real bad during a training exercise. Whole ear ripped off along with bits of his face. Off he went to the miracle Doc. And off I went to listen."

The cellist returned. Xia willed him to go away. She was hanging on to Burgs' every word, and he was taking his dear, sweet time letting her dangle.

"I listened as the Doc and some other military folk discussed his future in the military. How the injury had not only affected his ear, but part of his brain. Both the auditory and somatosensory cortexes were affected, and they kept saying 'The Operation' would likely be unsuccessful. At first, I thought they meant the operation to fix his ear. But the more the Doc and these other folks were talking, I realized they were talkin' about something else. Some operation that everyone had to undergo before they officially became a Force member."

She dangled, unable to drink, because the words stole her full attention.

Burgs took another swig and leaned back in his chair with an amused huff.

"Kid, you had found out that we weren't real slags. Well, slags? They aren't even real humans. Not anymore."

28

No Shoes

*R*ecomputing. Analyzing.

"It's the same issue with this batch as well. Surgical incisions underneath hairlines. Decreased gray matter."

The woman picked delicately between the brain folds, as if the answer to their conundrum were hiding in the squishy maze.

Initial hypothesis further supported. Dr. Nagawa is the root cause.

***

Xia waited for him to continue, but he let the words sit there, sizzling, frying, slowly beginning to burn.

"What do you mean?"

She hadn't even noticed the singer return. The room quieted further and Burgs' attention snapped back to the lady in red.

"Shh," he commanded, but his eyes widened with alertness.

"Come on, you can't leave me hanging on that—"

"Get down!" He yelled. The cellist stopped and a puzzled silence spread through the room as people looked towards Burgs in confusion. In the same moment Burgs pulled Xia down from her stool, the doors slammed open and a horde of slags rushed into the lounge, their Enforcers raised.

"EVERYONE. DOWN ON THE GROUND. DON'T MOVE. IRO NAGAWA. STEP FORWARD."

The room frantically obeyed the robotic baritone voice. Everyone stepped down from their chairs, huddling their glittered and well-dressed bodies to the floor. Xia whipped her head around the room. Iro Nagawa? Was the doctor behind the brain transplants here this entire time?

"IRO NAGAWA. STEP FORWARD."

There was a rustling towards the back. A man in a sharp blue suit scuttled along the floor, attempting to run for it. A ridiculous attempt. A shot through the air. Scattered screams. A hole blasted through his knee. One and a half legs. The man's deep-throated cries filled the room.

Two slags strode through the room towards the body, their movements heavy yet sleek.

"They aren't even real humans. Not anymore."

What had Burgs meant? Xia eyed them with newfound curiosity, trying to complete the mystery that Burgs had only begun to unfold.

To accept a life in the military was a somewhat mysterious endeavor. You were choosing to leave your family and your life behind—trading your difficult life as a civilian for a life of prestige. Because those that left for Military life didn't return; they lived outside the Walls in the Outer Hubs, places of supposed ease and comfort. Xia had never questioned it before. But as Burgs' words replayed in her mind, there was a new horror behind that mystery.

The slag stood over the man as he cradled his stump of a leg, the other half lying a few feet away. The red light blinked away at the temple of the slag's helm. The crippled man did little to hide his cries.

"NOT IRO," the slag spoke.

In unison, several other slags began scanning the room. ***"HE'S NOT HERE."***

The slags conferred among themselves in short, robotic commands, and then began to approach each individual in the room for in-depth scanning.

"Shit, Burgs," Xia murmured frantically. She had nothing to hide currently, especially in her tiny tight dress, but judging by Burg's newly revealed past, a deep-scan could be deadly for him.

The meatiest of the slags approached Xia first as she sat on the ground, her legs tucked underneath her. She gulped. Had they heard her gulp? Did they care? She stared up into the soulless visor. It wasn't hard to believe a human wasn't underneath there. Blinking, blinking, the red light blinked, it seemed to blink slower and slower. Finally, the blinking stopped, and the slag turned towards Burgs, his massive frame towering above him. Squatting on the floor, Burgs lost some of his gruffness. But there was still a little there. Or maybe it was something else.

Her heart pounded in her chest as the two stared off. Any second, they'd announce one of his infractions. He'd be carted off to the Void. Any second they—

But no. The blinking stopped. And meaty slag stepped over towards another cowering couple. Sweet relief cascaded over her. But if Burgs was able to get past a deep-scan, no doubt the notorious doctor could as well. She studied each individual in the room, wondering which one had the potential to be the despicable Dr. Nagawa. Then she noticed the two slags towards the back of the room. The only two not scanning the crowd. They were talking, but she couldn't make out the words. With the attention off herself, she tapped away at her temple and navigated to her eyescreen's audio maximizer settings, silencing the moaning cries of the shot man, and began to listen in on their conversation.

"UNIT 14, NO RESPONSE."

"LOCATION?"

"THE SUGAR TIT."

"WHY THERE?"

"PLACE OF EMPLOYMENT FOR HIS MOST RECENT PROSTITUTE."

"AND THE UNIT SENT TO HIS HOME?"

"HOME IS EMPTY."

"LOCATION CLOSE? WE GO THERE NEXT."

"11 NOKA CIRCLE. THREE BLOCKS DOWN."

That address rang no bells for Xia. And she just learned of the doctor's location today. Was it possible the slags had it wrong? As discreetly as she could, she checked through her messages and found the shared location from the blonde broad at the bar. 19 Advent Place. Had the slags already gone there? They were hell-bent on getting to him, but so was Xia. She cursed herself. She should have gone there as soon as she learned of his location.

"ALL CLEAR. MOVE OUT. SHARING NEXT DESTINA-TION."

And just as swift and thunderous as they came, the clog of slags exited the lounge. People slowly rose to their feet, with several of the staff rushing over to the newly maimed man.

"Well, that explains why good ole' doc wasn't here," Burgs said as he rose to his feet. He downed the rest of his drink in an exasperated gulp.

"What do you mean?"

"You think I only brought you here for the music? Nah, that ole' bastard loves to come here as much as I do. He'd never recognize me, though. But I'd recognize him anywhere."

"You mean he wasn't here?"

"I thought you were smart, dumb nuts. You think the slags would have missed him?"

"They missed you," Xia countered.

He waved his hand as if swatting a fly. "We should get outta here. It'll raise some eyebrows if people hear us talkin' about mechanical engineering after the slag fiasco."

Xia shook her head. As much as she wanted to know more, the 'slag fiasco' introduced a ticking time bomb. "I gotta go. If they're after Nagawa, I need to get to him first."

"What the? Are you outta your mind?"

She paid him no attention. "I'll pick up my suit later. Message you when I'm done. Here. No way I'm running in these." She slipped off the tight heels and tossed them into Burgs' arms. He barely caught them.

Before he could get in another word, she dashed out of the lounge, brazen and barefoot.

To the onlookers on the crowded city street, she was an upset one-night stand on a run of shame. Or perhaps a girl who backed out before going all the way. What didn't match that persona was the look of stoic determination on her face as she darted past the various people out and about for a night on the town.

For half a mile she ran through the cyber streets. Men yelled out after her in various cat calls ranging from inquisitive to obscene. The flashing advertisements and neon lights whizzed past in a colorful haze as she sprinted. Heart racing alongside her steps. A faint voice of reason nudged at her, reminding her she could have taken her cycle, but her body seemed to be moving ahead of her head. It was too late now.

She made it out of the heart of the Third Ward and into a subdivision with small, unassuming homes reminiscent of the homes she frequented with her Virgin clientele. But as soon as she scanned the street, the home of the doctor was made obvious. It blended in well enough from the outside, but it held a multitude of security measures. It was also the house with the most formidable gate.

She approached the house and scanned once more, looking for any hidden or weak spots. A camera sat by the front gate. Her head lowered as she eyed her attire. No boots, no suit, no weapons. Nothing except for her mods and cellchip. Even if she could break in, she wouldn't be able to fight past the security he undoubtedly had. She eyed the camera and took a gulp of air, wishing it was booze. No turning back now. She had to use what she had. Her scraped feet wobbled as she stepped towards the front gate and shook the bars. Before she could say anything, an intimidating robotic voice spoke from the camera.

"STATE YOUR NAME AND PURPOSE."

"I need to see Dr. Nagawa."

"STATE YOUR NAME."

She paused. "Xia Zuden."

"WHERE ARE YOUR SHOES?"

"Gone."

"WHY DO YOU SEEK THE DOCTOR?"

"I'm here to warn him."

The words came before she thought them. Uncommon for Xia. But the alcohol and adrenaline were a mixture for this recipe, whatever the recipe was. People came here seeking his abilities, and she guessed that people did not often come to speak of warning.

"WARN OF WHAT."

"Let me in and I'll tell you." It was the only leverage she had, and she hoped it would be enough.

Two scanners popped out of the gate and traced her body up and down. It found nothing, as she was practically wearing nothing. Once the scanners retracted back into the gate, it slowly opened. As soon as she entered, they shut behind her. She could barely believe it. She was in. The little black dress apparently had its advantages.

She approached the modest oak door and briefly debated whether to knock or simply go ahead and open it. Anxiety tapped away at the adrenaline. She was completely out of her element. A chill bit through the night air and goosebumps prickled up her arms. Was she cold? Or nervous? Couldn't be nervous. Not now.

Her knuckles floated a few inches from the door when it swung open revealing a man even meatier than the slag at the lounge. His eyes bore into her like cold steel. The goosebumps now goosemountains.

"Step aside, Gallo," a smooth voice purred from behind. The meaty man obeyed, but his eyes continued to bore into her. His massive feet thudded as he stepped to the side.

Xia stepped through the entryway, passing Gallo, and into the home. Its modesty halted at the front door. She had witnessed pure wealth in Burgs' apartment. But that wealth was a typical one. Here she felt as if she were transported to a different era. An era in the Before Times.

Emerald green swallowed the room whole, enveloping it in a rich velvet blanket. Velvet chairs, velvet couches, velvet curtains, all the same deep green. The walls were emerald, too, but barely visible behind the stream of rich ebony bookshelves, each shelf packed with hardbound books kept in pristine condition. Figurines and trinkets of pure gold and crystal gave pops of ornate opulence. Her eye caught the most glittering of all: a crystal carafe filled with a mossy green liquid. Seated behind the carafe,

in a large armchair, sat whom she knew to be the man she was looking fo
r.

"Dr. Nagawa."

His lips curled into a sly smile. "Xia, is it? Your name rings some distant
bells. Although I wouldn't expect you to appear so..." His beady eyes
traveled down her frame, lingering slightly on the hips, then falling on
her shoeless feet. "*Bare.* Had a rough night, did we?" His voice drawled
like a bored cat.

"You're going to have a rough night if you don't listen to me."

"Is that a threat?" Gallo took a thunderous step forward.

"Hush, Gallo. Darling, are you drunk? Your eyes look it. And your
clothes say it."

"I'm not drunk. I ran here from The Oasis. A bunch of slags stormed
in looking for you."

A flicker of intrigue shot through his eyes. Then it was gone. "And why
would they be looking for me?"

"I'm guessing it has something to do with the experiments you've been
doing. Swapping brains, and all that."

"So, you are aware of my talents." He crossed his thin legs, one twig
over the other, and brought the chartreuse to his lips. Xia could hear the
liquid as he smacked his lips. She twinged in disgust.

"You're putting people's brains into Virgin bodies. So that they can
get to the Revitalization Project. But that doesn't explain what you are
doing with the Virgins' brains."

His lips smacked again. "Like you said. I am an experimenter. I con-
duct experiments."

Dread panged at her chest. "So, they're not dead?"

He shook his head. "Who, the Virgins? Yes, they're all dead. Dead now,
at least. But you can do a lot with a dead brain. Or even one kept partially
alive. So many fun things you can do." His eyes glimmered with a childish
excitement that gave Xia the faintest urge to vomit.

"And the Daimyo?"

The glimmer deepened. He smiled. "The Daimyo allowed me to make
my breakthrough. His brain was the most fascinating to pick through.
Amazing how deep I've managed to cut into that family. I cut his daugh-

ter out of his wife, did you know? I saw her deepest insides. And I got to see the Daimyo's. Oh how I'd love to slice into that daughter. Closest I ever got was the umbilical cord. Shame, shame. But there's still time, no?"

The urge to vomit wasn't so faint anymore.

"Oh, don't look at me like that. You've cut into people yourself. Not nearly as many as I have. But after a certain number, they start to blur together. Isn't that right?"

She didn't take his bait. "What do you mean, breakthrough with the Daimyo?"

He eyed her with curiosity and stood. What Xia had thought to be a black suit was actually another deep shade of green, and it hugged his lean frame almost too comfortably. He stepped towards her, until they were less than a foot apart, his slender finger tracing along Xia's jawline as he stared down into her crimson eyes. Bile rose.

"You know, you've caused a bit of a hiccup for me. Your little faux mod business. My men had some difficulties narrowing in on some Virgins. Still do. It's a smart business you've established. The things we do for money, am I right?"

She recoiled and took a step back. "It's not about the money."

He laughed a high pitched laugh like a hyena. It hurt her ears. "If that were true, you'd be doing it for free."

"And be homeless? That money allows me to keep helping them. Help them from you. Because you're *killing* them."

"Touché, touché. But like you, I need to fund this lifestyle. And I found a way to do that. And I get to continue with my own endeavors. It's a win-win for everyone."

"Except for the people you're killing."

He smiled. "Sure."

"What was your breakthrough with the Daimyo?"

He sauntered back to the carafe and topped off the green liquid in his glass. "Why should I be telling you this? If you haven't noticed, it seems we are at odds with one another. Why should I share such things with the likes of you?"

The question came with genuine curiosity. As if testing her. She knew there was no reason for him to spill such secrets. And the leverage she had was minimal. But she noted the raw frenzy in his eyes. The pure joy in which he recalled his slicing and cutting. The obsession with green. This was a man gone mad by his dark passion. Without any weapons, this was what she'd need to lean into.

"Because you want to. Because it's groundbreaking and you have no one else to tell."

He chuckled. "I have Gallo."

"Something tells me Gallo doesn't quite get a kick out of it."

"And you will?"

"Try me."

They stared off, his green eyes glinting in the flickering candlelight's glow. She held the gaze.

"Sit down. Have a drink."

She hesitated for a moment, then grabbed the carafe and poured herself a small glass, pulling her dress down before taking a seat. The air stilled as her gaze lingered on the odd green hue of the liquid. It looked like poison. It could be poison. She wouldn't put it past the strange doctor to have built a tolerance and possibly even an affinity for it.

He eased back into his massive armchair, suit becoming one with the emerald velvet. "Do you know who I am?"

She sipped the poison. It wasn't poison, but it certainly didn't taste good. "I wouldn't be here if I didn't."

"Yes, yes, of course you know my *name*. And you are aware of my current business endeavors. But are you aware of my legacy?"

She cleared her throat. "I know you were a reputable doctor in the Virgin community. And I know you conducted surgery on military recruits."

His eyes flickered with the faintest of surprise. "Did you now? Someone has done their homework. Skipped the shoes, but not the research."

She curled her feet as much as she could under the seat. The more and more the buzz of the alcohol left her, the more exposed she felt.

"But are you aware of the nature of the surgery?"

"I can only assume it has something to do with their brains."

He took a long sip. "You assume correctly. It was a phenomenal feat. Continues to be. And it's the reason why I can rest comfortably here knowing those slags are running amok looking for me. Doubt they will find me. And they'll never act against me."

He topped off his glass, even though it was practically full to begin with. He was enjoying her curiosity, enjoying making her wait.

"The brain is a beautiful thing. Filled with so many delicious parts. Different parts have different responsibilities. One of the most special of those parts is the prefrontal cortex. Your choice to come here, to skip the shoes and drink my chartreuse, that's all possible because of this." His slender finger tapped three times on his forehead.

"So imagine what would happen if that part of the brain were tampered with? You mess with the cerebellum, your balance is gone. You play with the Broca's area, goodbye to your tongue. So I played. I played a lot. A lot of wasted brains, wasted potential. But then I got it right."

A drop of dread bubbled deep within her. Burgs' words echoed once more. *They aren't really human. Not anymore.* "What did you do?"

"I planted AI chips into their prefrontal cortexes, allowing the complete submission of will to an outside source. They don't answer to themselves. They answer to their chips."

So the FRF Force, the supreme military division of perfect robotic force is due to just that: a *robotic* force. Walking cyborgs with no free will.

"And who controls the AI?"

He smirked. "Oh, wouldn't you like to know."

The bubble frothed. "What about new slags? Clearly, you aren't still working for the military."

He crossed his other leg. "No. There were...*creative* differences. There was nothing left for me to do. I grew tired of the same procedure. I taught the procedure to others. I was bored. So, I retired. But I've continued my work. Continued to sell my services."

"And that's how you started the brain transplants."

"Precisely."

"And your 'big breakthrough'? With the Daimyo?"

She leaned closer with unfiltered anticipation. His ego allowed him to spill so much already. She prayed he wasn't about to hold back.

"Well, I needed to find out why the government wanted Virgins. I'm sure you've already figured out the fraudulence of the Revitalization Project."

She nodded, although this was the first time it was truly confirmed.

"Why were they enticing Virgins? And if they needed them, why not just take them? The opportunity was twofold. People wanted to become Virgins, and I needed a closer look at what made Virgins so special."

"But how did people know about the Revitalization Project? How did they know to come to you, that this was even an option?"

Nagawa looked with a strange fondness towards Gallo, who stood defensively by the door like a boulder. "Gallo is one of many *associates*. You of all people know the channels of communication run deep here in our Cyber City. I have access to many of those channels. It was quite easy to have Gallo and the others drop those seeds of information. A Utopia, an escape from this world, of brain transplants. Such a concept would reek terror mere decades ago. But with our world's obsession—no, our *dependence*—on such technology, the concept of brain transplants was welcomed. It didn't take long for people to come crawling to me—once I opened the door.

"So I studied. I sliced and studied. It's amazing how different a Virgin's brain is from our own. From the very first modular device implanted in someone, the entire framework of neural connections are altered in how they process information. And the longer one has mods, the less gray matter is housed in the brain. But still, I didn't see why they couldn't just *take* the Virgins. Why trick them? But my old friend the Daimyo held the answer.

"I never would have had my men target him in the first place. Too big of a star. And too good of a fighter. But he just happened to be at the wrong place at the wrong time. So that was his fate. But he wouldn't allow us to kidnap him alive. He committed suicide. The Daimyo was no fool, but how foolish for him. That final act of valor is what allowed me to complete the puzzle."

The green liquid swirled in his glass, then swirled on his tongue, wetting his mouth before he finished his monologue.

"The Daimyo was a man of pure discipline. Pure calm. His brain held no room for fear. And you know what fear does? It plays with your brain. Your amygdala, specifically. And every Virgin I took had a very messy amygdala. Because they were taken in fear. They *lived* in fear. But the Daimyo was as cool as a Virgin-grown cucumber. And so his amygdala was in pristine condition. And that is why they need willing Virgins. Willing *hopeful* Virgins. They need unaltered brains."

Xia eyed him with skepticism. Clearly, the man's obsession lay with the physical mind, but was that truly what the government was after? "It seems to be quite the leap to assume they want Virgin brains. What would they even do with them? What else do you know?"

His lips twisted nastily. "You asked before. Who controls the AI?"

A sudden bang outside snapped them from their exchange. For the first time, Xia saw concern on his thin face.

"Gallo, what—"

"Sir, slags are here. We need to get you in the basement."

A flash of indignation crossed his face. "What? Impossible! They couldn't be here."

"They are. Sir, the basement."

Nagawa regained his composure as quickly as it had attempted to escape. "That's quite alright. What better way to tell of my past accomplishments than by *showing* it? Let them come in."

Xia didn't know what game he was getting at, but she couldn't imagine any situation where a room full of slags would be good. Where would they be coming from? She scanned quickly. Towards the front. Blood pumped through her chest as she slowly began backing away towards the other end of the room. She'd find a back door, get out somewhere—

"Where do you think you're going? You don't need to worry. They won't lay a finger on you. Just like they aren't going to lay a finger on me—"

His words were cut off by the smattering of blood and skin exploding onto his own pale face as Gallo's head blew off his body. The slags were here, laser guns roaring. Xia dove behind the nearest cover, a large ebony wood desk in the corner of the room. She was so close to the door. If only she had been a few moments faster. Instead, she lay huddled under the desk as the commotion ensued. Behind her, atop a large buffet table with more crystal glasses and various liquids, was a large mirror in which Xia could see the slags enter the room one by one. The glasses shook as they kicked Gallo's large body out of the way.

Three, four, five slags crowded into the room, but she knew there were more outside. Was the drumming their bootsteps or her pulse?

"DR. IRO NAGAWA. YOU ARE TO BE TAKEN TO FHQ IMMEDIATELY."

The doctor straightened himself. "I don't believe so."

"IF YOU RESIST, WE WILL TAKE YOU BY FORCE."

Xia watched the exchange in the mirror, but she wasn't entirely sure what she was seeing. The doctor stared at the slag, eyes unblinking, as if waiting. But the slags had no reaction. One of the slags stomped behind Nagawa and grabbed his arms, placing them in obsidian cuffs.

Pure shock washed over the doctor's face. "This is impossible! No, what are you doing? I *made* you! Look at me!"

Again, the doctor widened his eyes, commanding them to look at him. No reaction from the slags. The one engaged in his staredown took out a syringe and slammed it into the doctor's side.

"How dare you!" His arms jolted manically as he attempted to fight the slag, but a second later his body slumped as the syringe's contents made its way into his bloodstream.

She needed to leave. Now. Whatever hold the doctor thought he had over the slags, he was clearly mistaken. It was now or never. She crouched along, making her way towards the door—

"SCAN FOR OTHER INHABITANTS. CLEAR THE AREA," The leader commanded.

Shit. She was almost there, but the last few feet would leave her in full view. There was no time. She rushed to the door.

"GIRL BY THE DOOR."

The slags turned and stared towards her, one by one, taking in her appearance.

"LIKELY ONE OF HIS PROSTITUTES." Their heads turned towards the leader.

He swung the limp body of Dr. Nagawa over his shoulder as he laid his final command. *"**KILL THE WHORE.**"*

29

The Mad Doctor's Lair

There was once a time when Xia found herself in trouble. Not the usual trouble. She was always in that. But a time where she truly thought that she was about to fall across the border between this world and the next.

She had no weapons. They had been knocked out of her hands and taken.

She had no allies. She had come alone.

She had no strength. The wound at her side sucked it all away.

The street was dark and hazy as her vision dimmed with her fading stamina. Her mods could barely stay powered. The gang leader taunted her, but she could hardly make out the words. Something about lies and weakness. Or was it flies and meekness? Something about a grave mistake. Or just steak? She thought of her grandfather's smile when she brought home that meat. How maybe she'd be seeing that smile soon again. She just had to knock on death's door. She was so close already, already on the street, just a few steps away from the reaper's house—

And that's when she saw it. The thing that sucked her away from Death's avenue, back to the grimy alley in Cyber City's Second Ward. Her vision cleared as she stared at the ticket to another day. The small slits at the bottom of his shoes, concealing hidden blades. Stepping closer.

Ready to strike. And so she knew how she'd strike. She led into her weakness, seemingly drifting away, while her senses only sharpened in anticipation.

She drew her eyes closed as his footsteps stopped before her. The world stilled as he drew his foot back, and despite the distant sounds of the street beyond, Xia swore she could hear the faintest of 'clicks' as the blade unsheathed from his boot. Not a second too late. Her eyes jolted open with every last ounce of newfound adrenaline as she maneuvered out of the way, grabbed his leg, and surged forward on top of him, her grasp on his leg only tightening. The leader yelped in surprise. The other members glanced between themselves, confused at the turn of events.

One of them pulled out a gun. Again, Xia let herself succumb to a moment of weakness, giving the leader a brief sense of security. A sense of security that was squashed as the bullet rang out from the member's pistol and Xia flipped herself over once more. Her body was already drenched in blood from the stab wound at her side, but now her face was too as the gang leader's face blew apart onto her own.

The members exploded in a fury of shock and confusion. Feeding off the adrenaline, Xia sprinted away into the night, her now crimson hair flowing behind her.

Now, with that final command from the slag to "Kill the Whore", Xia saw the border once more. How easily she could cross it. In a matter of mere seconds, an Enforcer would shoot a hole clean through her head. Her current spot on the floor called for it. But just like that other fateful day, it's in the moments of acceptance that clarity is found. That escapes normally hidden by fear and panic become apparent. She didn't even have to think. She pulled at the buffet table, having already noted that the massive mirror was attached to the piece of woodwork. In a colossal crash it came thundering forward, giving her the briefest moment to escape. She heard the electric whomps as the guns shot behind her. One hit close, too close, as the laser's trajectory burnt the hairs on her arm.

"341. FOLLOW HER."

Xia fell into the kitchen. No time to take in the room, to take in the jars of flesh on the table—until she picked one up to throw at the tinted window above the sink. She grimaced at the floating piece of organ. Then she smashed it through the pane, glass from the window and the jar shattering everywhere. She hopped onto the sink and jumped through the broken window.

Her lead was narrow. She sprinted in the direction away from the slags, towards the backyard, knowing damn well it could be a dead end. Her leg and arm bled from her jagged cuts. She may have escaped death's door inside the Doctor's house, but she was close to finding it again in his yard. Her breath wheezed in the chilly night air. The last of the alcohol that had been in her system evaporated with the appearance of the slags, and she was now left with nothing but regret at the stupidity of her actions. What the hell had she been thinking?

"Xia," a hoarse whisper broke through the yard.

Her head whipped around, but she couldn't see the source.

"Get in here," the voice said.

"Burgs?" She did a quick scan, and that's when she noticed the small break in the grassy terrain by the house. The ground lifted a crack, the terrain cut out in a perfect square.

"In, here," he commanded sternly, as if wrangling a stubborn dog.

She could hear the shattering of more glass behind her as the slag continued his pursuit. She didn't need telling twice. In three steps she swooped underneath the crevice and onto a narrow stairwell, illuminated only by Burgs' glowing holotech.

"What in the Hell's Void do you think you are doing here?" Burgs hissed. Xia snapped a finger to her mouth, signaling him to hush. He held up the small black box he used at the Oasis. "Nobody can hear us. And nobody can scan for us, either."

"What? How?"

"I may not be able to make my own of their deep-scanners, but I do know how to get around them." He tapped on his wrist, emitting a flashlight. His deep brown eyes trailed up and down her bloody frame. "You look like shit."

"I know."

"That's what you get for runnin' off on your own. Seriously, what the hell was going through your mind? I thought you were smarter than that."

She glanced away. "I did too."

The briefest of chuckles. "Seems spirits give you the ole' liquid courage. Don't drink before a job, do ya?"

"No, only afterward. Usually it just puts me to sleep."

"Well, I'm just glad you made it out alive."

She blinked. "You are? If I died, you wouldn't have to help me with this whole 'Save the Virgins' thing. And you could keep my gun."

He snickered. "Come on. I'm guessing you talked with the Doc, but I don't know the extent of what he told you. Best to see it yourself."

He descended the concrete stairs, slowly submerging himself into the black hole at the bottom. She gave one last glance upwards before following suit.

"Won't the slags find us down here? If you found this hole, I'm sure the slags can too."

His hand touched along the wall, trying to find the light switch. "Nah, I only found it because I knew what to look for. I had a hell of a time getting over that back wall. They'll see the mess I made and assume you ran for it that way. So, in the mean-time, we'll hole up here. There we go." His hand found the switch. The room's lights flickered on, and it took a moment for Xia's eyes to adjust. Once they had, she almost gagged.

Dozens and dozens of jars like the one she had thrown against the window lined the walls in a sickening exhibit of human anatomy. Pickled hearts, pickled lungs, pickled pieces of flesh and organs of which Xia didn't quite know what they were, but she knew they belonged on the inside of the body. Never outside. Never in a jar.

Her eyes flitted around the room, taking in the machinery, the surgical tools, the mountains of books and notes, purposely avoiding the headless body lying atop the operating table in the center. Finally, her eyes could flit no more and they landed on the exposed muscle and windpipe.

"Pretty awful, eh?"

She nodded. She had known what the doctor was up to, but to see it in the literal flesh brought an elevated sense of horror. It didn't matter how much she knew, how much she had thought about it. There was a veil shielding her from the true atrocity. And now that she was here, the veil was lifted.

She walked along the shelves lining the walls, reading the various labels on the preserved organs. The names weren't recognizable until she reached the wall of brains. Her stomach hinged. Genya, Ettaro. Genya, Leikko. The image of the beautiful babbling girl, eyes brimming with tears that brightened in ecstasy when the body of her husband walked through the door, played in Xia's own brain. And then the guilt. She could have saved them. But she had walked away. Leaving them to their demise. Leaving them to this.

She kept walking. She couldn't remember the Daimyo's given name, but she knew Mai's. And so she recognized his jar. Takamura, Masato. The source of the mad doctor's breakthrough. Xia couldn't coincide the memory of the powerful warrior with this lump of mass in the jar before her. But this jar lay different than the rest. While the other various pieces of flesh lay floating in a sickly tainted green liquid, the Daimyo's jar was red.

Burgs still stood by the switch, watching Xia as the faintest of emotions flickered across her paling face, her body leaving a trickling trail of blood from the cuts on her arms and leg. A bloody cherry on top of the fleshy cake of horror. Even Burgs felt the remnants of alcohol in his stomach rumble a bit. Just a bit.

"Kid, what all did he tell you? Any of this come as a surprise?"

She unpeeled her eyes from the Daimyo's brain. "No. Except he didn't get into just what he was doing on the brains of the slags. When they stormed in, it was almost like he expected them to...obey him or something. He was surprised they'd act against him."

Burgs crossed his arms across his thick chest. "Checks out. He likely put some type of code into the AI chip that recognizes him as a decision-maker. Was likely overwritten."

She nodded. "He mentioned that. Right before the slags came in.

"That's the reason why I say them slags are barely even human anymore. I suppose you could ask, 'what makes us human?' Question as old as time. Done my time thinkin' about it. That's for sure—"

"Burgs," Xia cut in. She could tell the alcohol was still buzzing in his system. Seemed he was one to drink before the job.

"Right. So, once you graduate the Military Academy, you get an AI chip implanted into your brain. It was sold to us as a chip that would further enhance our abilities. But I had caught wind of the intention earlier, once I made that bug and heard just what the hell this crazy doctor was up to. These weren't special ability enhancing chips. They were command centers. Stuck into the decision-making part of the brain. Relinquishing all autonomy to the commands of the little chip in their brain. Whatever the chip told them to do, they would now do. The entire military is essentially a squad of robots."

Those visors always did seem like a soulless void to Xia. Little did she know it practically was. "Are the people inside aware? Is it like being trapped in your own body?"

"I don't know, kid. I sure as hell hope not. But I don't know."

30

Time Ticking

The two sat in uncomfortable silence in the corner of the concrete room, the only corner not adorned with some type of dead flesh. The view of the body was slightly better. Xia only had to stare at the poor sap's toes. She looked for something to cover the body with, but found nothing, and grew sick of looking. Didn't want to walk past the brains more than she had to.

Burgs passed his flask towards Xia, which she declined. Potentially the first time she had ever turned down the stuff. But she still felt the buzz of danger and didn't need any more reckless encounters. He raised his brows but said nothing more.

In the past 24 hours, their relationship had morphed from slight intrigue and annoyance to a whole different beast. He told her more than he'd ever told anyone, even Fay. It took Fay years of just being a constant presence to know all she did. But Burgs had told the silver girl everything. He wasn't exactly sure why. Was it the intrigue? Was it the bourbon? Or did he just like the kid? She held a gall and level head that he wished for his own son. But that was his own fault.

Xia wasn't thinking about Burgs. Or the bourbon. Or the now scarring cuts, worsened by her lack of clothing. She was thinking about the headless body, and how she needed to move more quickly. Because the threat wasn't gone. It was only delayed. And soon it would come full force.

She now understood why Kibou had told her not to pursue Nagawa. The wise old bastard knew more than he let on. Getting rid of the doctor would halt the snatchings, sure. But it meant the market of supposed 'Virgins' signing up for the project would dwindle. And the government would catch sight of that. And eventually, they'd pursue more severe methods in taking them. Because, as Nagawa exposed, the government wants pure Virgin brains. Lots of them. Supposedly, the government couldn't simply take them, because they needed the brains free of any trauma. That's likely why they went after Nagawa. They figured out the volunteers for the project didn't have those untouched brains, and that Nagawa was the cause of that problem.

It all seemed so fantastical, so *horrible.* The image of Prime Minister Zoke came to her. Could he truly be the spearhead behind such a horrendous operation? Because while the FRF held the potential for wicked, and there was evidence for it every day, there was something harmless about Zoke—something almost pathetic. It was exacerbated by the fact that he was rarely seen on the news anymore, and never seen inside the city proper. Maybe that's because he wasn't the leading figure, but just a mere puppet. He certainly looked like it.

So what would the FRF's next step be? Whatever it was, it would come fast. She needed to move faster.

"C'mon, I think they've cleared out by now." Burgs stood and Xia followed swiftly behind, not wanting to be in the grisly room a second longer than she needed to be. As they neared the top of the stairs, Burgs scanned for several seconds before confirming the slags were gone.

"It's possible they left some type of traps around. Unlikely, but possible. We'll go back the way I came. Want to avoid the camera out front. Keep scanning as you go. Note your nose. One of the best indicators of an out-of-the-ordinary electromagnetic presence, especially of the slags' kind, is a slight tingling in the nose."

Her nostrils inadvertently flared. Then she followed Burgs further towards the backyard. The chilly air stung at her cuts. The terrain changed from grass to rock as they approached the massive crushed hole in the wall that wrapped around the yard.

"Can see what you mean about having a rough time getting into the place."

"I didn't do this. Slags must've when they were following you. Told you they'd head this way. Now we make a run for it."

And so they ran. The adrenaline and potential for safety carried her along. Feet hitting dirt, grass, stone, passing homes, groves of S-trees, and eventually people as they made it back into the Third Ward. And her feet cried with every tender step. Xia ignored any and all glances that went her way. Which was quite a lot, considering it looked like she escaped a sadist's basement. She pretty much had.

"Shit, what happened to you guys?" Leonardo's expression morphed from amusement to concern as his eyes registered the wounds.

She ignored him. "Leonardo, I need you to get Mai. She can't walk right now because of the surgery. You need to get her and bring her here. Grab my injections out of the fridge. Message me when you are there and I'll unlock the door. Fast as you can. Go."

He asked no questions. Just gave a nod and ran off, his handsome face not showing an ounce of his usual foolery. His scar grew more fitting.

She turned back towards Burgs. "I don't know if the slags were able to get a good scan on me. I also don't know if they even would care enough to pursue me. But figured it'd be safest to hole up somewhere else. Don't worry, we won't stay here."

Burgs huffed. "I think we're past that point. It's alright. Just keep it clean. I like it tidy."

She smiled. "Thanks."

As the water drenched Xia's skin with an enveloping heat, and the steam filled the room like a hot spring, Xia was thankful for the night. Because it meant that she didn't have to go back home. It meant she could stay here. Stay in this divine bathroom. There was no limited supply of water here. There were no frigid showers as the water slowly rose in temperature. It came out piping and limitless. The cuts and tears littering her arms and leg were forgotten. All she could feel was the steaming aquatic droplets from heaven—

"Put me down! Put me DOWN! Where is Xia?! XIA!"

And the bliss was gone. Xia groaned and shut off the water, then proceeded to wipe herself off with a towel. Even the towel was fluffier than a cloud. She threw on a t-shirt and shorts, courtesy of Fay, and left the sauna of a bathroom, into the battleground.

"Has she been whining the whole way?"

Leonardo set the cursing Mai onto the couch. "No, she's been knocked out the whole way. Even slept in the med pod. Of course it was right in the elevator that she decided to throw a hissy fit."

"What the hell was I supposed to do?" Mai snapped. "What would you do if you woke up in this buffoon's arms?"

He smirked. "I'd expect a kiss at the least."

Mai ignored him. "Xia, what the hell is going on? Why are we here?" Her eyes widened. "What happened to you?"

The story was told in bits and pieces. Between Mai drifting in and out of medicated sleep, and Leonardo and Fay running off to swap places with the others (who then needed the story told as well), Xia was exhausted by the time light broke through the sky. Today was one of those glaring days when you could almost make out the blinding lemon in the sky. But at that point, Xia was desperate for sleep. And Mai wouldn't allow for it. She had too many questions.

"So Dr. Nagawa figured that the government needs...pure brains?" Her nose shriveled at the word. Mai sat up on the white couch, the life and vitality she always carried slowly coming back to her. "And that the mods somehow affect our brain matter?" She gulped at the prospect that now her brain was somehow altered.

"Apparently. I had my skepticism at first. But with his experience with the government, and after seeing his basement, I'm guessing he got it right."

Burgs nodded from across the room, an entire cup of espresso in his hand. Seemed he was alright with swapping some caffeine for a night's sleep.

Xia continued. "And with him gone, we need to move fast. I want that scouting mission done as soon as possible. Like, tomorrow fast."

Mai straightened herself, wincing while she did so. "Tomorrow? There's no way I'll be able to go!"

"I know. Which is why you won't."

She exploded. "What?! After all I've gone through? You're telling me I'm not going? Like *hell* I'm not going! If I could walk I'd slug you Xia!" With her unkempt hair and sweat-sheened, pale face, she looked like an absolute lunatic.

"Relax. It's not for nothing. You'll still be involved. Burgs is still making your suit. I'll record the entire mission. It'll be like you're right there. But from the comfort of this nice couch." She kicked the white piece of furniture with her bare foot for effect. Mai frowned.

"Can I watch it while it happens?"

"No. We won't be able to transmit any signals out. Need to be as elusive as possible." Xia glanced towards Mai's arm. "Have you taken your injection for today?"

"Yeah, Leo helped me," Mai grunted.

"Good. But that does remind me..." Xia glanced uneasily towards Burgs. "Holotech. To use the suit, you'll need ret-mods. We'll get you the most basic, least invasive. Basically a starter pack to be able to use connector tech."

Mai looked crestfallen. "Connector tech?"

"Yeah. That's what allows you to use special mod devices. Like the slag helmet. If you put it on right now, you can't use most of its features. So we'd have to get you some basic ret-mods."

"What's one more thing, right? Add it to the list!" She threw her hands up and tried to smile, but the smile fell into a wince. Xia pretended not to notice.

The plan was both simple, and very much anything but.

The trio stood in their slag fits. Fay, the most curvaceous of the three, Renjiro, the skinniest, and that was really the only distinction between them. The three were essentially identical, both to each other and to any true slag.

The revelation that slags were seemingly controlled via artificial intelligence made the scouting mission even more daunting. Humans are inconsistent. They can be bribed, influenced, intimidated; AI can't. Above all, the group didn't know the full scope of the AI's power. But they did know it was limited. And that was one advantage.

One thing Burgs did know was that the artificial intelligence chips run on processing power—a power that is finite. They speculated that was the reason their entire fake slag operation at the Pagoda could last for so long: keeping tabs on what slags were hired and where was not a priority on the AI's list. Due to this, they were able to keep guard unbothered by other slags. It also meant they should be able to scout the area unsuspected as long as they kept themselves in line.

Xia's head buzzed with information and caffeine. Burgs had given the three of them data chips containing every piece of military intel he knew from his academy days. How the slags operate individually and as a unit. How to identify a Divisioner, and how to avoid them. How to walk. How to talk. How *not* to talk. It was so much. And yet it was already go time. Fay had suggested waiting another day, but two had already whizzed by. Time was a finite resource. And the clock was ticking.

"Alright," Burgs said, standing before them. He took a long drag from his cigarette. "Scan me." Fay and Ren immediately emitted their scan replicator signal, red lights flashing in synchronization. It took Xia a second to access the command on her visor. "Damn it Xia, faster! Those slags will detect the faintest of abnormalities. You must be perfect."

She hadn't had time to be perfect. "Right. Sorry."

"You fuck up, you're done for. These slags are operating under precision. Automation. Something we don't have. So your objective is simple. To remain undetected. Fly completely under the radar. Follow your objective, stick to your script. Fay, you'll be recording. Constantly. Ren, you'll be scanning. Constantly. And Xia, you'll be taking the lead on scouting. Questions?"

Xia could tell he was enjoying this. Barking out orders like a commander himself. A real fervor bubbled up from deep inside him over the past two days as he delved into every step and point of their mission. There was a light in his eyes Xia had only caught the faintest glimpses of. Perhaps he hadn't only joined the military back in the day for the tech. A part of him truly wanted to lead.

Their IDs made them Majors. Not grunts, yet not leading Commanders, they'd be able to venture independently without having underlings seek them out for instructions or approval. It also gave them access to the facilities, and free use of the trams.

The first step was to acquire a tram. And once that was acquired, stay in there as long as possible, as that was the one spot they'd be safest. They'd be able to talk freely, since there were allegedly no surveillance bugs inside a tram. When Xia asked why, Burgs had said the military ran into interference issues with having so many mods and tech all utilizing communication tools. Thus, they needed to be selective in where it was placed. When asked how he knew this was still the case, it led to the second objective. To pick up Commander Young.

"Commander Young is the entire reason this is a scouting mission and not a suicide mission. When asked your objective, answer that you are transporting Commander Young. When asked for what purpose you are transporting him by anyone but a Divisioner, answer that it is restricted information. If a Divisioner asks, state that you are transporting him to HQ."

"What's HQ?"

"I don't know."

"How do you not know?"

"Don't question me, kid."

And those were the instructions. Leave the outer wall into Outer Hub C, one of the six outside hubs housing military and government officials. Not technically within the confines of Cyber City, but still not free in the outside world. That was the last step.

"It's a scouting mission. So, scout. Take your time in there before picking up Commander Young. Study their points of entry, their points of exit. Take everything in. And when it's time, meet with Young."

He wouldn't say who exactly this Commander Young was. He was clearly a slag of some importance. How the hell could they trust one of those? Whatever the reason, he didn't give it. Fay had given Xia the slightest of headshakes when she was about to press further. So she held her tongue and accepted the cryptic script.

"If, at any point, you are given a question you can't answer, what do you do?"

In unison, the trio cocked their heads down and repeated in their robotic baritone voices, "RECOMPUTING."

Burgs nodded. "And then use as much time as you need. Issues with the code can happen all the time. Especially with interferences between the brain signal and the chip implant. Remember. You only get one Hail Mary. One chance out of an encounter. And if you use it, it's a doozy. You all have access to it, but you can only use it once."

The saving grace was labeled *'Help'* on their command screen. What that help exactly was, Burgs wouldn't say. "It's better you're just as surprised as the slags."

"Rely on your instincts. They may have the power of artificial intelligence on their side, which means they'll be looking for any abnormalities. But they are missing intuition. You've still got that. Use it. Any questions?" He glanced between the three of them. Xia shook her helmeted head. There were questions, but none that could be answered now. Do or die. It was time to do. "Alright, get on out of here. We'll be waiting."

The three shuffled outside the door, and as Burgs watched the three of them leave, cigarette hanging from the corner of his lips, he wondered if that'd be the last time he'd see them alive.

31

THE SCOUTING MISSION

If Xia hadn't felt she was a slag by the uniform, she'd have felt it by the looks of the people passing by. The crowd along the city streets naturally moved as far away from them as possible, as if the trio held a 10-foot radius electrical forcefield. Most kept their heads down and eyes averted. But she could still see the fleeting emotions of disgust, of envy, of fear. Lots and lots of fear.

She had the soundbox, but the trio kept quiet as they paraded through the block. At the corner of Main and Giroko, with skyscrapers so high they could touch the city's dome, they took a left towards the Northern Military Block. A direction Xia never took, as she never had a reason to. Not until now.

Unlike other parts of the city, where the switch from the bustling and populated parts would slowly morph into its broken-down and dilapidated counterparts, the military blocks were different. One street marked the difference from ordinary civilian life to military mania—between chaotic urban neon and the bellicose order of the Freesian military. Xia stole a glance behind her at a machine massage parlor that likely didn't get much business given its suboptimal location. Then she looked forward towards the base's metal monster of an entrance. She gulped. Then they proceeded.

The massive wall of steel encompassed the entirety of the base with a set of titanium doors allowing for entry. Surprisingly, there was nobody standing guard at the entrance. Perhaps nobody needed to. The tech and steel were seen as security enough.

As they approached the doors, and Xia began taking in the scanners and various devices that littered the panel beside them, Ren stepped forward with methodical confidence and placed his hand atop one of the scanners. The doors registered the unique frequency of the uniform and instantaneously opened, revealing the base inside.

They entered.

The base made Cyber City feel cozy. It was expected of the slags' quarters, but as she watched the hordes of military trainees in their green jumpsuits mill about, she felt a twinge of gratitude that she never pursued the military track. Living here for a year would have been rough. Their suits kept their bodies at a steady temperature, but Xia could tell it was a solid 10 degrees cooler here, for whatever reason. The buildings loomed over them with imposing grit, the concrete walls gray and identical. No need for any pleasing aesthetics. No need for individuality. As they walked along the main road, Ren broke away from the trio and approached one of the military trainees.

"YOU. NAME."

The gangly boy stared upwards with sunken eyes that rounded in fear. "I-Ivan Toren, sir." Xia noticed the golden circled "C" sewn into the chest of his top. Demeanor reflective of his rank.

Ren nodded and continued walking. Xia didn't know what the hell he was doing, but she continued behind him. Her eyes darted around from person to building, looking for the nearest uninhabited tram as well as keeping an eye out for potential dangers. Yet she couldn't help but take it all in. She couldn't believe where she was. She was actually there. And it was all thanks to Burgs.

Xia was well aware of the pitifulness of her situation. Oh, how she had been in over her head. The more she studied for the scouting mission, and the more Burgs had gone over the plan, the more she realized how little grasp she had on the situation. Her entire life she had worked alone. The fods were entirely her doing. Kibou had sought her out to help the Virgins, *alone.* And yet what chance did she have at success without

Burgs' help? She had suspected he would have some useful intel. But this was more than some aide. She had taken a backseat.

She didn't like that.

"THERE." Ren voiced, the first time they had spoken to each other since leaving the apartment. Up ahead, outside a particularly large and depressing building, sat an unoccupied tram. An enormous black **C** sat atop the massive double doors to the building, marking the housing quarters for the lowest-ranked individuals. Like he had done it a thousand times before, Ren approached the side of the boxy vehicle and placed his hand atop a sleek blue panel, signaling the door to slide open. A moment later, they were inside. A collective breath was taken.

Xia activated the soundbox from Burgs. While he was sure that the trams would be a safe place to talk, one could never take too many precautions. The tram featured a driver's and passenger's seat, and two rows of seats facing each other in the back, pure black enveloping them. The three sat along the bench seats, temporarily leaving the driver's seat empty.

"We made it," Fay said. Even with the slag voice distorter, Xia sensed the relief in her voice.

"Still have a ways to go. That was the easy part," Xia replied.

Fay slid into the driver's seat, her previously designated role.

Ren spoke. "You can sit with Fay."

Xia shrugged. "I don't mind."

"Go sit with Fay."

Without his face, Xia couldn't place the intent behind the words. Not that Ren showed much expression anyway. She knew nothing about him. And until now, that never bothered her. But now she wished she at least knew a little—that she had a couple scratches on his hunk of ice. Was it even ice? Maybe he was just dull. Still, she obliged and took the seat next to Fay.

"I'm gonna drive around a bit. Get a layout of the land. Then we can head into the Outer Hub."

"And look for this Commander Young guy?"

"That's right."

Fay maneuvered the tram around a tight corner, slowly driving past trainees and slags alike. Nobody gave them a second glance.

"Do you know who he is?"

It took Fay a few moments to answer. "Yes. It's his old roommate. From the academy. I'm not sure what all Burgs told you. He seems to like you. But he's a tough nut to crack."

The booze seemed to crack it just fine. "The one that got injured? And they weren't sure if he'd be able to undergo the procedure?"

"That's the one. Seems he has told you some things. Well, he had the procedure. And it...kind of worked. The only one who knows that is Burgs."

"*Kind of?*"

"Yeah. He'll hear and feel the commands from the chip. Kind of like an intrusive thought that the body just obeys. But with a little effort, he can ignore it. He's the reason why Burgs is able to stay up to date on so much of the slags' doings. They don't keep in touch all that often, but after you recruited us for help, he got in touch with Young immediately."

A true slag on the inside. Again, Xia was struck by how much she was relying on Burgs. "You guys are more help than I anticipated."

Fay laughed, the sound resembling a monster through the voice modifier. "Yeah, without us there's no way you would have been able to do all this."

"Well, I didn't know slags weren't autonomous. Bribes and stealth can go a long way." Her hand caressed the Enforcer at her side. Burgs had returned it to her for the mission. She'd still never gotten to properly use it. Something told her that would change soon. "But you can't bribe a robot."

Fay took another turn, now riding alongside the steel outer gate. "Don't think of it as a debt. Honestly, Burgs was itching at the chance to do something like this. He's been wanting to stick it to the FRF for ages. Lurking around right under their noses was right up his alley. And he's grown very sick of our charade at the Pagoda. We all have. But we do it for the money. It's kinda nice to do something for a *different* reason."

What an odd sentiment. Every mission, every perk, every exchange Xia had made, in any setting, involved one of the parties getting *some-*

thing from the other person. Money, a favor, a bottle of booze. Always something. She wasn't used to this kind of dynamic. Such altruism was unnerving.

"You got a good layout rendered, Ren?"

Renjiro nodded, then activated a small holographic display a foot from his visor. A small map layout of the military hub floated in the air. "Traffic increases closer to the main path, around the trainees' housing buildings, and the dining facility. Haven't detected any patterns in movements."

"Great. Alright, step 2. To the Outer Hub. Xia, get in the back. If we're picking up the commander, he'd be in the front."

Xia nodded and went in the back, taking a seat across from Ren.

"Any way I can get that map—" She was cut off by a small notification on her eye screen, signaling a file was sent to her via her direct channel. "Thanks."

"Keep that in your secure database on your suit, not your personal one."

"Right."

"Commander approaching," Fay spoke from the front. Xia's heart rate quickened, so she activated the pulse steadier in her suit, one of the dozens of handy features installed. As they approached the gate, a commander walked towards the tram and Fay came to a slow stop while lowering the window.

"STATE YOUR PURPOSE FOR TRAM USAGE."

"Retrieve and Transport Commander Varen Young."

"NUMBER OF PERSONNEL."

"Three."

And just like that, the commander stepped back towards the gate, and it opened. Just like that. Xia's mouth fell open in disbelief. No scanning of any kind. They didn't even have to step outside. Everything was going well.

A little too well.

They drove through the gate, and at first, Xia thought something happened to the windows of the tram.

"Did they tint or something?"

Ren shook his head. "The plasma sphere surrounding the city doesn't extend over the Outer Hubs. Instead, it's covered by titanium. Permanent nighttime here."

The city's skies were nothing to marvel at. But there was still the semblance of the sun on a blinding day. There was still color through the smog. Permanent darkness didn't seem ideal, especially for the government elite.

Ren read her thoughts. "I'm sure the Hub makes up for the darkness in other ways." He glanced around. "We won't be able to scan the perimeter in here this time. We'll need to do so on foot."

"Why?" Xia asked. Burgs said she was supposed to lead, but so far that hadn't been the case.

"Trams may not have bugging surveillance, but they do have trackers. Since we've given our objective as retrieving Commander Young, it won't look right if we're driving all around."

Xia nodded slowly. "Would they be checking that?"

"Don't know. Don't know the extent of the AI's surveillance. Better to be on the safe side."

"Right. So that means—"

Fay turned around in her seat. "I'll keep driving. You two get a lay of the land."

Xia had almost begun to feel a sense of safety inside the tram, and it literally went out the door as she and Ren exited.

Even at nighttime, it was never this dark in Cyber City. While she knew it was titanium plating that cast the black sheet above, she imagined it to be similar to the night sky outside the city's bubble of smog and pollution. Golden lights speckled around them, hanging on invisible wires, providing an almost eerie illumination over the block. Streetlights and slags' glowing tech were the only other sources of illumination. The brick buildings, which stood a story and a half tall and fit snugly together, were dark on the inside. There the windows *were* heavily tinted.

As the two of them walked, Xia glanced around the brick buildings and wondered who might be inside. She knew that this was where many government officials lived. Through the low-lit lights, she could just make out an enormous black block of a building, about a quarter mile ahead towards the edge of the sector. Presumably, where the slags resided. And presumably, where Commander Young would be. With Fay making it that way, Xia and Ren veered to the left and began their scanning of the land.

Fear hadn't crept in yet. But a different feeling had. One that she got when she imagined the centipedes that must be living in the depths of her home. Like little buzzing gnats were burrowing into her skin and tickling her nerves. She had often imagined what the Outer Hubs would look like. Considering the military and government elite resided there, and opted to distance themselves from the grime of Cyber City, she would have expected much more glamor. More spark. But this place didn't even look like it belonged to Freesia. It was otherworldly, like from a different time.

The Before Times?

Besides the glowing tech from the slags that patrolled and marched about, there was not a speck of modage. Or electricity, for that matter. The roads were an odd cobblestone. The trees were real, not synthetic. How was that possible? Trees supposedly couldn't grow properly in the city due to the smog, hence the synthetic ones. But how were they able to here, without the sun? Were the trees why the air here seemed so much fresher?

A drone flew overhead with a rectangular box hanging below it. Xia watched as the curious device hovered by the door of a nearby building and dropped the box in front of it. A moment later the door swung open and a man in a textured gray suit picked up the box. His eyes followed Ren and Xia as they walked past. Ren paid no attention. He was preoccupied with scanning and recording a layout. But Xia's eyes met the man's. He gave a brief nod. Xia didn't return it. Her eyes traveled further behind him, catching a glimpse of the home inside. She couldn't see much, but it reminded her of the Doctor's home. She could see a bookcase and a crystal chandelier. Laughter rang from inside as he shut the door behind him, the sound ringing across the dark street like a chime in the wind. As soon as the door shut, the air stilled in silence once more.

They continued their lookout. More drones revealed themselves, dropping off similar boxes. Food service. Seems the personnel didn't venture outside much if they didn't have to. They'd walk past the occasional slag, none of which paid them any attention, until they made a loop around and began to approach the military headquarters.

As the number of boxy buildings and hanging twinkle lights decreased, the number of groups of slags increased. Her skin prickled underneath the suit. Groups of soldiers walked with purpose from one area to the next, their heavy boots clomping over the stony path. A group of four slags walked with special purpose, but it seemed they were walking right towards the duo. She kept waiting for them to change their direction, head into a building, towards the main gate, anything, but they kept approaching, until the group stopped right before them.

Ren and Xia simultaneously pumped their fists into their chests, the sign of respect given when speaking with a commander on foot.

"RECRUITING OPERATIVE 29676 FOR OPERATION EPSILON 35-D. FOLLOW."

Xia's mouth hung open as she mulled over the command. 29676 wasn't her, it was Ren. They were recruiting Ren for a mission. Just like that.

She ducked her head and said "Recomputing", expecting Ren to do the same. Expecting Ren to hit the *Help* command on his command center. But instead he said something else.

"AFFIRMATIVE."

The most she could do was scream with her eyes. What the hell was he doing? Her eyes hovered over the *Help* command on her screen. Just one willing flare of the eyes would trigger it. But the commander began to walk away, with Ren walking with them. She watched them as the moment slowly slipped away, silk slipping through her fingers. She needed to grab onto it, but it kept falling until it was gone, flying away with the wind. The moment was gone, and so was Ren.

Fuck. She stood there, alone. Heart rate rising, she activated the pulse steadier once more, feeling as if her veins were thickening under her skin. Before she could plan her next move, a tram approached her.

Another *Fuck* to herself. Her nerves were artificially calm, but she could still feel the bells of alarm ringing in her mind. The door slid open and with a breath of authentic relief, she recognized Fay in the front seat.

But she wasn't alone. Another slag sat in the front passenger seat. His helmet bowed slightly to avoid hitting the roof of the vehicle.

She slid inside. Once the heavy door shut behind her, Fay turned around.

"Ren?"

Xia shook her head as she pulled out the soundbox. "Recruited for a mission. Operation Epsilon 35 - D."

"And you didn't think to use the Hail Mary?!" Her voice rose, sounding all the more intense with the voice modifier.

"He went willingly. I could have. But we may still need it."

Fay didn't press further. "Fucking Ren..."

Xia turned towards the slag in the front seat. He sat there stationary, like a massive robot doll. "You're Commander Young?"

His helmet slowly nodded, the top scraping the roof of the vehicle. The man had the build of a synth tree. Limbs long and lanky, almost too tall to be human.

"Operation Epsilon 35 - D." A pause. **"You won't see him for a while. If at all."**

"Why? What is he going to do?"

The commander simply shook his head. **"We move. Proceed to the Main Gate. Keep speed under 5MPH. Never take eyes off the road. When they ask questions, don't answer. I answer. Only answer if they call your ID. Now, drive."**

32

HAIL MARY

There are places throughout the world where the silence is deafening. Where the sound of a breeze is the only element to stir the thick depth of stillness. Such places don't truly exist in Cyber City, but if you knew where to look, you could get close. Youle had found one of those spots. He ventured there every day for his morning walk, across the old stone bridge, past the abandoned park, and towards the grove of authentic trees that somehow managed to grow despite the lack of true rain and sun. It's where his spirit left the city and joined the stillness of death.

Xia found the silence boring when she was young. *"Hush,"* her grandfather would say as she exhaled too loudly or scuffed her large feet against the grassy ground. But after her grandfather left the physical world, she began to appreciate the lull. How her thoughts could amplify, reverberating like speakers. Or how her thoughts could empty, her mind unifying with the emptiness. But that was really the only place she felt such a feeling. The sounds of the city were perpetual.

But she faced that silence in the back of the tram. In tense situations, *really* tense situations, she'd feel the blood pounding in her ears. But now there was nothing. Total and pure suffocating silence as she waited for the commander to approach the tram. The windows slid down. As they approached, the world suddenly turned blue as the commander activated a soundsphere, making their words inaudible to anyone outside of it. Even slags didn't leave the Main Gate just for any reason.

"STATE YOUR PURPOSE TO EXIT MAIN HUB."

Commander Young turned towards the slag. **"Objective Delta 35-D."**

The slag turned towards the back of the tram and stared. The red light signaling the deep-scan flashed on his visor.

"CLEAR. PROCEED."

The silence enveloped her as the tram crept forward, inching towards the titanium double doors. They opened slowly, as if being wrenched apart, revealing pure blackness beyond.

They trekked forward into the darkness, the wheels of the tram trudging below them with a thunderous excursion. Xia scanned and began recording. They were in a tunnel, with the only source of light being a glowing thin line in the center of the path, lighting the way. A way that went downwards. Underground.

Only a few meters in and they reached a fork in the dark road; to the left the line continued glowing yellow, while to the right the light morphed blue.

"Yellow is Leaving. Blue is Returning. Turn Left." Commander Young stated. She knew he was with them, but it still perturbed her to be on the receiving end of a command from a slag. They took the left.

They continued for another minute and met another fork. This time, the light on the right morphed green.

Xia turned towards Young, expecting an explanation.

"We are leaving. Take the Left."

"Where does the green go?'

"Left."

Fay took the left. Xia settled back into her seat. Then she figured. He may not answer all her questions, but that shouldn't stop her from asking them. She channeled her inner Mai.

"Why are there no other slags down here? Don't they come out here often?"

"Usually come out in groups for missions. Don't leave the walls often."

"So what is mission Delta 35-D?"

"Objective 35-D."

"Right. What is it?"

Silence.

"Are you able to tell us and don't want to? Or does the AI implant make it difficult?"

A moment of silence. **"Both."**

Xia scanned around her but received error signals and interference. If only Ren were still here. "What is the surveillance like down here?"

"Minimal due to being underground."

"Can I get out of the tram to explore?"

"No."

She leaned back in her seat, annoyed. "Where does the tunnel lead?"

"You will see."

"Does it lead outside?"

"It can."

"Is that where we are going?"

"No."

That was the ultimate point of this scouting mission. To figure out how to get outside. The annoyance deepened. "How do you get outside?"

"Red leads outside. Rarely go outside."

Xia took a beat. "Can we take the red path?"

"No. Tram is not authorized to go outside. Must follow Objective Delta 35-D."

"You do. But we don't. Can one of us go? And the other goes with you?"

"Can't stop the tram."

That was answer enough. "Fay. Swap places. I'm driving. When we reach the red path, you'll get out and investigate. Record everything. I'll need to review it later on. I want to tag along with Young. See where he's taking us."

Without a word, Fay shifted the gear into neutral, letting the tram coast, then slid out of the seat and squeezed past Xia into the back. Xia stole her spot and took a moment to familiarize herself with the controls. She scanned. She nodded. She took control of the gear and kept driving.

As if on cue, they met another fork in the road. To the right, the line on the ground glowed red. In one swift motion, Fay slid the door open and hopped out. Xia watched as she walked along the red line, further into the darkness, until she disappeared completely. Xia continued down the yellow line.

"So where are we going?"

"Headquarters. HQ."

"Headquarters? Didn't we just leave Headquarters?"

"Living Quarters are in Outer Hubs. Headquarters is under-ground."

The tram's wheels rumbled against the ground as they continued along the narrow tunnel. Commander Young's body remained unmoving. Without Fay, Xia felt a weight lift off her shoulders, but not in a good way. She felt flimsy. Fay was a safety blanket. And now that safety was gone.

"HQ is approaching. Never speak. Stand on my side at all times. No scanning."

"Can I record?"

"Only on private cam."

The tunnel slowly widened until it expanded into a cavernous room with multiple other tunnels snaking into it. Trams parked along the dark wall. Xia watched as one tram pulled into a spot and six slags piled out, the flickering lights of their suit forming shadows against the wall. She wondered if one of them was Ren. One of the bodies hung especially lanky and seemed to walk with the similar controlled cadence that Ren did. But without scanning, she couldn't tell for sure.

She parked the tram next to the one that had just parked. Then she made her spot next to Commander Young, making sure to match his pace and keep her gaze forward. Ahead was a massive dark wall of unknown material, with a set of likely titanium double doors barring the entrance. Unlike the previous doors blocking the Inner and Outer Hubs, Xia saw no control panel for the entrance. Instead, Young simply stood directly before the doors and waited. A second later, they flung open with a monstrous THWOMP.

The room swallowed them whole. Xia stared above at the monstrous cavern. She hadn't thought they were so deep underground, but the expanse of the ceiling above proved differently. Electric scarlet wiring and glowing metal rods extended from the top of the cavern walls like mechanical jungle vines, joining together into a massive mech-like sphere that hung from the center of the ceiling. Xia resisted the intrinsic urge to scan the mysterious structure. Whatever it was, it used a lot of power. At least she was recording.

What was most unsettling wasn't the electrical humming of the sphere, or the sheer volume of the room, but it was the lack of other slags. Where was everyone? An electric buzzing sizzled in her chest.

Young proceeded forward, the sound of his heavy boots reverberating across the room. As they walked underneath the sphere conglomerate, Xia glanced upwards. Inside the mech structure was a gleaming crimson orb, hanging like a teardrop. She only looked for a second. But in that second, she could have sworn the orb was moving, almost like it was breathing. The buzzing in her chest amplified. She thought she heard Young say something under his breath. But maybe it was just the buzzing.

More footsteps. Several holes in the cavern walls created entryways in the circular room, and through one came a group of slags. Not led by a commander, but by a very ordinary-looking person.

She walked with prim and proper steps, echoing her prim and proper attire. Her nude blazer shone pink in the ruby light of the room. Matching heels clacked against the floor, but even with the tall pumps, she was barely 5'2. Black hair slicked behind her into a tight bun. Her small frame grew larger, larger, until she stood directly before the trio. A petite hand flicked upwards and signaled the slags to quit their marching behind her. Xia noticed how the thin and lanky one seemed to stop their marching a second too late. Just the splitting of seconds. But still late.

Ren.

"Commander Young." Her voice seemed to shoot from the nose. "You've received instructions regarding Objective Delta 35 - D?"

"Affirmative."

"Hm." Her nose twitched. "Then why did you not come immediately?"

Suddenly, the walls rattled. Xia tensed herself, but the woman didn't even bat an eye. It felt similar to the rumblings up in the city, although now they were underground. Yet it almost felt as if something was causing the rumbling, something right on the other side of those walls—

"Command not marked as infra code. Finished other Objectives first."

The rumbling stopped. The woman narrowed her eyes. She turned towards Xia.

"You. ID number."

She straightened slightly. "747282."

The nose crinkled again. "This one's never escorted you before, have they?"

"No."

"I don't want new ones in the control room. And especially not in the labs. From now on, keep your escorts in the same rotation. You." Her silver eyes penetrated right through Xia's helm. "Return to the Outer Hub."

"Affirmative," Xia responded. Without a second's hesitation, she turned on her heel and left Young alone with the woman. As she walked underneath the orb, Xia made sure to take a full glance upwards this time. Not only did the inner teardrop seem to be breathing; the crimson coating looked almost flesh-like. She would have given anything to scan it. Her eyes gave no clue as to the purpose of the floating structure.

Several other slags walked through the room from one hole in the wall through another. Labs and a control room. What other places lay hidden down here? Is this where the infamous Void was? For now, she wouldn't get to know. But she was ready to see what Fay had figured out.

Back into the tunnel she went. This time, the path glowed blue, signaling the way back to the Outer Hub. She reached various forks, each with a different color signaling a different type of route. Time slugged by as if covered in molasses, the darkness thickening that molasses. But then time quickened as Xia noticed the distant red line up ahead. The tram barreled along slowly, and as the red path came into view, Xia's heart stopped as she saw an empty path. No sign of Fay.

She lowered the tram window. A shadow formed against the wall as Fay stepped forward, the lights of her suit suddenly illuminating. She pulled the door open and came inside.

"Had to camouflage myself from other passing trams. Only one passed by. And then you. You weren't gone long."

Xia picked up the pace. "I know. Got kicked out. But I'm pretty sure I saw Ren."

"No kidding. Glad to know he's okay. For now, at least."

A pause. "So, what did you find out?"

"Hard to describe. I *think* I found the exit. You'll see soon enough. I recorded it all. Where did Young take you?"

Xia tapped her helm with her index finger. "You'll see soon enough."

Fay let out a laugh, a garbled sound that made Xia shudder. "Touche. Man, can't wait to turn these damn voice changers off. And get out of this suit. I'm feeling a little too slaggish, if you know what I mean."

Xia did know what she meant. The suit was beyond comfortable. A smooth melted skin. But just knowing what she was wearing was enough to cover herself with a constant film of discomfort. "But you wear these things every day."

"It's not the same. At the Pagoda, it's almost like playing dress up. Here, it's different. I've been using the pulse steadier this entire time. I don't think you're supposed to use it that much. Got chest pains. What we're doing is crazy, you know."

Xia nodded. It was beyond crazy. It was insane. She wondered if anyone else had managed to get an inside peek into the FRF Force. She doubted it. Not a single soul in the massive metropolitan did what she did. It was daunting. It was exciting. But also disappointing. Years and years of perseverance and blood-soiled work, determination and will, got her to where she was. But here, at this very moment, this was all due to Burgs. Burgs handed her this adventure. No blood-soiled work here.

"What do we do about Ren?" Xia asked.

"We hope for the best."

The path sloped upwards as they reached the end of their journey through the tunnel. The blue path merged with the yellow and led to a solid gray wall. As the tram approached, the wall cranked open. Xia drove the tram forward and looked around.

Something wasn't right.

"Where are all the slags?" Fay muttered.

Xia scanned. There were no slags. Not a single one in sight. Dread mixed with the darkness. If none of the slags were there, *they* shouldn't be there either.

"You think we should be on foot? No other trams moving around, either," Xia said, eyeing the parked trams along the gate exit.

"Yeah," Fay agreed.

Xia parked the tram next to a few others and the two exited the vehicle. She glanced around. The place had an air of eeriness before. But now, with the lack of slags, it was downright chilling. They wasted no time and quickly set foot on the main path towards the gate to the Inner Hub.

But then they weren't alone. She barely even noticed them coming in the darkness, their uniforms pure obsidian, save for the small glowing red light on their helm. Every expletive ran through Xia's thoughts as she recognized the trio of slags.

Burgs had told them what they looked like. Pristine obsidian, the lack of glowing tech, the size of their builds. The chance of running into one was low since their numbers were so few. Few rose to the ranks to commander. And even fewer rose above to become Divisioner. Rumor has it they were the ones who'd escort you to the Void. But nobody knew for sure, since they were as elusive as the Void itself. But here they came, stepping towards the duo. The pulse stabilizer worked harder than ever.

"WHY ARE YOU OUTSIDE?" The tallest of the three spoke. Xia got the impression he didn't need the voice modifier. The tone reverberated through her, rattling her bones.

"Escort for Objective Delta 35 - D. No new instructions given." Xia held her tone steady.

The tallest of the three turned towards the shortest. The red light blinked on his visor. But it blinked more rapidly. Her heartbeat fought against the stabilizer, hammering at the soothing wall of equalization, now crumbling away.

The silence weighed upon them like a tram. Crushing her. Her breath hitched as she waited.

"ANOMALY. TAKE THEM."

Xia sensed Fay freeze beside her. Two of the Divisioners moved towards them. She wished a mental apology to Ren. Then she accessed the "Help" on her screen.

Halfway through their step towards Xia, they suddenly stopped, as if their bodies were physically restrained by an invisible force. They dropped their heads and cocked them sideways. The tallest grunted.

When it came to the Hail Mary, Burgs had given one instruction and one instruction only. _"Once you activate it, run. Max you'll get is 3 minutes."_

And so they did. Xia never ran so fast in her life. Fay lagged slightly behind her. They ducked a right into a side street filled with Government housing. A small bud of relief blossomed as she recognized the street. This was where she saw the first drone delivery. They continued to run, the street dark save for the twinkling golden lights above, Fay following closely at Xia's heels, before looping back around towards the main gate.

Xia approached the control panel, but it was completely dark. Had the saving grace somehow disabled it? Xia scanned it. It had been functioning normally up until 2.2 minutes earlier, exactly when she triggered the Hail Mary.

Fay pulled Xia. "We need to hide."

Xia shook her head as she turned off her suit's glowing lights. "Just wait. Wait." She had faith in Burgs. Every second ticked at her with an agonizing pang, each heartbeat thumping to the stagnant pace of time. Her eyes fixed to the control panel, waiting. She could hear a distant door open. An even more distant robotic yell.

_39. 40. 41._

Fay urged again. "Xia. We _need_ to hide."

Xia ignored her. _49. 50._

"Xia!"

On 55, the control panel buzzed as the screen powered back up. Xia slammed her hand down onto the panel and the doors opened not a second too soon.

Never before had the hazy smog felt so safe and welcoming. Trainees milled about looking confused and anxious. Slags stood around, looking around slowly, some holding their helmets with their hands.

As the door to the Outer Hub shut behind them, Xia copied the other slags. She reactivated the lights on her suit and grabbed her helmet, walking slowly, glancing around at the scene around them. Snippets of conversations caught her ear.

"What the hell just happened?"

"Is this a part of some drill?"

"Should have used that time to snag one of their helmets."

"Sh! They'll hear you."

But none of the other slags paid the trainees any attention. They seemed to be slowly coming to consciousness. Whatever Xia had done, it had affected all the slags. She continued walking along, steps perfunctory, ignoring slags and trainees alike. And in turn, they were also ignored.

33

AN ANGEL'S SYMBOL

Xia had expected to feel the comforting waves of relief once they stepped back into the proper of Cyber City, leaving the military delirium behind the titanium blockade in their wake. But instead, as she stared upwards into the browning heavens, sky rich with caramelizing density, she felt its weight crush down on her. Fay clearly felt the opposite. As soon as the doors shut behind them, she let out a whooping laugh of relief. It began as a guffaw. Then transformed into wheezing. Xia stood as stationary as a stone, only slightly perturbed by Fay's mania. Xia'd never laughed like that before. Not since she was a bumbling kid. Now they were anything but. Eventually, the wheezing prolonged the acceptable amount of time, and Xia gave Fay a push as she began walking ahead. Walking back to the apartment. Walking back without Ren.

This time, the glances and stares from the citizens of Freesia bothered Xia. She wasn't sure why. Perhaps because the starers knew so little. Could they ever imagine the depths she had just delved? The incredible risk? They knew nothing. Their stares were empty.

Xia entered the apartment behind Fay, taking their helmets off in unison. The smell of roasted meat and vegetables suctioned her nose, triggering her stomach to let out a ravenous growl. She hadn't realized how starving she was. Fay ran off towards Burgs, who stood at the stove stirring a pan of herbs and vegetables. Xia added chef to the ever-expanding list of Burgs' shining qualities. She let them have their reunion and walked up behind the white couch where Mai lay sleeping. But she wasn't alone. Leonardo lay on the floor beside her. Left hands intertwining.

My, how things could change in a day.

Xia flinched at the feeling of a heavy hand on her shoulder. Burgs stood with the widest grin she'd ever seen.

"Back in one piece. That's a hell of a feat, kid. Gimme that data."

Xia gave a small nod and a smaller smile back. She didn't have the energy for much else.

Ocean waves of blue bamboo swaddled her as she gazed upwards toward the shimmering ceiling. Xia wasn't sure what it was exactly that Fay had installed overhead, but in the darkness it seemed to glimmer and swirl.

A knock at the door. "Can I come in?"

"It's your room," Xia responded. She sat up as Fay flicked the lights back on.

The shimmering swirls stopped.

"How are you feeling?"

Xia shrugged. "Fine. Tired. But fine."

Fay's eyes narrowed. Eyes bluer than her hair. "Come on, really. I fail to believe that you're as stony inside as the outside."

She shrugged again, but it felt more like a twitch. Her shoulders felt somehow uncomfortable. Her whole body did.

"Is this how you talk to Burgs?"

She smirked. "Sometimes. You two are quite alike."

"Quite a compliment."

"I didn't mean it as one."

Silence.

"I appreciate you letting me rest in here. The blue is nice. Calming."

Fay looked around the room as if taking it all in for the first time. "Yeah, I'm a sucker for cobalt. Always been one of those people that when you really like something, you go all in and let it become your personality."

"Is that why you latched onto Burgs? Let yourself become his caretaker, so to speak?"

Xia enjoyed flipping the tables of conversation back onto the other. The other person rarely did. But Fay rolled with it.

"Yeah, I guess so. Plus the poor guy needed one. Dallek too."

"Dallek?"

"Oh, that's Grimer's actual name. I'm pretty much the only one that still calls him that, though. Usually only in private. But it slips out."

"Sounds a lot nicer than Grimer."

Fay's turn to shrug. "You know, when we were back there, I really thought that was the end. That we'd be killed. Or worse."

"Like the Void?"

"You believe the Void is real?"

"Yeah, why wouldn't I?"

Fay crossed her arms. "Is that really a question?"

She was right. With all the lies they'd discovered by the FRF, truth was a rarity.

"Void or no, the government's got a high threshold for cruelty. A quick death would be a kindness."

"You didn't seem scared."

"Hard to tell with the helmets on."

Fay shook her head. Blue ringlets fell out of her loose bun. "No. I could tell. Behind all the gear, you were as cool as a cucumber. And at the gate too. It was a good thing I listened to you."

She couldn't think of what she should say. So she said nothing.

"Burgs watched our recordings. Wants to go over everything. And I figured you'd want to see the video of what I saw."

Xia nodded. "Mai awake?"

"Yeah. Woke up about an hour ago. She watched it all with Burgs. Well, she made him restart it. He wasn't too pleased."

"Seems she and Leonardo smoothed out their differences." Xia narrowed her eyes in confused disdain.

Fay chuckled. "I'm not surprised. He's a good soul, you know. Obnoxious. But honestly, he's got the best heart of all of us. And Mai's got an eye for a good heart." She motioned with her head. "Come on when you're ready."

She allowed herself another minute of rest in the heavens before following Fay into the living room. Burgs sat in his usual chair, hunched over with a glass of bourbon, examining a holographic display of the Outer Hub. It was incomplete, as that had been Ren's job. Leonardo and Mai sat on the couch, their thighs touching. Xia's recording floated above the walnut coffee table on a holographic screen, paused at the moment she entered HQ.

As soon as Xia entered, Mai exclaimed with a childlike glee.

"Xi! Look at this!" Leonardo gave the faintest of pushes upwards while Mai eased herself off the couch. She began walking towards Xia. Although it was a bit more like hobbling, like her legs were filled with marbles. Despite the marbles, she stood before Xia with a grin that threatened to open her beautiful face. "How amazing is that? How do I look?"

Her glee was infectious. Xia smiled back. "Tall. Very nice."

The grin somehow widened. Leo walked up beside her.

"I'm surprised. A day ago all you could do was complain."

"Well, Leo's been helpful." She attempted a twirl but the marbles sent her off kilter. She stumbled, but Leo caught her without a second's hesitation.

"I can see that," Xia mused. There was a giddiness behind Mai's smile that seemed unrelated to her renewed ability to walk.

"Enough of the chit-chat. Get over here," Burgs barked.

The three obliged and made their way to the couch. The closer Xia got to the floating image, the tighter her chest felt. Fay leaned against the window with a glass of aqua liquid in her hand. Even her drinks were blue. The girl was undeniably consistent.

"Feels empty without Ren," Grimer spoke up from the smaller armchair across Burgs.

Xia disagreed. Ren was barely enough of a presence before. Always quiet, always to himself, always seeming to wish he were asleep instead. For her, this crew felt more than enough. "I expected him to use the Hail Mary when he was recruited to follow the other slags. But maybe it was good he didn't. It came in real handy for us."

"What did it do?" Mai asked. "I still don't understand. I saw the recording. It looked almost like the slags were shut off or something."

Burgs' chest practically swelled with self-satisfaction. "A virus. I'd been concocting it for years. I'd hoped you wouldn't have to use it, but it sure is nice to see it worked so well. A blackout virus. Latched itself onto every single device in the slags' network, inhibiting its use. That includes the AI command chips in all their cortexes. Worst case scenario, they'd be able to overcome the virus in just a few seconds. But it did its dirty work."

"That explains their odd behavior once the command chips came back online. Basically, their brains rebooting."

"Can it be used again?" Mai asked. "Maybe Ren could still use it."

"No, the network is essentially immune to it now. I can probably splice it up enough that it could work again, but that'll take time. Don't worry about Ren. He knew what he was getting into, and he was more than willing to run off with them. Little bastard." There was a twinkle in his eye. "Xia. You managed to set foot in HQ. That's incredible. Did you feel anything out of the ordinary?"

Fay cocked her brow, but an answer immediately popped into Xia's mind. "My chest. It was almost an electric fluttering. And I felt it more when I was under that weird...thing on the ceiling." She made a small gesture to the floating screen.

Burgs hummed to himself. "Definitely a power source. Massive one."

"What is it powering?" Grimer asked. His voice rang with trepidation and a touch of eagerness.

Burgs drank.

Xia leaned closer. "That reminds me," she said, just remembering it since it happened. "I could have sworn Young said something to me when I walked underneath the ceiling orb."

Grimer didn't need telling twice. He leaned forward and sped through the recording to the moment just prior to Xia's fleeting glance towards the giant sphere. Then he played with the audio settings, isolating the sound frequencies from the direction of Commander Young and maximizing the audio.

The word came clear as neon. *"OMEGA."*

"Omega?" Leonardo repeated.

"Is that what the sphere thing is called?' Fay asked.

Burgs snapped his fingers. "Your mission name was Delta 35-D. When the slags would corner you. Right? Did you hear any other mission names repeated at any point?"

Xia thought for a moment. "Epsilon. That was the mission that Ren was recruited for."

Burgs' eyes narrowed. "I'll follow up on that."

Mai stirred beside Leonardo. "I don't get it. This Commander Young guy. You had him on the inside this entire time? What was even the point of this entire mission? He could have just told us all this from the get-go. Xia didn't need to risk her life for it."

Burgs huffed. "Don't try to flush when you don't have shit. It's hard enough to get two sentences from Young. Poor guy's gotta have a battle with his brain every time he wants to act autonomously. We're able to communicate briefly on the channel server he's got access to. But sending entire video files? 3D layouts? There was no way. No, if you want to be able to leave that way, you needed to go about yourselves. Now. I want to go over the exit point. Fay, display your recording."

She nodded as her eyes danced from one side to another, accessing the data on her eye screen. Then Xia's recording disappeared as Fay's recording replaced it.

For several minutes, all that could be heard was faint breathing and careful footsteps as they watched Fay walk along the darkness, the only light coming from the red line on the pathway. The room stilled as everyone watched with intensity.

The darkness grew more opaque. The red line stopped. Fay had then altered the camera settings, changing the lighting and allowing everyone to see the blockade.

Xia had expected some type of overtly technological door, with scanning devices and locking mechanisms. But instead, Fay met with a smooth obsidian wall, with no noteworthy aspects except for an odd angular design in the middle—two intersecting loops inside a lopsided diamond.

Xia snapped up straight. "I know that symbol."

"You do?" Fay turned. "I couldn't find a single record of it. Not in any archive, no public database, nothing."

Xia's mind wandered back to *that* job. The job she'd never forget—because she had almost died.

She had been hired to take out the leader of the Butori Gang. It had not gone well. But in her last moments, she noticed the hidden blades in his shoes, and was able to counterstrike and snag her victory. But she had still been wounded. Severely.

She hobbled along a back alley, pellets of rain descending in a drenching fury. Rain always seemed to visit Xia at her lowest moments. Was it a positive sign of renewed rebirth? Or was it one final cackle from the gods of misfortune? She didn't know. She was just thankful it wasn't acid.

No matter how many waves of rain washed at her wound, blood continued to pour out, seeping through the hole in her suit. The alley was growing darker. She walked past the occasional druggie or prostitute. None of them paid her any attention. Not until she heard a voice.

"Hey, you! Silver-haired!"

Xia thought she'd imagined it. The voice seemed to come above her, floating down with the gusts of rain. Perhaps her mind was wandering across the border, out of this world—

But no. She jolted back to reality when a hand wrapped around her bicep. She glanced down and a miles-long length of fingers wrapped around her. Her body was slow to turn around, but the hand yanked her into facing the source.

Xia's eyes traveled upwards, upwards, continuously upwards, eventually landing on the face of the titan of a woman before her. The long fingers now made sense. Her ashy blonde hair fell in waves behind her, completely dry and unaffected by the rainfall. Her tight jacket and leather pants threatened to burst over her muscular frame. She seemed older, but you wouldn't be able to tell from the face. Not a line or wrinkle in sight. Just smooth peach complexion with eyes as pink as the neon ramen signs.

"Are you...an angel?" Xia croaked.

The woman let out a throaty laugh before scooping Xia up into her arms like a newborn child. Xia didn't protest. Even if she had the energy, she didn't need to. Something about this strange large woman exuded peace. So she let herself be carried off, and she let herself fall into unconsciousness.

Xia stayed at the woman's home for three days. She never learned their name. The woman refused to give it. The woman was no doctor, yet Xia was stitched back up and fully healed before she left. She could tell that the woman held some tech background. It wasn't obvious by the small place at all. There wasn't much out of the ordinary. A cot, a kettle, a few faux plants. Everything was unassuming. A little *too* unassuming. Xia was free to roam (as much as she could) except for one room. The woman spent most of her time in that room. When Xia tried to scan, there were a plethora of scan blockers and signal disruptors making the room immune to such attempts. But every time the woman left the room, the hum and buzz of electric equipment was unmistakable.

Xia never pressed. Never asked. And when she noticed the symbol tattooed on the woman's back when she was swapping jackets, Xia never mentioned it. But she remembered it. And that same symbol was plastered on the otherwise unremarkable wall.

"Yeah. It was tattooed on someone. A woman. In the middle of her back."

"Who was the woman?

"I don't know."

"What do you mean you don't know?" Leo piped.

"I was injured. She helped me get back on my feet. But when I left her place, she had my vision obscured so I wouldn't know where she lived."

Fay hummed to herself, Grimer leaned back further, Burgs took another sip.

Mai's voice came soft. "Xia, what did the woman look like?"

"Really tall. Bordering 6'6. And very muscular. Had kind of sandy blonde hair."

"And pink eyes?"

Xia raised her brows. "Yeah. Don't tell me you know her?"

"Not exactly. My father did. And I think Kibou does as well."

Xia smirked. "Sounds like it's time to have a meeting with the old man."

Burgs clicked his tongue. "Damn straight. Bastard needs to send another payment, too. Just because we ain't there right now doesn't mean we don't get last week's pay!"

34

LORENA

Kibou stood in the lobby of the apartment building, more out of place than a cat in a doghouse. Which is slightly what he resembled. The long flowing robes and matching flowing beard gave him a perpetual air of elegance and fortitude, much like that of a well-groomed cat. He stood at the espresso machine with a bemused chuckle.

"Buy me one, please." He said without turning around. For a man with no mods, he held a peculiarly strong sixth sense.

Xia tapped the necessary buttons. A moment later, the warm toffee liquid poured into a small cup. He took it with grace and sipped. No waiting for the drink to cool.

"It's been a bit," Xia said.

"Ah, for what is time but just a simple passing of the sun?" His beard smiled underneath the teacup. "Now, shall we? I am quite eager to see the likes of our protectors' domain."

After getting to know Burgs and the crew a bit more, it was odd to hear them called 'The Protectors'. Xia waited for two ridiculously attractive and equally similar-looking young women to step off the lift before entering with Kibou.

"Did Mai fill you in enough?"

She was ready for a flowery response about her gifting him with the blossoms of wisdom, but he just gave a solemn nod.

"How are the other monks doing? And the samurai?" With the disappearance of the Daimyo and the unknown future steps of the government to pursue Virgin brains, Kibou deemed it best to pause operations inside the Pagoda.

"They are adapting to the best of their abilities. It is hard to be forced away from the only place you've ever truly known to be home. We understand it is necessary. But still. Without movement, without acting on one's calling, one grows restless. They are restless." He blinked slowly like a cat. "Especially Buko."

Xia recalled the hot-headed samurai with little trust for her. She believed Kibou full-heartedly. As the two ascended the dozens of floors and entered the penthouse, the apartment's air thickened with an unbalanced discomfort at the presence of Kibou. Like everything else, it didn't faze the wise old man.

"Hello everyone," he said with a deep bow.

Burgs shuffled over, mouth open, about to give a piece of his mind regarding the lack of funds. Before the words could leave his throat, Kibou pulled out a small sack of phys.

"It is my understanding that this choice of lifestyle requires consistent funding," he said with a rye smile.

"It damn well does." Burgs snatched the pouch and sat in his armchair to count it.

"We have much to discuss, it seems."

After the group got settled, Fay showed the recording. She paused as the symbol on the door came into full view. "You know a person with this symbol?"

"Ah," he said as he set down his empty cup. "Indeed I do. The Lovely Lorena."

"Lorena?"

"Yes. A very kind soul. A kind soul cursed with a dexterity too talented for her own peace."

"Always speaking so flowery, aren't ya old man?" Leo chuckled with a bit of spright.

"The world could use a bit more flora, wouldn't you agree?" The twinkle never left his eye. "Lorena. She came from a long family line of software and machine learning engineers. Her parents had left those ways behind. They embraced the ways of Virgin life. Lorena learned those ways. She rejected those ways. She delved into the cyber world. And she excelled. The government took notice. They used her work. They used her." His finger motioned towards the floating recording. "Only she knows how to open that door."

"Where can we find her?" Fay asked.

"I'm afraid that knowledge eludes me. She cut her ties with us after Lord Daimyo cast a harshness upon her that she deemed too much. I have not seen her in many moons."

"Kibou, what is her last name? Any aliases?"

"Her family name is Nox. That is all I know."

That was enough for Xia to work with. But it involved some outside help. Some of which she wasn't in the best place to ask for.

She parked her cycle in the alley beside the bar she had used to frequent so often. A part of her felt the tendrils of guilt, as if she had abandoned a long lost friend. But was it the bar that was the source of her self-reproach? Or was it Dames? Things had never felt so off between them.

She entered Mickey's with haste, as if the sooner she could enter the place the sooner she could cut through the fog of unease that lingered. She had an objective. She sat down with a thud. Being midday, the bar was nearly empty, just as she needed it to be. Her fingers drummed against the sticky bar top as she waited for Dames. And waited. Dames had never kept her waiting for so long. Never left the bartop so sticky either.

"Look who's here," Dames spoke as he finally arose from the back.

"Hey. Yeah, I've been a bit busy."

"I can tell. Same old same old?" He wiped the bartop and ignored her eye.

"Uh, not the old old stuff. The new stuff. Unless that's what you meant." She scratched the back of her head, although it wasn't itchy. "I'm here because I need some more help from you."

He continued to wipe. "Seems I've been helping you a lot lately."

"You have. I really appreciate it." She stared at him, waiting for him to meet her gaze, but he just kept wiping. "Are you upset with me or something?"

He exhaled. "No, no. Just tired. What is it you need help with?"

"I need to find someone. Someone who helped me back a while ago. Her name is Lorena Nox. Does the name ring any bells?"

"Doesn't ring any bells. What line of work is she in? Freelancing like you?"

"I don't think so. She's got a computer background. Software and artificial intelligence. Some engineering as well?" She held out her wrist and displayed the image on her cellchip. "She has this symbol on her back."

All of a sudden, Dames' eyes widened and his residual hardness dissipated. He cleared his throat. "Yeah. I know a girl with that symbol."

"You do? Is it Lorena?"

He cleared his throat again. "I don't know. I don't know her name."

"What does she look like?"

He squinted his eyes, recalling the memory, the lines deepening around his eyes. "Blonde. Dark blonde. And tall. Because I didn't have to bend over too much."

"Pink eyes?"

"I think so. I didn't see much of her eyes."

"You didn't see much of her eyes? But you did see her back? How do you know her?"

For the first time in a long time, Xia felt true annoyance. Not the pangs of annoyance that Mai held a special skill for. No, this was the annoyance that seeped in from every corner. So suffocating that the source is questionable. Xia had a few ideas. The surrounding blazes of flashing red lights and half-naked women were a clear source. And her recent job of consistently playing errand girl was another. But were those the true origins? Or was it the fact that Xia had to envision Dames and this Lorena gal in the throes of passion?

He didn't want to go into detail. But she wasn't a prostitute, despite him meeting her at a brothel. And he was sure she would still be there. Why? Because he had gone there quite recently. According to him, he hadn't gone there with the intent of getting off. That it just ended up happening. And with who? The owner of the fine establishment. Who, supposedly, was Lorena Nox.

Xia approached the small, unassuming entrance. It blended in with the rest of the whore houses, a string of scarlet lanterns outside adding to the district's name. She walked beneath it and entered *The Lovely Lions*. She had only been inside a handful of brothels throughout her life, (always for business' sake), and each one had its own gimmick. This one seemed to be...lions. Plush fur covered the floor, the walls, even the people. Although just barely. The prostitutes themselves seemed to resemble the majestic beasts, with mighty frames and flowing hair. If Dames' had lied about the intent of his visit, it seemed this was his type.

A man with a leopard print loincloth that did not quite cover his lengthy girth sauntered over to Xia, red mane flowing. "Hello there beautiful," he practically growled. "Lion or lioness? Or perhaps both?"

She recoiled. "I'm here to meet with someone." She dropped her voice. "Lorena Nox?"

The lion's scarlet brow furrowed. Lip jutted. "Don't speak that name. What do you want with the owner?"

"I need to speak with her."

"Why?" It came out as a statement. A very cold statement.

"I know how important she is. More than just the owner here. Right? Scan me, check me, do whatever you need to. But it's vital I just speak with her. Please." Her eyes pleaded with him, prey to predator.

He glanced behind him, towards the hallway which led to the private rooms. Which also led, Xia guessed, to Lorena's room.

"I won't make any guarantees."

He began to walk back towards the hall when Xia added for extra measure, "Tell her I know Dames!"

And that was her ticket.

When Xia opened the tall wooden door, she was quite relieved when it opened into an office and not a bedroom. Unlike the rest of the place, the office was every tech fanatic's wet dream. Multiple massive monitors, holographic displays, a dozen keyboards both physical and haptic. This was an upgrade even to Burgs' place. Why the hell she had an office like this inside a brothel, Xia didn't know.

Even as she was sitting, Xia could notice the length of the woman sitting at the U-curved desk, her blonde hair in an intricate braid resting just where her tattoo would be. And although her back was facing the door, Xia recognized the woman instantly.

"Lorena?"

The woman spun around slowly. Face initially curious and calm, but recognition dawned on her.

"Xia?"

Xia nodded. "Wasn't sure if you'd recognize me. Or even remember me."

"Of course I remember." She smirked. Eyes raking Xia up and down, up and down, taking her all in. "You must be curious as to why I own a place like this."

Not curious. Incredibly confused. "Yeah."

"You say you know Dames."

Her hand twitched. "Yeah."

"He's quite a man. In many ways. Maybe you know some of those ways." She raised a brow.

"No. Not like that."

Lorena narrowed her eyes, gauging the truth to Xia's denial. Likely scanning. Her eyes were even pinker than Xia remembered. Almost fuschia. Her hair was blonder too. Other than that, she hadn't changed a drop.

"Well, I recommend it sometime."

A shiver. "I didn't come here to talk about Dames. He's just how I happened to find you."

Her expression hardened. The air hardened with it. "What do you want?"

Xia displayed the symbol from the door above her cellchip. It hovered in the air for less than a second before Lorena exploded from her chair.

"What the fuck do you want?!" She roared like the lions the place was named for.

Xia dropped the symbol and raised her hands in defense. "I need to know about that symbol. About a certain project you were contracted for."

"How do you know about that?"

She was walking on very thin ice. "I was there. I saw the door. And I need to know how to get through it."

The connections to Dames and Kibou certainly helped in bridging the gap of trust between the two. But deep down, it was the mending of the silver girl's wounds that fateful night that allowed for the possibility of help. Because if anyone else came walking through that door asking about that symbol, they wouldn't have left back through it.

People live with all sorts of walls that work perpetually to stave off any and all types of closeness. Natural repellents of insincerity and disregard. Perhaps in a different time, things were different. Perhaps without the constant flurry of mods and morphing of bodies, it was easier to see the human. In Cyber City, it wasn't humanity that ruled the world. It was technology. Fear. Pleasure and survival intertwining beneath the walls of a cybernetic web.

But when one bleeds, those walls are nowhere to be found. The physical flesh is melted away to reveal an inside that should never be seen. It reveals pain, angst, sometimes hopelessness, sometimes hopefulness. Through the cuts, one can catch a glimpse into the person below. Lorena caught many glimpses as she tended to Xia.

She noticed how no matter how hard Xia suppressed the groans of pain, she couldn't control the contortions of her face as she'd wince with every touch of the wound. She noticed how the girl had to be force-fed a meal, but wouldn't refuse some medicinal liquor. She noticed how Xia whimpered in her sleep, calling out for the ghosts of her closest loved one.

Lorena enjoyed these glimpses into humanity. She hadn't always. She hadn't cared. Her parents had tried to instill in her those values. But she hadn't wanted to garden. She hadn't wanted to meet with the monks and meditate. She was dazzled by the ever-evolving technological advancements around her, and she wanted to make her own advancements with them. The only one who had recognized such skill in her was Kibou. It was because of him that she was given the opportunity to develop her skills in software and circuit design. And even he could tell she was beyond proficient.

So now, after decades of immersion into the cold world of unfeeling machinery, she fed on these glimpses like a starving child, healing her own wounds behind eyes forever branded with the electronic anesthesia.

"Why lions?"

"And why a whorehouse?"

Mai turned in her seat. She was able to do so with ease now. "We prefer the term *Pleasure Den,* thank you. And isn't it obvious? Nobody would suspect she was there. If she needed to work under the radar, that's a prime spot to do it. And prime for funneling true sources of income."

"Exactly," Xia said. "She agreed to come by tomorrow morning, but only if Kibou would be here. Mai, you think you can arrange that?"

"If there's espresso waiting for him, he'll be here." Mai let out a chuckle and eased into Leonardo on the couch, the two making no attempts to hide their newfound intimacy. Fay retreated back into her room, and Grimer followed a few steps behind to his own. Xia exhaled a solid breath. It felt as if they were getting somewhere. As if pieces were falling together, and that everything might turn upside. And that maybe they could snag a solid rest for once. But not a moment too soon, Burgs flipped it back down.

"Hey, you been busy, so you may not have realized. But your radio friend? The Nightcrawler? Haven't heard a broadcast from him in over a month. And I track 'em all. He's never missed one before."

A weight sunk deep in her chest. She kissed the night of rest goodbye.

35

Missing Manic

Xia ignored the pleas from Mai wanting to accompany her. And she ignored the scolds from Burgs to slow down as she gathered her things. The only person she reached out to was Kibou, and that was a call she made inside her helmet as she raced through the city. A shooting star with one purpose: to get to Opell as fast as possible.

"Have you spoken with Opell recently? He hasn't made any broadcasts in over a month."

For the first time since she had met him, Kibou's response came after hesitation. And for the first time, his voice didn't come with his usual breezy contentment, forever void of any manic emotion. He responded with urgency.

"I am on my way. Get there now."

Xia took a corner too quickly and narrowly dodged a behemoth of a man.

"Watch your fucking roll you dirty spinster!"

Xia felt the pang of a bottle pitched against her backside. She paid it no mind as she raced through the street, leaning from side to side as she weaved in and out of people's way. She hadn't known Opell very well, but the thought of something happening to him, something inhibiting him from his crazed hobbies, filled her with a gnawing worm of pity that kept biting at her insides. One of the many perks of working alone. No gnawing worms of empathy.

As she approached Opell's dumpy building, she could sense a difference. Nothing visible. Nothing tangible. But a phantom feeling of invariable unease. A gaggle of drugees lay along the side of the building, eyes rolling and mouths foaming. But other than them, the street lay deserted. She remembered the centipede. She shuddered. Then she entered the building, flew down the narrow stairwell, and approached Opell's door.

She scanned. Nothing. Not even a lone bug. Her bandaged fist pounded on the door as she called out. "Opell!"

No answer. She pounded once more and the door rattled beneath her fist. She glanced downwards and noticed the lock. Or rather, the lack of lock. She turned the handle and the door opened with ease.

Her eyes saw nothing in the dark. Pure enveloping darkness. She scanned. While there was nothing dangerous, and no signs of life, nothing was where it should be. Her retscanner registered a toaster on the ground, cables ripped from the wall, a tablet broken on the floor. She flicked on the light switch on the side of the wall. The darkness remained. Either the lights were broken, or the power was out

.

"Opell?" She called out after shutting the door behind her, this time more softly. She activated the flashlight on her wrist to examine the room more closely.

"What the hell," she muttered to herself. Everything lay everywhere. The couch was tipped over, its cushions and pillows splayed about. Broken glass, garbage, notebooks, empty syringes. The kitchenette wasn't any better. She stepped over the toaster and examined the appliances. The fridge was empty with the door hung open. No cooling. Seemed the power wasn't on. The stove's burners were removed. A large blue stain pooled along the countertop.

What happened? While it was very much possible the government caught wind of Opell's discrepancies, they wouldn't have left the place like this. When the slags are finished going through someplace, they leave it pristine. Untouched. This had everything touched. There didn't seem to be anything that *wasn't* touched. It was almost manic how everything had been moved.

Manic. She tucked that suspicion to the back of her mind. Flashlight on, she proceeded to the rest of the apartment. She braced herself as she pushed the door to Opell's bedroom and scanned once more, expecting the worst. But instead she found more of the same. The blankets from his small twin bed lay scattered on the floor. The mattress sat flipped over on its side. Dresser drawers open. Mirror shattered.

She retreated slowly and made her way to the room she was most worried about. While she was worried for Opell's safety, she was equally as concerned with his tech and gadgets. The door creaked as she opened it slowly, expecting to see every precious piece of equipment in shambles. She didn't see it in shambles. She didn't see it at all. It was all gone. Except for one thing.

Her eyes adjusted from the pitch-black darkness of the hall to the dimly lit room, RGB lights from the keyboard fading from violet, blue, green, looping back in a constant rainbow. The power seemed to be working in here. The humming of the computer mixed with her slow exhales, creating the only sound heard in the room. But even those noises felt like they were too much. She kept her footsteps silent as she approached the main monitors where Opell had shown her the satellite images.

She was about to scan when her eyes squinted as the sudden illumination of the monitors before her filled with electric blue. *What the hell?* She felt confusion before. Now she felt paranoia. As if someone was watching her. She scanned, but once again, found she was alone. The room was empty save for the computer and monitors, but she wasn't able to properly scan it. Whatever had triggered the monitors to activate came from the computer itself.

She tapped on the login and her breath hitched in her throat. The computer asked for a password, and above the password field, read the username.

XIA.

She stared at the screen for several moments before racking her brain for a potential password. She first tried Nightcrawler. Incorrect. Then every variation of it. Each attempt met with *Password Incorrect.* She noticed the touchpad on the side of the keyboard. Perhaps it used biometric data. She placed her fingerprint on the pad.

Invalid Biodata.

She scraped the corners of her brain, reviewing the memory of her first visit with Opell. The laughs. The teeth. The lingering stares towards his precious toys. Then she remembered something. The tiniest ping at the back of her scalp as he plucked one of her long hairs. *"Silver smarts on a silver head."*

She snatched one of the hairs from her head and placed it onto the small pad. Within a second, the screen changed from the blue login screen to his home screen. A smile. She was in. And whatever was inside, Opell had wanted her to find.

She explored the interface and found nothing except for two lone folders. Opening the folder, she found it contained satellite images, with the date and time collected as the file names. The other file contained the same dated and timed images, but stated *EDITED* at the end of each file name. Xia tapped her cell chip to the transfer port of the computer to collect the data. The files began their transfer slowly. That's when she felt eyes behind her.

She whirled around in the blink of an eye, simultaneously drawing her weapon.

"Such quick reflexes," Kibou mused.

She stowed the Enforcer back into her suit. "How did you get here so fast?"

"One has their ways. Was that an Enforcer?"

She nodded. "Still haven't gotten to properly use it yet."

"Thankfully I wasn't your first victim." His smile glistened in the monitor's light. "Find anything out of the ordinary?"

"Yeah, actually." Xia beckoned him closer and showed the account's username. Kibou's face eased into satisfaction.

"Ah, that delightful soul. What brilliance. I don't suppose you've figured out what happened here?"

She glanced back to the monitor. "He wanted me to find this. And the place is ransacked, but there doesn't seem to be any rhyme or reason to it. And in here..." Her eyes swept the empty room. "Everything is gone. All he cared about. I'm thinking that he left himself. But wanted to make it look like something happened to him, so as to throw off any potential trail."

The wrinkles around his eyes deepened as he smiled once more. "Precisely. And knowing Opell, I question his affinity for the theatrical."

"What do you mean?"

"I would say, once you've extracted all the files you need, leave with haste. And once we leave, there is no returning."

Her mouth parted slightly as she understood the gist. At that moment, the file transfer *pinged* with completion.

"Shall we?" Kibou moved with an agile grace towards the door, Xia right behind. Right on cue, as the door shut behind them, the sound of a *CRASH* boomed behind them as the computer self-destructed.

***

"Can we talk?"

It was two in the morning. Too late for a message like this. Especially one from Dames.

Xia sat on the edge of Fay's bed, staring at the message like it was poisonous. She was going to view the images from Opell, but the incoming message had frozen her to her spot.

Then came heat. And for the first time in a long time, Xia was grateful for it.

"Knock, knock," Mai said, without knocking, and opened the door to Fay's room. Fay had moved temporarily into Burgs' room, kicking Burgs out onto the couch.

Xia looked up as Mai entered. She did a small twirl. "I basically feel back to normal. Even the weird eye stuff. They said my eyes could hurt for a while, but they only did the first few hours. Leo had a few tips for that. Told me not to move my eyes around too much, and to let myself 'sense' something first before moving my eyes towards it. I think it helped. I'm basically ready for my suit!" She said it all with a smile on her face. Then it faltered. "I feel like we haven't really gotten to talk much recently."

"We haven't. That's fine. You've been recovering. And I've been busy."

"Busy is one thing to call it! Hell! From the escape at that creep of a doctor's house, to the mission, all your narrow escapes, I can't believe I missed it all!" Her shoulders drooped. "But I would have held you back. Those escapes likely wouldn't have even happened if I were there."

Xia scooted on the bed, giving Mai comfortable room to sit down. Mai sat. "You'll get your chance to prove yourself soon enough. Not like you can't hold your own. Remember that guy at the bar?"

"Unfortunately, the skills that combat horny folks aren't quite the same as the ones that are useful against the military."

"We'll see," Xia replied. The conversation lulled, and like wading into shark-infested waters, Xia asked the pressing questions that had been wading in her mind. "So, you and Leonardo?"

Mai's cheeks immediately reddened. Red suited her. "Oh. Yeah. I have been wanting to tell you all about it. But also not."

"Why not?"

She chuckled. "Does that even need to be asked? You're not exactly a romantic, Xia. I feel awkward."

"Oh. Yeah, I guess. Well it's an awkward thing, isn't it?"

Mai's head cocked in perplexity. "No. It's not awkward at all. I mean, it started out a little bit that way. Mainly because I was so confused that my initial feelings of dislike at the guy were being pulled away. No, not that. They were morphing. Morphing into excitement. Butterflies, you know?"

"Butterflies? Like, the bug?"

"It's an expression. A fluttery feeling. In your gut. Or maybe your heart." Mai brought a hand right below her chest, to her sternum. Then she placed it on Xia's. Xia's breath hitched. "Right there. Makes you feel almost sick. But in a good way. And when the source of those butterflies touches you, or even better yet, kisses you, they all fly away. In an explosion." She flung her hands in the open and danced her fingers in the air, mimicking her words. Xia was familiar with the sick feeling. She thought of when Mai saw her naked body. She thought of herself and Dames alone in her apartment. But the explosion. She had never felt that.

For her, she didn't really think it was possible.

"So who made the first move?" She didn't really care to know, but she couldn't make the logical jump from hating someone's guts to suddenly wrapping yourself into them, both physically and emotionally.

Mai's reddening face turned scarlet. "It was me. I had been bickering with him so much, but he was so patient. Nothing I could say got him. And the way he looked at me. Butterflies. So, I planted one on him. He was so shocked! Just stared at me. Didn't even kiss me back. But then later, after my dose of painkillers, he kissed me on the forehead. And I had been going crazy in that time, because I didn't know what he thought of what I had done. So when he kissed my forehead, I grabbed his face and kissed him again. But this time, he kissed back."

Xia listened to the recounting with nothing but the pits of hollow antipathy in her gut, but she couldn't help but notice the buds of love and joy blossoming in Mai's voice. And because of those buds, Xia also felt the faintest touches of happiness for her Virgin friend.

Well, not a Virgin anymore.

"You really think you are almost back to normal? Are you sure you'll be ready for the real deal? Because that time is going to come soon. I'm kind of surprised it hasn't already."

Mai cocked her head once more. "What do you mean?"

"The government was already onto Dr. Nagawa. They knew the reason their 'Virgin brains' weren't working is because he was swapping them. But their attempt at having Virgins volunteer to come to them willingly hasn't worked. The Revitalization Project has only attracted people with mods. But they can't kidnap Virgins since that will alter their brain chemistry. But the government still wants to take you guys. What are they going to do? And when are they going to do it? That's the burning question. And we need to act before we discover the answer."

She nodded solemnly. "Have you looked at the files from Opell's? Leo told me what happened."

Word traveled fast. Xia was bombarded with questioning by Burgs as soon as she returned, but luckily he respected her wish to view them in private.

"Not yet."

A flash of excitement. "Can I look at them with you? Before the rest of the group tomorrow morning?"

Xia smirked. "Sure." The two rose from the foot of the bed and approached Fay's computer. Like everything else, the keyboard and background were a deep royal blue.

"Fay really likes blue," Mai mused as she took a seat beside her.

"Your room at the VL was all pink." Xia gulped at the memory of her first encounter with the girl.

"Yeah, well each of us had to pick a color and stick to it. Make it our brand at the place, so to speak. So I got kind of stuck with it."

"You also bought a pink couch for my apartment."

Mai raised her eyebrows with a nod in defeat. "I suppose I did."

Xia transferred the files to the computer and began opening the images. The satellite images showed the nearby forest closest to Freesia, each image gradually getting closer and closer, until the images pixelated as they got close to the city.

"Seems the same as before," Mai said.

"There's another folder. Same images, but modified."

She opened the new folder. On these files, text notes were displayed at the bottom of each image.

Interference from ground, not from plasma dome

Next image. Arrows drawn pointing to the green stretch of land between the forest and the city.

COMING FROM THE GROUND.

Next image. The stretch of land was circled.

0.4 MILES, move FAST

Next image. The garbled one.

WHAT IS HIDING UNDERNEATH? NOT JUST GOV. MOVE. THE RUMBLINGS. NOT QUAKES. FROM THE GROUND. MOVE FAST. WHAT IS IT? WHAT IS IT XIA? DON'T TRY TO FIND OUT. JUST RUN.

"The rumblings aren't quakes? Meaning, not earthquakes? What does he mean?"

Xia didn't answer. She stared at the screen, eyes narrowed, flicking back and forth between the images. Then she took the image right before the garbled one and zoomed in.

"Do you see something?"

"I need an incon scanner. Don't know if Fay has one on here," she looked through the short list of programs on Fay's computer. Wasn't much on there except for multiple music and media file players. Seems she was appreciative of the arts along with Burgs. "Go ask Burgs."

Her face paled. "W-what?"

"He'll know how to do it. Go on."

"He's probably sleeping."

"Burgs never sleeps."

The paling continued. "Don't you already have one on your fancy cell thingy?"

Xia rolled her eyes. "I need one installed on the computer itself in order to properly scan for any inconsistencies. You need to practice talking to the guy."

"He hates me," she huffed.

"He doesn't hate you. And if he does, who cares?"

"I care!"

"Go." She gave Mai a push. "I promise you, he doesn't hate you."

Mai shuffled with reluctance as she made her way out the door and across the hall. A moment later Xia faintly heard Burgs bark "whaddya want?!"

Xia glanced back down towards her cell chip, Dames' phantom message lingering.

Can we talk?

Why was she feeling so damn nervous? And why could she not think of anything to respond? It was a simple question. Wasn't it? When did things not get simple?

A few moments later, Mai returned with a small drive in hand, interrupting Xia's conundrum.

"This better be worth it," Mai said as she took a seat with an exasperated *thud.*

Xia shook her head, as if that would clear the gnats of anxiety. "It will be."

Mai's toil was worth it. After Xia installed the software, she ran the images through its various modes, testing for any inconsistencies unnoticeable to the naked eye. From digital tamperings to natural flaws in an image, it tested for anything and everything. A list of numbers and codes popped up, all looking like unintelligible jargon to Mai.

Mai leaned in further. "What's it all mean?"

"There," Xia muttered as she highlighted one of the lines of results. She then highlighted a small area of the ground in the expanse of field, roughly halfway between the outside of the city and the neighboring forest. She ran the program once more and a smaller line of jargon popped up. "See this area right here?"

Mai stared. There was absolutely nothing noteworthy about it. She nodded.

"The ground isn't uniform. It should be completely seamless. But instead, it's as if it were gutted and then replanted."

"Okay," Mai hummed. "Could that be the exit? The tunnels are underground. Which means you'd be coming up from the ground."

"Potentially, but that's pretty far from the Outer Hub. Plus, why would it be covered?"

"Maybe because they want to make sure nobody leaves right now?"

The thought sent a depressing shiver down her spine. Rattling each vertebra. Was there a chance that getting past the gate would get them nowhere? That the exit to the outside world was holed in? But then she remembered the captions from Opell.

WHAT IS HIDING UNDERNEATH? NOT JUST GOV. MOVE. THE RUMBLINGS. NOT QUAKES. FROM THE GROUND. MOVE FAST. WHAT IS IT? WHAT IS IT XIA? DON'T TRY TO FIND OUT. JUST RUN.

"Or, this is what Opell is warning about. That whatever is under there is causing the quakes. And once we're outside, we need to get away. Fast."

36

THE PLAN

"She's late."

"Are you sure she's coming?"

"She'll be here," Kibou stated with a calm confidence. He sipped on his third espresso.

Mai paced back and forth along the couch, practicing her steps, Leo watching with a mixture of pride and the seedlings of love. Even after learning how they came to be, Xia couldn't tell exactly what Mai saw in the good-looking blonde. And as she watched them interact, she couldn't help but feel pangs of distaste.

Fay spoke from her usual spot at the window. "I'll go check on Grimer. He's been stuck down there waiting—"

But she was cut off by the *DING* of the approaching elevator. A collective breath was taken as the doors opened and Lorena entered through them, Grimer trailing behind like a nervous dog.

Xia never noticed just how low the penthouse ceilings fell before seeing Lorena's towering presence inside. She briefly thought of Dames and how he'd likely have to bend over.

"Blonde. Dark blonde. And tall. Because I didn't have to bend over too much."

His words lingered in her ears, and she felt the same pang of distaste that she'd become familiarized with when watching Leo and Mai. She coughed. She wanted some water. Or some bourbon.

Lorena's pink eyes swept over the room before landing on Kibou. Her face softened. "Kibou," she said as she rushed forward. Her long legs took her before him in three brisk steps. She hunched over and enveloped him in a tight embrace. The size difference between them was comical, but the heart warmth overshadowed such awkwardness.

"You've grown," Kibou chuckled. He reached his hand upwards and caressed her cheek. "And the beauty with it."

"It's been what, over 15 years now?"

"17 years and three moons. Too many moons, my child." A misty haze glossed over Kibou's eyes. A fog around the ever-stoic mountain.

"Let's cut right to it," Burgs said as he took a few formidable steps toward Lorena. While he was much shorter, he still held a solid presence in her midst. "Seems like you're some kind of tech guru. I won't test your skills. Old man here's done enough talking to vouch for you. And being contracted by the gov, well, that speaks for itself. Doesn't it?"

He glared toward her. There was almost a sense of animosity in his glare, his deep brown eyes unblinking. The hairs on Xia's neck stood at careful attention.

"It could. In my case, it does. Trust me. But why should I trust you? My insight is more valuable than all of you lot combined." She made a twirling show with her finger.

"Now now," Kibou chastised. "Let's not play such games. Clearly a foundation of trust has been established for you to even walk through those doors, Lorena. And my presence is enough, is it not?"

A playful grin danced on Lorena's lips as she glanced at Xia before turning to Kibou. "As always, you're never wrong. But I'm not sure how I can help you. You're going to need me there to open the door. Xia told me about your little slag costume charade. I have no interest in playing dress-up. And that door sends an alert every time it's opened. As soon as they know there's an unauthorized exit, they'll be on your asses in two seconds."

Xia figured this. But she was one step ahead. "Lorena, you created that door. You can get past it. Can you break it?"

Lorena's pink stare narrowed on Xia. "Why?"

"I can't imagine how skilled you must be to have had the FRF contract you to create such a door. And from the few things I know about you: your skill, your secrecy, and your pride, I am guessing you wouldn't leave that project finished. I'm guessing you would maintain some type of access to it. And it's why you've worked so hard to keep yourself hidden."

The group glanced between them.

"Am I right?"

Lorena smirked. "Yeah, yeah you are."

"So you could break the door? In a way that the FRF couldn't fix?"

"Yes—"

"Wait a second," Leo piped up. "If you have remote access to the door, why not just open it remotely?"

"Use your brain, pretty boy," Lorena snapped, eyes sharp. "That door has more security and deep-rooted locking mechanisms than half of Cyber City put together. You think I could just open that with a click of a remote?"

Leo shrugged. "I have no idea. I have no idea how any of that stuff works."

"You don't need to to know that I can't do that. What I can do is send a self-destruct signal via the private channel I created when I first installed the door. The FRF won't be able to detect what's wrong with it. They'll call me up. They'll send out a slag escort to pick me up and supervise me fixing it."

Xia nodded. "And when they come, we're going to take them out."

"We're gonna what?" Grimer's eyes widened.

"Burgs, you always said you wanted a slag helm so you could get your hands on the deep-scan tech? Well, this'll be your chance."

***

With some back and forth and bickering between them, the mission was drafted.

Lorena would remotely disable the door. Once that occurred, it would be a small matter of time before FRF officials would reach out and demand her to fix it. She'd oblige wholeheartedly. Being the vital person she was, it was likely that several slags would come to fetch her. She'd give the address of one of several hideouts she had scattered over the city— a hideout that she and Grimer would make fully signal-proof. Couldn't have any slags sending out an SOS when they were faced with a sudden ambush.

The group was iffy about the ambush. It would be a difficult fight. They needed to ensure that the helms of the slags were untouched, since they would be stealing those helms and wearing them themselves. This way the same slags that would leave to fetch Lorena would be the same ones returning with her. Except it wouldn't be— it'd be the motley crew.

The tram would be their Trojan's horse. The exact number of slags coming to fetch Lorena would be unknown, but she suspected four or five. Xia and Fay were necessary, and Leonardo was the next obvious choice. And while Xia had hoped Grimer or Burgs would push for a spot, the next one went to Mai. Mai had to go. She had gone through so much to be a part of this. Given up so much. Yet Xia couldn't deny the girl was a liability. And even worse, the thought of something horrible happening to her was something Xia couldn't think about. The final spot would potentially go to Grimer, but the entire crew hoped that wouldn't be necessary.

One "lucky" Virgin was tasked with accompanying them on this trip in order to make trustworthy contact with the Lost Samurai on the outside. Xia had foolishly assumed this entire time that the lucky person would be Kibou. But Kibou was old and much too valuable, and his disappearance would raise too many brows. And Kibou only had one man in mind for the job: Buko. The same samurai who held such opposition to Xia when she first met Kibou. The same samurai who didn't want Xia in the Pagoda in the first place. He would be tasked with the ultimate mission.

He also was one of the only ones who could operate a cycle. Which was the other important part of the plan.

It was far enough of a trek to their destination. But Xia trusted those cryptic messages from Opell.

"MOVE FAST. WHAT IS IT? WHAT IS IT XIA? DON'T TRY TO FIND OUT. JUST RUN."

What better way to move fast than a cycle?

And so, like the scouting mission, the plan was both simple and anything but. They'd move through the Inner Hub to the Outer Hub, then travel underground and take the red-lighted passageway to the door that led back outside. The door that only Lorena could open.

There was room for two cycles in the tram. Both would be installed with anti-scanner cloaking mechanisms by Burgs, and Buko'd be forced to wedge himself in between them, shielding himself as well. It was inevitable that the tram would be deep-scanned at one point, and so the interior needed to be clear of anything conspicuous. (Two cycles and a Virgin were quite conspicuous.)

While two people could fit on a cycle, Buko's one condition was he would be riding alone. So it would be Buko and Xia each riding solo. (Mai didn't like that.) The two would race to the Lost Samurai via the coordinates from Opell's satellite images. Originally, they planned to communicate with Opell and Kibou via that same satellite: two large broken tree branches forming an X on the north end of the forest if there was a successful way to get the Virgins out of the city, or an X on the South end if hope was lost. But with Opell missing, that part was made temporarily obsolete. Kibou remained confident that Opell would make himself visible in due time.

"But...what if there is no way back in?" Mai had asked. It was the question that forever loomed above them, too dangerous to even ask. "What will you do?"

Xia's face remained forever unchanged. "I'll figure it out. Like I always do."

The mission was significantly more dangerous than the scouting mission, both due to the contraband inside the tram and the lack of escort by Commander Young. Above all, there was no saving grace mechanism from Burgs. Hopefully, being Lorena's escort would be enough.

"You must be outta your goddamn mind." The raspy voice barked through her cell.

"Russel—"

"That's my baby, my goddamn baby. You ain't takin my baby—"

"Russel, I'm not asking for you to give me your bike." Although he had three, so technically he could spare one, Xia understood the love he had for each individual cycle. "I just need you to fix mine up like yours. And one more too." Any minute now, Fay would be leaving Neyo's, the small motorcycle vendor, with a brand new cycle. Two were needed for the mission, and they both needed to be fixed up in order to work with electromagnetic interference to ensure they could run outside the city walls. Something Russel had done for all three of his bikes.

"I want ten cartons of them cigs. And a slab of meat. Two slabs. And a case of beer. Two cases."

"Deal." Then she ended the call.

And so, the place turned busy as everyone delved into their newfound tasks: Burgs began working on the anti-scanner cloaking mechanisms; Lorena and Grimer outfitted one of her hideouts to inhibit outgoing radio signals for the ambush; Fay went to purchase the new cycle; Kibou acclimated Buko to the entire situation; and Leonardo further helped Mai get used to the mods.

An invisible clock was ticking. And nobody could see the time.

37

Back to My Place

"Get off my lawn! You know how hard it is to grow grass out here?"

"Grass? You call this grass? Those specks of green hidden in the dirt?"

"Watch it, tough guy. You think you can just parade around like you own the place? Let's not forget who's garage you're usin'." Russel took the cigarette out of his mouth and spat, perfectly landing on one of the few blades of grass that barely littered the 'lawn'.

"That how you water 'em? No wonder they can't grow for shit." Burgs let out a tight-lipped snicker.

"Where the fuck is Xia? She got a leash on you?"

Not a moment too late, Xia sped down the dusty road, cruising a little too fast, and swerved in front of Russel's. Even from across the bare yard Xia could see the tension between the two men. Fay stood off to the side, leaning on the side of the small house, arms crossed with a stern look of disapproval.

"You get the other bike here?" Xia called out as she dismounted the cycle, sliding off her helmet.

"Not even a hello? Well fuck me, Xi."

"I'd rather not. Hi Russel. Thanks again." She gave a brief smile before turning towards Burgs and Fay. "The bike?"

"Underground in that garage of his. If you can call it that."

"Oh, for void's sake, Burgs!" Fay shouted from behind him. She made eyes with Xia. "They've been bickering since they first laid eyes on each other. Like watching two school kids try to prove who's the bigger bully."

"I ain't no bully. But I am bigger," Russel mused as he swelled his chest. That wasn't exactly true. Russel was taller, sure, but he had the frame of a lamppost. Burgs could knock him over with a heavy belch.

"Russel, knock it off," Xia said, half placing herself in front of Burgs. She could sense the waters of rage simmering beside her, and she wasn't about to let Burgs bring it to a boil. "We are very appreciative of you working on those cycles. Another token," she tossed a pack of *Smokettes* at him, the premium brand of cigarettes that Russel could never afford.

"What the—those are mine!" Burgs objected.

Xia rolled her eyes. "The bikes, everything look like it'll work okay?"

Russel lost some of his gumption. "Well, there's actually an issue. Your so-called 'cloaking mechanisms'," he shot a nasty glance towards Burgs, "interfere with the tech I've installed. Let me show you. You can still bring her on down though." He motioned towards Xia's bike.

"*Him,*" Xia corrected as she pushed the bike into the open garage, Fay and Burgs following behind. Inside held nothing out of the ordinary. Tools and gear lined the walls, hanging on metal hooks. Cobwebs littered the corners and the ceiling. Xia inadvertently shuddered. Then Russel pulled on one of the empty hooks and a panel revealed itself in the wall.

"Everyone move on back," he said. The trio obliged and Russel stuck his thumb onto the pad. An electric whirring began as the ground slowly began to slope downwards, the once flat ground now a path underground.

Russel pulled on his hat. "Shall we?"

Xia had only been in Russel's home and garage a few times. It was clear where all of his money and passion lie because his home was as barebones and run down as they came. But his garage?

They entered the massive underground space as the driveway floor lifted back to an unassuming upper floor. Bright golden spheres of light lined the walls. The dirt floor and paneled walls insulated the place allowing for a toasty temperature. It was almost cozy. Three cycles sat on pedestals of various heights for no reason other than for pleasurable viewing. Those were Russel's. Xia wanted to take a closer look but she kept her attention towards the cycle in the middle of the room, that one pedestal-less. That one theirs.

Xia pushed her own cycle beside the one Fay bought. It was nice: sleek and a bit smaller than hers, but more gadgets up top.

She liked hers better.

"So here lies the issue. My tech installed no problem. Easy peasy. This bad boy can ride anywhere, completely immune to outside electromag forces. But as soon as you activate the shitty anti-scanning whatchamacallit—"

"Watch your lopsided mouth!" Burgs spat.

"—it don't work no more."

"Do you guys know why?" Xia asked.

Fay spoke up. "Basically, Russel's tech is an EMI absorber, and it generates its own electromagnetic field to counteract any interferences. Burgs' tech relies on manipulating magnetic fields. So basically, Burgs' tech warps the EMI absorber's own signals, making it useless."

"So they can't work simultaneously? Couldn't we just disable the EMI absorber until we get outside the walls? We shouldn't need both technology at the same time."

Burgs crossed his burly arms. "That's not an option because this *idjit* here made it pervasive tech. It's always on. Only way to disable it is to uninstall it."

"Besides," Fay cut through Russel's inevitable rebuke. "We *shouldn't* need it at the same time, but we might. Would be good to have that option."

"So how do we fix it?"

"Easiest way would be a Nanoparticle Harmonizer Module," Burgs replied.

"I don't know what that is."

"Neither do I," Russel said.

"It ain't that crazy of a piece of tech, and it would be the quickest to install. But I don't have the time to craft one up though, or the materials handy. We need someone who is well-versed in electromagnetic engineering *and* nanotechnology. Not an easy ask."

One person immediately came to mind.

"Let me make a call..."

Xia stood outside the garage, the oppressive heat sinking into her suit as she explained her request to Flux over her cellchip.

"No."

"I can pay—"

"I don't need your money. I got people payin' up the wazoo for a hundredth of what you're askin' for."

"Your work is good. Beyond good." Xia spoke urgently into her cell chip.

"Flattery'll get you nowhere. I know my work is the best. Don't need you to tell me that. Call me if you have problems with your bike's EMF. Otherwise, leave me alone." Flux ended the call before Xia could say another word.

A memory sparked. *If there's one person I trust in this god-forsaken city, it's Dames.*

She called down towards the trio below. "I'll get us that tech!"

It was a mile and a half to Mickey's. She considered having Mai tag along. The girl was useful when it came to such social situations of persuasion. Especially with men. But Xia figured this was something she should do alone, so she left immediately from Russel's to the bar.

Lively chatter met her ears once she opened the bar door. She let out a small groan. She was hoping for a dead night, but Mickey's was poppin'. And the reason why stood behind the bar himself.

Mickey was an old man. A very old man. Much too old to still be alive. People didn't live as long as they used to in the city, but Mickey defied the odds, his alcoholism somehow fueling his lifespan as well as his bank account. He didn't come into the bar often. But when he did, it was always a special affair for the regulars.

Mickey spoke to a gaggle of regulars crowded at the bar and they all let out a whooping laugh. Dames stood beside Mickey, (there was no way he could man the bar himself), laughing along with the crowd. The smile didn't quite reach his obsidian eyes. A moment later, his eye caught Xia's. He turned back to Mickey and joked further.

Xia took a seat at the end of the bar, away from the noise. She waited. And waited. And it was Mickey who told Dames to tend to her.

"Hey," she said. A bird of anxiety fluttered its wings in her voice.

"Hey," he parroted. "What can I get you?"

"The usual."

"What's that again?"

Her shoulders tensed. "Make me whatever you want. I need to talk to you." The rest of her body tensed. "Another favor."

Dames let out a hollow laugh. One she'd never heard before. "The hell, Xia. That all I'm good for? That all I'm worth to you? Fuckin' favors."

Dames wasn't one to swear. He was one of the few souls she knew whose vocabulary wasn't oozing with profanity. She didn't like the way it sounded coming from him. What was his deal?

"Of course not. It's just…" Her voice trailed off as she looked to the side, staring at nothing. "A lot has happened. A lot is going to happen. If I can get some help from a certain friend of yours, that is."

"Who?"

"The one who made the barrier for my bike?" She didn't use Flux's name aloud. Dames stared at her, something flashing in his eye. He turned around towards the opposite side of the bar. At first, she wondered if she had set him off, but he began concocting her drink, the same pour of whiskey with some mystery syrup and a fat cherry.

He returned and placed the drink before her.

Men like to feel wanted. Everyone does. Mai's savvy came back to her from the last time they had come to the bar together. Oh, how things had changed.

"So, Mickey's still kickin' I see."

Dames glanced over to the old man. Mickey laughed again, gums bare from his lack of teeth. He could easily get some fake ones, but Mickey lived through it all. The fall of the Old Times and the rise of Freesia. The advancement of mods and glorification of all things technology. Something told Xia Mickey hadn't changed much in that time, that there was a reason his passion and profession was one of the oldest. Alcohol producer and consumer.

"Would be interesting to pick his brain," Xia said.

"Not much left to pick. The man's got his jokes, got his stories, but he doesn't get into much else. Every time I think it's his last time here in the bar, I'm proven wrong."

Xia smirked. "I always think the same thing. How long have you known him?" She knew Dames had been a bartender as long as she first started drinking. But Xia had no idea of Dames' true age. With modage, it was often hard to tell.

"Since I was but a young babe."

Xia cocked her head in confusion.

"He's my grandfather."

The answer came as a slap in the face to Xia, even though she knew it had no right to. "Mickey's your grandfather? And you never told me?"

He shrugged as he began cleaning a glass. "Never came up. Not like you ask much about *me,* anyways."

A pang of guilt hit them both.

Dames didn't let it stew for long. "That friend of yours, Mai? You still hanging around with her?"

Xia took a sip, debating just how much to tell. Her friend, Mai. The Virgin. But no longer a Virgin. Took a sip. Currently holed up in an apartment, but not her apartment. Because they dropped out of there out of fear of the slags checking them out. Another sip. Why would the slags be checking her out? Why, because she was in the home of Dr. Nagawa, the renowned ex-surgeon of the FRF Military, who had been harvesting Virgin brains before the government got the chance. Another sip. Why was she there? Because she's trying to help these Virgins. Help them before it's too late. She brought the glass to her lips a final time, but nothing but the bare cube met them.

Dames peered down at her with a mixture of intrigue and concern. "Are you *trying* to get drunk?"

She eyed him back, noting the initial callousness he held was drifting away. "Gimme another." She shook the glass with a snicker. Dames needed no telling twice.

Two hours later, Xia was thankful she didn't have her cycle. She wasn't *wasted,* per se, but even in her swirling state of inebriation she knew that cycle was her baby and there was no way she could ride it. She was careful to steer clear of any personal topics and took advantage of the fact that she had never pressed much into Dames' personal life in the past. And it wasn't all for personal gain. No, the questions came naturally. Partially due to the booze, sure. But mainly due to the curiosity that had dwelled inside her ever since she met the gentle giant. He was a mess of contradictions that she never put any effort into sorting out because there was no reason to—and because talking to people like that was scarier than any violent job she'd been on.

But as he told her about his grandfather, who was very much unlike her own, she was swept into a sea of nostalgia as she recalled memories of her own grandfather. The booze added to the sea, rocking the wistful waves. She got swept up in the stories of Mickey. And then lost in the memories of Youle.

Mickey had seven children, but only two survived through the rise of Freesia, one being Dames' father. His father, like many in Cyber City, fell into the lifestyle of constant and insistent pleasure, spending most of his time and money in the Red Light District or gaming cafes. And that's how a certain prostitute became Dames' mother. It was incredibly uncommon for a prostitute to get pregnant; there were a plethora of mods to inhibit conception. But the risk was greater if you didn't use mods.

"Your mother wassa Virgin?" Xia asked with a faint slur.

Dames nodded. "She kept working right up until I was born. That was right at the time the government began instituting child-care programs for unwanted kids. She wanted to send me there. My dad did too. But Mickey wouldn't hear of it. So he raised me. Although I still saw my parents occasionally. Circumstances were awkward, to say the least."

Xia swallowed every detail he shared along with the drinks he kept placing before her. And by the end of her last drink, she was so close to divulging about her own grandfather. Her own life. So close to opening the rusty box inside her chest that siphoned in every fear, every loving memory, every hope and desire.

"I don't think you can drive," Dames said with an apologetic smile.

"Yeah, thanks a lot. Don't have it right now anyway." She staggered off the stool. "Ah, fuck," she muttered as the floor rocked beneath her. Still lost at sea. "I need to get back."

"I'll walk you back."

She shook her head, the movement dizzying. "I'm not at my apartment. Haven't been there in over a week."

He puzzled. "Why? Where are you staying?"

She waved him off. "It's a long story. I'll walk. It'll take a few hours, but I'll manage." She could manage. But the thought was daunting. And then the memory of her apartment resurfaced. Longing combined with curiosity. She had purposely stayed away from her apartment. The prospect of it being invaded was awful. If she left it alone, keeping that question unanswered, that prospect would never come to fruition. But now, as she stood in the bar with the floor rocking beneath her, that fear was gone. And the much shorter walk was all the more enticing. "Never mind. Back to my apartment."

Dames closed his eyes with a silent chuckle. "Come on, let's go."

"No, it's fine," she hurried towards the door but her big foot caught on a barstool and she began to fall forward. But of course, Dames was quick and hooked his arm around her middle, preventing her from completing the fall. The lurch into her stomach almost made her wretch. "Fine," she groaned in defeat, still hanging over Dames' massive forearm.

The chilly night air helped to sharpen her senses. Her steps were a bit more formidable. She didn't want to have to lean on Dames. The two walked in silence. As the number of passersby lessened and the street grew dumpier, dumpier, they eventually made it to Xia's apartment. She gazed upwards towards the towering building. Had the slags drawn the connection between the runaway "whore" and Xia? Had they been inside? As both the question and the apartment loomed over her, she had the sudden realization that she didn't want to find the answer alone.

"Come upstairs with me?" Xia asked. Dames looked at her with surprise, then quickly wiped the expression away.

All he did was nod. And it wasn't until they stood in the elevator, creaking past each floor, that Xia realized just how her question came off.

Oh, fuck me. But not literally. Anything but literally. Unless sleeping with Dames could get him to speak to Flux? It probably would. But the mere proposition was impossible for her to pursue. Oh, if only Mai were there.

Xia's terror was temporarily replaced with a dark anticipation as they exited the elevator and approached her apartment's entrance. Even in her hazy vision, she could see her hand was shaking as she brought up the cell chip to unlock the door. There was a click. She inhaled. She opened the door. They stepped inside. She could hear Dames was about to speak. She whipped up a hand to silence him.

Her eyes swept over the room, taking in every detail. The leftover takeout container of ramen from the night she left for Burgs. The blanket thrown to the floor from when Leonardo came to fetch Mai. The fridge door left ajar after Leonardo grabbed her injections. She scanned the room. Nothing out of place, but nothing perfectly *in* place either. The slags hadn't been here.

Relief came like an ocean and she moaned along with it. "Thank the spirits..."

Dames coughed. The tension returned. She needed to slice through it with something. Anything. Then she remembered the small black box gifted from Burgs, kept snugly inside her suit. While she was sure the slags hadn't been here, she could never take too many precautions. She took out the soundbox and activated it, ensuring anything they said was warped into a different conversation. "I haven't been here in a week. I had to leave it for a while. With Mai, too. Safety concerns. I... had a run-in with slags. I barely escaped." She wandered over towards her window of a wall, staring out through the glass below. She missed this view. It was bigger and grander in Burgs' apartment. But this was home.

"You what?"

"Yeah. I got lucky. If it hadn't been for Burgs... although, Burgs was the reason I was there in the first place."

"Who's Burgs?"

"He's—uh—he's a guy I'm working with. With helping the Virgins."

"Like with the fods?"

It dawned on Xia just how much had happened since she last spoke with Dames. "I've moved on from that for now."

"To what?"

What a question. And if she had been sober, she wouldn't have dared say the answer. "To help the Virgins escape."

"Escape where?" He now stood beside her.

"The city." She stared out towards the distance. Past the massive metropolis that she had never truly second-guessed, never dreamed of stepping out of. And here she was, so close to doing it.

"That's impossible," Dames looked down at her as if she was pulling his leg. Or maybe he thought she was stupid. Xia couldn't tell. She used her emoti-scanner. "Quit using that damn thing," he snapped.

She startled and abruptly stopped. Her eyes lingered on him. Then the room started rocking once more, like wading through the ripple from a large wave. "Oh no," she groaned. She rarely reached this level of drunk. Usually, she'd have stopped drinking before this point, or she'd have had another which would have thrown her into a blacked-out oblivion. Her stomach churned. She had the faintest urge to cry.

"Xia?" He asked, this time with more concern.

She waved her hand dismissively, expression growing fiery. "I'm fine. And it's not impossible. I'm so damn close. I've been inside there already."

"Inside where?" Dames grew impatient with her half-tellings.

"The Northern Inner Hub. And the Outer Hub. And the tunnel. You know there's a tunnel? That's how they leave the Outer Hub. They go in trams and they go along these dark tunnels, and there's forks in the road, and I don't know where they all go, but when I went, I ended up at HQ. Headquarters. And there's this massive electric sphere thing that's almost fleshy. I don't know what it does. But it freaks me out. And I'm gonna get them out through there. The Virgins. 'Cause if I don't, the government's gonna use their brains. Why? Hell if I know. Because they're sick. They're sick and controlling and they lied about the Revitalization Project. They lied about the outside world. They lied about trees. Trees, Dames! Trees can grow. Real ones, not the stupid fucking S-Trees. They lie and they control everything. Even music. You know music can be so damn beautiful, Dames? It almost made me cry. I almost cried…"

Xia didn't notice how loud her words had gotten until they grew softer than a whisper as her last sentence faded, and her shoulders shook, and her eyes began to flood with tears. Of what exactly, she didn't know. The next thing she *did* know was her being wrapped into Dames' colossal arms, and her tears soaking through his tight black shirt. She felt his hand wrap around her head, holding it close to his chest, her hair pressing warmly into it. And while the tears were confusing, and the feelings were confusing, she couldn't deny that this closeness felt anything but. It just felt nice.

Their hold was broken as a sudden piercing flash of red burned in Xia's vision. It came from everywhere, invading every sense, electricity firing in her ears, her eyes, her head. She screamed. Her knees buckled. And Dames did the same as his entire body felt the electric flames.

38

The Scarlet Signal

Cacophony. Pure, absolute, mayhem. The screaming. The wails. The city fell into chaos as people were brought to their knees, various joints and orifices sizzling with white-hot pain. The massive screen in the center city square that continuously looped various advertisements was replaced with a blank red screen.

Some slags stood on, their bodies forever stoic. They appeared to be watching the mayhem unfold. But while the AI chips told their bodies to stay still, it didn't stop their joints from tensing as they, too, felt the debilitating pain.

***

A Virgin teen gazed upwards towards the foggy sky as she gingerly slid the needle into her forearm. It didn't take long for her to see stars. That used to be a normal view, according to her great-grandparents. Stars in the sky. Now she needed drugs to see them. The high that came from a shot of nexanine was like no other. Her head lolled and she looked back down to her friends in front of her. Friends was a generous term. She knew close to nothing about them. But they got her drugs, and they got high together before stumbling back to their respective homes. The two men looked equally zonked. Eyes glazed, lips parted, breathing slow.

"Do you see the stars?" She asked. Well, she thought she did. Her words got lost somewhere between her mind and her lips. She wasn't sure. Then she started laughing.

The other two laughed with her, but then stopped in unison. Their eyes grew wide. One slammed his hands over his ears, and the other covered his eyes. They groaned and moaned as the pain swept into their senses. The source was far. They couldn't tell from where. The drug dulled their awareness. All they could feel was pain.

And then it stopped. As quickly as it started.

***

The effects weren't quite as drastic in the Red Light District due to the lack of screens. A sweaty and near-naked Levi Leonhart laid upon a mess of pillows while a lavender-skinned prostitute rode him in reverse. It hit her first. Her body seized as the pain enveloped her whole. She locked up with Levi still inside her. Then the pain hit him. It was light in the eyes. But his penis. His poor penis raged as fire consumed it.

***

The signal was a calculated risk. But it was needed.

***

Xia vomited. Dames was soaked. He barely noticed. What he did notice was the screen in the corner of Xia's apartment was no longer a blaring scarlet, but back to blank black.

"What just happened?" Dames asked. Voice low.

Xia brought her hand to her mouth, her stomach threatening to upheave itself once more. "I don't know. It hurt a lot. My eyes still hurt."

"My whole body felt like it was on fire."

"My eyes..." She rubbed her dirty gloved hands on them. "I'm so confused."

"You should get some rest," Dames said as he half led, half pushed her onto the couch. She protested a little, but the come down from the pain was making her very tired. And so was her drunkenness.

Her eyes widened in a moment of sudden, horrified clarity. "My injection!"

"You got one on you?"

Her face softened as she nodded, head lolling like a ragdoll, and pointed to her ribcage. Her eyes began to flit closed. Dames gulped as he slid a hand inside her pocket, right below her chest, and took out a syringe. Of course she had to be covered from neck to foot. He removed her glove and began to roll up the sleeve to inject the serum but his hands paused as he noted the scars on her hand. Some were fresh, and he was reminded of her saying she just barely escaped the slags a week prior. But the others were old, resembling acid scars. He thought of how she always wore a glove, but he never thought of a deeper reason for it. He should have realized. With Xia, there was a deeper reason for everything. His hands moved with delicate apprehension as he rolled the sleeve upwards. More scars. Deep and harsh and fresh. Jagged lines of violent hurry.

The syringe was tiny in his hand, but he inserted it with a delicate skill—one that came with concocting many cocktails. Then he rolled the sleeve back down and put the glove back on, one careful finger at a time. He wrapped her in the blanket on the floor and watched as she instinctively curled into the pink couch with the woven cream knit. She looked nice against the pink. Dames had never seen her in anything but black. But he imagined she'd look lovely in pink. He left her to make a cup of boiled water. When he returned, she was deeply asleep.

Xia awoke not of her own volition. She was shaken out of it. Literally. *A rumbling.*

The thought came instinctively. But this time, an alarm bell came with it. She remembered Opell's notes.

THE RUMBLINGS. NOT QUAKES. FROM THE GROUND. MOVE FAST. WHAT IS IT? WHAT IS IT XIA? DON'T TRY TO FIND OUT. JUST RUN

She had the instinct to obey, to run. She shifted. But she was met with pain.

She groaned as she slowly opened her eyes.

It was still dark. The rumbling stopped. To her mild surprise, Dames stood in the corner of the room, watching her.

"The rumbling wake you?"

She sat up slowly. "Yeah." Then she shuddered. "I need some water..."

Dames beat her to it and brought the cup from before. "You want some pain meds?"

She eyed him. "You got some?"

"I saw some on the counter."

Leftovers of Mai's. "Yeah, I'll take one."

He fetched the bottle and brought it to her. She wasn't sure if the pain in her head was just from the alcohol, or the lingering effects of whatever the hell had happened a few hours prior.

"Do you have any idea what that...*thing* was? I don't even know how to describe it. It was just pain. Like my eyes were fighting off something and electrifying themselves in the process."

"I'm surprised you remember. You were pretty out of it."

"Hard to forget something like that."

Dames nodded slowly. "True. Well, it wasn't just us. It seemed to happen to everyone. The whole city. But you said it was your eyes?"

"My eyes and my head."

"For me it was all over. My buddy mainly felt it in his arm."

"His arm?" There was something there. Her head was too foggy to decipher what.

"Yeah. And the signal came from there." He nodded towards the visionscreen in the corner. "I barely noticed it at the time. But the screen turned red. And in the center square, the main ad screen turned red. That's where it came from."

"You said it's a signal?"

"I have no idea what it was. Vision screens turn red, and everyone feels electric pain. Some type of malfunction maybe?"

Knowing everything that had been happening, Xia knew the conclusion wouldn't be so benign. "Dames, you said I was out of it last night. And I mean, I was a bit," she cringed at the memory of her letting everything out in a blubbering cascade. "But everything I said was true."

He eyed her, saying nothing.

"It's crazy. I know. But it's why I've been...distant. And a part of me regrets telling you because those are dangerous words to have said. Dangerous things to even be aware of. If you cared most about your safety, you'd throw me off to the slags."

He huffed. "As if I could ever do that."

She gave a half-hearted smile as she checked her cell chip. Multiple messages from the others, but the most recent came from Russel, informing her that her bike was done, but that it still needed that nano-proton part.

She blinked as she remembered the entire purpose of this endeavor. The blood rushed from her head as she stood and approached Dames. She was still slightly tipsy. "Dames, I desperately need Flux's help. He'll only help if you talk to him. And I don't know if we can pull this off without him. Not in time, at least."

His eyes soaked through her, bleeding with emotions he didn't know he could ever say. "Sure. Just don't be a stranger, all right?"

"Done."

They left her apartment. The sky began to lose its twilight and turn its classic shade of daylight gray when they reached the passing to go separate ways. Xia didn't know where Dames lived. She assumed it was closer to the bar.

"I'm this way. Remember, don't be a stranger."

Xia nodded. For the briefest, strangest moment, she felt the urge, or maybe it was an obligation, to embrace him once more. Her body faltered forward, but then she stopped herself. The movement shriveled with awkwardness. Then she settled for a punch on his elbow as she said, "See you, Dames."

He bit back the chuckle as she jogged away.

Xia wasn't sure what to expect when she entered Burgs' place, but she wasn't expecting everyone to be stationed in the living room, already waiting for her.

"Where the hell were you?" Burgs barked from his usual chair. He paused from typing on his holographic keyboard.

"Xia!" Mai exclaimed. She rushed forward and threw her arms around her silver friend. Xia was surprised the girl was able to run and brace her with full impact. She was healing well. "I was so worried when you weren't here and that awful *thing* happened!"

"Yeah, about that," she said as she came forward and stood behind the couch. Lorena sat on one end, fingers furiously typing on her own keyboard. "You all felt it too?"

Fay shuddered. "Like my eyes and head were all on fire."

"I felt it all over. It was worse than the nanobot surgery," Mai lamented.

Xia's eyes narrowed. Mai felt it in her whole body. So did Dames. But Fay only felt it in her eyes and head, like Xia. She turned towards Mai.

"Have you spoken with Kibou? Or any other Virgin friend of yours?"

"Not since yesterday," she replied.

"Call him up and ask him what happened to him and the other Virgins when the signal went off. Then tell him to come over. And do it on your eye screen. You need the practice."

Mai huffed a bit but obeyed nonetheless, shuffling out towards Leo's room.

"Were any of you by a telescreen when it happened?" Xia asked.

"Grimer and I were working on the room. We were lucky not to have been in the middle of something. Wiped us both out for a sec."

"I was sleeping. Almost slept through it. Thought I was having a nightmare," Leonardo said.

"You think that's where it came from?" Burgs asked.

Xia nodded. "I didn't see it myself. But Dames saw the telescreen in my apartment turn red when the signal went off. And you know that giant ad screen in the main square? Apparently, it turned red too."

"You were with Dames?" Lorena asked, turning towards Xia for the first time since she entered. Her face sheened as pink as her eyes.

"Yeah. He knows Flux, the guy I called yesterday about helping with the nanotech. Flux told me no, but I managed to convince Dames to talk to Flux. It looks like we'll be getting the nanotech we need."

"So, the signal came from the telescreens? Do you think it was some weird malfunction?" Grimer guessed.

"Doubt it. I'm sure the answer is more nefarious. But whatever it was, I don't think it affected the Virgins."

Fay eyed Xia with curiosity. "What do you mean?"

"We'll know in a second. But it seemed to target everyone where they have mods. I'm guessing, Fay, that you don't have any body mods? Since you only felt them in your head?"

"Yeah," she said slowly.

"So did I. But Mai felt it all over. And so did Dames."

Lorena shifted once more. "Did you tell him we're working together?"

"I didn't," Xia replied. The disappointment was visible. "Sorry, I never really thought of it." That was a lie. It had popped up constantly throughout the night with Dames. Like an itch she wasn't able to scratch. But for whatever reason, their relationship was not one she wanted to delve into with him.

A moment later, Mai stumbled back into the room. She looked sick. Face pale, eyes wide. Like she had seen a ghost. Like she *was* a ghost.

Leonardo noticed just as quickly as Xia. "Mai, are you—"

"What did the old geezer say?" Burgs interjected.

Mai's response came slowly, her mind in one place but her voice in another. "He, uh, he said he hadn't felt anything. When the thing went off."

"Looks like Xia was right!"

"But what does it mean?" Grimer piped.

Xia approached Mai more closely as her face continued to pale. "Hey, are you alright?"

Mai's eyes danced around unfocused as she whispered. "My father. He said my father is back."

39

THE RETURN OF THE FATHER

Little could unnerve Kibou. But this. This unnerved him.

It wasn't due to the physicality of it all. He was certain that this man who resembled the Lord Daimyo wasn't *actually* the revered samurai. Kibou held little importance of the physical self. So while it was the Daimyo's physical body, he knew his old friend was no longer there. And he was sure that if he saw the samurai disrobed, that he would see the fatal scar from the Daimyo's honorable suicide.

Nor did the malice shake him. He already knew the government's capabilities for depravity.

No, what unnerved him was what this meant for the other Virgins. While Kibou was the head monk of the Pagoda, and he was sought after for wisdom and guidance, the true leader was and always has been the Daimyo. To speak against the Daimyo would be unfathomable in the Virgins' hierarchy. And to tell the other Virgins that the Daimyo was not truly him would be speaking against him.

Kibou knew his community was not stupid. But hope is blinding. And what better hope than for the Daimyo to return? He could hear that blinding beacon of hope in her voice. It was dim. Clouded by the truth, clouded by the pain she had endured. But he could hear it. That fearful shaking as she whispered, "My father?"

If the Daimyo knew that Kibou did not believe him to be his true self, Kibou had no doubts he would be killed. He did not fear death, but leaving this realm before he saw his people's safety ensured did pick at his nerves.

That is what unnerved him.

"I have to go see if it's true."

Xia's thoughts raced a mile a minute. "Kibou told you this?"

"Yes. I have to go see him. Even if it's not really *him.*"

Xia shook her head in disbelief. "What do you mean *if*? Of course it's not. You know that." Yet still, she couldn't understand how or *why* he was back. Hadn't the Daimyo killed himself? Even if a brain were transplanted, surely that needed a living body to do so?

"Sounds like a trap," Fay said. "The government needs Virgins. Couldn't they be using the Daimyo for that?"

"Like luring them back to the Pagoda? Since Kibou told them to steer clear?" Grimer added.

"Better reason for me to see him first hand," Mai's voice gained some traction.

"No, even less of a reason. You're not going anywhere—"

Her head shook violently as the words poured out in a frenzy. "Like hell I'm not! I am so damn *sick* of being cooped up here while everyone else does everything! These are MY people at stake. I went through hell with that surgery and what have I gotten to do? Absolutely nothing. This is my father. I need to see him. I need to see him."

Xia wanted to scream, *It's not him!* She wanted to shake the girl, she wanted to slap some sense into her. As Mai made a move for the door, Leonardo reached out and grabbed her arm.

"Mai, I really don't think—"

"Let go of me, Leo!" She tugged her arm out of his grasp with brute force, knocking him off kilter. A second later, she was out the door.

Xia groaned. There were already so many moving pieces and Mai just had to derail the entire train. "Alright. Burgs, I'm forwarding any calls from Flux or Dames to you. You figure out how to get your nano proton thingy and install it. Grimer, act as liason between Burgs and Russel. Leo, you're errand boy. Fetch any of the things they need. Lorena, go over the satellite images from Opell with Kibou when he gets here. See if there's anything I missed." She glanced towards Fay. "Fay, uh—"

She gave a lazy two-fingered salute. "I'll keep the boys in check."

Xia nodded and bolted out the door. If there was one thing Mai wasn't going to do, it was to go on this endeavor alone.

Mai hadn't made it far. The streets weren't too crowded, likely due to the early time and the painful signal, so Xia was able to spot the flowing black hair a block up the street. She sprinted up the street and pulled on Mai's elbow as she breathed out, "Mai, hold it."

"Leave me alone, Xia." Mai kept herself facing forward, but Xia could just see the glossiness in her eyes.

"I won't try and stop you. But I am coming with you."

A gust of wind whipped at their faces. Mai brushed at the hair in her face. She also used that as an opportunity to wipe her eyes.

"I'll keep myself back. Give you two some privacy. But in case it is a trap," Xia's voice trailed off.

Mai gulped. Then nodded.

The entire city felt off. Without the cycle, the two made the trek by foot, and in doing so, were able to fully take in the state of the city. They walked past the Main Square. Normally, hundreds of people shuffled through the square no matter the time of day, bumping into and squeezing past each other in a claustrophobic expanse while the massive ads for new tech blazed above. But not today. The usual neon ads blazed, but Xia could actually see the ground of the square. The signal seemed to scare people enough to stay home.

But not Mai.

Her eyes toggled between tearful and dry, but the determination never faltered.

Xia was impressed at the girl's silence, as it was the longest she had never heard her speak. But even that couldn't last long, as Mai finally broke the hush.

"No cycle?"

Xia activated the soundbox. "It's at Russel's. They need a part. Did the group fill you in?"

Mai scowled. "Barely. Burgs views me as a nuisance."

It was no surprise the two didn't mesh. "You try on your suit?"

"Yeah. It's fine." She drew in a deep breath. "Is this going to affect our mission at all?"

"You mean the Daimyo situation?"

"Y-yeah."

"If anything, it means we need to start it sooner."

Eventually, they reached the Pagoda. Mai insisted he would be there, not at her home. They walked past the main gate—no faux slags this time—and into the front garden. Some of the plants were wilting, but three Virgins knelt on the soil, working hard to revive the plants that had been neglected since Kibou told everyone to stay away. Because someone had told them to return. That someone being, supposedly, the Daimyo.

One of the gardeners looked up. "Mai!" The middle-aged woman exclaimed. "Surely you've heard the news about your father?"

"Have you seen him?" Mai didn't hide the eagerness in her voice.

The woman shook her head. "I haven't. But Roshi and the samurai have. That is word enough for me." She smiled to herself as her nimble fingers returned to pruning.

Xia followed Mai as they entered the Pagoda itself. Samurai trained in the courtyard and monks sat cross-legged before the center bronze statue as if no time had passed at all. Couldn't they sense this wasn't right? Perhaps not. Hope is blinding.

Xia and Mai ascended each flight of stairs, past each story, until they made it to the fourth floor, the room empty. Mai made a move for the final set of stairs when Xia stopped her. "You talk to him alone. But here." Xia tapped at her temple, scrolling through her eyescreen interface before selecting the audiolink option. "Did you get a notification?"

Mai's eyes widened as a little blue bubble appeared in the corner of her vision. She wasn't used to her eyescreen mods yet. She gave a small nod, as if moving her head too hard would make the bubble disappear.

"Select it."

Her hand moved tentatively towards her temple, tapping delicately, before the task was completed. "Done."

"Alright. Go. I'll be listening."

Xia stood in the corner of the room with bated breath. The ornate room was silent. Statues of ancient men stared ahead, eyes faded with time. Despite their eyes being stony and lifeless, the feeling of *someone* looking at her tickled her hairline. She turned. She scanned. Nothing. The feeling remained. Then the voice of Mai played in her ear.

"Father?" Mai finally broke the silence. She had reached the top of the stairs and saw the backside of a man. The recognition was instant. The robes the same. Dark hair braided the same. He stood at the window, looking down upon the sparring samurai, just as he had always done. Once she spoke, he slowly turned towards her.

For a fleeting moment, the stare was blank. She had almost missed it. Then he let out a graceful smile.

"My child," he said, his tone as calm as it always was.

Mai stiffened. "Where have you been?"

He stared off into the distance. "You know the dangers that face us."

"What do you mean?"

And then his eyes met hers. "You know what I mean."

Her blood chilled. Those were her father's same brown eyes. Yet something, something was off. "I don't."

"You've never quite known how to lie. I know what plagues our people. And I know how to protect them. They are safe." His eyes narrowed, gaze darkening. "But you. You are no longer one of us. What have you done to yourself?"

She took a step back. "What are you talking about?"

He came forward. Mai's narrow frame shrunk beneath him. A coldness emanated from his towering build, dark clouds circling a lifeless mountain. "You've poisoned yourself with the infections of humanity. For what? You'd abandon your people to save yourself? After all I've taught you?"

Every sentence uttered by her father was a fear that had plagued Mai's mind since she underwent the modifications. She had taken small comfort in knowing she'd never get confirmation because her father was gone. Yet here he was. Bringing these dreads to fruition. Each sentence a shard of ice piercing into her chest.

She couldn't speak. She lunged forward. Half wanting to feel her father close to her one more time, and half wanting to feel a robotic body underneath. Because there was no way that this was her father. But as her arms wrapped around him, she felt his same toned flesh that she knew from a thousand embraces over the years. And as she felt his warm flesh inside her arms, her heart fell into the depths of the Void.

He broke free from her embrace with nonchalant ease. "You are no child of mine anymore. Leave here. And take your tainted friend with you."

Her hands balled into fists as tears welled in her eyes. There were so many things she wanted to say. But she let those fall into the Void as well as she let him have the final word and descended the stairs.

Mai didn't wait for Xia. She fled down the stairs and kept going, never looking back. Xia followed at her heels. It wasn't until they were outside the gate and Xia pulled out the soundbox that they broke the silence.

"That didn't go how it was supposed to go," Mai's voice strained.

"There was a rustling at one point. What happened?"

"I hugged him. I was hoping it wouldn't be him, you know? But that's his body."

"It's his body, but it's not him. You know that."

Tears welled again. "But everything he said. That's what my father *would* say."

"How did he know you were no longer a Virgin?"

"I don't know."

"You can't tell just by looking at you. And not only that, but he knew I was there. He told you to take your tainted friend with you. That's me. Somehow, he knew I was there." Neurons made faint connections as she began to put pieces together. "We need to get back and talk to Kibou. I have an idea of what's going on."

They returned to Kibou, Leonardo, Fay, and Burgs. Lorena and Grimer left to connect with Flux regarding the nanotech. The only person who cared for Mai's emotional well-being seemed to be Leonardo. The rest wanted to know what happened. Mai wasn't keen on sharing and left Xia to give the gist.

"You did not speak with him, Xia?" Kibou asked after a long sip from his espresso. He dribbled a small amount of liquid onto his robes, invisible against the deep brown fabric.

"I didn't. But he knew I was there. I don't suppose you noticed anything off about him, Kibou?"

"Nothing these five senses could determine. Only the sixth. The sixth sees something very wrong."

"When did you receive word the Daimyo was back?"

"Before the dawn. By dawn, we all returned."

"And nobody in your community felt anything last night? Around 1 in the morning?"

Kibou's eyes closed as he shook his head slowly. "I was deep in slumber. And from those I have spoken with, they too remained in slumber. Whatever plagued you all seems to have neglected us."

"So a signal is sent out only affecting modded people, and a few hours later, the Daimyo shows up, and he is able to detect modded people around him. I'm betting they're connected."

"You think the signal instilled some type of tracking mechanism?" Fay asked from beside the window.

"It's possible. Or maybe the Daimyo simply has a scanner on him, and the signal did something else. I don't know. But since it's not truly the Daimyo, we don't know what all he's capable of."

Mai stood from the couch, leaving Leonardo's cradling arms. "You keep saying it's not him. But how do you know that? Maybe something was done to him. But it's his body. And he knew me. Clearly some of his brain's up there too."

"Ah, the age-old query. A query that has only grown more convoluted in our recent years. What truly makes one them *self*? The brain? The mind? Is the mind solely in our brain? The spirit? Is there truly such a thing?"

"I don't want no philosophy lesson, old man," Burgs huffed from his chair.

"Not a lesson, just mere questions. Questions that heavily pertain to the situation at hand."

"Isn't that a core notion in your community?" Leonardo asked. "That your true nature of humanity comes from your spirit, and the body and creations of it, especially mods, are a hindrance to your spirit's growth?"

Kibou smiled. "Precisely. A core conviction that Mai knows in and out. She'd do well to remember it."

40

EMBRACE THE DARKNESS

Xia thought the walls were thick. She rarely heard anything outside Fay's room. She never had to endure distant sounds of passion or late-night ramblings. But that night, she heard Mai cry. There was an obligation to check on her, to comfort her. Xia ignored it. Well, she tried her best to. She didn't get up from the bed. But she didn't sleep well either.

She thought of Kibou's words. They spurred an unsettling existentialism that she had never given the briefest of pondering. Who had the time or energy for that when your only focus was how to survive? How to make enough money to pay the rent? How long could you shower if you want to maintain your water supply? But the ceiling's enchanting swirls of navy noir seemed to capture her thoughts and trap her within them.

Brain transplants were the revelation that had started this all. When Dames uttered those words to her in the bar in what felt like eons ago, she felt her world shake. Because despite growing up in such a tech-saturated and cybernetic world, that was a step too advanced. A step too far. Because, really, what made Xia, *Xia*? If it lay in the brain, wasn't Kibou right? That the modifications took away from her true self? Or was there something else?

Those slags with AI chips—where were their *selves?*

She had heard about the *soul.* Where was that thing? And what were people doing to them?

***

"It's done."

"Are you sure?"

"Yes." Lorena stared down at her with conviction. Xia felt so damn small.

"No hiccups between Russel and Burgs?"

"Didn't say that. But the tech's installed, and the bikes are ready to go."

"What did you think of Flux?"

"Interesting character."

Luckily for Xia, Flux was not one for formalities or flattery. Flux appreciated people who could understand and appreciate his work. Lorena was someone who could do both. And so it wasn't hard to win him over.

"Speaking of," Lorena's eyes diverted, almost nervously. It was hard for the strong-jawed beauty to appear anything but angelically stoic. "Dames connected you with Flux?"

"Yeah."

"How is Dames?"

Xia gulped. "Is there a reason you can't ask him?"

"How could I? I don't even have his cell."

This confused Xia. What exactly was the extent of their relationship? "You could always visit him at the bar."

"What bar?"

The extent didn't reach far, it seemed. "Once this is all over, I'll take you. Deal?"

***

"Tomorrow's the big day," Burgs said as he handed Xia a small glass. It was the good stuff that she brought him in exchange for the softening of his gruff exterior. It wasn't very long ago, yet it felt like eons. Time was a fickle thing.

"Can't say I'm ready." She took the glass.

"That's because you aren't." The electric city buzzed below them through the window wall, seemingly unchanged and unbothered. The night seemed darker. The sky true obsidian. An ad for a sexual planetary VR experience flashed below them on one of the dozens of ad screens that littered the sides of the buildings. Xia averted her gaze back to the black sky.

"Are you nervous to have Dallek on the mission?" It felt odd to say Grimer's true name aloud.

Burgs didn't react. "It's complicated."

She nodded like she understood. "I still don't understand why you even helped me. Again and again. The Enforcer isn't worth that much. Fay gave a few reasons. I don't buy any of it. I don't get it at all."

"Why are you helping the Virgin girl?"

"She's not one anymore." Xia side-eyed him. "And her name is Mai. Call her by her name."

Burgs laughed. "She could get every modification in this damned city and she'd still be a Virgin girl. Same way she's been fucked every which way in that whorehouse and she's still a Virgin." Crass but light. "You didn't answer my question."

Her grandfather came to mind, but it was no longer the only explanation. "I had my own reasons. But at this point, I don't have a good answer. It just seems like what I should do. And once I decided to do it, I haven't felt any regrets."

"Well, I suppose my answer's the same. Don't always need a grand explanation for shit. Hard enough to understand the world around us, understanding ourselves is even harder. But when you live your life one way for so long, always feeling empty, and something comes along and says 'hey, you should do this instead', well, then you do it."

"So simple."

"That's because it is. Besides. Something tells me this isn't the end of things. Somethin's brewin'. You must feel it too."

The brains. The signal. She nodded.

"So don't fuck this up. 'Cause I like having you around. Like you said. No regrets."

***

"I'm just so grateful to have you back, Lord Daimyo. We've been so lost without you. Roshi has worked valiantly in your stead, but it hasn't been the same. It hasn't been right. Now, all is right."

The Daimyo led the woman further into his home.

"The way in which I was called away was regrettable. But you may rest assured. All is well now."

The woman's eyes gazed around in wonder, taking in all that was before her. She had never stepped foot in the Daimyo's home before. When she was asked to, she was shocked. Excited. Nervous. But also very confused.

His home was much larger than her own. That was to be expected. He was the Daimyo after all. Yet everything inside was simple, purposeful, modest. Fitting for the Daimyo. He led her down a hallway and opened one of the sliding doors into the traditional dining room. Upon the floor table was a steaming pot of tea with two yunomi. He gestured towards the floor pillows.

"Come, sit down."

She gave a hasty nod as she knelt down rather clumsily. He poured her some tea, his face relaxed as his eyes followed each of his hand movements. The suspense was strangling her. She watched as he took a sip of the steaming liquid. Then she did the same. The silence lingered.

"Lord Daimyo, I must ask," her eyes shifted back and forth, not willing to meet his. His eyes bore into her. She could feel them. Her throat tightened. "Why exactly did you want to meet with me here?"

He set his cup down. "Neoko, your work at the Pagoda is one of utmost diligence, care, and beauty. Without your tender care, our temple would wither, surely. My daughter's berries are of little sustenance in comparison to yours. I ask that you share your wisdom, your expertise."

Neoko visibly relaxed as a smile lit up her youthful face. "Of course, Lord Daimyo!" And as if swept up in a lighthearted dance, her words of cross-pollination and soil preparation poured from her mouth, her eyes and lips afire with content passion. She loved the garden, she loved her work. She loved that the Daimyo saw it. Appreciated it. Her eyelids grew a little heavy. Her words began to slow. But she didn't even notice. She didn't even notice the two bodies creep behind her. Or the needle that slid into her throat.

Her final words, 'Allow the sunlight', rang softly across the room as her body fell into the slag's arms, her spirit embracing the darkness.

41

Fighting Friends

"For a hideout, there isn't much here," Leo said as he sat back down on the thin gray futon.

"I've got several all over the city. I'm not going to deck them out like your apartment, sorry to disappoint," Lorena spat. While it didn't need the luxurious flair of Burgs' place, it was barer than bones. A gray futon, a small fridge, an even smaller sink, a tight desk and folding chair, and a small metal partition shielding the toilet were the only points of interest in the concrete room. That would have bee n sufficient if it weren't for how large the room was.

Nestled deep in the outskirts not too far from Russel's place, any nefarious activity would blend right in. Xia walked past three drug dealings alone just on the walk over, and yells, moans, and gunshots peppered the air outside. But the room itself was made completely soundproof.

"How long do you think we'll have to wait?" Mai asked from the futon. She adjusted her slag helm. Everyone else had theirs temporarily off, but Xia insisted the girl needed as much practice as she could get navigating all the features. But once the slags came to escort Lorena, everyone would be fully suited up.

"Shouldn't be long," Xia replied. It had been six hours since Lorena sent the destruct signal.

"Are you sure it even worked?" Leo asked.

Lorena's eyes shot a few daggers. "Yes, it worked." As if on cue, her cell chip buzzed. "Everyone, shut up." She stepped to the corner of the room and spoke.

"Aexus speaking."

Aexus?

"That's impossible... Have you tried rerouting the nexus circuit board?... Are any of the lights activated?... Alright. When do you need me?... I'm not going there. Pick me up at 90 Oraku, in the Western Outer Slums... Either pick me up here or it stays broken."

Xia's brow raised in surprise. Who was she talking to that she could speak with such gall and make demands?

"I'll be ready in an hour." Lorena ended the call and returned to the group.

"Aexus? Is that your alibi?" Mai asked.

"Of course. I never use my real name. Imagine my surprise when someone came to the Lion's Den asking for *Lorena*," she glanced towards Xia with a wry smile. "They'll be here in less than an hour.

59 minutes later, the door pounded.

Lorena stepped towards it. Leo stood by its side and would be invisible once it opened. She glanced behind her. The place looked empty. The gray partition once used to wrap around the toilet was now split and placed in various positions around the room with the rest of the group hiding behind them. Except for Xia. She crouched behind the futon, ready to make her shot with the Enforcer. Besides that initial firing shot months ago, the weapon had laid dormant. Now she'd wake it from its slumber with a bang.

If all went well, the rest of the group wouldn't even be needed for the fight. While she hadn't used a gun in a little while, she still made a good shot.

Lorena opened the door slowly. Xia could just see past her large frame. Three slags stood ahead. Even now, hidden from vision and fifteen yards away, Xia could sense the coldness they brought with them. Her neck twitched.

The slag in the front scanned Lorena, red light blinking. *"**AEXUS. YOU ARE TO BE ESCORTED TO THE INNER HUB.**"*

"I'm gonna need to bring some things," she replied with confidence. "Help me get them." She motioned for them to follow. They paused for a moment, and Xia wondered if the plan would fail. If they'd demand Lorena to come outside. If they'd refuse to enter. But no, one by one, they followed Lorena inside. And as the third and largest entered, Leo shut the door behind them, enacting the signal barrier around the room, initiating the ambush.

This was it.

Lorena darted to the side as Xia simultaneously raised the gun from behind the couch. Her heart slammed against her ribcage. The steady *thwomp* was the only thing she could hear as she raised the barrel and steadied her hand. Her eardrum now a war drum. She aimed directly at the slag's broad chest. Then she pulled the trigger.

A ten-centimeter hole appeared in the center of the slag's upper body. A perfect shot. The beam passed through their body, disintegrating every piece of flesh in its way, including the bicep of the slag behind him. Before the second slag could register the turn of events, Xia shot once more into their chest.

The third eyed the barrel. Xia's finger buzzed in anticipation, ready to feel the sweet jolt of electricity as she fired the final shot. She aimed at the colossal cyborg with a confident conviction. She pulled the trigger.

Nothing happened.

The conviction faltered.

She pulled again. Nothing. The group was quick to realize the failing situation. Leo rushed forward behind the slag, but the slag was quicker and flung their massive fist backward like a trebuchet, striking Leo square in his helm. He fell flat on his back.

With robotic precision, they pulled out their own Enforcer.

And this one worked.

Xia rolled to the side as an electric beam blasted through the futon. They were just about to fire once more when Grimer charged at the towering slag. Seven feet of pure power, the perfect blend of flesh and mech, a prowess of computerized rigor. Equipped with a weapon that, with one shot, would kill instantly.

Grimer closed the distance just as the slag detected his presence. He parried the slag's left arm, bringing the gun to point down towards the ground and away from Xia. He had one advantage: the size variance. And he used it with a surprising skill that Xia never would have expected from the ever-anxious Grimer. He slammed himself with an explosion of force into the slag's stomach, using his lower center of gravity. And it worked. The slag was momentarily brought off kilter. And that moment was enough.

Knocking the metal partition to the ground, Mai came sprinting from the other side. She launched herself onto the back of the slag. It was all too fast for the slag to properly react. Even with the power of computer processing, the sudden change in events was too stark. Mai's legs wrapped around the slag's midsection as her arms squeezed around their neck. With the added distraction, Grimer was able to successfully execute a wrist lock and attempt to take the gun for himself.

Any human and it would have been easy. But the slag was so damn strong. Grimer used every drop of adrenaline and fury to fuel his grip. The gun loosened itself from the slag's grasp, but Grimer wasn't able to secure it. It dropped to the ground and slid across the floor.

The slag's now free hands pulled at Mai's clutching arms. Grimer sent a powerful kick into the slag's stomach but they absorbed it with ease. The titan pulled Mai's arms and flung her to the side like a ragdoll.

At the same time, it was Burgs who made the sprint for the fallen gun.

The slag sent a powerful fist flying towards Grimer. He barely dodged it. Then another. He barely slipped that one. Grimer countered with an elbow to the slag's sternum, slicing into him with his arm now a dagger. Then he spun and sent a thunderous kick to the back of the slag's knees.

Burgs now held the gun. With Grimer's spin, he was now out of the line of sight. It was a perfect shot. But as Burgs watched his only son fight the monster slag, he hesitated.

The slag turned and kicked Grimer down, knocking him to the ground.

"Shoot, Burgs!" Fay yelled from the sidelines.

Xia couldn't see Burgs' face behind his slag helm, but she noticed the quivering of his hands as he held the gun before him. The sound of plasma bursting through the air electrified the room, but the slag still stood. The sink crumbled at the edge.

He missed.

He shot again. The sink exploded. The slag fell to his knees, not due to the gunshot, but to straddle Grimer and send another fist pummeling into his face. The helm cracked under their mighty fist.

The gun fell from Burgs' trembling grasp.

Xia was about to leap to Grimer's defense but another electrifying shock crackled through the air. It was Leo who grabbed a gun from the second dead slag's body and shot through the colossal slag's torso. He shot once more. The slag's entire midsection disintegrated as his upper body split away from his pelvis.

Fay ripped off her helmet and sprinted towards the motionless Grimer. Leo rushed towards Mai, who was now resting against the wall, massaging her lower back. Kneeling down, Fay gingerly pulled off Grimer's broken helmet to reveal his bloodied face. The helmet had cut deep into his eye and cheek.

The horrible question of death was answered by Grimer's signature whining groan.

He shifted and Fay helped him sit up. Burgs came tumbling over like his legs were made of jelly.

"Dallek," he muttered as he fell beside Grimer.

"You alright there buddy? Looks like you're gonna have a scar like mine," Leo called out.

Grimer gave a winded chuckle. Relief cascaded over the room.

"We don't have much time, folks," Lorena called out from beside the broken sink. "Move the bodies, grab the guns, and get in position."

Fay and Burgs helped Grimer out of the way behind one of the partitions as Xia looked down towards her own faulty Enforcer. She had no idea why it jammed. Out of charge? Shots too quickly linked together?

She knelt beside the body of the first fallen slag and observed their helm. The differences in military ranking were subtle (save for the Commanders and Divisioners), the only differences being the markings on their helm. This one was a Brigadier: a step above Major, and one below Commander. Hopefully, that ranking was the highest in the group. As she removed the helm from the body, her gaze fell upon the face of the dead slag. She was young. Maybe thirty. Olive skin smooth. Green eyes wide and empty. Freckles speckling a strong nose. Chapped lips parted and full.

Xia averted her gaze and swapped her helm with the dead Brigadier's. They fit surprisingly similarly. But as Xia used her eyescreen to connect with the helm's tech, numerous numbers and commands filled her vision, displaying various options that she could use. She minimized them, took the Brigadier's Enforcer, and began pulling her towards the corner of the room.

Mai and Leo pulled the second slag, and Lorena carted off the two halves of the third, carrying a leg in one hand and an arm in the other. Mai's gaze lingered on the split body.

"I'll get out of the way and make the first shot. If there's more, Leo, you'll be the other shot. Got it?" Xia said as she headed towards the door.

"Yes ma'am!" He called out.

She left the room and entered the dingy hallway. It was a pathetic building with flickering bulbs and cobwebs galore housing the lowest functioning addicts of the city. But Xia felt a sense of calm as she marched down the hallway, the adrenaline from the fight beginning to ebb away. Down the stairs she went. A movement to her left scuttled. She glanced. A centipede. She kept walking.

At the end of the downstairs hallway was a hazy window beside the door, and through that hazy window Xia saw the outline of a large black cube. The slags' tram.

She stepped outside. Pellets of rain fell from the sky and splattered against the jagged concrete, the tram, her new visor. She approached the front passenger window and waited as it slid down.

Just one slag sat in the front. A lone major. She hoped that was all that was left. "NEED YOUR ASSISTANCE," Xia said, her voice unwavering.

Not a second of hesitation. The small slag simply exited the vehicle and began following behind her. The two's heavy footsteps reverberated down the empty hallway. Yet something felt off. Xia couldn't place it. She scanned. Nothing. Then she *deep* scanned.

She almost lost her footing. Her vision warped, as if the world were covered by an electric blue film. Her ears, her nose, her tongue all buzzed with a tingling fire, almost unpleasant, yet oddly satisfying. Then the film lifted and the results of the scan scrolled on the right side of her visor. Nothing out of the ordinary. Many centipedes.

They approached the hideout. With zero hesitation, Xia opened the door and walked inside, leading them into the trap. The door clicked behind. Xia spun to the side and pulled out her Enforcer.

But something was still off. She hesitated to shoot, eyeing the final slag down. Eyeing the curvature of their back, the stiffness of their legs, the motion of their hands. Hands that didn't move towards an Enforcer, but raised upwards, almost as if motioning to stop—

Xia put her gun down. Leo raised his. "Leo! Don't shoot—" Xia yelled, but it was too late.

The plasma beam shot through the air with a resounding ZHWMP.

"STOP!" Xia yelled.

The slag fell to his knees, then onto his back, clutching at the chunk of missing flesh at his side. Xia rushed forward, but the confused Leo still held the gun at the ready. Xia yanked the helmet off with brute force, revealing the missing member.

"REN!" Leo cried. He dropped the gun and sprinted across the room towards his lost friend. "Ren, Ren, oh my God Ren, I'm so sorry." Even with the helm, it was evident he was crying.

Ren ignored Leo, his vacant eyes falling on Xia. "How did you know it was me?" His voice was barely audible.

"Just knew."

Fay appeared at the ready. "Don't strain yourself, Ren. Thank goodness the laser blasts cauterize the wound. Thank goodness *you* missed!" She glared at Leo. "But you're missing part of your large intestine. I can't believe you're here. I can't believe you're okay."

"I'm not okay," he said dryly.

"You will be, you will be buddy," Leo chanted. "Burgs, Burgs! Can you believe this? He's back!"

Burgs came hobbling over as Grimer leaned on him for support. "Well, how's this for a reunion," he muttered with a smile.

Lorena brought the clarity that an outsider unfamiliar with the situation would. "We don't have time. We need to go. Four slags means four of us. Xia, Fay, Leonardo, and Mai. The rest will take care of the bodies." And just like that, the reunion was cut short.

The crew exited the building. There wasn't any time to acclimate themselves to the new helms, but thankfully, Burgs had created a formidable copy. Aside from the new menu options and the integral deep-scan, the helms fit just the same, and used the same software that connected to their vision screens.

Fay carried a dummy (a sex doll now used for more honorable purposes) dressed in a slag uniform created by Burgs. Since Xia would be leaving but not returning, they needed a body to replace her for any potential deep-scans. The dummy would have to do.

As Fay entered the tram, Leo and Xia rounded the corner to move the cycles they had hidden in the narrow alleyway. Then they pushed the bikes towards the tram as Mai opened the back. Lorena was quick to spot the handle at the side of the tram, triggering a ramp for them to move the cycles inside.

The entire process took less than a minute.

Buko then appeared from down the block. He had been waiting the entire time, ever ready. He approached the group, completing a sight that had never occurred in the city: four slags, a samurai, and a sex doll.

If only someone had taken a picture.

Buko's face remained impassive, representative of the years of training at the Pagoda. He followed behind the group as they all entered the tram with Fay and Lorena in the front, and Xia, Mai, and Leo in the back.

"Buko, you'll need to—"

"Between the two cycles. I know," he said as he walked towards the back and crouched between the two stationary bikes. Xia appreciated the obedience. Fay tossed the dummy uniform back and Xia stashed it atop her bike.

"You know, you could wear it," Leo joked towards Buko.

If looks could kill, Leo would have died before the mission even started.

"Okay, give me one second," Xia muttered as she activated the barrier around the bikes. Then she exited the tram and stood to the side, initiating a deep-scan. She had to be sure it all worked.

Her vision warped once more as the deep-scan turned the world blue. As she stared towards the tram, outlines inside emitting various frequencies blurred in her vision. A slag and human up front, two slags in the back.

No cycles, no Buko. She smiled.

Let's fuckin' go.

42

TREMBLE

The city blazed neon, its electric lights shimmering through the pristine window glass, meeting Burgs' eyes for the thousandth time as he watched below. Yet this time it felt different. It wasn't due to the fact that he ignored his usual chair and opted to stand. It wasn't because this whiskey was Xia's gift and better than his usual bottle. No, it was different because he was a changed man. He just couldn't pinpoint how.

The guilt was insurmountable. He had a perfect shot. A direct line to his son's assailant. And yet his hands shook. He *missed*. He never missed.

Burgs had killed more people than he could remember. Stabbed, strangled, shot. The shots were the easiest. And yet when it mattered most, when his son was at stake, he couldn't do it.

What the hell was wrong with him?

He couldn't figure it out. But deep down, the answer was there. Seeing his son on the brink of death—that moment unlocked a hidden pool of trauma in the very depths of Burgs' subconscious. Because the last time Burgs was in a life-or-death situation, his wife was murdered shortly after. And here he was about to lose his son. That trauma, holed up for so long, was momentarily brought to the surface. And as it rose, it shook his nervous system, shook his very nerve that connected the control center of his brain to his index finger. The nerve trembled. The finger quivered. The gun missed.

"Dad?"

Burgs slowly turned. He couldn't remember the last time his son hadn't called him *Sir,* and in this moment Burgs was glad the boy didn't.

"Have a sip," Burgs pushed the glass into Grimer's chest, avoiding his son's eyes.

Grimer took a wholehearted taste. His eye was patched up, opting for the old-fashioned way of healing.

"How's Ren doing?" A friend had arrived earlier to fix the wounded boy up, and Burgs let the boy rest before picking his brains about his time undercover. Grimer had been holed up in Ren's room, and occasionally Burgs could hear a bout of laughter between the two boys. Because that's what they still were to him—boys.

"He'll be alright. At least physically. I can tell there are some things bothering him. He's good at hiding it."

"I'd be shocked if there weren't things bothering him. Can't imagine what he's been up to out there." He took the glass back and swigged. "You handled yourself well, kid."

Grimer's eyes glistened.

"I didn't. I was shit."

"Dad—"

"And I've given you so much shit over the years. Been so hard on you. And then here I go, and fuckin'..." His words caught in his throat.

Grimer's eyes widened even further. He'd never seen his father like this. Never heard him talk like this. There was no hesitation. He threw his burly arms around his father's stoic figure in a tight embrace.

Burgs tensed momentarily before easing himself into his son's grasp. Then he brought his own arms around his only son, almost dropping the glass of bourbon.

"It's alright, Dad. We're good. We're good."

Eventually, Burgs broke the embrace and gave a gruff cough, easing his throat with another swig of liquor.

"You think they'll be good?" Grimer asked as they both looked out towards the city.

"Only time can tell, kid."

43

INTO THE LION'S DEN

Xia remembered the calm confidence with which Ren walked right up to the control panel and placed his hand on the massive scanner. This time, it was her turn. She exited the tram, approached the panel, and placed her hand atop. A second later, the machine registered the material unique to slags' frequency-emitting uniforms and the doors slammed open.

The tram trudged along into the Inner Hub. The vehicle gave a false sense of protection. But as Xia looked out the window, she sensed the seedlings of danger.

"Remember to use the pulse stabilizer if you feel your heartbeat rising," Xia said.

"Is it bad if I have to use it already?" Mai asked.

"Go ahead."

They passed group after group of trainees, each led by at least two slags. There seemed to be more people moving around than the last time.

Fay continued to drive up the wide gravel path. No need for exploration this time. Just a straight shot to the next gate. Just as long as they weren't stopped—

The sound of a low-bellied siren filled the air. The slags leading the groups of trainees immediately changed direction and began marching toward the open training field.

"Damn it," Xia muttered.

"What's going on?" Mai asked.

"Follow the tram up there. We do whatever they do," Xia commanded Fay and then turned back towards Mai. "RCD. Random Compliance Drill. Burgs told us about this. The slags check the trainees for anything out of the ordinary."

"Why do we need to diverge if they are only checking trainees?" Leo asked.

"Because all missions and movements are temporarily halted during one. Whatever the other slags in trams do, we do. But whatever happens, we can't let anyone else inside. Remain calm. Blend in. Buko, you'll stay inside."

The tram moved along the main road as the hordes of trainees converged onto the massive field, lining up in neat rows. Towering poles cast blazing, synthetic lights upon the oval field, compressing any comfort that the soft daylight might have gifted them. The slags formed a semi-circle around the sea of military hopefuls. The tram ahead of them parked along the back of the field, alongside several other trams, the inhabitants standing outside.

"All of us, outside. Stand tight. Don't speak unless spoken to. Follow any commands from a commander." Burgs knew the science behind these drills. The siren wasn't just a sound; it would emit a signal to the AI chips to pause their current objectives and give them a temporary overriding one. A safety measure to ensure not a cog is out of place.

They stepped outside the tram, one by one, Xia exiting last. The thick suits protected against the chilly air. The trainees didn't have that luxury. Their baggy long sleeves and pants offered minimal warmth. Not a shiver could be spotted; the trainees stood with perfect rigidity. The only one who stood out in the sea of statues was a prisoner standing outside a few trams down, who even from afar, Xia could see shuffle and twitch with fear.

Off to the Void, perhaps?

From the northern end of the field, a group of commanders began walking along the slags. It seemed height was a requirement when climbing the ranks to commander. There were only seven of them, yet their massive builds seemed to multiply them as they thundered along, giving commands to each passing slag. Some remained standing, unmoving, while others would leave their stance and begin walking among the trainees, deep-scanning them for contraband.

Two of the seven marched toward the groups of slags outside the trams. They approached closer, closer, and Xia could hear her heart pound in unison with their crashing boots.

The two stood before their group and lifted a heavy gloved hand. ***"YOU TWO. SCAN TRAINEE RANK C."*** Xia inwardly grimaced as she saw who the other finger was pointing at. Mai.

Xia didn't waste a second and began marching toward the end of the group. She correctly assumed C to be at the end, as they were the lowest ranking. It was almost amusing seeing the variance of facial expressions among the kids. Most of them were barely 18. Not a wrinkle or beauty mod in sight. Most looked on with a faux confidence, but many looked as if they were about to crumble. Eyes wide and lips tight with fear. Xia walked along, deep-scanning each trainee. Little did they know they were blessed with the perfect slag for the job; if Xia were to find anything out of place, she wasn't going to say a thing.

The girl in the next row wasn't so lucky.

"That's not mine! I swear! That's not mine!"

The slag scanning her held up a small electronic device. ***"POSSESSION OF LEVEL 3 OR HIGHER CONTRABAND RESULTS IN IMMEDIATE EXPULSION AND DISPOSAL. CYPHER LINKS ARE LEVEL 2. ITEM WILL BE CONFISCATED."***

Xia looked on past the trainee in front of her and toward the ginger girl.

She shook her head frantically, violently, screaming through tears. "It's not mine!" In the same movement that the slag slid the device into his side, she bolted past him and into the next row over.

Xia didn't have time to think. The girl sprinted into her row, right past Xia. She had no choice. In an instant, Xia grabbed the girl around her waist and twisted her around, placing her in a lock. The poor girl continued to kick and scream. Xia willed herself to ignore the pleading of the dying animal and keep her grip strong. Because that's what the girl was. She was going to die.

The slag who scanned her along with a commander relieved Xia from the hold and carried the girl away, her screams the only sound breaking through the field. Xia continued her scans down the row of terrified trainees. Even the tough ones looked rattled now. If only she had been one row over.

Due to the commotion with the girl, Xia was one of the final slags to reach the end of her row. Instead of returning to their spots on the outside of the field, they stood stationary at the end of the row, facing the line of trainees. She mimicked the others and stood at the end of the line.

Silence weighed down upon the field, thick and overbearing, but the screams of the ginger girl seemed to echo inside her ears, haunting her, mixing with the oppressive silence to create a sickening hellsong.

After a small slice of eternity, the splitting siren returned. Miraculously, Xia didn't flinch. The trainees did. Especially the C Rank. With the siren came the resumption of the previous objectives slags were conducting, along with new objectives commanded by the AI. It was her prime opportunity to return to the group. She could see the various slags shuffling back into the trams. The trainees dispersed. It was over. Now to just get back—

A behemoth in her corner vision began to approach her. Her heart sank as she realized she was sucked into another encounter, likely a commander wanting to do something about the run-in with the ginger girl. But as Xia turned toward the approaching giant, her heart didn't just sink. It plummeted into the deepest pits of her chest as she saw not a commander approaching her, but a Divisioner.

Her mind filled with the memory of the scouting mission and the use of the Hail Mary virus. There was no Hail Mary now. There was just her.

She stood tall and brought her middle and index fingers to her helm in a strong salute. The Divisioner stood before her, no more than two feet away. A horrified thought assaulted her. What if this was the same one to have stopped her and Fay during the scouting mission? Could he somehow sense she was the same person?

The pulse stabilizer fought hard to keep her heart rate steady as her chest tightened, tightened, tightened as he approached.

"**_ID_**," they commanded.

Her heart skipped as she recited the new ID of the dead brigadier. "550101".

He stood there. Unmoving. Each stagnant second burned. She knew better than to say anything. Never speak to a Divisioner unless spoken to.

"**_REACTION TIME CONCERNING INCIDENT WITH TRAINEE LELA MONOT 1.2 SECONDS OFF._**"

She kept her composure while her mind raced. 1.2 seconds? Did Divisioners study everything that intently? She didn't have the help of artificial intelligence, but she could have sworn her reaction was instantaneous.

"**_AVERAGE REACTION TIME TO OUTSIDE STIMULI WHEN CONDUCTING OTHER OBJECTIVE CONSISTENT AT 1.5 SECONDS. YOUR REACTION TIME 0.3 SECONDS._**"

She blinked under the helm. 0.3 seconds? Was she really under scrutiny for being too _fast?_ It was all because she had her eyes on the girl the second the altercation started. A true slag would ignore such a debacle until it interfered with them. But she had felt for the woman's screams. She had anticipated her running. She reacted too fast.

Suddenly, his head snapped in the other direction and he took a hard left, away from Xia. Her eyes followed him as she saw a horde of trainees sprinting towards the other end of the field with their shirts off.

What the hell? Her eyes surveyed the field. Almost everyone was gone. The trams were veering away. But there was one slag standing in the middle of the field, their leg popped out slightly, their hand curling and uncurling. Xia recognized them immediately.

Mai.

Xia picked up the pace, nabbing the opportunity of the distracted Divisioner beelining for the trainees. What the hell was going on? Why wasn't Mai with the rest of their group in the tram? There was no time and no way to ask her. The distance closed between them as they walked in silence off the field, away from the trainees and back towards the Main Gate that led to the Outer Hub.

"What are they doing?" A trainee with a bold **B** on his chest asked another.

"I don't know. I saw Wints go up to them and then they all started stripping," a bronze trainee replied.

"Wints? The top S ranker?"

"Yeah. I don't—" The B-ranked boy shut his mouth as Mai and Xia approached, and then exhaled in relief as they kept walking.

Xia still didn't understand what happened. They continued walking down the side of the main pathway, spotting a parked tram a few yards down. Their tram. The pulse stabilizer took a break. The trainees milled about, some following behind slags, others wandering in groups and straightening their forms when Xia and Mai walked by. Then they reached the side of the sleek black tram.

The mass that had been weighing down on Xia's shoulders ever since she stepped foot out of the vehicle lifted as she stepped back inside it. She took a deep breath and a seat as Mai shut the door behind them. Leo made a move towards Mai but thought better of it, repositioning himself back on the seat.

"You're back, you're okay," he said. The voice modifier couldn't hide the breathless relief in his voice.

"I saw a Divisioner coming towards you right as we had to leave. What the hell happened?" Fay asked.

"I don't know. The Divisioner told me my reaction time in stopping the girl was too fast. And then a bunch of trainees ran off half-naked, so he followed them. Then Mai and I left. But Mai, what were you still doing on the field? You had time to get away."

"Because I was the one who helped you," she replied. "I remembered seeing on your recording of the scouting mission how Ren walked up to those trainees and started ordering them around. They'll do anything a slag tells them to do. And I noticed the Divisioner had his eye on you as soon as the girl was taken away. So I found the closest S rank trainee and told him to get a group of at least 10 C Rank trainees to remove their shirts and sprint to the mess hall."

"Why didn't you tell the C rank trainees directly?" Leo asked.

"To create a longer trail," Xia responded. "So that when they're questioned, there's another point before leading back to Mai. And you chose the mess hall because that's the farthest building from the training field. And you did all this on the fly, based on what Ren did?"

Mai nodded.

Buko shifted between the cycles. He hadn't uttered a word the entire time. "Can you all turn off those awful robot voices?"

Xia shook her head as the tram reached further down the dusty road.

"Xia," Mai muttered. She was trying to speak quietly, but the voice modifier made it difficult. "What do you think will happen to that girl? Will she be okay?"

"Who knows? Maybe."

No. She would not.

They approached the Main Gate.

"Alright, Step Two."

Fay stopped the tram as Xia hopped out.

The two slags standing guard approached them. ***"STATE YOUR PURPOSE TO EXIT MAIN HUB."***

After the encounter with the Divisioner, she didn't feel as nervous. Her voice remained steady as she replied, "Classified."

As she expected, the two slags stepped closer to her and activated a soundsphere, similar to the soundbox Burgs developed. The concrete maze of buildings and distant trainees wandering looked warbled, like a thin smoky veil encased them, warping any sounds they made.

"Escort Aexus." On cue, Lorena rolled down the passenger window and gave a brief nod.

The two slags deep-scanned, red lights blinking. Then it stopped and the soundsphere deactivated as one of them uttered, ***"CLEAR. PROCEED."***

The colossal titanium doors wrenched apart slowly. Too slowly. As if mocking their progress. The tram barreled forward. Xia stole a glance behind them just as the doors closed. It was far in the distance, but she recognized the figure instantly. The Divisioner from the training field, watching her as the doors shut.

She shivered. They entered the Outer Hub.

Xia watched as the darkness enveloped them. It was daytime; yet it was that same midnight black on the dome above, with the same twinkling specks of gold for lowlight. Was it really perpetually dark here?

Again, something was off. The main road before them was empty. Fay drove along, the tram rumbling against the cobblestone, the cycles in the tram jostling against Buko's crouching frame.

"Where is everyone?" Fay broke the eerie silence.

Lorena gazed out the window. "I don't know."

Xia deep-scanned outside the tram. Her vision couldn't reach far, but she noticed dozens of slags and trams parked along the side streets. "Veer left, up here."

Fay posed no questions. She followed the instruction and turned left onto the residential side street. They passed four trams parked along the narrow lane, with various slags standing beside them.

"What's going on?" Mai asked.

"Looks as if they're waiting for something..." Xia muttered.

"Think this is related to the drill at the Inner Hub?" Leo wondered.

Fay parked behind the fourth tram, mimicking the other slags' habits.

"What's with the guy out front?" Leo mused as he peered out the window. The people residing in the Outer Hub seemed to stick inside for the most part. But as if to prove the notion wrong, a lone man lounged in a thin, reclining chair underneath a thick cherry tree upon his front lawn. Most of the homes were tall and thin, stacked against each other like the bricks that formed them. But this house stood fat and girthy, taking up substantial space on the narrow street.

There was something eerie about it. Perhaps it was the gangliness of his frame, or the paleness of his face emitting an almost milky glow. Or perhaps it was the book resting in his spindly hands, which his narrow eyes somehow read intensely despite the shade of the tree and noir of the sky.

"I'm going to watch outside. You all stay here." Xia hopped outside and slid the door shut when a hand grabbed and stopped it from closing. Mai pulled the door back open and hopped out with Xia, taking advantage of the fact that her friend was unable to scold her. The two took similar poses along the tram, mimicking the other slags that stood outside.

Xia eyed the man with caution. Then she scanned the book. *The Psychology of the Unconscious Mind.* His gaze lifted from the book and stared right back at Xia. She felt a jolt in the back of her neck—centipedes racing down her nervous system. His lip curled upward in what could have been a smile or a sneer. He tapped at the cover of his book with a skeleton finger before returning his sharp eyes to the pages.

Xia's disturbance lingered as she turned towards Mai, wondering if she had caught the odd interaction. But Mai's focus was elsewhere— on the full and fruitful trees that adorned the tree belts. The *real* trees, not S-trees, thriving despite the permanent lack of sunlight.

The silence was broken as they heard a faint commotion down the road. A few moments later, the now-familiar sound of a tram made its way down the central road. All this for a tram? Who was inside?

She had an inkling of an answer before she saw it. As the tram rolled by their view, the back side window was opened, giving a clear view of the man sitting inside.

A clear view of the Daimyo.

44

The Twisting Frontier

The slags stood off the main road of the Outer Hub. Dome sky black, faint lights emanating from the twinkling dots and street-lights mixing with the slag's neon contours. In any other context, it might almost be cozy. But it was eerie. They watched on as the lone tram proceeded past—watching the sad, lone parade of one.

The slags held varying degrees of knowledge of the inhabitants of the tram. To some, the dark-haired, sharp-eyed man was a stranger. To others, he was a useful tool. A tool for what, even fewer knew. But it didn't really matter if they knew or not. The small pockets of will in their mind could scream all they wanted. Nothing would happen. The AI decided the route of action. And for now, it was telling everyone to wait. Wait until the man in the tram passed. Let nothing happen to the man in the tram. Precious cargo is in there.

Because the people who were once in there were no longer that. Now they were cargo. Cargo for a very, very important task. A task that had failed due to some lacking intel. The Revitalization Project was a failure. An unaccounted failure. The Virgins hadn't latched. But it created an opportunity for this. For this man to become a very useful tool.

One slag looked on in horror.

***

Mai looked on in horror. The air froze as Xia's eyes darted from the Daimyo to Mai. *Don't move. Don't move.* The father was the girl's soft spot and they couldn't afford another setback. But the girl didn't move. She froze with the air.

They couldn't see, but the tram was clearly headed for the Main Gate. And if Xia could bet on it, she'd bet they were headed to HQ. And that it had something to do with Omega.

But there was no reason to focus on that. They had their mission. And as the other slags began returning to their trams, Xia and Mai did the same.

Inside, Mai said nothing. Nobody said anything for several moments until the tram ahead of them began to move.

"Shall we?" Fay finally asked.

"Let's go."

The tram in front took a right in the direction of the Inner Hub. Fay took a left towards the Main Gate. The gate was barely visible through the low lighting, especially with the faint tint of the tram windows. Xia wondered why it was so damn dark. If they could have real trees here, they clearly could have some type of light.

She jolted her head. What wasteful thoughts. She needed her mind on the mission. Especially since they were now at the Main Gate.

The commander approached the tram. Identical to the scouting mission. But this time, there was no Commander Young in the passenger seat. There were now cycles hidden in the back. Fay rolled down the window. Everyone in the back stilled. Even Buko resembled a watchful statue.

"STATE YOUR PURPOSE TO EXIT MAIN HUB." The slag asked as the now familiar veil of sound-blocking signals enshrouded them. The gate appeared smoky beyond the shroud. They were so close. So damn close.

"Transporting Aexus."

Lorena gave a two-fingered salute as the commander turned towards the tram, their visor's red light flashing as it conducted a deep-scan. Xia waited with bated breath for something to go wrong. For the commander to call out to other slags for reinforcement. For an order to exit the vehicle. She was ready for the delicate plan to shatter. But the blinking stopped. And then came the sweetest words she'd ever heard as the world fell back into focus.

"CLEAR. PROCEED."

Leo pumped the air with his fist. Mai let out a relieved sigh. Xia didn't allow herself to succumb to the false respite. They were not yet in the clear, so there was no use acting like it. The towering wall before them split in two, heaving itself apart as it revealed the pure darkness below.

They descended. The wall shut closed behind them.

The slag visor adjusted immediately to the claustrophobic darkness of the tunnel. The lone lighted path would be barely enough for the naked eye.

"Alright, just like last time. Follow the line until we hit the intersection with the red path. Fay, you'll need to back into the path and drive in reverse so we can get the cycles out. Lorena will open the door. Fay, you'll take my helm and get it ready on the slag dummy. Mai and Leo, you'll help us push the cycles since we can't start them until we're out of the outside. All good?"

Buko gave a silent nod.

"Yeah," Leo agreed.

Mai stared onward.

After seven tense minutes, the faint glimmer of red in the distance marked the designated fork. The tram's wheels reverberating in the silent tunnel were the only sound that cut through the thick layer of tension. They reached the fork and, as if she'd driven it a thousand times, Fay seamlessly began to reverse into the crimson path.

The tram made the trek much shorter than when Fay ventured on foot, giving the group minimal time to mentally prepare themselves. Traveling backward, Xia had a clear view of the approaching door through the rear window. It began as a glimmer. Faint specks of electric green that faded in and out of darkness grew larger, larger. Those were the only sources of light besides the ruby glow of the path. It wasn't until Fay parked the tram and they all hopped out, one by one, that the symbol on the slate gray wall became clear. The same symbol on Lorena's back.

For a door with such a grand purpose, it was quite plain. It barely even resembled a door. The specks of fluorescent green seemed to melt into the slate gray of the wall before bleeding back out. Besides the pulsing lights and large black symbol, there was nothing else to indicate this slab of wall was anything special. But it was more than special.

It was the door to the outside world.

Xia pulled out the soundbox and activated it. "Leo and Mai. You two get the cycles off the tram. Remember, you'll need to manually push them."

Due to the inner workings of the cycle that omitted various electro-magnetic frequencies, it was vital that the bikes were not turned on until they were outside the walls.

"It doesn't look broken," Fay mused as she eyed the stone wall. "It looks just as I'd remembered it."

Lorena ignored her as she tapped on her cell chip, casting a holo-graphic display above her wrist. Her nimble hand moved at the speed of light as she began typing away at the virtual key display. Her hand skillfully moved back and forth between tapping various specks of green on the wall and typing at her cell chip display. Back and forth, back and forth. Then a glimmer of green seemed to shine a hair brighter than the rest. Lorena pressed it with her index finger. Then the lights faded completely and a small hole suddenly appeared in the wall, as if the solid alloy vanished into nothingness.

Lorena pulled out a knife. "To get through, you'll need to give it some of your blood."

"What?" Fay said.

"You said it needed our biometric data," Xia said. "Nothing about blood."

"Right. Your biometric data via blood. It's how I made the door."

Xia didn't question it further. Instead, she grabbed the blade, pulled off her glove, and sliced the pad of her ring finger.

"It's going to need at least a teaspoon's worth."

"Didn't want to tell me that first?" Without hesitation, she sliced the back of her hand near the webbing and slammed it into the hole in the door.

The green lights returned. Flickering, fading, then disappeared once more.

"Alright. Now you're good. Who's next?"

Buko took a solid step forward and nabbed the knife from Xia. With even further precision, he sliced his hand and placed it into the door.

"Won't the FRF be notified that new blood samples were input?" Fay asked with trepidation.

Lorena rolled her eyes. "You think I don't have that figured out? All new inputs first pass through my closed channel. The same channel that I broke the door from in the first place. I can stop that information from traveling further. Which I have. Relax and have a little faith."

Fay had faith, but relaxing was out of the question. She took a hesitant step forward and cut through the flesh of her hand.

Mai needed no prodding. After the bikes were settled, she swiped the knife from Fay and mimicked the same cutting with cool confidence. Then she passed it to Leo. His hand moved gingerly. With trepidation or care, Xia didn't know. She wanted him to move more quickly. This was it. This was the final step.

Hurry up and slice, damn it.

Finally, Leo cut into his hand and placed it into the hole. The lights returned and disappeared a final time.

"Are you ready?" Lorena asked.

Xia nodded and turned to the rest of the group. "Alright. I'll lead ahead. Lorena stays behind and mans the door. The rest of you will need to push the bikes up. It'll likely be a steep incline. Once we're out, we'll get the bikes ready. Fay will take my helm. Then Buko and I are off. The rest of you get back to Lorena and get the hell out of here. Got it?"

The group nodded, and Lorena placed her hand in the center of the large symbol. Then the symbol moved downward and the wall slowly descended into the earth. The group stared on at the pitch-black void before them.

Xia started forward. It was too dark even with the tech of their helms. She turned on the flashlight attachment. Rocks and dirt formed the walls and the ground. The terrain was rough. Infrequently traveled. Xia looked behind them. No footprints, but the bikes left tread marks.

"Buko and Leo, move the bike yourselves. Move slowly. Fay and Mai, cover the tread marks. I'll scout ahead." The group's pace slowed as they awkwardly moved along, the two women dusting over the marks left by the bikes while Xia jogged up ahead.

Partly, she wanted to ensure the group's safety and be on the lookout for potential dangers. But mainly, she wanted to see the world for *herself* first.

In the distance, the ground sloped upward and faint flickers of warmth lit up the tawny dirt. She turned off her flashlight and it became even clearer. "There it is," she muttered, barely audible in the deep tunnel.

Her heart hammered in her chest but Xia let herself feel it, disabling the pulse stabilizer. This was a different kind of adrenaline. Fear and trepidation mixed with anticipation into a fury of exhilaration at the prospect of the sight they were about to see. The feat they were about to accomplish. And it was only 10 yards away.

Five yards.

One yard.

Xia began the steep trek upwards. The incline felt like nothing as the adrenaline pushed her every step, practically flinging her forward. The passage grew brighter, brighter, the ground turning grassy, sweet vibrant blades of green, not the artificial neon of fluorescent lights, not the faux imagery of minuscule pixels, no. Real, fresh, true green. Multiplying. Scattering the rich brown dirt until it was more green than brown. Until it was a sea of green. And then a sea of blue above the grassy green as the sky met her eyes.

Holy mother of midnight.

***

The old man poured the tea into his clay cup, the liquid's earthy notes mixing with the pure, clean air. Despite the act becoming a habit of over 50 years, he never took it for granted. He still remembered the days without it. As he brought the tea to his lips, something shifted. He shriveled his wide nose. Had the tea gone bad? He rose slowly from his wooden chair and approached the canister beside his wood stove. He sniffed. No, fresh as ever. A bird chirped outside his window. He returned to his tea and continued his 50 year-long ritual.

Little did he know, everything was about to change.

45

Epilogue

Xia didn't get to bask in the world long enough before the voice of Mai called out from the base of the tunnel.

"Are we good to go?"

"Yes, Yes!" Xia called out, her voice initially stuck in her throat. It was like the first time she was speaking. She was reborn in this beautiful world.

That same adrenaline that fueled Xia powered the rest of the group as they pushed the bikes up with ease, breaths hot and heavy and excited. Leo almost dropped it as the clear blue came into view.

"Oh my God," Mai gasped. She ripped off her helmet as she gazed upwards into the brilliantly blinding sun.

"You should keep it on—" Xia began, but Leo ripped his off as well. Even Fay took off her helm. The sunlight glazed the blue of her hair in no way any lighting in the city could. She looked younger. So did Leo. He was always the epitome of handsomeness, but underneath the sunlight he reached practically godlike beauty. But it was Mai who was truly breathless. Skin that had seemed so pale and lifeless since the surgery now seemed to glow, her features softening yet also intensifying under the golden sun.

Xia gazed at the horizon. Soft white clouds floated beyond, while the fresh green grass stretched on towards hills and forestry. That's where they'd be headed. The distant cluster of evergreen to the east.

She turned towards the bikes and began to reactivate them. All of a sudden there was a pulling at her face as her vision blurred. Her hands reacted defensively before she realized it was Mai, pulling off her helmet.

"You need to feel the air! Breathe it! Look at the sun!" Xia glanced up but now the sun pierced at her eyes. She squinted and turned. "It's beautiful, isn't it?"

Mai's smile was infectious. Xia couldn't help but return it. Her eyes drifted behind Mai. Leo was wandering.

"Leo, get back here. Stay by the entrance."

He ignored her as he spun, raising his hands in a circle. "This is amazing!" He flopped down onto the grass, feeling it as much as he could through the slag suit. His inner child was squealing and he couldn't help but act on it.

Xia remembered Opell's warning. She remembered the images. She yelled at him again. "Leo, stop! Get back here."

Mai's smile faltered. "Leo, stay over here!"

He stood again and jogged away even further. Mai took a step forward to follow him but Xia crossed her arm in front and blocked her.

Leo turned back around to face them. His smile was just visible in the distance. "Why even go back?" He called out. The sudden fresh air and freedom were intoxicating. He was drunk with it. This was beautiful. The world was beautiful. The air was clean and the sun was warm and he laughed in pure and innocent glee.

But the smile ripped from his face as he was suddenly flung into the air as the ground opened beneath him and a twisting, mechanized tentacle erupted from the ground.

The rumblings.

The tentacle raised several stories high before shooting back down and scooping up the barely conscious Leo.

Mai screamed as she attempted to run towards him. Xia pulled her back.

"Buko, drive towards the trees, now!" He needed no telling twice. He swung his leg over and raced the bike in the opposite direction from the mechanized creature and towards the evergreen trees.

The tentacle curled itself around Leo, the tip of the robotic tendril just thin enough to wrap itself around him. The burgundy mechanisms linked together giving chain-like dexterity, able to snake around with flexibility. The hole in the ground crumbled and sunk further as the tentacle grew wider and wider toward the base. How long was the thing? How far down did it go?

The mechanical horror sunk back down into the hole, taking Leo's limp body with it, but not before snapping it in two just as it reached the ground.

Fuck, fuck fuck, Xia chanted as she wrapped her arms around Mai as the girl's knees buckled, her body convulsing with tears. There was no way she'd be able to keep it together and head back into the slag's den.

"Fay, head back, now! Tell Lorena it's just you. Give Burgs the breakdown," she shouted over Mai's wails and the distant rumblings of the mechanical beast in the hole below. It could be back up any second.

Fay swallowed, bit back her own tears, and gave a solid nod before slamming the helmet back onto her cobalt locks and sprinting back towards the tunnel.

"Come on, we have to go," Xia urged. Mai attempted to stand but her knees gave out. Xia grabbed her by the hair and gave her a solid *SMACK* as the silver freelancer slapped her across the face.

"Cry later. We have to go *now!*"

Xia pulled Mai and forcefully yanked the girl onto the cycle as she swung her leg around. She threw her slag helm back on and clipped Mai's onto the side of the cycle before telling Mai, "Hold on tight!"

In a burst of lighting, they sped off into the expanse.

Buko was far ahead. The strange monster hadn't gone after Buko. Was that because it was busy with Leo? No, that was clearly just one of many different limbs. Xia hoped the same grace would be extended to her as it was for the samurai.

That wasn't the case.

The ground rumbled as Xia began to weave left and right. A few yards behind her the ground collapsed as another tentacle shot through the air. The sound was deafening. Even through her slag helm, she could hear the monstrous mechanical whirring as its links maneuvered the massive weight of the machine monster. It hovered several stories above before slinking back down like a snake on the hunt. On the hunt for them.

"Xia!" Mai screamed. Her survival instincts finally overcame the sorrow.

"Hold on!" Xia waited. Waited. Just before the tentacle was about to touch them, she smashed the turbo accelerator and they shot forward with a burst of speed. Mai choked as her head whipped backward before slamming into Xia's helmet. The beast didn't react in time. It attempted to reach for them, slithering and skating through the air, before it suddenly yanked back.

That was the end of the tentacle's length, it seemed. Xia didn't dare turn her head, but her eyes glanced at the small rear mirror on the side of the bike. She watched the tentacle loom above the ground. Hovering. Watching.

Not this time, she taunted.

Succumbing to its loss, the tentacle burrowed back into the ground. Mai's body further melted into Xia. Her jaw bled from the impact with her helmet. The tears mixed with the blood. Xia's eyes intensified as she locked her gaze forward toward the evergreen, her resolve deepening and darkening.

ABOUT THE AUTHOR

Nina is not Xia, as much as she'd like to be. But she does bleach her hair into oblivion to get that silver tone, and she does ride a motorcycle for those otherworldly thrills. She makes drinks like Dames. She loves music like Burgs. She's motherly like Fay. She adores the cyberpunk aesthetic like many trapped in Cyber City. She's been to Japan and dreams every day of going back, but for now is stuck in Midwestern Milwaukee.